THE ARIZONA TRIANGLE

T0176343

THE ARIZONA TRIANGLE

A JO BAILEN DETECTIVE NOVEL

SYDNEY GRAVES

HARPER

NEW YORK . LONDON . TORONTO . SYDNEY

HARPER

THE ARIZONA TRIANGLE. Copyright © 2024 by Laurie Kate Christensen. All rights reserved. Printed in the United States of America. No part of this book may be used or reproduced in any manner whatsoever without written permission except in the case of brief quotations embodied in critical articles and reviews. For information address HarperCollins Publishers, 195 Broadway, New York, NY 10007.

HarperCollins books may be purchased for educational, business, or sales promotional use. For information please email the Special Markets Department at SPsales@harpercollins.com.

FIRST EDITION

Designed by Jamie Lynn Kerner

Art on title page and chapter openers
©Arroyan Art/stock.Adobe.com

Library of Congress Cataloging-in-Publication Data has been applied for.

ISBN 978-0-06-337999-2 (pbk.)

24 25 26 27 28 LBC 5 4 3 2 1

FOR BRENDAN

THE ARIZONA TRIANGLE

ONE

ONE FRIDAY MORNING IN JUNE, I WAS CROUCHED IN SOME MESQUITE bushes outside a suburban bedroom window, sweating in the sun, photostalking a middle-aged housewife named Tiffani Cortez, who was, at the moment, getting spectacularly banged by her much younger boyfriend. She had lizard-tanned skin, bleach-blond hair, and a Realtor's license, and she had rented this cookie-cutter tract house in Sabino Canyon with cash up front for her extramarital activities.

Her not-born-yesterday multimillionaire soon-to-be-ex-husband had figured this out. He wanted custody of their ritzy Catalina Foothills spread—and their two kids, George Jr. and Willow, as an extra twist of the knife. That's where I came in.

The boy toy seemed to be genuinely enjoying his own performance, plying his surreally sculpted body above hers like a dancer, swiveling his hips and tightening his butt cheeks and undulating his stomach, while Tiffani clutched the sheets and arched into a full-throated orgasm that rattled the windowpanes.

Frankly, I was on her side: I had met George Cortez, a shlubby little weasel. I wasn't here to have opinions, just earning a paycheck, but I made sure to shoot Tiffani from flattering angles.

As I clicked on a few glowing close-ups of her postcoital face, my phone buzzed rhythmically in my hand. A text from my boss: Call me asap. I duckwalked out to the driveway, toddled to my car, and heaved myself into the baking-hot interior with a flashing awareness of the sordid absurdity of my line of work.

My name is Justine Bailen, Jo for short. I'm a licensed private detective in the state of Arizona, and I work for the Taffet Detective Agency. Our offices are in a strip-mall storefront on Campbell, just north of the university. The agency's owner, my boss and mentor, is Veronica "Ronnie" Taffet, a seasoned, locally renowned private eye. The entire outfit consists of four women: Ronnie, of course, and me, as well as Erin Yazzie, our third PI, and our so-called executive assistant, Madison Taffet. So you'd think it would be awesome to work at a small, all-female agency. And you would be mostly right.

But here I was, almost forty years old, hiding in shrubbery taking illicit sex photos of strangers. Hoo boy.

As I drove out of the development, icy air from the dashboard vents blasting my face, I called Ronnie back.

Her voice shredded my ear. "Jo!"

I adore my boss, but she's a piece of work. "What's up?"

"New case for you. Missing person. The family asked for you specifically."

I looked longingly at Charlie's Drive-In Liquors as I streaked by. "Back in twenty."

I screeched into a spot in the parking lot and left the glacial climate of my car for the parched blast furnace of a typical spring afternoon in Tucson, then just as fast I entered the office, which the strip mall management keeps as frigid as an Arctic dawn. Everyone in Arizona has haywire internal thermostats because of this schizoid air-conditioned desert lifestyle. Madison was huddled at her desk in a denim jacket, whispering into her phone. She's a pallid twentysomething whose favorite thing to do outside of work is to make TikTok videos of her pet rat. She's astonishingly inefficient. She's also Ronnie's niece.

Madison looked up as I came rushing in and gave me an unenthused half wave without stopping the flow of whatever she was saying into the phone. I scuttled fast into my dim, tiny, cluttered office, where

I could hear Ronnie loud and clear through the shitty particleboard walls, telling some lowlife to go fuck himself. Or maybe she was cooing sweet nothings to her true love. Who could tell? She talked to everyone in that same raucous blat. Erin's office was empty because she was on a stakeout all week up in Phoenix. As I emailed the photo files and my invoice to Madison to send to George Cortez, Tiffani's cuckolded but now vindicated husband, I looked at all the end-of-week paperwork on my desk—reports to type up, expenses and time sheets, including some from the week before I'd been putting off. I had to do this myself because I could not trust Madison with the simplest receipt, or anything for that matter.

My desk phone rang, caller ID blocked. I picked up the handset. "Taffet Detective Agency, Jo Bailen speaking."

There was a whoosh, and then came a sound like a fire burning. Or maybe it was just static from a bad connection.

"Hello?" I said.

No response, just more crackling, so I hung up and stepped out into the short hallway and rapped on Ronnie's just-ajar door, then stuck my head in. She was still on the phone.

"I'll call you back," she shouted and abruptly hung up and motioned me in, shaking a scrap of Madison's message at me. "This woman's been missing two days. Her mother called, asked for you. She seems to think her daughter is in some kind of trouble, but who the fuck knows."

"Why didn't she call the cops?" I plunked myself in the chair across from her desk.

"She did," Ronnie said, her raspy voice belying the vision of loveliness from which it emanated.

Happily single and child-free, Ronnie's a forty-six-year-old Long Island native who majored in communications at the U of A and took a liking to this town and never left. A workaholic, bourbon-drinking, chain-smoking, sunbathing junk-food addict, she's also a freak of nature who should be a dried-up wrinkled handbag at this point. But her skin is radiant. She's a bombshell according to even the most stringent standards of female perfection: a five-foot-seven package of ash-blond hair, symmetrical bronzed face with big blue eyes and rosebud mouth, firm pneumatic boobs, tiny waist, cute butt, and long, slender legs. Her feet are normal, and I have no reason to think her genitalia aren't as well, but those are the only differences between her and Career Barbie that I can see. And then she opens that angel's mouth and out comes the clamor of a buzz saw peppered with the filthiest words in the English language. "She says she's talked to them several times, but they're being fuckwads about it, as usual." No one in our agency had any great respect for the cops of southern Arizona. "She says she wants to hire you in particular. Says she knows and trusts you."

Anxious parents of missing adult children are legion in our line of work. More times than not, the kids just don't want their parents to know where they are. To be fair, it's generally the same with the missing elderly parents of anxious adult children. And of course it's our job to locate them anyway.

I leaned over and took the slip from Ronnie. "Laura Gold," I read out loud. My blood did something in my veins, chilled or curdled or both. "Holy shit. I know her. I know her daughter. From Delphi."

"Yeah," said Ronnie. "Home sweet home. So how'd it go, the Cortez case?"

The fact that Rose Delaney was missing and I was being hired by her mother to find her was taking up all my brain cells. I had to force myself to remember what case I'd just finished. "Madison has the photos. She should be sending them to George Cortez right now, although, of course, who knows."

Ronnie narrowed her eyes at this. She did not find my little digs about her niece's work ethic amusing. Madison was the spoiled only child of her much-adored younger brother. Also, Ronnie has no sense of humor, not a shred, and zero tolerance for nuance or irony. She deals in facts and unequivocal truths. And she's also an incredibly good detective. She taught me most of what I know.

"I hate custody cases," she was saying now. "They're so dirty. Who fucking cares who fucks who? What difference does it make?"

"By the way, the boyfriend is stupidly hot."

"Good for her. She's better off without that dickbag anyway."

"Agreed."

"Call the mother back. Get up there."

"I can't. It's not ethical. Rose was my childhood best friend. I grew up with these people."

"Ethical? Fuck that. You know this person, right? So you'll have a better chance of finding her than a stranger."

"Rose has barely spoken to me since we were fourteen. She hates me."

Ronnie steamrolled me. "Anyway, I already took the case. So if you had weekend plans, now you don't. Go find her."

I did, in fact, have weekend plans, a date I would now be canceling. "Roger that, Captain."

"Who's Roger? I'm not a captain," Ronnie said as her phone rang. "Hello? What? Who's this? How the fuck should I know if Sniffy is depressed, Ma? I'm not a pet therapist. He probably needs prune juice."

I beat it out of the office and slid back into my hotbox of a car that had been baking in brutal direct sunlight and cranked down all the windows for the short drive to my apartment, a one-bedroom basic dump in a mid-twentieth-century stucco complex a few blocks from the office. Three separate buildings surround a swimming pool. The laundry room is next to the manager's unit. I live on the third and top floor, which is reached by external staircases and outdoor walkways. My apartment is what's called in real-estate lingo a one-bedroom efficiency, and what I call a litter box. Over the years I've lived here, I've never bothered to upgrade from the furniture I bought when I moved in, a minimalist mélange of IKEA, the local

Sam Levitz Furniture warehouse, and Craigslist. My housekeeping skills are spotty, but luckily no one cares. It's just me.

In the kitchenette, parched and ravenous, I chugged some cold iced tea straight out of the bottle, palmed a handful of roasted salted peanuts into my mouth, and, crunching away, went into my Spartan little bedroom and collected my go bag, which I keep packed with underwear and a toothbrush and a few other necessities, along with my two guns and ammo and PI tool kit: lock picks, binoculars, handcuffs, GPS tracker, digital scanner, and pepper spray for good luck and bear attacks. I usually stow my go bag in the back seat of my car, but I recently brought it inside to refresh the laundry and replace the toothpaste and tampons.

In the bathroom, I peed and washed my hands and didn't bother checking my reflection in the mirror; nothing of interest there. I'm pretty much one neutral unicolor—short auburn bed head, tawny skin courtesy of my Mexican father, cinnamon red–brown eyes—which is handy in the Southwest, because I'm basically the same color as the ground, just a lighter shade. I can blend into the background when I need to, also an advantage because I'm five foot nine and mostly muscle, not a small person, so I need all the camouflage help I can get.

That night's date, the one I had to cancel, was with a chick named Lissa Jordan I'd known since we'd worked together as chambermaids at a Miracle Mile motel in our early twenties. These days, she was a lawyer who specialized in environmental protection cases against developers and corporations. We were supposed to go out for tacos and a show at the Rock, some local band I'd never heard of. After the workweek I'd just had, nonstop scrambling around after no-goodniks and adulterers, I felt a hard desire for spicy food, strong booze, loud music, sweaty dancing, and kinetic sex. So I deeply regretted having to break this date, which had promised all of the above. Lissa was a hot little snack, sharp and funny, with a curved, foxy mouth I had been fantasizing about since that morning, watching Tiffani get stud-

THE ARIZONA TRIANGLE 7

muffined. Lissa and I were friends with benefits, or as I called it, lovers
with borders. Oh well.

Another time 4 sure, she texted me back. So that was that.

Standing by my front door, bag slung over my shoulder, having
put it off as long as I could, feeling deeply uneasy about this, I called
Laura Gold.

"Justine," she said, "thank God, I'm losing my mind."

"I go by Jo now. I heard Rose is missing."

"It's been more than two days, maybe three by now. She left her
car, all her stuff, her laptop—and she was supposed to come for dinner last night. It's not like her to just forget or blow me off."

"I wouldn't worry yet," I said. "That's not long. She probably went
off with a friend and forgot to tell you. I bet she'll be back."

"Call it a motherly hunch," said Laura, who was frankly one of the
least maternal people I'd ever known, besides my own mother. "Ben
said to call you. He hates it when I worry. But this time, he thinks I
might be right to."

Ben was Rose's half brother, the younger of Laura's two sons with
her second husband. I'd heard he was a junkie, and then he went to
rehab and got clean. "My professional opinion is that she'll turn up tomorrow or the next day. My services aren't cheap, Laura. I really don't
want to waste your money. Can we give it till Monday?"

"It's worth it to me to know you're looking for her."

"There are a couple of reputable investigators closer to Delphi I
could recommend."

"No. Ben and I both agree you're the best person for this. You
know Rose."

"We haven't seen each other in years."

"Well, at one time you knew her better than just about anybody.
That has to count for something."

There was a silence on the line as I tried to find another excuse
and came up empty. Ronnie had ordered me to take the case.

And Laura wasn't backing down. "Please, Justine. Something's not right. I can feel it."

I caved. "Madison talked to you about our fee and retainer." It was phrased as a statement, but this was optimistic.

"Yes, and I gave her my credit card number. She said she'd email me an agreement to e-sign, but I don't have it yet."

"I'll send you our standard contract right now, hold on just one sec." As I texted the file as an attachment to Laura's phone number, I made a mental note to double-check the card number when I was back in the office. Madison had a highly annoying habit of muffing one digit. Exactly one. Not transposed, just flat-out wrong. It boggled the mind. She wasn't dumb. I suspected she was doing it on purpose, to mess with us. "In addition to the agency's hourly fee, we also charge for travel and expenses."

"Of course," Laura said. "Are you free to come up this evening?"

In no way, in any universe, did I want to touch this case, anywhere, with any length of pole. It freaked me out, because my history with Rose was messy and painful. But I had already agreed to take it. I couldn't back out now. And maybe there was a part of me that was secretly excited to intrude on Rose's life. At our core, we detectives are just nosy little fuckers.

"Sure," I said. "I'll be there as soon as I can."

"Thank you," Laura breathed. "If anyone can find her it's you." She seemed to have no idea of the rich irony in this statement.

"See you in about an hour," I said, locking my door behind me.

During the drive north, I put myself on autopilot, hardly aware of the traffic, the heat waves rising from the tarmac, the mountains hulking to my right.

Admittedly, Laura was right, there was a lot that I knew about Rose, because she was my inseparable best friend for ten years, until she dumped me in ninth grade. She was born Catherine Rose Delaney in Trenton, New Jersey, the only child of Laura and James Delaney, born on June 14, 1982, exactly two months before me. She moved to Delphi, Arizona, with her mother at the age of four, which was when our friendship began. After we graduated from high school, she went to Evergreen College up in Washington State, then she moved back to southern Arizona to get her MFA in poetry at the U of A and stayed on, living in Tucson and working as an adjunct professor of creative writing and English comp at Saguaro Early College. This last part I knew through the Rancho grapevine. I had also learned that she was a published writer with two books of poetry, and that in her spare time, she fronted a supercool, hard-rocking all-female band called the Sisters of Percy.

But this was all incidental knowledge, little shards of fact gathered from the internet, mirror of all things, which only served to remind me how little I really knew about the real Rose Delaney, at least the adult version of her. And now my job was to locate her, whether she liked it or not. And she wouldn't like it. Well, neither would I, for that matter. If I could find her remotely, without having to interact with her at all, that would be ideal. For the moment, I had to assume she was out there somewhere, having a lark. I knew Rose well, or at least I used to, and could easily imagine her heading off somewhere without telling anyone, jumping into a friend's car for a few days in Mexico, or walking dreamily into the mountains with a notebook and pen and sleeping bag to commune with nature. Anything was possible. Rose was impulsive.

To fuel my body for the unwanted task ahead, I stopped at In-N-Out for a rare and indulgent treat: a double-double cheeseburger Animal Style, an order of fresh, starchy fries, and an Arnold Palmer, which I mixed myself at the bank of soda nozzles. I took a red plastic stool at the counter by the plate-glass windows, dredging my fries in multiple little paper cups of ketchup and trying not to get any of it on my face or clothes. The mountains sat straight ahead, rising in my field of vision like living beings, grand and spiky. Their vivid colors were flattened by the harsh midday sunlight, their ridgelines etched like a sci-fi planet's weird landscape against the deep blue sky. It felt like a cartoonishly grotesque incongruity to sit in this fifties-style diner looking out at what could easily be the surface of Mars. For more than fifteen hundred years, this land had belonged to the Hohokam, masters of the desert, who left behind evidence of a peaceful farming culture and a sophisticated irrigation system. In college, a few friends and I hiked the hard, ass-kicking Baby Jesus Ridge Trail to look at their petroglyphs in Sutherland Wash. It was all that remained of them now. Despite their ability to channel and husband water, they had been undone by drought in the end. They left because the water disappeared. In fact, "Hohokam" is a Piman word that means "exhausted," "tired out," something I very much sympathized with at the moment.

Back on the road, the taste of fresh grease and lemonade lingering on my tongue, I navigated northbound traffic past one new development after another. Sand-colored ranch houses proliferated through the desert like cancer cells, each containing a set of humans sucking up water and electricity and spewing out shit and trash. Just past the enormous megamall in Plato Valley, the road narrowed to four lanes through a couple of nondescript little towns. Then all this commerce and human presence gave way all at once to the lonesome high country. The highway abruptly halved itself into a narrow two-lane blacktop and ran due northeast, parallel to the jagged mountains on the right, through mostly empty desert, punctuated in the near distance by rock outcroppings and saguaro and ocotillo forests. A solitary Ford dealership loomed out of nowhere with its rows of shiny, steroidal pickup trucks. When I passed the state tourist information bureau, then the turnoff to the Ecosphere Museum, I was almost home.

I felt a jolt of dread. Going back to the Rancho almost certainly meant seeing my mother. After my father's sudden death in a car crash when I was little, my mother, not the most touchy-feely person to be-gin with, started treating me as a vestigial and traumatic reminder of the lost love of her life. My presence seemed to cause her nothing but pain, which caused me pain. As I got older, I accepted that the best I could achieve with my mother was a neutral pleasantness, the warm-and-fuzzy train having long ago left the station. I was already steeling myself against the disappointment in her face when she inevitably saw me. I vowed to put that moment off as long as I could.

It was nearly five o'clock when I hit Delphi, population 3,867, perched high in the foothills of Mount Lemmon. Delphi used to be a gold- and silver-mining town back in the Wild West days, but now it's a sleepy, scruffy, semi-interesting mix of working-class families, artists, and retirees. Houses, most of them small midcentury cinder-block ranches, sprawl through the high foothills, tucked into hollows and perched on ridges through the desert. I turned off the highway onto Arizona Avenue and slowed down to an obedient forty-four miles per hour, the tacitly legal nine miles per hour over the speed limit, and crawled past the all-too-familiar Dollar Store across from the trailer park, the first of two Circle Ks, the Apache Motel with its cement teepees, Juan Carlos's Mexican Restaurant, the Delphi Inn, a couple of churches. Nothing ever changed here.

At the second Circle K, I took the right-hand turn onto Bella Luna Road. Two miles in, just past Tom and Celia Dixon's rammed-earth farmhouse with its shrieking army of chickens and organic raised-bed vegetables, I pulled into the long, bumpy, heaving driveway that led to Rancho Bella Luna. It's a former dude ranch that found a new life as an artists' colony in the early 1970s, when a bunch of idealistic baby boomers, including my parents, bought it outright, pooling their savings and inheritances, scraping together whatever they could kick in, then staked out plots and refurbished outbuildings or built their own houses and art studios on the land. They were all getting old now, but most of them were still here, still going, my mother included, living on their savings and Social Security checks and whatever artwork they could sell. They did what they could to keep the place in working order, but upkeep had been sporadic and iffy for years.

For various reasons, mostly because I was pretty much estranged from my mother, I hadn't been back here in almost a year. With a low-level hum of tension in my chest, I steered my ten-year-old Honda around the ruts and over the cattle guard, jouncing through the rough open courtyard, and parked below the dilapidated old ranch house that sat on a small bluff right above the parking lot. It had once been a grand home fit for entertaining robber barons and heiresses. There had been talk at the Rancho for years about fixing it up and turning it into a guesthouse, but by the looks of things, it still functioned as a place to store old furniture and cast-off junk.

I emerged from the chill air of my car straight into the evening heat. The Rancho was laid out like a beehive, a tight cluster of adobe casitas and bungalows rising above the old main house on the flank of the broad hillside. As I passed my mother's little house, a refurbished adobe casita in its own landscaped patch of desert, I thought I saw a curtain twitch and felt the cold laser beam of her gaze on me. I didn't look directly at the window, just kept walking until her house was out of sight. As I went, I felt that old familiar pang of wistfulness. For so many years, I'd wished things could be different between us. But even if she'd shown any sign of wanting this too, which she hadn't, I didn't have the slightest clue how to bring it about.

At the top of the hill, with the best view, but also the most exposure to the scouring winds, stood Laura and Leo Gold's house, a modern architectural statement cantilevered over the wash on steel beams. I crossed the short, polished concrete bridge that spanned a shallow gully to the front door and rang the doorbell. Laura opened the door. She wore a pale-blue caftan made of some light, fluttery material. She looked even tinier and skinnier than the last time I'd seen her, as if Rose's absence had shrunk her two full sizes. In the best of times, she was highly strung. Right now, she was vibrating at a frequency too high for humans to hear.

As she gestured me into the foyer, I hesitated briefly. I hadn't set foot in this house since Rose and my best-friend breakup more than twenty-five years ago, in our freshman year of high school, and I wondered whether Laura had any clue that her missing daughter would have a fit if she knew I was here.

TWO

LAURA LED ME PAST A DANISH TEAK CREDENZA INTO THE LIVING room. It was a rich, cultured space, all polished, poured-concrete floors and soaring ceiling and enormous fireplace, the kind of room you would associate with muted cool jazz on the stereo and old, expensive red wine. A wall of huge windows and glass sliding doors gave onto a stone-paved patio, and beyond, a view of the wild mountains stretching back into the sky.

I was remembering the day Laura and Rose arrived at the Rancho, two exotic wanderers from the east, smelling of foreign lands and perfumes. I'd fallen in love with both of them at first sight. Rose and I were both four. Finally, a girl my own age to play with. I took Rose's hand and showed her all my hiding places. We were an inseparable dyad, until we weren't. Memories rose up like a flock of birds in my head. The slumber parties, Rose and me in sleeping bags down in the old Airstream by the horse stables, with a thermos of cocoa and our Ouija board. Our made-up world, Jag-Brolla, when we were eleven and into science fiction, with its own language and customs and history. That sort-of friend we had for a while when we were twelve, a glamorous girl our age named Natalie, who came in a camper van with her dad and a few other hippies, taught us to smoke cigarettes, and told us all about sex, and then was gone again just as suddenly. Spying on the grown-ups at Sunday open-studio parties. Getting our first periods at the same time, running to Patty, who happened to be

Leo's first wife and Laura's best friend, for advice and equipment so we wouldn't have to tell our mothers.

And most of all, I remembered the make-believe games we used to play, sometimes just the two of us, and sometimes letting Rose's little brothers in on the fun: dress-up games imitating artsy ladies in old-time costumes we found in the attic of the ranch house, or running through the gulches, Native hunters tracking game, as swift and quiet as spies. Our favorite game was pretending we were outlaws, hiding back in the foothills in an old shack we told each other used to be Crazy Davy's hideout.

Rose had an amazing imagination. She was ringleader and director of all our games. The magic she created for all us kids was all-consuming, powerful. Whatever we were pretending at any given time felt more real to us than our so-called real lives. Whole afternoons passed, deep in Rose's made-up worlds. It was all I could do to shake myself back to reality in time to go home for dinner, not that my mother would have noticed or cared if I stayed out all night. I stumbled home anyway, dazed through the darkening desert, as if I were waking from a vivid dream.

Rose had always had as complicated a relationship with her mother as I did with mine, just as fraught and chilly. Laura Gold was the Rancho's movie star. I knew her glamorous story by heart, had internalized it as a kid. She grew up in Southern California and at sixteen was discovered by a talent scout and became a Hollywood starlet with a series of ingenue roles. I had watched a few of her movies. She was a gorgeous sylph with genuine talent, but she chucked the whole thing at twenty ("that town is so superficial, and oh, the awful men") and went east. In New York, she joined an avant-garde dance company that performed in underground theaters and toured Eastern Europe and India, then married Jimmy Delaney, a Jersey boy from an Irish crime-syndicate family, settled with him in Trenton, and gave birth to a daughter. She eventually got antsy being a mob wife, with nothing to do all day but get her hair done and redecorate the den, so she left Jimmy and headed back out west with four-year-old Rose, to turf up at this scruffy artists' commune in Delphi, Arizona. She bought into the collective; stole the Rancho's doctor away from his wife, Patty, and married him; built this house with him; gave birth to their sons, Jason and Ben; became a sculptor by sheer force of will and a surprising gift for three-dimensional abstraction; and here she still was.

Now, her hands trembled in midair. Her small face was all vivid eyes and wide, mobile mouth, and otherwise a pale oval of fine clay she molded at will into a series of expressions. She stood hovering like a nervous hummingbird by the shallow steps that led up to the open kitchen-dining room. "Would you like red or white wine?"

"I forgot how stunning these views are."

"We designed the house around them, of course."

"Red, please."

She flitted back into the kitchen, and I wandered around, glad for the chance to be alone. Displayed on the walls and shelves was a lot of local artwork, Laura's own carved stone sculptures, a few of my mother's startlingly, incongruously sensual drawings, an abstract steel cactus by Pablo, Solo's ceramic bowls, a portrait of Laura signed by Patty, a photograph by Giselle, five of Suzie's odd little figures. Leo Gold loved art; his role at Bella Luna was to support his wife and her cohort and collect their work. On the bookshelves was a preponderance of historical nonfiction with a heavy emphasis on World War II, along with a wide-ranging assortment of novels and poetry collections. A cabinet held a stereo with a record player and a collection of CDs and albums, jazz and classical. Two facing long, white couches and a couple of metal and chrome low-slung armchairs and several Moroccan poufs were arranged on a large rug around the fireplace.

I'd always loved this house. After my father died, when it was just my mother and me alone together in our incompatible grief, I spent as much time as I could over here, not only because Rose was my best friend, but also because a real family lived here, three siblings, two parents, a noisy, fun whirl of squabbles and dinners and shoes in the foyer. Luckily, Rose seemed to love having me here, in fact, she never wanted me to leave. She and I leaned on each other so much as kids, two lonesome girls stuck in the high desert, both of us with distant mothers, missing beloved fathers, intractable singular personalities.

Laura handed me a wineglass. Her hand trembled. I had to grab it from her to keep her from dropping it. "Please, sit down." She landed on the edge of an enormous Eames lounge chair, alighting like a dancer, with her legs tucked to the side, spine erect. "Thank you so much for coming on such short notice."

I plunked myself on one of the hard modern couches.

"I wanted to tell you one thing before you see Leo." She looked down at her own glass of white wine. "He has dementia. We just found out a few weeks ago, so maybe you didn't know."

This was the worst imaginable news. The population of Rancho Bella Luna is like a fleet of rebuilt, stripped-down, Mad Max diesel-punk vehicles, rattling over the sand, churning through the rocks. Everyone carries heavy loads of accrued experiences, weathering the years—high-tech machinery swapped in for worn-out joints, titanium bars holding splintered bones together, kidney and liver transplants, heart stents and pacemakers, along with all the tumors and malignant growths dug off their skin, cut out of their bodies, excised from their brains. They've undergone invasive surgeries, regimes of dialysis, chemotherapy, and radiation. Some of them have limps from childhood polio. Women have scars where their breasts used to be. They joke a lot about spare parts and jerry-rigged chassis. But the one thing that's never funny around here is dementia, that's the great terror. Not breaking your back, not cancer. The old people I know all carry their brains inside their skulls like fragile cargo.

"I'm so sorry," I said. "I didn't know. Is it Alzheimer's?"

"That's what they think. Anyway, so there's that. And now Rose. I'm just beside myself right now."

"You said she was due over here for dinner last night?"

"Yes. She would *never* not come without calling to let me know. That's when I first knew there was something wrong. I called the cops at midnight last night after she didn't show up, and I've tried calling her phone a dozen times since then, but it goes straight to voicemail every time."

I could imagine their reaction: She's been gone two days? Seriously? But I kept my face impassive. "What did the cops say?"

"They came by this morning, but only to tell me they can't open an official case until she's been missing for at least seventy-two hours. That's when I decided to call you. No one has seen Rose since Wednesday morning. It's Friday evening now! What if she's been kidnapped, what if she's lying hurt somewhere? Seventy-two hours could be too long! Is that true, that rule?" She peered at me.

As Laura knew, I used to be a cop, but I didn't want to get into what the local police should or should not have been doing. "You mentioned that Rose left her things here. Can I take a look at them?"

"Well, not *here*, here. They're over at the Triangle A. She has been staying in their visiting artists' casita this month, doing a residency. She also rents a house down in Tucson."

"When was the last time you saw her?"

"Last week. She came over briefly to borrow a pair of hiking boots. We wear the same shoe size."

"She was going hiking?"

"I'm not sure. She didn't say what she needed them for. But I assume so."

"Does Rose live with anyone down in Tucson?"

"Her friend Mickey, who hasn't heard a word from Rose since Rose came up here. Apparently they were fighting."

"Is it a love relationship?"

Laura looked consternated. "I don't think so. Mickey is a woman. I mean, she goes by they and them pronouns, but she's . . . female? I think? And Rose likes men, as far as I know. So probably not. They are very close, I do know that. Gosh, I don't know, Justine. I feel like I don't know anything at all about my daughter right now."

"How has she seemed to you lately?"

"She has been having some troubles lately. Besides fighting with her roommate. She lost her job." Laura's face was bone white and gaunt with strain. I was increasingly curious about the source of the intensity of her anxiety. Back when I was her daughter's best friend, she'd always seemed somewhat remote from our childhood world, mysterious, a glamorous cipher, and I was in awe of her mythic coolness and romantic complexity. This was the first time I'd ever had a reason to feel compassion for her, ever seen her as entirely human. "Also, she's been suffering after a romantic breakup . . . well, she didn't confide any of this in me," she added, as if this pained her to admit. "Ben told me yesterday, when I called him to let him know Rose went missing. He was really worried that she might have done something to"—her nostrils flared—"hurt herself. I can't believe she would, but Ben knows his sister better than I do. It was his idea to call you after the cops came this morning."

Aha. So that would explain the urgency. "Who were the cops who came?"

"Eddie Gomez and Tyler Bridgewater."

At the sound of Tyler's name, I gave an involuntary start. Tyler was my high school sweetheart, the boy Rose had decided I'd stolen from her, the reason our friendship ended so painfully and abruptly. "Have you talked to anyone at the Triangle A about where they think Rose might have gone?"

"A little," Laura said, clasping her own elbows and hugging her arms to herself as if she were cold. "I spoke to Angela, she's the caretaker over there. She has no idea, she says."

The front door opened and closed, and I stood up to greet the two young men who walked in. It took me a second to recognize these tall, strange new versions of Jason and Ben Gold. I hadn't seen them since they were kids. Girls are women-in-waiting, but boys metamorphose from small, sweet-smelling, soprano-voiced pip-squeaks with adorably vulnerable necks into hairy, large, deep-voiced adults. Jason and Ben had both inherited their dad's broad-shouldered, medium-tall build. Jason was angular and slim, with a narrow face and a neat, corporate haircut and Warby Parker glasses. When he was little, he looked like a cute little chipmunk. As a grown-up, his rodent features looked too small for his face, as if they hadn't grown along with it. He had a pinched little mouth, close-set eyes, and his nose was roughly the size and shape of one of those little hard-rubber doorstops, affixed vertically to his face. His hairline was beginning to recede.

Ben was stockier, softer, his features broader than his brother's. He sported a wild half-fro of curly brown hair, and the lower half of his face was peppered with dark stubble that scratched my cheek as he gave me a hug.

"Hey, Ben."

"How are you, Jo?"

"Okay. It's been awhile. You grew up."

He grinned. "Only on the outside."

Jason's phone rang. "I have to take this," he said, striding from the room without acknowledging me.

"My big brother the wheeler-dealer," said Ben. "His new pet project is an old-age home."

"Ben! It's an eldercare facility," said Laura. "And it's exactly what we old fogeys need right now. He's doing a great thing for the Rancho."

Jason's voice boomed somewhere off in the house, loud and officious. Ben caught my eye, and I had a flash of the impish, shaggy-haired kid he used to be. Laura leapt up and levitated up the steps to the kitchen. Leo Gold emerged from the hallway and fixed me with a blank look, as if he had no clue who I was. I was shocked by his appearance. He was fairly well along on the declining end of the male metamorphic timeline. Back when he was younger, he had been a vital, imposing man, with a large head of wiry salt-and-pepper curls, a barrel chest, and strong arms. Now he looked like a straw broom, bald and rickety and skinny, as if his brain's deterioration had caused him to shed and wither. His eyes looked fixed in their sockets, so he had to turn his head to aim his gaze directly at whatever he wanted to examine. He was seventy-eight, but so was the organic farmer across the road, and so was my old friend Solo, and those two dudes were still doing physical work, still stringing coherent sentences together, still flush and hardy.

It was sad to see him like this.

"How are you, Leo? I'm Jo Bailen. I haven't seen you in a long time."

"Well, I'm just fine, how are you," he said in a reedy voice, higher than I remembered.

I sat down again. Laura reappeared with a tray and gestured to Leo, pointing at a chair across from me, raising her voice and enunciating as if he were deaf as well as demented. "Come, dear. Sit over there."

Ben seated himself at the other end of the couch I was sitting on. Jason walked back in, pocketing his phone, wearing the smug look of a guy who had just closed a deal. "That was Chad. He said everything with Sunset Shadows is on track and we just need one more signature and it's done."

"That's wonderful, Jason," said Laura. She was fussing with the contents of the tray, handing Jason an opened bottle of beer, a can of seltzer to Ben, and a small glass of what appeared to be prune juice to Leo. The tray now held only two small dishes of olives and peanuts, which everyone ignored.

Laura arranged herself again on the Eames chair, sitting side-ways, right on the edge, as if she were about to leap up again.

I palmed some peanuts. "What's Sunset Shadows?"

Jason looked directly at me for maybe the first time since I'd arrived. His expression was flinty. I felt hostility coming off him like smoke from dry ice.

"It's his planned community," said Ben. "My brother and a couple of his college broski friends are trying to quote-unquote 'buy' a hundred-acre plot of Rancho land for literally one hundred dollars so they can go and develop some crappy, cookie-cutter complex of 'senior condos' and in return all the residents of Bella Luna get to 'age in place' or some shit. Did I get that right, Jase?"

"No," said Jason, sitting next to his father. "And also go fuck your-self."

"Justine is not here to talk about Sunset Shadows," said Laura. On that large chair, dwarfed by the men in her family, she looked tiny and fragile. I couldn't help suspecting that this pleased her. "She's here to talk about Rose."

"Sure, Mom," said Jason. "Let's talk about Rose." He cocked his head and stared at me, arms crossed. I was not a fan of this titan-of-industry adult version of Jason, who used to be a good kid, quiet, a little shy. How had he turned into such a douche?

"All right," I said. "But just out of curiosity, what does your sister think about Sunset Shadows?"

"She thinks it's evil," answered Ben. He was clearly relishing having me as an ally in what appeared to be an ongoing, lifelong fraternal battle. "And a tragedy. If she were here right now, she'd be outraged. She has been, all along."

"Rose is fine with it," said Jason, not taking the bait. "And she's not missing."

"Jason," said Laura, "you don't know that. It's not like her not to come for dinner, not even a call . . ."

Jason bared his teeth in a cold smile. "She probably just flaked off somewhere and forgot to turn on her phone."

"She never turns off her phone," said Ben. "She's always on it, every second."

Both brothers looked at me as if I were the arbiter here. Jason's close-set eyes were narrowed behind his expensive glasses, whose lenses I would have bet anything were nonprescription. Ben leaned forward, his elbows resting on his knees, and I felt him willing me to share his sense of urgency. The airy, high-ceilinged room felt as if it were shrinking, drained of oxygen by these two contentious brothers.

"Well," I said with a glance of apology at Ben, whose side I wanted to be on, "she hasn't been gone very long. The logical starting assumption is that she decided to go somewhere without telling anyone. The majority of missing-person cases don't involve foul play."

There was an odd, terse silence. Jason looked smug, Ben started to say something, thought better of it, and clammed up, and Laura gazed at me helplessly. Leo looked around at us as if we were all strangers speaking a foreign language.

"That said," I went on, feeling uncomfortable and off-kilter and way too personally involved in all this, "if any of you can think of anyone who might want to harm Rose in any way, enemies, rivals, anything at all, I am all ears." No one said anything, but the silence bristled. I tried again. "Laura mentioned some trouble in her life. She had a recent breakup? She lost her teaching job?"

"Yeah, she got shit-canned for faking Navajo heritage," said Jason.

I stared at him, not sure I'd heard him correctly. "I'm sorry, *what*?"

"I just can't believe she would do that," Laura said. "I don't understand it."

"That was smart, if you ask me," Leo barked with a canny gleam in his eye, as if the clouds in his brain had parted briefly.

Jason snorted. "Not smart. How stupid can you be? She should have picked Penobscot or Seneca, something far away and harder to prove. You know? She's from the East Coast, originally. Who would have questioned that? But faking being Navajo in Arizona, that's just asking for it."

"In Rose's defense, she's always been empathetic to the plight of minorities and the oppressed," said Laura.

"Um, no she hasn't," said Ben.

"She's so full of shit," said Jason, snorting again.

The brothers exchanged a rare split second of shared mirth.

"Lately I got the feeling she was starting to believe it herself," said Ben. "She was pretty convincing. Last winter, I went to a talk she gave on collective cultural trauma. I almost believed her when she started referring to the Navajo as 'my forebears.' And I'm her brother."

"Half brother," said Jason. "Hey, maybe Dad secretly has some rare Jewish Navajo blood in him."

"Jew-vajo," Ben said.

"That makes no sense," said Laura. "Leo's not her father."

"Where the hell is Rose?" Leo asked loudly, looking around the room at his wife and sons. "Why is she always late?"

"She's missing, Dad," said Ben in a patient voice. "That's why Jo is here. She's going to find her."

I stood up, feeling antsy. Rose's family had nothing more to tell me about her, at least not now, at least not as a group. Maybe one-on-one with each of them I'd have more luck. "Thanks, Laura," I said. "I'll talk to Angela first thing tomorrow morning and go from there. I'll be in touch with you all."

"I'll walk you out," said Ben. At the door, he held out a pack of American Spirits. "Do you have a minute before you go?"

"You still smoke actual, real cigarettes?"

"I'm in recovery from booze and drugs, not nicotine. And I hate vaping."

Lighting up, we strolled over the ridge and sat side by side on a big rock under a nearly full moon. It was dark already, and the sky bristled with stars, the desert splashed with bright cold light. I nudged Ben's shoulder with my own. "How are you? I heard through the Rancho grapevine that you were having some tough times. Are you okay now?"

"Yeah. I've been an addict since I was a teenager." He said this with the rote assurance of someone who regularly announced this in front of a roomful of people. "Now I'm in every twelve-step program in existence. I have eighteen months clean and sober. It's been an uphill journey."

"Good for you."

"I'm in school too. Getting my degree in social work. I want to mentor troubled teenagers, maybe run a group house with my girlfriend, Savannah. We're pretty serious. She's studying theater at ASU, so I've been living up in Phoenix."

"Is she sober too?"

"Yup, she got into drugs hard and early, got sober at eighteen. I met her in NA, actually. She was a child actor, like a freaking prodigy with voice parodies. She started out doing local radio commercials, voice-overs and stuff. After she gets her degree, she plans to move to Hollywood and get into TV."

"An actress, huh."

"I know. Classic Oedipal shit, right? Actually, I was an actor for a while, too. I got some parts in local theater, but that lifestyle is too conducive to using. Too emotionally intense."

"How long have you and Savannah been together?"

"Six months. She's twenty-one." He added with a spark of defensiveness, "But she's a grown-up."

"Do she and your mom get along?"

He looked sheepish. "They haven't met yet."

"In half a year of dating?"

"We've been too busy to . . . Anyway, I was planning on bringing Savannah down here to introduce her to everyone tonight. But then with Rose disappearing and all, it didn't feel like the right time. Maybe tomorrow."

I got out my phone. "Before I forget, what's Rose's cell phone number?"

As he read me the digits from his own phone, I punched them in and tried to find a more comfortable seat on the rock. Rose and I used to sit here as kids. I was smaller back then. "What else can you tell me? You and Rose are close, right?"

"We are. I talk to her almost every day. Sometimes it's just to check in. She's been good about helping me stay clean. And by good, I mean in my face. Tough love. I need it."

"How did she seem to you lately?"

"She's been kind of a mess."

"How so? Your mother mentioned relationship problems, in addition to losing her job."

"Well, there's something else. Something I haven't told anyone. I wanted to talk to you about it in private."

I looked around at the vast, empty night—no eavesdroppers anywhere. "What's that?"

"Rose has been talking a lot about you recently. You and Tyler Bridgewater. Like, obsessively. She claims you ruined her life. Both of you. Some kind of high school drama–type shit. She blames it for all her problems, literally."

I was amazed at how much this accusation still simultaneously hurt and outraged me. "Seriously?"

"I wish I were kidding, but I'm not. What exactly happened between you two? I know her side of the story, which I'm sure is totally delusional and blown way out of proportion."

"Which is?"

"That you stole Tyler Bridgewater away from her. She talks about it like it was this epic betrayal of biblical proportions. The original sin."

"Oh God. We were fourteen. High school freshmen. I went on a date with a boy she secretly liked, which according to her broke the girl code, which wasn't fair, because I had no idea she liked him, because she never told me, even though I was her best friend, and then suddenly we were enemies. I mean, if she'd just told me that she had such a big crush on him, of course I would have stayed away forever, but I had no clue. I offered to cancel the date and never speak to him again. But for her, the damage was done. She said she'd never forgive me. It was so crazy I actually thought maybe she'd secretly hated me all along and was looking for a reason to lash out."

"Wow," said Ben. "Women really know how to fuck with your head, don't they?" He crushed his cigarette butt under his sneaker and pocketed it.

"Tell me about it," I said. I took a deep final drag of my cigarette and stomped it out under the heel of my boot and picked it up. Ben held out his hand for the butt automatically, like a soccer mom collecting gum wrappers. "It was good seeing you again. Call me anytime, night or day."

I headed down the moonlit path. As I passed my mother's little house, I glanced at her front window and saw lights on behind closed curtains. For a moment, I considered knocking on her door, but she hated to be dropped in on, and I wasn't feeling confident enough at the moment to face her irritated, impatient expression when she saw her daughter unexpectedly on her doorstep. I was frankly yearning for a warm hug right now, and my mother's hugs were forced rather than heartfelt. She hugged me because you were supposed to hug your daughter, but she didn't seem to like it.

So I continued on to the main courtyard, got into my car, and shut myself inside. I drove up the rutted driveway slowly, my headlights picking out a pair of glowing eyes off in the rocks, the glint of a beer can.

THREE

THE NEARBY APACHE MOTEL WAS THE EASIEST SOLUTION. THE AL-
ternative was to drive back down to Tucson tonight and then drive
back up here again first thing tomorrow morning, which seemed like
a lot of trouble. Exchanging minimal grunts with the stumpy, balding
gender-indeterminate garden gnome behind the counter, I handed
over my credit card and ID and filled out a form and in return got my
cards back along with an old-timey room key, a long brass-toothed
jobbie on a triangular plastic fob with the room number stamped on
it. I was in Teepee #3. All the other teepees were empty. I shuffled
along and unlocked the particleboard door set into the slanted concrete wall and went in and flicked on the overhead light and looked
around at my new palace: stiff chintz drapes, stained orange carpet,
rust marks in the bathroom sink, an overall smell of harsh disinfec-
tant with a moldy underbelly, but on the whole, clean enough for my
low standards. I flopped on the red-white-and-black polyester Navajo-
patterned bedspread, flesh-eating microbes and residual bodily fluids
be damned, and stared up at the ceiling.

Ben had brought it all back, the bewildering psychodrama of being Rose's best friend one minute and then her worst enemy the next.
For the rest of high school, after accusing me of betraying her, Rose
turned a group of girls against me and went around with her cote-
rie, her coven, giving me black looks. I covertly, wistfully, enviously
watched her with her new gang of friends, that bunch of smart, arty
girls who ran the literary magazine and acted in the theater produc-

tions and played in the school jazz band. Yearning to be allowed to join them, to win my friend back, I tried to talk to Rose a few times, awkwardly attempting to apologize, to explain, to say whatever it took to make things right. But she cut me dead every time.

So I wrapped myself around Tyler. He was my social safety shield, my friend as well as my boyfriend. Compared to Rose, he was straightforward and uncomplicated. What he felt, he felt. He was nowhere near as interesting as she was, but to compensate for his limitations, he was devoted, consistent, and physically beautiful. He had glinting dark-blue eyes and full pouty lips and silken skin and a snake-hipped whip-lean body and thick wavy chestnut-brown hair. He smelled like raw apples and musk. His voice was like hot honeycomb. And he adored me. I'd lost my father and then, for all intents and purposes, my mother, and now my best friend was gone as well. I had no siblings. I was a loner. So Tyler became everything to me by dint of necessity: boyfriend, best friend, family.

But I never stopped missing Rose.

I pried myself off the bed, went into the little bathroom, washed my face, brushed my teeth, and put on my pajamas, which consisted of an extra large T-shirt and undies. It was still early, but I turned out the lights and climbed into bed and lay staring into the semidarkness.

After Rose and I went our separate ways, we had an almost preternatural awareness of where the other one was at all times, like the inverse intensity of our friendship, its negative. At school, we existed in our separate social bubbles with no overlap, like our own John Hughes movie. We managed to avoid each other almost entirely for the rest of high school, until that one night.

What the hell even was that?

Reluctantly, I retrieved the memory from the depths of my internal data drive, dusted it off, and let it play: prom night senior year, when Rose showed up at the Triangle A after-party in her white dress and green gloves. Dateless, she glommed on to Tyler and me as a bunch of us shit-faced kids left the party to watch the sunrise out in the desert, bouncing around in Tyler's pickup truck in the dark, headlights careening off the cactus and creosote, liquor bottles and pot smoke and laughter, a bunch of amped-up seniors carousing one last time. I was sitting in the cab next to Tyler, who was driving, and somehow Rose had managed to insinuate her way into the cab next to me, on my other side. I was caught off guard by this sudden about-face, but so happy that she was being friendly again that I was ready to go with it, no questions asked. "Look what I have," she said as she pulled out a little plastic baggie and shook it at us. There were three pills in it.

"Whoa, what *is* that?" Tyler said with that confused, scared expression teenage boys get when they're confronted with something new and strange, probably the same one Adam had when he asked Eve what that red thing in her hand was with the bite mark in it.

"Relax, dude," said Rose, nudging me with a grin that made my heart balloon with joy. "It's Ecstasy. But I only have three, so don't tell anyone."

"I don't do pills," said Tyler. Drunk and high and acting on impulse, I swallowed the one Rose handed me, then took the other one and turned Tyler's head toward me as he drove along the rutted track, kissed him, and tongued the pill into his mouth and held his lips closed while he swallowed it as if I were medicating a puppy. Rose watched us and laughed.

We parked and ditched the truck when the road got too rough, and about seven or eight of us hiked down to the wash and lit a camp-fire in a ring of rocks with mesquite we collected. While everyone else passed a bottle of tequila around, looking up at the sky and waiting for the first rays of sun, Rose pulled Tyler and me away and led us around a bend in the arroyo. The moon was almost full, the desert awash in cold bright light. Rolling hard now, we lay under the leafy branches of the biggest cottonwood tree for miles around, a pile of three warm adolescent bodies in the cold sand in a long, slow free-for-all of kissing and pawing and rubbing and, as I now vividly recalled, some pretty intense and full-on three-way sex. It was also clear to me, replaying this memory now, that Rose was the instigator all the way through. It didn't feel accidental. Rose had orchestrated it. But I was a willing participant. So was Tyler, for that matter, but he didn't count because he was a guy and, as we all know, teenage boys will get a hard-on if anyone comes over and sits on their lap, even their own mothers. Yes, I was on drugs. But I wanted it too. Not out of guilt, but out of love. At the time, if I thought about it at all, it was in the context of Rose and me together, as an intense and albeit twisted way for us to work out our feelings for each other under cover of a drug, with Tyler as our foil and mutual lust object. Nothing overtly sexual had ever happened between Rose and me before. Even during the most intense romantic make-believe games as kids, we always laughingly put one of our hands between our mouths when we pretend-kissed. I was aware that I was attracted to girls as well as boys from an early age, but for some reason, not Rose. It wasn't like that with her. My feelings for her were familial. She was my ally, my familiar, my sister.

So fooling around with Rose was totally new for me, and unexpected, but it wasn't as weird as it might have been. I didn't mind sharing Tyler with her. If she'd asked, I might have done so from the start. More than anything, it made me hope our friendship could resume again. It made me think I might get her back as my best friend.

Silly me.

As the sun came up, a strong chilly dawn wind blew, and the three of us lay in a drowsy heap in the sand together, cuddled up for warmth. Rose lay between Tyler and me with her arms around us, wide awake, still rolling, running her hands through our hair, telling us both how much she loved us, staring into our eyes. Rose had always been intense, that was how she was, full of hate, full of love, both at the same time, out of proportion but genuine. In my even-keel drama-free relationship with Tyler, I had missed this intensity more than I cared to admit to myself.

Afterward, we sobered up and all went home to sleep. To my pained disappointment, the next time I saw Rose, she snubbed me coldly, acted as if nothing had happened, as if that whole night had been a hallucination. So we were sworn enemies again. That was my history with Rose Delaney: We loved each other, probably more than either of us realized because we were so young, and then she hated me for "stealing" a boy I'd had no idea she even knew existed, and then she and my boyfriend and I had intense drug-fueled sex, and then it was a cold war again. Our relationship felt like a snarled tangle, I guessed fraught for her, and definitely confusing and painful for me.

Years later, in our midtwenties, on a whim, because I missed her and was curious, I went to one of Rose's poetry readings in a bar downtown. She was gussied up like a retro-punk princess, with a shock of pink in her jet-black hair, thigh-high boots, and a black leather bustier minidress. She read her poetry in a breathy, pretentious voice that made me chomp on my lower lip to keep from laughing. I thought it was cute, how self-serious she was. I wanted to elbow the old Rose, who would have grinned at this new version of herself. But this new Rose was much too cool for the likes of me. After the reading, she sat in the back of the bar in a small crowd of friends, probably fellow poets, drinking and talking. As I was skulking out the door, our eyes caught and held for a split second, and I felt a powerful surge of re-membered love. Then we both looked away, and I hustled along the street back to my car.

A few years later, Rose was walking into a trendy downtown thrift store as I was heading to the Congress Hotel to meet with a prospective client at the Cup Cafe. She saw me, too, but she wouldn't meet my eyes this time, so I just kept going. I remember suppressing a pang of sadness mixed with something else, something rougher. Anger maybe. Why did it have to be that way? As an adult, Rose looked interesting, full of exuberance and life, like someone I'd like to know.

Only once as adults I tried to talk to her. It was at a Christmas party at the Rancho. We were in our early thirties by then, both grown-ups, but there we were, still skirting each other, still making sure our paths didn't intersect. It felt flat-out stupid to me. After a few glasses of wine, I walked up to her and looked her in the eye and said, "Come on, Rose, we were just kids. Can we be friendly again?" Without a word, she walked away from me. I stared after her, stung. And that, as the saying goes, was that; I was damned if I was ever going to try again.

Holding on to that defiance, I fell asleep. My dreams were slow-moving and blurry and restful, and I woke up bright and early with a clear head. I sat on the unmade bed in a clean pair of underwear, my hair wet from the shower, and dialed Ronnie's cell number while coffee dripped in the little coffeemaker.

"Hey, Bailen."

Just the sound of her brusque, raspy voice bucked me up. There was no reason to call my boss right now, but I needed some moral support in the form of an expletive-laden brush-off. "Hey, Taffet. I talked to the family last night. Turns out the missing woman lost her teaching job for faking Navajo heritage."

"No shit?"

"None whatsoever. Listen, seriously, this case is literally too close to home for me. I don't think I can be objective here. Can you or Yazzie take over for me?"

"We're both tied up." She knew I knew this. She also knew I was just calling to get my hand held a little. "This is all yours. Don't let feelings get in your way. You're a professional."

"Okay," I said. "Roger that."

"Who's Roger?"

We hung up, and I called Erin Yazzie.

"What's up, Bailen?"

"Hey, Yazzie. I'm on this missing-woman case. Turns out she's been faking Navajo heritage, among other things."

"So you're what now, trying to get some Native insight?"

"If you have any." I was smiling. Ever since Erin had joined the agency, I'd been trying to strike up a real friendship with her. She was hard to pin down, but I had a feeling she liked me too.

She snorted. "My Native insight is that it's fucked up. White girls keep doing it, ever since it started to be socially advantageous to have melanin, and why do you think that is?"

"For attention. They want the oppression cred because they're pissed that no one cares about white-girl pain anymore."

"You don't need any help from me. You got this." I heard the squeal of tires on pavement. "I gotta go, I'm tailing a sleazebag in a lowrider."

After we hung up, I slammed two cups of acidic, weak motel brew, brushed my teeth, then pulled on yesterday's jeans, clean socks and bra and T-shirt from my go bag, and last but not least, my cowgirl boots. I own fifteen pairs, both new and vintage. They are my only fashion obsession. My current pair were 1960s era, black with textured red feet and pulls, and curlicue cream inlays, midcalf rise, low heels, slightly pointed curved toes. I felt like a badass in them, like Rattlesnake Kate headed to the saloon for a night of whiskey shots and Texas Hold'em.

Resigned to doing this job as well as I could, at least for now, I pointed my car at the Triangle A Ranch, which was just out of town, across the highway, a cluster of old buildings tucked into a grove of juniper and cypress in the open desert. The Triangle A was a cattle ranch turned art commune, like Rancho Bella Luna. But unlike the Bella Luna, which ran on fumes and nostalgia these days, the Triangle A remained a functioning business, well maintained and profitable. The bed-and-breakfast was popular with tourists, and the adobe Art Barn had a gallery, a theater, and an outdoor sculpture garden. The grounds were landscaped with native plants and rocks, whimsical artworks catching the light, mobiles turning in the breeze. All the paths were lit at night with solar footlights and fairy lights overhead. The Triangle A's parties had been legendary since I was a kid: summer bonfires by the Art Barn with openings and dance or theater or musical performances, and New Year's Eve parties in the main house with a live band and the entire town of Delphi dancing on the floorboards and getting drunk together.

I pulled into the parking lot and trundled through the sun-blasted early morning to the main house, a big, square, two-story nineteenth-century place with a red-tile roof, painted white with blue trim. I climbed the steps to the deep porch that spanned the front and knocked on the big wooden front door, old and intricately carved, with a mullioned window at eye level.

After a while, I heard footsteps inside the house on the wooden floorboards, getting louder. The woman who opened the door was about my age, slim and red haired, dressed in a short silk flowered kimono over white cutoffs and a white tank top, pert little nipples clearly visible. Because I am a sucker for beauty, I was momentarily struck mute. Her hair was long and loose and glinting with gold highlights, her eyes a strong, direct green. Splashes of paint streaked her hands and forearms. There was a finger of magenta going up one thigh, disappearing under her shorts, which made me suddenly aware with electric interest that she'd been painting naked; the delay in answering the door must have been because she'd been getting dressed.

"I'm Jo Bailen," I said, trying to recover my cool. "I'm a private investigator. Rose Delaney's mother hired me to find her."

"Come in," said the woman. Her voice was husky. "I'm Angela Geiger, like the counter. Can I offer you some coffee? Have you had breakfast?"

"No. I mean, yes. That all sounds great."

I followed Angela through the two large, dim, cool parlors with their original plaster walls and moldings and fireplaces, furnished with Queen Anne love seats, brocade fainting couches, big leather armchairs, Oriental rugs, and lamps with fringed shades, through the formal dining room with its long mahogany table and matching cushioned chairs, old hutch, and sideboard. Off the dining room was a smaller room that had clearly been turned into Angela's painting studio, a half-finished painting on an easel and a strong whiff of turpentine. Paintings hung on the walls of all the rooms in the house. Every surface and windowsill and shelf was crammed with artifacts, carved sculptures, vintage glass bottles and tobacco tins, peacock feathers in fish-shaped vases, leather-bound books, dream catchers, beeswax candles in Mexican pressed-tin holders. An old upright piano sat by the fireplace in one of the parlors, and chandeliers hung from the plaster medallions in the ceilings. The wide-board floors were uneven and creaky.

The big old-fashioned kitchen had Formica countertops, green flecked with gold. A white cast-iron double farmhouse sink was installed in the pantry. In one corner was a vintage Frigidaire, and under a big casement window sat a 1950s eight-burner chrome stove, skillets of various sizes stacked on its surface. Pots hung from hooks above. All my life, the Triangle A was the youthful counterpoint to the more settled, structured Rancho. Life here always struck me as a free-form, ongoing, communal art fest, people coming through for a night, a month, a couple of years, and even as high school kids we always felt welcome to join the fun. When I was a teenager, coming to Triangle A parties on weekends, we used to cook drunken midnight suppers in this kitchen, spaghetti or bacon and eggs or chilaquiles. We'd eat in the front parlor, sitting on the floor by the fire, someone playing guitar, people dancing, singing along, playing cards, someone crashed on the couch. Now, there didn't seem to be anyone around at all. My car had been one of only three in the lot.

I took the cup of coffee Angela handed me and sat in the break-fast nook. She turned a burner on under a skillet and flipped a pat of butter into it, let that melt, then cracked a couple of eggs into the hot fat. While they sizzled and spat, I drank some black coffee and split open a muffin. It smelled like cinnamon and was chock-full of healthy ingredients, shredded carrots and chopped walnuts and dried apricots. Sunlight lay in slanted oblongs on the linoleum floor. The overhead ceiling fan spun currents in the air, stirring the edges of Angela's kimono. She slid the fried eggs onto a plate, reached into a pan in the oven and added a few strips of bacon alongside, and set it in front of me.

I picked up a strip of bacon, dipped it in hot yolk, and crunched it down. The edge taken off my appetite, I got to work. "Where is every-one? This place always used to be full of people."

"It's been really quiet. COVID hit, and now we're closed for ren-ovations."

"How long have you been the caretaker?"

"Since 2019. I took over when Kumar and Ellen left. Did you know them?"

"They're after my time. But I grew up in Delphi, I used to come to parties here in high school. Rose and I grew up together at the Bella Luna."

Angela shot me a look as she poured herself some coffee. "Well, the last time I saw her," she said before I even had to ask, "was Tuesday night at dinner."

"How did she seem?"

"Normal." Angela sat across from me and gave me a cool, apprais-ing look. "Acting like the superstar of the Rose Delaney Show. I tuned her out, but she didn't even notice."

"Sounds like she was a little manic."

"You can call it whatever you want." I heard an edge in her voice. "She talked about herself nonstop."

"She's been going through a lot of stress, I understand." For some reason, I felt defensive of Rose. "What was she saying about herself?"

"She was going to show them, whoever 'they' were. The people who hurt her. She arrived here about three weeks ago acting like a tragic heroine, and as time has gone on she's pumped herself up into some kind of brave survivor, the victim of persecution. She likes to say 'turn pain into poetry,' like her mantra."

Well, good for her, I thought. It sounded to me as if she were waging an intense battle against self-pity and shame right now with everything she had. "After dinner, did she meet anyone? Go anywhere?"

"Not that I know of," said Angela. "I assume back to her casita. I didn't see her again. She wasn't at breakfast on Wednesday morning. I haven't seen her since. Kylie and Babette both got worried yesterday and called her mom to see if she was over at her place."

"Who are Kylie and Babette?"

"Oh, I thought you knew them. They're Rose's bandmates. They both work here and live in the Art Barn. They were the ones who got her the residency."

"Did you know Rose before she came up here this month?"

"Never met her before."

"Who else is living here right now, besides you three?"

She gave me a sharp look.

"I don't mean to sound policey and nosy." I held up my hands to reassure her she wasn't a suspect. "I'm just curious."

She backed down. "At the moment, no one, just us. We're opening up and expecting some guests next week, but like I said, it's been quiet."

"Have any other people come by recently, deliverymen, visitors, anyone?"

"Nope. Just us chickens. We do our own shopping. We keep to ourselves." She reconsidered this. "Well, of course, Noah," she said. "He's around a lot, but he doesn't live here."

"Who's Noah?"

Before she could answer, there was a kerfuffle at the back door, and Angela leapt up to open it. An old, grizzled, skinny mutt came in, walking with regal detachment, his legs stiff, a hitch in his hip, eyes bright and game. Behind him stumped a tiny black thing with a monkey face and a fluffy teddy-bear body on short, sturdy legs.

"What the hell is that?"

"That's Rose's dog," said Angela. "Our best guess is that she's an affenpinscher mix. Her name is Ophelia."

She poured kibble into two bowls, and a duet of canine crunching filled the room.

"Who's Noah?" I asked again.

"He's Kylie and Babette's friend."

When the little troll finished her breakfast, she made a beeline for me and leapt up into my lap, leathery black snub nose twitching, button eyes drilling into mine. She was not cute. She was a bearded freak. Hot and compact, she leaned her paws against my breastbone and licked my chin with her raspy, dry little tongue. Grasping her stout torso in both hands, I pried her off me and set her back down on the floor. She was heavier than she looked. I felt a flash of fondness for her. I had a soft spot for unlovely creatures.

"Could I see the room where Rose was staying?"

Angela nodded and led me behind the Art Barn, down a short path lined with succulents and paved with adobe bricks, and unlocked the front door to a small casita. "Let me know if you need anything," she said and headed back up to the main house.

In the far corner was an iron bedstead, mattress covered with a Navajo blanket. A worktable abutted the front window, which looked out over the bare foothills, up to the snowy peaks of Mount Lemmon. There was an armchair with a standing lamp, a small bookshelf, and a wooden chest of drawers. It was a simple, spare, cozy little room.

Rose had made herself at home here. The worktable was covered with books and papers. On a trunk at the foot of the bed was an open backpack exploding with clothes. The little bathroom was cluttered with toiletries, jewelry, hand-washed lingerie draped over the shower-curtain rod. The bed was strewn with clothes. Shoes littered the floor, along with a puddled scarf, a few stacks of books.

Ophelia stumped through the open doorway. After she lapped at a water bowl on the floor in the kitchenette, she jumped up to settle herself on the bed, her head on her paws, watching me.

Rose's laptop was on the worktable. I sat down and powered it up. I didn't know her password, of course, but I could get around that. When it booted, I pressed the Command and R keys to put it into the Mac OS recovery mode. When the Language screen came up, I clicked my way through the steps to the "reset password" prompt, entered "Ophelia" because it was the first word that came to mind, restarted the computer, entered the new password, and I was in.

"Hello there, Rose Delaney," I muttered, looking at her jam-packed, messy desktop. "Let's see what you were up to."

In the disappointing absence of desktop WhatsApp and Messages, I went through her recent email correspondence, working my way through the Inbox, her archived emails, and the Sent folder. It wasn't surprising that there wasn't a lot of personal correspondence, since everyone texted and IM'd and messaged these days. What I really needed was to get my mitts on her phone, but until that turned up, most likely along with Rose herself, this was all I had to work with.

An hour later, I had learned enough to confirm my impression of Rose's current life as a hot mess, even adding a thing or two to the list of troubles her family had given me. "What the hell," said the email she'd sent to Jason on Tuesday. "I can't get Mom to listen to me. PLEASE don't do this, Jason. I can't believe you're 'on board with this.' Who even talks like that? How did you turn into such a douchebag?"

If Jason had written back, Rose must have deleted it, or else he had called or texted her about it, or maybe he'd ignored it. In any case, this email was a stand-alone with no preceding note or response.

Next came a short exchange with someone called Lupita, her Gmail handle GGonzalez. As far as I could make out, because it was all hastily written in a kind of shorthand, Lupita and Rose were talking about Sunset Shadows, commiserating about how horrible it was, and trying to figure out how to stop it.

Just under that was a letter from someone named Lena Duby, who turned out to be the academic dean who'd just fired Rose for passing herself off as Navajo. It tersely confirmed an in-person conversation referred to as "yesterday's meeting on this issue." I read through the attached paperwork that constituted Rose's official dismissal from her teaching job at Saguaro Early College. Rose's reply to Dean Duby, sent four minutes after the email came in, was short and to the point, acknowledging receipt and agreeing to remove her belongings from her office right away.

The email from Rose's publisher, Felix Mantooth, dated a week ago Friday, was equally merciless and abrupt: Due to the ongoing misrepresentation of her identity and the appropriation of Native culture in her work, Catalina Press would be unable to publish this book or anything else by Rose Delaney ever again. Of course, Rose was welcome to seek another publisher.

In the rest of her emails, I found nothing to or from her roommate Mickey, no correspondence of any interest, and nothing further concerning Sunset Shadows. The rest of her recent emails, going back a month, were an assortment of receipts for online orders of books, clothes, and shoes, subscriptions, and automatic bill payments.

On the desktop I found a JPEG called THAT FATEFUL NIGHT. The photo was of Rose sprawled on a couch in a darkened room with a very young man, more of a kid really. Rose wore a slinky charcoal-gray pantsuit, the top unbuttoned to show a white lace camisole underneath. The boy was dressed in jeans and a T-shirt, his arm around her. She nestled against him and held his arm more tightly around her with both hands. They appeared to be in a public lounge of some sort, a bar or club.

I espied a bound manuscript on the worktable. I picked it up. It was slight. The title on the front was *Changing Woman at the Rainbow's End*. I flipped through it, stopped to scan one poem called "Foremothers, Sing to Planet Earth." It was a prayer, a lot of "Harness your ancient powers, Great Matriarchs," and so forth. Despite the highfalutin old-timey diction, and words like "geniculate" and "auscultate" and "soliterraneous," and some lines in what I guessed was Diné, the Navajo language, I was pretty sure I got the gist, which was essentially "smash the patriarchy for ecological healing." I scanned the next page, and the next, and turned to the last one. The poems all seemed to be about environmental despoilment and extinction, the "ravaged, poisoned, raped, trash-choked planet." Cheery stuff.

The back cover was stamped with a one-line logo, the outline of a jagged mountain ridge, and the words "Santa Catalina Press, Tucson, Arizona." A local publisher, small indie press from the looks of things.

Reading contemporary poetry isn't my favorite leisure activity, but I had a job to do, this was work, and I've always loved to work, even if it meant reading a long poem called "Bitter Sea of Sand." As I turned pages of painfully overwrought, despairing, existentially anguished poetry, I felt a powerful twinge of discomfort. I was used to snooping, part of the job, but not with people I knew so well. Or used to know. And Rose wouldn't want me here any more than I wanted to be here, privy to all her recent humiliations, pawing through her life, assessing her self-inflicted damages. It felt almost like a violation, my sitting here in the intimacy of her clothes, reading her emails. But I was just doing my job, helping her family too.

Rose's little monkey-dog growled from her perch on the bed as a female voice came from the doorway, lightly accented. "Hello? Are you the detective? I am Babette Pelletier."

FOUR

"JO BAILEN." GLAD FOR THE INTERRUPTION, I GOT UP AND SHOOK her hand. She had a narrow face, dark eyes close together, an elegant little hawk's beak of a nose, straight shiny brown hair in a high ponytail. She was as tall as I was but skeletally thin with knees like knots, and she wore a pale-blue T-shirt, cutoff shorts, and leather huaraches.

I recognized her as a member of Rose's band, the Sisters of Percy. I'd watched a few of their videos. It was a four-woman outfit, Aerosmith on estrogen, self-consciously nineties retro. Rose was front and center in a long black slip dress and black fingerless gloves, red lipstick, heavy eyeliner. Babette played bass in metallic eye shadow and a cobweb minidress, a blond-pigtailed adult Lolita in a Catholic girls' school uniform was on guitar, and behind the drum kit was a redheaded person who looked like a lumberjack crossed with a fire hydrant. While the three musicians played a funky, hard-rocking beat, Rose, wild black hair snaking around her head, sang a gamut of coloratura yowls and slinky purrs and kittenish mews. In that Halloween goth-cat getup, slithering around the stage, she channeled her intensity and made it hot, kinetic. Watching her gave me an odd, proprietary mix of pride and anger and a strange, unwanted envy.

"Angela said you were camped out here," said Babette, settling on the bed amid all the clothes as if she did this all the time. She lifted the little monkey troll up to look her in the face. Ophelia licked her nose. I was getting the feeling that life at the Triangle A was basically an ongoing slumber party having homemade tattoo sessions and blowing dust up each other's noses and all-night thrash-dancing. I wanted to move here immediately.

"You're in her band, right?"

"Not her band. Our band."

"I've watched some of your videos."

"We're better live. You should put on some fucking makeup and come to a show. Quite possibly it'll kill you." Sudden grin. "In a good way."

"You're French?"

"Quebec, lady. Not a stuck-up French-from-France douche."

"Didn't mean to offend."

"No, you're just interrogating. But I'm here to help. From Montreal originally, but I've been in the States for years."

"All right, if you want to help. How long have you known Rose?"

"God, I don't know, like ten years now? Is that possible?"

That was possible. "When is the last time you saw her?"

"Tuesday night dinner, a lentil hippie salad with fucking quinoa. She didn't come to breakfast the next morning." Her opaque eyes glinted. "We weren't worried at first."

"Is it normal for her to disappear?"

"Define normal."

"Does she go off by herself a lot?"

"Rose does what she likes."

"Are you worried now?"

As fast as I fired questions, she snapped her answers back at me, staccato, as businesslike as a vulture pecking a carcass, no apparent feeling or inflection in her tone, except contempt. "At first, we figured, maybe she got lucky, you know? But then two nights? And no word from her. That's *bizarre*." She said that last with full Gallic flair.

"Any idea where she might have gone? Who she might have gone with?"

Babette gave the slight shrug that means "no fucking idea" in French.

"How has Rose seemed to you lately, while she's been here?"

"Trying very hard."

"I heard from her family she's been having a lot of problems."

"I would say, a lot." Babette ticked them off on her fingers. "Her new book was canceled. She lost her teaching job. And there was something with a student."

"Like what?"

"She was sleeping with him."

That explained the photo of Rose and the boy on the couch.

Whoa. This was some serious shit. Not only had Rose been pretending to belong to an Indigenous culture for her own gain, she had seduced one of her students? Despite the fact that everything that had happened to her, all of it, was entirely of her own making, I could not entirely suppress a small pang of sympathy for her. How mortifying. How crushing. Poor Rose, sort of.

But whoa. "Has she seemed suicidal to you?"

"Not at all." Babette paused. "Well, her book."

"What happened with her book? Why was it canceled?"

"She wrote it in the voice of a Navajo woman."

"I understand she claimed to be part Navajo."

"I have First Nations ancestry myself. Rose and I connected through that." She blew air upward through her bangs. "But fuck her. It was a big fat lie."

"Right," I said.

"Anyway, someone ratted her out."

"Who was it?"

"Not me." Babette shook her head with a decisive inward expression. "An anonymous letter."

"What did it say?"

"I don't know. The dean asked for proof, her certificate of Native blood. Which she couldn't give them. And then . . ." Babette made a *tsk* sound, tongue against teeth. I got a strong feeling that this had called into question her decade-long friendship with Rose. "The publisher of her book also found out."

"Who wrote the letter?"

"She says she has no idea."

"It seems odd she wouldn't have some idea who did it."

"Most people thought she was Navajo. I know I did. She knows the traditions. The history. She even speaks some of the language."

I tried not to snort at the image of Rose using Diné words and earnestly respecting the ways of her Native ancestors. She was the daughter of a blond SoCal WASP and an Irish Jersey boy. I also recalled my entire history with her, during which she showed not one whiff of any interest in or personal association with Navajo or any Native culture whatsoever, let alone a claim to tribal identity.

I kept a straight face. "How did she get this residency so fast?"

"This place was empty. We invited her."

"Has she seen anyone, gone anywhere, had any visitors lately?"

"She came up here to be alone and work, she said she needed a retreat. She mostly stays in here working except for dinners, walks in the desert."

"She hasn't seen anyone or gone anywhere since she's been living up here?"

"I think she visited her mom maybe? She was out a few evenings these past weeks, not sure where. She might have seen a friend or gone to a movie, I don't know. But she's been here every morning at breakfast."

"Did she say anything to suggest she might want to take off? Or that she was afraid of anyone?"

Babette squinted at me as if the question were absurd and shook her head. "No."

"Anything out of the ordinary that you can think of?"

"Just that she missed our rehearsal yesterday and her mom says she didn't show up for dinner."

"Hey," said the blond-Lolita guitarist, bursting through the doorway, a little out of breath. "I'm Kylie Frost." She was small and curvy, with a kewpie-doll face, big brown eyes, her hair in two little braids. She wore powder-blue corduroy overall shorts over a pink baby tee. She had a slight twang, I guessed from West Texas. She was so cute she made my teeth hurt. "I heard you're looking for Rose."

I introduced myself. "Do you mind if I ask you some questions, Kylie?"

"Can we talk outside? It feels wrong, being in here. Like we're invading her privacy."

I followed Babette and Kylie out to the small patio. We sat in the shade in rickety metal lawn chairs in a semicircle, looking out at the desert. The landscape around us was dusty and parched. It was June, so the world should be turning lush and green soon with seasonal rains, unless the monsoon winds arrived bone dry again this year.

"I'm wondering about those anonymous letters," I said. "Could it have been the student she was seeing who reported her to the dean?"

Kylie and Babette exchanged a look. "I don't think so," said Kylie. "Maybe?"

"What's his name?"

"Chayton Griffiths," said Kylie, enunciating each name so I'd be sure to get it straight. There was something people-pleasing about her, eager and golden retriever–like. "He's called Chay."

"Have any of you met him?"

"He came to one of our gigs a while back with a few friends," said Kylie. "He was a sweet kid. Nice."

"Saguaro is an early college," I said. "High school juniors and seniors can leave high school early and earn an associated degree in two years there, so Chay was only in his late teens, I'm assuming."

"Eighteen," said Kylie. Her tone was a little defensive, as if Rose was on trial and she was on the witness stand in her defense.

As it happens, the age of consent in Arizona is eighteen.

"What happened between Rose and Chay?"

"She was his mentor. They were close. I think she might have. . . . Maybe they slept together?"

"Then he turned on her, of course," said Babette. "He wanted to bring her down."

"Did he know she wasn't Navajo?"

Kylie shook her head. "No clue. He probably thought she was legit, like the rest of us. No reason not to."

I was aware of something subterranean going on between Kylie and Babette, an unspoken communication transpiring in the air between them. I had no idea what it meant, couldn't pick up any of its flavor. I was just aware of it. They were thinking something. It was almost certainly about me. My antennae prickled.

I looked at them. Kylie's expression was innocent, but I caught something in Babette's face before she wiped it away, a residual smirk.

"Anything else you want to tell me?" I asked.

Kylie looked startled. "What?"

Babette's face was blank.

I asked on a hunch, "Do you guys know who I am? Did Rose ever talk about me?"

"Yes," Kylie said quickly, as if my question relieved her. She wasn't someone who liked keeping secrets. A compulsive confessor. My favorite kind of person in my line of work. "She has a thing about you."

"What did she say?"

Babette twisted her mouth a little and made a clucking sound, tongue against teeth. "You betrayed her," she said with sardonic melodrama. "You crushed her heart."

"Two sides to every story." My tone was light but firm.

Babette muttered something in French. It sounded exquisitely skeptical.

"Rose is still so hurt," said Kylie.

"We were fucking fourteen years old," I said, feeling a wave of weary, defensive sadness. "How can she still hold that against me?" Kylie and Babette watched me with wary alertness. I forced myself to detach, switch gears. "Has either of you talked to Rose's roommate since she went missing? The drummer in your band?"

"Rose and Mickey had a huge fight," said Kylie in a helpful rush, as if to make up for her and Babette's smirkiness about me back there. "I don't know what it was about, neither one of them is talking about it, but Rose is obviously pissed, and Mickey has blown off all our rehearsals this month. They kind of hinted that they might quit the band."

"Both of them?"

"No, just Mickey. They go by they/them pronouns. And Rose might move out of their place."

"Neither one of them will tell us," said Babette.

I cocked my head, not buying this. Rose had lived at the Triangle A for the past three weeks. The Sisters of Percy were all obviously extremely tight with one another, and bands are hothouses of drama and gossip. "You really don't know what this is about?"

"Rose did say Mickey has their head up their own ass," said Kylie. "And I quote, 'It's so far up there they can lick their own kidneys.'"

"Which is totally disgusting," said Babette. Her phone rang. "I have to take this," she said, glancing at the screen. "It's Noah."

"How long have you and Babette lived here?" I asked Kylie after Babette wandered off down the path.

"A couple of years. We live upstairs in the Art Barn, the old hay-loft is full of beds, we call it the dorms, in exchange for running the B&B. It's easy, mostly taking reservations, changing beds, cleaning the guestrooms, laundry, grocery shopping, cooking breakfast. We've been closed since December, though, so now it's mostly just keeping everything running. It's a sweet deal."

We could hear Babette laughing loudly at something going on in the phone call with Noah, whoever he was.

"Who is Noah?"

"He runs CHIT, the theater." CHIT, short for the Community House of Improvisational Theater, was housed in an old Baptist church on Arizona Avenue, just down from the Dollar Store. It was, as the name suggested, an improv troupe, with a dash of burlesque and a touch of Tennessee Williams. Their performances were free-form and experimental and charming. Last time I went was a few years ago to see a drag king lip-synching competition.

"Where does he live?"

"He lives at the theater, but Babette and I are in a relationship with him and each other. We're in a throuple."

Very briefly, I considered what it might be like to be part of a three-way relationship. I imagined that it might be emotionally thorny and complicated at times, but on the upside, probably not lonely.

Kylie stood up and started drifting toward Babette with an antic-ipatory smile, as if she already knew what the joke was and wanted to be part of it. "Let me know if you have any more questions," she said politely as she went off.

BEFORE I CLOSED UP ROSE'S CASITA, I WENT BACK TO HER LAPTOP and sent the academic dean and her editor each a quick email explaining who I was, asking them for any information that might help me determine the identity of the person who'd sent anonymous tip-off emails about Rose.

As I walked back to my car, my boots crackling against the gravel path, I hauled out my phone and called Freddy Lopez. He's a technical wizard with legitimate superpowers. He plies keyboards as if they're extensions of his fingers, mind-melds his brain with hard drives, becomes one with data, leaps over tall statistics with a single bound. Years ago, he worked for the Tucson Police Department, around the same time I did. Around the same time that I quit, he slept with the wrong captain's wife and was sent home to be a highly paid freelance consultant. Our friendship is based on a shared mistrust of the police department, a total lack of sexual interest in each other, and a mutual urge to bring criminals to justice.

"Hey, Freddy," I said when he picked up. "I need you to track a mobile phone for me." Leaning against the hot metal of my car, I gave him the number of Rose's phone and briefly explained where I was and what I was doing.

"How is it up there? You okay?" Freddy thinks anyplace north of Ina Road is the lawless wilderness. He lives in his grandmother's hacienda in the Barrio Viejo with his entire extended family. I'm not sure he's ever left central Tucson. His daily life is his bank of computers, his clients on the other end of his state-of-the-art phone, and the meals his grandmother cooks for him. When he goes out, it's within a very small radius, either to hit the gym or dance in a downtown club with his latest hot young girlfriend. These beautiful sexpots never last long, because Freddy, who is handsome, fit, and hardworking, is also high on the autism spectrum, and he's never been great at empathy or commitment. He's my age, around forty. We understand each other. I have his number and am neither attracted to him nor put off by him, and this is mutual. I joined his gym a few years back, and twice a week, Monday and Thursday mornings, he's my weightlifting buddy. He spots me and I spot him, and he politely refrains from pointing out how much more he can bench-press than me. Anyway, I do all right for a girl.

"I'm riding bareback firing a six-shooter at outlaws as we speak," I said.

"That's funny," he said flatly, not laughing. "Okay, GPS is not active, the phone is turned off, I'm getting nothing."

"Can you do me a favor and keep a tab on it and let me know if it's turned on?"

"No prob."

As I opened my car door, Ophelia hopped into the driver's seat ahead of me. "Oh, no you don't," I told her, scooping her up and depositing her on the ground. She fixed me with a stare, her four paws planted far apart. I drove out of the parking lot carefully, making sure I didn't run her over. I took the dirt road back up to the highway.

FIVE

I PARKED IN RANCHO BELLA LUNA'S MAIN COURTYARD AND HIKED up to Laura's house and knocked. Ben opened the door.

"Come on in," he said. "My parents should be back soon if you want to wait, they just ran across the street to get some eggs from the farm."

"It's okay," I said. "I'll come back. I've got nothing real to report, I'm just nosing around Rose's life to see what I can find out."

"I could use some moral support," he whispered, glancing over his shoulder back into the house. "I brought my girlfriend over to meet them. I feel like the timing isn't ideal, but she was on her way down to Tucson today anyway."

"Who's that?" came a young female voice.

"It's the investigator who's looking for Rose," said Ben. "Come in, Jo, meet Savannah."

Reluctantly, I stepped into the foyer and beheld a very young woman approaching from the living room. She was tall and slender, with rectangular gold-framed glasses and a captive bead ring piercing her bee-stung lower lip. Her long brown hair was glossy and thick, cut in tiny bangs that framed a tender forehead with fierce eyebrows. She wore a green minidress and little black ankle boots. She smiled shyly at me. "Hi," she said, offering me her hand to shake.

"Nice to meet you," I told her. Her hand was soft and warm and felt boneless in my grasp. She was so young, she hardly had any features yet, any personality. Behind her glasses, her eyes were large and blue. Her skin was perfect. She looked like she might be a nice girl. That was as much as I could ascertain at first glance. I was sure Laura would instantly size her up as much too young and dismiss her as Ben's little poppet. "Ben says you go to ASU?"

"I'm majoring in theater performance," she said. Her voice was clear, her accent generic American.

"She's talented," said Ben with what felt to me like avuncular pride, just skirting the verge of creepy, the older man showing off his talented niece or protégée. He was only about ten years older than she was, but the difference between thirty-one and twenty-one is vast. "She writes too."

I nodded, smiling, wondering how to get out of there before Laura and Leo got home. "Well, I'd better get back to finding Rose," I said.

Savannah's expression slid easily from friendly to solemn. Her face was like Laura's, motile, fluid, her expressions coming as easily as ocean waves, stage- and camera-ready, practiced. "God, it's so worrisome, I hope you find her!"

"Thanks," I said, unable to suppress a grin.

Ben caught my eye. He knew perfectly well how young his girlfriend was, and he seemed amused by my reaction, not at all offended or daunted. He clearly thought I was underestimating her and saw my reaction as a litmus test of my own character, not hers, and no doubt he was right.

"Okay, Jo, give a call as soon as you learn anything," he said.

I DROVE OFF CHUCKLING TO MYSELF, IMAGINING AS I TRUNDLED along Arizona Avenue the likely undercurrents about to ripple between Ben and Laura and Savannah and Leo, who might blurt out something wildly inappropriate about Savannah's age, which Laura would hastily cover up, which would make everything even more awkward. As I sat at the stop sign with my blinker on, waiting for a rush-hour line of cars to pass so I could swing a left onto the highway, I heard screaming sirens, saw the cars on the highway start to pull over to the shoulder. A moment later, an ambulance, two cop cars, and a fire truck whipped by in a motorcade, red and blue lights swirling, sirens Doppler shifting as they sped through the turnoff and headed into Delphi.

Impulsively, I did a quick U-turn and followed them, staring straight ahead through my windshield, not blinking, as I aimed myself at whatever we were all rushing toward. Whatever it was, it was big enough to send the whole cavalry after it.

Back on Bella Luna Road again, almost to the turnoff to the Rancho, I saw a flash of a lot of metal glinting in the sun in a cleft in the foothills. Guessing this was where the emergency vehicles had parked, I passed the Rancho driveway, keeping a bead on the spot when the vehicles dipped out of view. I veered through an open gate over a cattle guard onto a rough dirt hunting track that snaked its way through Rancho land, skirting the valley near the Ecosphere, dipping down to cross the broad, sandy arroyo bed before heading steeply upward into the high hills, running along the ridges and going way, way back into the mountains.

With a queasy dread in the pit of my stomach, I realized I knew this road. The last time I'd driven out this way was prom night of senior year with Rose and Tyler.

As I rounded a bend, I came upon the two police cruisers, fire truck, and ambulance parked in a hurried jumble at a sharp bend in the road, right where it started to climb up toward the mountains, rutted and washed out, impassible for all but the hardiest ATVs. I pulled in next to the empty vehicles and made my way on foot down to the clump of trees in the dry wash, where I could hear voices carrying on the air. I knew the way so well I probably could have found it blindfolded. My footsteps crunched in the red, rocky sand. The cows were let to graze in this part of the ranch's fenced land, so there was no grass underfoot to trip on, just barrel cacti and ocotillos to skirt, the short round Aunt Sponges and tall skinny Aunt Spikers of the desert. To the south and east, through the vast mountain range stretching toward Tucson, were the wild ridges and valleys of desert highlands. Outlaws used to go to ground back in these mountains, most notably Crazy Davy Thatcher, a local legend Rose and I used to be obsessed with.

The Cowboys were a gang of outlaws who operated along the U.S.-Mexico border, stealing cattle and robbing stagecoaches. Their leader, Crazy Davy, ran afoul of his criminal brethren for reasons unknown, maybe a shoot-out gone wrong, a nefarious poker game, a fight over a woman. Whatever it was, he was kicked out of the gang and had to go it alone. He famously hid out in a rough shack in the foothills above Delphi and died during a frenzied dance here at the Inn. The circumstances surrounding his death have always been disputed and hazy. Some accounts say he was possessed by the devil. Others say he drank too much rotgut whiskey. One account even claims to have seen him speaking in tongues, setting his hair on fire. The most credible of these theories, to me, is jimsonweed poisoning.

I scrambled along the slope, the hot wind steady in my ears, and clambered over the boulders that tumbled down to the dry waterbed, hustled along the sandy bottom of the wash. The air was still and heavy down here. I passed old, charred circles of piled rocks, remnants of campfires like the ones we used to have. I was running now, toward the bend in the wash, breathing heavily, my throat parched and tight, on full alert, propelling myself forward.

As I rounded the bend, I came upon a scene so dreamlike and surreal I didn't understand what I was looking at for a moment. A woman in a white dress dangled from the big cottonwood tree. Three cops and two EMTs stood around the hanging body, staring at the ground or off into the bushes, while a fourth cop with his back to me was doubled over, one knee on the ground, dry heaving. In the background, a herd of curious cows looked down at us from the hillside, chewing their cud. The kneeling cop stood up and turned, wiping his mouth, and I recognized Tyler, sweaty and pale faced from retching. Even in this state, even from a distance, he looked offensively hot, still as studly and gorgeous as he'd been when we were younger, maybe even more so, that prick.

Then it hit me in the gut with a *whomp*. The dead hanging woman was Rose.

Here we were again, Tyler and Rose and I, together in this same spot, under that exact same cottonwood tree. Time folded over in a gruesome mockery of itself.

I looked directly at Rose, taking it in. She was hanging by the neck from the strongest branch, her long black hair stirring in the rising evening wind. In this bone-dry air, her face and body looked weirdly normal, as if she were sleeping or had staged a piece of performance art. She was wearing a long white dress. Her body swayed a little. Her bare feet dangled about a foot above the ground, which made it seem almost as though she were levitating. I stared at the old tree with a restless sense of wrongness, as if a fundamental law of the universe had been broken.

Superimposed on the sight of her, another quick, sudden memory rose up in my vision and burst like a soap bubble: a game we used to play, outlaws, a pretend-hanging we'd staged a few times, not here, but back in the hills by his old hideout shack, Crazy Davy Thatcher being strung up by the sheriff, hanged by the neck for his crimes. We'd made it feel so real, we spooked ourselves. We were nine or ten. Rose always got to be Crazy Davy, the star of the game. I was the cruel sheriff, and her little brothers were my henchmen. As Ben and Jason pretend-strung her up, Rose pretend-died in a spectacular spasm, clutching her throat, gasping for breath and choking before she fell to the ground, motionless and limp. The first time we played this game, Rose died so convincingly that Ben burst into tears and couldn't be comforted even after his big sister sat up laughing and alive to reassure him.

And now she was here, hanged for real. My arms were cold in the dry heat.

"Holy shit, Jo," I heard Tyler say hoarsely. "What are you doing here?"

"You guys passed me on the highway and I followed you. How did you know she was here?"

"One of the Gonzalez herders saw her and called us. But seriously, what are you doing here?"

I heard something in his voice. "It's nothing fishy, Tyler, I'm investigating, I'm on the job. Rose's mother hired me to find her. When I saw you on the highway, I had a hunch."

Tyler cleared his throat, ran a hand over his face, straightened his collar, trying very hard to pull himself together. A couple of junior cops were hovering near us, and the EMTs stood by, waiting for some direction, an order, anything.

I glanced over at his partner, Eddie Gomez, a skinny older guy with a neat little potbelly and a shit-eating grin under a wispy mustache. He was circling the tree, staring up at Rose's body. "I'm going to call the coroner," he said. "Let's just get her cut down and covered up before he gets here."

"Wait!" My voice rang out, as sharp as a whip crack. "How can you be sure it's a suicide?"

"Look." Tyler jerked his head toward the tree. "She hanged herself."

"But you can't say that definitively. Until you can, this is a potential crime scene. Tell me I'm wrong."

I was pushing it, questioning Tyler's and Eddie's authority in front of their underlings, but I didn't care. Homicidal hangings have a frequency of one percent compared to suicidal ones, a small percentage, but not vanishingly so. Tyler knew that just as well as I did. I expected him to follow basic procedures and secure the scene, log details, and take photographs before moving the body.

But his hands were trembling. His skin was pale green.

"This was suicide, Jo," he said. His voice was so low and shaky I could hardly hear him. "Obviously. Look at her."

I stared at him, trying to figure out what was going on in his head right now. Maybe he was thinking about prom night too and was still so emotionally stuck in high school that he couldn't detach to deal with the situation. Or maybe he was too overcome with emotion over the death of someone he'd known all his life to function. Both options made him a shitty cop. And it was unfair to Rose. She deserved better.

"I'm going to take some photos," I said. "I need two minutes before you take her down, that's all." Eddie grunted, which I took as permission. Before Tyler could object any further, counting on his evident mental distress to slow him down, I whipped out my phone and started snapping everything: the tree, Rose's position on it, a few close-ups of the knot and the rope, the ground around the tree. I photographed her body and head, the bottoms of her feet. I worked as fast as I could while cop radios squawked and the EMTs prepared the stretcher and Eddie got on his phone, I assumed to call the coroner.

As I aimed my phone at her neck, angling myself underneath her to get the right shot, my attention was caught by a red mark on the inside of her forearm. I looked closer. It was a triangle, about an inch tall, freshly scabbed. It looked as if it had been drawn with a straight pin or the tip of a knife pressed hard and dragged over her flesh. I took several shots of it, then her neck, then her face, then I stepped back and took a few more of the whole scene from all angles.

I forced myself to swallow every single strong emotion I was feeling, push it all down hard. I wanted to fall to the ground and scream with grief, but I owed it to Rose to keep it together, so I did.

Done here, I headed back toward my car. Tyler caught up with me around the bend, out of sight and earshot of the others. "Hey," he said, out of breath. "Jo, wait. I'm sorry I freaked out. Seeing Rose like that.

And then you showing up. The whole thing, our history with her. It threw me. I'm okay now."

"The bottoms of her feet are smooth, Tyler. No abrasions, no sign of walking barefoot over this terrain. Where are her shoes? How did she get to the tree? She was living over at the Triangle A. Her car is still there. Her phone is missing."

"Her phone is missing?"

"I want you to look at her left forearm, on the inside. There's a scabbed triangle, you have to really look to see it. Either she did it herself or someone else did. Ask the coroner to figure out whether it was before or after she died."

He rubbed his dry mouth with the back of one hand.

"Wake the fuck up, Tyler!"

He jumped. "Yeah," he said. "I know."

"Go and do your job. Forget you knew her."

He nodded hard and started back toward the scene. Then he turned again, hangdog, asking me for something. "I have to notify the family—"

"I'll do it. I'm headed over there now anyway."

His lips were cracking they were so dry. "Can I buy you a beer later?" His voice was still scratchy from puking.

"I'll text you," I said.

SIX

BACK AT MY CAR, I FIRED UP THE ENGINE AND DROVE BACK TO THE Rancho, my tires spitting over pebbles in my haste. I turned into the driveway, drove over all the ruts and cattle guards, climbed the hill, and parked next to Laura and Leo's house.

The next few minutes passed in a slow-motion blur of raw emotion. Laura answered the door, looking haggard, bereft, shocked. She was home alone; apparently Ben and Savannah had driven Leo down to a doctor's appointment. I told her as gently and clearly as I could. Even so, the news hit her like a bomb going off, spraying shrapnel that would stay in her psyche for the rest of her life. She collapsed onto the floor. I helped her to the couch and called her best friend, who lived in the Airstream just off the main courtyard.

Patty burst through the door a few minutes later, all ramrod spine and iron-gray pageboy and beetled brows and loyal attentiveness to her best friend, the glamorous movie star and dancer who had stolen her husband all those decades ago.

As Patty rushed to Laura and cradled her head in her arms and crooned to her, I left them there and hotfooted it to my car. As I chirped the driver's side door unlocked, old memories of Rose erupted in my brain, molten lava that burned and hurt. I remembered her loud, wild laugh. The way her rough black hair tickled my cheek when we lay on our backs on the ground, heads together, looking up at the clouds. Her funny gait when she ran, like a galloping horse, uneven and forceful, her feet slapping the ground. Her evil grin when we did something sneaky or forbidden, sweet and beguiling and itching for trouble, eyes flashing at me. We were allies. We were so close, so aligned, so inseparable, we breathed in unison, communicated without talking sometimes, got our first periods the same damn day.

My heart was painful in my chest. It felt swollen and tender, as if it had been punched hard. All my old, unresolved feelings about Rose exploded in a blast of heartsick regret. Why wouldn't she forgive me, those times I begged her? What the hell had I even done? We were kids! And I never had the slightest clue that she liked Tyler, so how could she have held that against me so hard for all these years? And more importantly, why the hell hadn't she told me she had a crush on him, the one person she confided everything in, or so I had thought? I believed we were closer than sisters, our bond unbreakable. Why had she kept such an important secret from me and then accused me of not knowing and ended our friendship over it? And prom night— what was that *about*? Why did I still not get it? What *else* hadn't she told me?

I would never be able to ask her any of this. So I might never know.

Instead of getting into my car and driving away, I looked up at the old main house, where the ranchers used to live in the old days, perched up on its ledge just above the dry, rocky, rutted expanse of the main courtyard. There was something about the house, something I wasn't remembering. The first floor was a long rectangular box of joined formal rooms with enormous multipaned windows, a screened porch along the left side. Two sets of sharply peaked roofs sat side by side atop either end of the first floor, forming two separate second stories, two sets of bedrooms, two attic crawl spaces. I stared up at the little round window at the tippy-top of the left-hand side.

Finally something nudged me, a hunch, a memory, and I climbed the crumbling stucco steps and crossed the patio with its old wrought-iron white table and chairs and opened the front door. I headed past the wide, curved, balustraded staircase that led up to the right-hand second floor and through the cavernous main parlor with its huge fireplace and canvas- and sheet-covered furniture and large windows looking out over the desert, the old wooden floorboards creaking and echoing under my boots.

The joists and beams were settling, so all the floors in the house sloped, and the plaster walls and ceilings were cracking. The house shook if you stepped too heavily. It was a beautiful place, built in the 1880s, back when this was a working 125-acre sheep and cattle ranch. But it needed a structural overhaul, along with everything else. I could feel it quaking under my tread.

I opened the French doors into the big glassed-in side porch and squeezed through piles of boxes and old lamps and stacked tables and chairs and overstuffed wingback armchairs crammed into a corner, through the dining room with its long oak table and oak hutch and sideboard and upholstered mahogany chairs that didn't match the table and striped faded wallpaper peeling off the walls, heaped with unused sports equipment and boxes and piles of dusty books. The long-unused kitchen at the back of the house smelled of dust and old paint. I climbed the rickety back stairs off the kitchen up to the second-floor landing. The bedrooms were crammed full of junk and in even worse shape than the downstairs, with water stains and damage from monsoon rains exposing horsehair plaster and lath and God knew what resident wildlife, snakes and mice and bugs.

I pulled down the creaky trapdoor in the second-floor hallway ceiling and climbed carefully into the low-ceilinged crawl space, ducking through the attic itself toward the front of the house, toward the little closet where Rose used to sit, tucked under the eave, wedged beneath the peaked roof, looking out the small round window. Years ago, she had told me that this was where she went when she needed to be alone. I'd always understood that she kept her diaries up here, or rather, journals, as she called them. And I would have bet that no one had been in this hidey-hole since Rose's last visit.

I pulled open the small door of the closet and stuck my head into the space, which was daylit by the grimy small window, just enough to write by. And sure enough, there was a low wooden table against the window, a purloined couch cushion big enough to sit on by the table, and a carved wooden box with a hinged lid next to the cushion. I stepped gingerly, hoping the floorboards would support my weight, and opened the box. I lifted out a small stack of bound notebooks. Bingo.

I carefully descended the ladder, clutching my booty to my chest. I closed the trapdoor and retraced my steps back down through the creaking, empty house. Outside, I dashed through spatters of warm rain to my car, threw the notebooks on the shotgun seat, and gunned it up the rutted driveway.

Back in the surreal privacy of my room at the Apache Motel, I sat on the edge of the bed and methodically read through all of Rose's childhood journals, keeping my mind as blank as I could make it, still pushing away all the feelings that welled up in me. If I let them swamp me, I would be paralyzed with inchoate grief. And that wouldn't help Rose, or me, or anyone.

A few hours went by while I turned pages. I read chronologically, from Rose's seven-year-old oversize baby scrawl with its creative spelling all the way up through high school. She described her excitement and joy when each of her brothers was born, her touching, curious musings about the meaning of life, and her insecurities about her body, which I had always felt were caused by all the seemingly offhanded comments from her beautiful pixie dancer of a mother. I read her sharp, sly, often funny opinions about food and people in our class, and teachers, as well as various pop stars and books she was reading.

And there it was, written in exhaustive detail, in heartbreaking entry after entry: Rose's ongoing, unrequited crush on Tyler. It had started in sixth grade and deepened over the years. She could barely get up the courage to speak to him. "He doesn't know I'm alive, and worse, if he did, he wouldn't care" was a common refrain. "I can hardly bear to look at him. He's so beautiful. I think he likes Suzy. Or maybe Amy. I can't bear it. Why am I not like them? They're both so confident and pretty. I cannot go on." In seventh grade, she wrote, "Tyler picked me first for his dodgeball team in PE today and high-fived me when I blasted Dougie so hard he fell down. BEST DAY OF MY LIFE!!!!!" A week later: "I said hi to Tyler before Arizona History but he ignored me. CRUSHING SHAME. I want to die . . ." And so it went, painfully and obsessively and at great length, through the rest of seventh grade and on through eighth and into ninth, when we all left Delphi Junior High and started high school in Plato Valley.

As for me, I was friendly with Tyler, and I always thought he was cute, because who didn't, but I had no idea he liked me until mid-December 1997, our freshman year, when he somehow got my number and called me on the phone and asked me to go and see *Starship Troopers* at the Plato Valley mall with him during winter break. I said yes. The instant we hung up, I ran excitedly up to Rose's house to tell her about my date. It was still afternoon, getting dark but not night yet. And it was cold, but we went for a walk through the gulch. We stood under the fateful cottonwood tree as I announced that I was going to the movies with Tyler Bridgewater. I assumed Rose was quiet because she was so breathlessly eager to hear all the details of my new romance.

Then she burst out, "I hate you." Her face was stony. Her voice was harsh.

"*What?*"

"How could you do this to me?"

I don't remember what I sputtered. My shock was total and immense.

She spat at me: "You broke the girl code. I'll hate you forever."

"I won't go. I'll call him the minute I get home and tell him I changed my mind. I had no idea you even liked him, Rose, or I never would have said yes! Not in a million years!"

"How could you not know? It's so painfully obvious."

"I'm just a big idiot, I guess. I feel sick to my stomach now."

"It doesn't matter anyway. He picked *you*. He likes *you*. So I *hate* you."

She turned and headed up the gulch without a word.

At home, I called Tyler and broke the date, saying I was too busy, then wrote Rose a note to tell her what I'd done, since she wouldn't speak to me, and put it in her mailbox up by the road. She tore it up and pushed the scraps into my locker at school. Our friendship was over, but it took me a stupidly long time to realize it.

Meanwhile, Tyler asked me out again, and again. Finally, since Rose was already punishing me for this betrayal, I figured I had nothing to lose anymore and agreed to go to the movies with him. While we waited for his mother to pick us up at the mall afterward, he asked me to be his girlfriend, and I said yes to that too. Without Rose by my side, I was suddenly alone. Tyler's passion for me confused me a little, but it also flattered me and made me feel a little less like the evil monster Rose seemed to think I was. For the rest of high school, Tyler and I were joined at the hip.

There was nothing in Rose's journal about any of this. She stopped writing about Tyler in the winter of 1997, as if she had suddenly forgotten he existed. There were two other things she didn't mention. She didn't write a word about her summers in Trenton with her father. Maybe there was a simple explanation for this. Maybe those summers were so busy and fun she had no time to write, no angst to write about. Or maybe her journals stayed here in the attic of the Rancho's main house when she was back East. But even so, this omission was a big question mark for me, to be investigated along with everything else that wasn't adding up about Rose's life, and all the other question marks that kept piling up.

But even weirder to me, the other thing she never mentioned was me, her constant companion and closest friend. Not once, not even in passing. She described experiences we had had together, places we'd gone, things we'd done, but in her recounting, she was apparently alone, because there was no sign in anything she'd written that her best friend was by her side, right with her through everything, all of it. She didn't mention all the hours and hours and hours we spent talking, playing games, all the times we complained about our mothers, did our homework side by side on her bed, danced and sang along with the radio pretending to be rock stars and watching ourselves in her bedroom mirror, the times we walked out into the desert and daydreamed aloud about our futures and pretended to be Natives and outlaws.

If I were a stranger reading these journals, I would have assumed that Rose was a total loner, friendless, stalking through this dusty Arizona mining town, cultivating a gimlet eye and a barbed wit, hiding in corners watching everything, all alone. It gave me a weird feeling, a sense of not fully existing all those years. Maybe I hadn't been as important to Rose as she was to me. Maybe I was just a sidekick, a needy dork with no siblings or friends, who tagged along with her all the time. Was it possible that she hadn't loved me at all? The possibility that this could literally be true took my breath away. I gasped for air, my sore heart thudding slowly in my chest.

It was so hot in this stuffy room, the air felt thick and almost mineral, but I didn't turn on the AC, I was too paralyzed with mounting, wounded confusion, still absorbing Rose's total silence around the fateful day when I told her Tyler had asked me out, the day she told me our friendship was over. The next entry picked up after winter break and was all about our Spanish teacher's son, John, a rawboned blond football player. Mr. Kurtz apparently made Rose say, "*Juan es muy guapo*" and "*Juan me gusta mucho*" in Spanish class just to torture his son, who always sat next to her with a big shy grin. I remembered that day. It had made Rose blush and go silent with confusion. But in her journal, she was cool and in control. She wrote about telling John Kurtz, "*Eres un perdedor patético*," calling him a pathetic loser in fluent Spanish while the class looked on in awe and admiration.

I kept reading, struck by the total change in Rose's focus. After obsessing about Tyler for years, rhapsodizing about his grace and charisma and beauty, she stopped writing about him entirely, as if he had vanished from the face of the planet after he and I got together. Instead, she suddenly adopted a serious, self-consciously erudite, literary tone, as if she believed that these journals would someday be published to great acclaim throughout posterity. Her erasure of her feelings about Tyler, as if he'd never existed for her, was, in a way, far more telling than pages of heartfelt devastation would have been.

It occurred to me that maybe the real reason Rose never wrote about me was that I hadn't existed for her. Or rather, I didn't exist independently of her, I wasn't a separate person; I was an inextricable part of her, fused to her. So maybe the real betrayal was that I turned out to have my own agenda, my own desires, my own damn self, totally independent of hers. And my real crime was that I didn't belong to her, because I didn't belong to anyone, because nobody did, and that was what she could never forgive me for.

The last entry was dated May 4, 2001: the day of senior prom. Rose wrote all about her dress and gloves, how she planned to make an entrance, make a splash, but of course there was not a word about the three doses of Ecstasy she had stashed in a plastic bag. And there was also nothing about the encounter she engineered for us three, because her voluminous ten-year spate of journal writing ended right there, before the prom, as if she'd come home from that night and put away all childish things forever.

I PUT THE BOOKS ASIDE AND STARED INTO SPACE FOR A WHILE, coming back to myself in stages, rising slowly through the underwater layers of pressure so I didn't get the bends. It was getting dark. I got up and drank some water. I realized that I was hungry and in powerful need of some booze.

I fumbled for my phone and texted Tyler: Beer?

He texted back right away: See you at the Inn in 20 minutes.

SEVEN

THE DELPHI INN LOUNGE AND STEAK HOUSE IS A RENOVATED HIS-
toric relic, with an old-timey western-style wood-paneled saloon
through swinging doors next to a large dining room with a terra-cotta
tile floor; whitewashed brick walls hung with dramatic paintings of
cattle, horses, and cowboys kicking up dust and galloping through
the barrel cactus; a huge, blackened brick fireplace; a low, raw-beamed
ceiling; and multipaned windows draped with heavy red velvet curtains. There's a display case full of gold and silver ores, veins gleaming
in quartz.

The Inn used to be known as a "fightin' bar," back in the days
of cowboys and miners, since evidently the two factions didn't like
each other much. There's a local story that the place is haunted by the
restless ghost of Delphi's local legendary outlaw. There's a life-size,
painted, carved-wood statue of Crazy Davy in the entryway, right by
the cigarette machines. He's depicted as a lean, broad-shouldered fellow with a handlebar mustache, dressed in a wide-brimmed hat and
long overcoat with a bandanna around his neck, double-breasted vest,
jeans, two pistols in his hip holster, and leather boots. He looks like
your standard-issue stock outlaw from central casting, including the
mad glint in his eyes.

Because I was early, and my long-vanquished nicotine habit had
been reawakened by that cigarette I'd smoked with Ben, I bought a
pack of American Spirits from the cigarette machine and palmed a
matchbook. I went back outside and sat smoking alone on the de-

serted covered side patio, watching smoke float from my mouth up into the red glow from the strings of chili lights along the underside of the eaves. The air smelled of dry mesquite and minerals, the thirsty, expectant aroma of the desert before the monsoon rains. It was the smell of my childhood.

The fact of Rose's death kept hitting me. It was the full-stop end to our story, no resolution or reconciliation or redemption, just over. I had thought, in the back of my mind, that we had time. I'd nursed a subconscious fantasy that we'd befriend each other again as old ladies, laugh at the stubbornness of our younger selves. Now I realized how strong and pervasive this fantasy had been: this was why I kept up with news of Rose, why I went to her reading that time, why I watched videos of her band. I had thought she'd come to her senses and remember that she loved me, even if it took till we were fifty, or seventy, or ninety. And now she never would. Never, ever.

I broke up with Tyler just after high school graduation, but we stayed close anyway. Rose went to college up in Washington State, but Tyler and I both stayed local and went to the U of A. We couldn't seem to let go of each other, more family by now than friends or lovers. We rented a bungalow together near campus. I majored in English lit, and he majored in psychology. In retrospect, it was a bad idea for me to live with an ex-boyfriend who hadn't gotten over me, if only because whenever I brought anyone home, male or female, he always found something to criticize, anything from an annoying laugh to a defective personality, which Ty felt comfortable diagnosing because he was a psych major. And Tyler's problem with keeping his financial shit together threatened to balloon into a major issue. More often than not, I had to lend him his half of the rent, and I eventually lost track of how much he owed me. In the end, I decided to just let it go. It was only money.

After college, Rose moved back to southern Arizona and started the poetry MFA program at the university; I got a minimum-wage job as a bookseller at Barnes & Noble, and Tyler enrolled in the police academy. That had been his plan since the end of our senior year of high school, after an all-night party at the Triangle A, the usual weekend rave with bonfire and electronic music and swaying crowd of tranced-out touchy-feely kids on Ecstasy floating around stroking one another's hair, when for some reason the cops decided to pay a visit. Everyone scattered except Tyler and me, because we were having sex in the bushes and didn't hear them coming. The two of us emerged blinking into the swirling red and blue lights like idiots, all our friends long gone. Sitting in the back seat of the cop car together, looking at the cops in the front seat, Tyler turned to me and said, "I'd kill to be on the other side of that glass right now." I could feel the wheels of his brain spinning, and by the time we'd talked ourselves down from a citation for underage drinking, drug use, and public nudity to a stern warning and a slap on the wrist since the cop was an old friend of Tyler's uncle, becoming a cop was his life's plan.

As for me, I quickly got bored selling glitzy paperbacks, celebrity memoirs, and self-help books at about the same time I realized I had zero interest in pursuing the usual English-major careers, teaching or writing. I was primarily interested in rebelling, which might be the real reason I joined the police academy shortly after Tyler did. To my mother, becoming a cop was as bad as being a Republican, a doomsday cult member, or a born-again evangelical Christian. Her disapproval galvanized me, immature though this may have been as the underlying motivation for an entire career.

But I was also instinctively attracted to the gray areas and ethical complexities inherent in law enforcement. I've noticed that most people who claim to be Moral with a capital M are actually judgmental and small-minded, lacking in imagination and empathy. Cops, whatever else you care to say about them, and there is plenty to say, are generally not Moral. The wheels of policedom are greased with payoffs and kickbacks, bent by broken rules, clogged with dubious-quality procedural shortcuts. Most of the cops and private detectives I've met in my life have fallen somewhere on the spectrum that runs from freethinking to psychopathic. Some cops are violent, racist, scary motherfuckers, high on power and the pleasure of inflicting pain, and they are everything that's wrong with the profession. But decent cops, the hardworking ones who try to do the right thing, who actually sort of, on a good day, believe in the principles of justice and fairness, they're not cops because they're moral, or Moral. The system itself sees to that. You enforce the law because you understand the criminal mindset. Look at Tyler and me: druggy, oversexed, shoplifting, trespassing teenagers one day, cop wannabes learning how to break into a house full of armed drug dealers and shoot guns at moving targets the next. I had to think there was a character arc here, some cause-and-effect thing going on.

Tyler didn't think about any of this the way I did. He just wanted to have a good job, stay out of jail himself, and retire early with a good pension and benefits. When I used to try to talk to him about all this, his face went blank. It made me chafe.

As it turned out, I lasted less than a year as a cop. My push out the door came when I caught Tyler and two other rookies pocketing wads of wrapped hundred-dollar bills during a drug bust. We'd done everything else by the book, cuffing the dealers, reading them their rights, and shoving them in the back seats of the cruisers to await transport to the precinct. And the next thing I knew, my colleagues were casually helping themselves to the cash, as if this were just another part of collecting evidence.

When our sergeant, a huge dude from Tombstone named Guppy Valdez, grabbed a wad and tossed it to me to catch, I almost slipped it into my pocket as I was clearly expected to do. But instead, more because I hate doing what's expected of me than out of any sense of ethics, I chucked the wad of money back at Guppy without a word. They all watched me do it. There was silence. Guppy's eyes drilled into mine, then without turning his head, he reached over and clapped the money into Tyler's chest. "That's her cut," he said to Tyler, not joking around. "You gotta keep your woman in line."

I couldn't decide what I was more pissed at, Guppy calling me Tyler's woman and telling him to keep me in line, when Tyler and I weren't even remotely a couple, just friends and housemates, and I was as much a cop as any of them, or Tyler just accepting the money without any respect for my decision not to touch it, or the fact that, even though I would never in a million years rat them out and I hoped they knew that or they knew nothing about me whatsoever, there was now a thick, silent divider between me and the rest of my fellow cops. I think that last thing was what got me most of all, the fact that they now saw me as a potential snitch and always would, just because I wouldn't split an illegal windfall from a bunch of low-life heroin dealers with my supposed band of brothers. I refused to take the first step on the easy slope down from being a straight cop to being a crooked one.

Two days after the bust, after suffering the stony silence of the guys at the station, I quit the force, turned in my badge and gun, just walked away from the whole tamale. It was a clean break, the only kind worth making, no mess, no psychodrama. I was good and pissed at Tyler, though, as well as hurt, for not saying anything, not standing up for me. I moved out of our cute, cozy bungalow into a shithole apartment, found a part-time job as a PI apprentice to Ronnie Taffet, and supplemented the low training wage she paid me by working as a motel chambermaid while going to night school and studying criminal justice. As soon as I qualified, I got my license and joined Ronnie's agency full time, and that's where I've remained to this day, and in the same apartment. I like being a private eye more than I liked being a cop, just like I like being single more than I liked living with anyone. I like working alone and living alone because I'm independent and self-reliant to a fault. In fact, I'm more like my mother than either of us likes to admit.

Of course Tyler stayed a cop. And of course he got married a couple of years after I quit the force, and of course he and his wife, Linda, instantly had kids, not one or two, but four of them, and of course they were still together fifteen years later. Somewhere between kid two and kid three, Tyler had left Tucson and moved back up here to Delphi to raise his family, joined the Plato County force. And here he still was, like everyone else around here, walking around half asleep in a snoozy little town in the hills.

EIGHT

I WATCHED TYLER'S CRUISER PULL INTO THE PARKING LOT. HE SLID
into the spot next to my car, opened his door, and got out slowly, looking dazed. Before this afternoon, our paths hadn't crossed in four or
five months, maybe longer. We weren't close anymore, nowhere near
like we used to be.

"You're here already," he said, approaching the patio as I stubbed
out my cigarette. I wasn't sure from his tone if this was a good thing
or not. Maybe it was hard for him to see me after everything that
had happened between us through the years. Or maybe he'd hoped to
have a little time to himself, off the job after a very tough and emotionally upsetting day, away from the wife and four kids, snort some
whiskey and think his thoughts undisturbed, the way I had just enjoyed my contemplative cigarette.

We went inside and took an empty table near the unlit fireplace.

I peered at him. "You okay?"

"I'm just . . ." he said, and for a split second his face dissolved
and I saw again how deeply messed up he was by Rose's death. But
he snapped out of it, stalling, getting us on familiar footing first.
"Drowning in paperwork."

"Paperwork," I said, giving him time to breathe. "Never your
forte."

We exchanged a frank look.

The waitress appeared with pen and pad and an inquisitive expression. I ordered a Southwest chicken salad and a draft beer. Ty-

ler ordered a burger and fries, a shot of whiskey, a beer, and then he tacked on an order of jalapeno poppers.

"How do you keep your girlish figure, eating like that?"

"Baby carrots," he said. "I crunch out my frustrations." He added, a little defensively, possibly referring to his vomiting and freaking out earlier at the scene, "Seriously, though, I'm burned out. I'm already dreaming about retirement, less than four years to go."

I darted a quick look at him. He had been a cop for going on seventeen years now. Four kids, fifteen years of marriage, long hours on the job, paperwork, stress . . . and who knew how many instances of grift he'd been peer pressured into by his less ethical fellow cops. I couldn't blame him for wanting out.

Our drinks were set in front of us, a squat tumbler of liquid amber and a couple of sweating-cold pint glasses with foam on top. We knocked the beers together and drank.

"So about Rose," I started to say.

"To be honest," he interrupted, "I've been thinking about doing what you do. Private detective."

All right. If he wanted to stall, I'd play along. "My line of work is not without its own grind and paperwork. I've had a few too many insurance fraud cases. And I've photographed and tracked enough cheating spouses to put me off marriage forever. Not that I was ever a candidate."

"For marriage?" he said. "Or cheating?"

We exchanged a look. I was craving physical contact with a familiar, warm, living body, his body. In his face was an odd, panicky yearning, maybe for the same thing. We brushed antennae, and then we moved on. It was time to cut the shit and get real.

"What is up, Tyler?" I asked him. "What was going on with you today? That was a mess."

"I know," he said. He took a nip of whiskey and wiped his hand over his mouth. He looked agonized. "I have to tell you something."

"Okay." I dreaded hearing it.

His mouth opened and closed. His eyes were shiny. "You're the only person on earth I can tell this to."

I waited.

"Linda would . . ." He licked those big, dumb, sexy lips, gave me a stricken sideways look. "A couple of weeks ago, I got a call from Rose. Just out of the blue. I hadn't seen her or talked to her in years and years."

All at once, I got it, like a writhing mass of black widow spiders in my stomach I got it, but I waited for him to spit it out.

"She told me she was back up here again, living at the Triangle A. She wanted to get a drink." He exhaled hard. "I figured, why not, she's an old friend."

"Rose was never your friend. She was obsessed with you."

"Yeah, well." He made a strangled noise in the back of his throat like a dog getting a shot at the vet. "We ended up . . . in the back seat of my cruiser."

"You had sex with Rose."

"It happened a few more times."

Jesus. "Still in your car?"

"Motel room."

I shook my head. "You were having an affair with her."

"I told her it had to stop. That was last weekend, a week ago, Saturday night. I ended it. It was over."

"Got it," I said. I wanted to smack him, hard. "So now she's dead and you're going crazy with guilt."

"I had just ended it with her," he said. "And then she kills herself."

"I admit, I'd be freaked out if I were you. Very. You need to recuse yourself from this case, Tyler."

"I should. But I can't, because that would mean telling why."

"Okay," I said, rolling my eyes. "Listen. I've been sniffing around all day. I've learned a few things that might make you feel a little less personally to blame for this."

"I know she was fired from her teaching job," he said. "Was there anything else?"

While he shoved jalapeno poppers into his mouth, I filled him in on everything I knew about Rose's recent life: her fake Native identity, losing her job, the cancellation of her book, the affair with the kid, her fight with her roommate.

"Wait," said Tyler. "An affair with a kid?"

"According to her bandmates, she was sleeping with a student."

He winced. "And she said she was Navajo?"

"She claimed to be. A lot of people believed her."

"She wasn't, right?"

"Nope."

"Then why would she say she was?"

"Maybe for attention. Maybe because it helped her teaching career. Rose always loved pretending, taking on other identities. We used to play games, as kids, and aside from outlaws, her favorite was being Native. She really got into it."

"But that was when you were kids. She was almost forty."

"I know," I said. "It's fucked up. Oh, and I wanted to mention something else. Do you know about the old-age home Rose's brother is working to build on Rancho land? Sunset Shadows?"

"I know about it," he said. His expression was cagey, but I let it go and plowed on.

"They were talking about it when I was at Leo and Laura's for drinks. Then later, I read some poetry Rose wrote about environmental devastation. In an email to someone, she wrote that she'd quote-unquote 'do anything to stop Sunset Shadows from happening.' Do you think . . ." It sounded crazy even to me. "Maybe it was some kind of protest. Like those eco-activists who set themselves on fire."

"That's pretty far-fetched," he said.

"Yeah, it sounds that way to me too."

"I swear to you, Jo, I didn't want to get involved with her like that, I never once cheated on Linda before. I don't know how it happened."

"Rose was hot? Your life is stressful and you needed to blow off steam? You're a shitty husband?"

He ducked his head. "When I told her it had to stop, she went insane."

"Insane how?"

"Crying. Yelling at me. Calling me a womanizing scumbag and threatening to tell Linda. So then I had to promise her I'd have a drink with her one more time just to get her off the phone."

"When were you supposed to have that drink?"

"Wednesday night. Here, actually."

"So you waited here."

"That's right."

"What did you think happened when she didn't show?"

"I thought—I don't know actually. I was relieved."

"So the next night, her mother called to say that no one had seen her since Tuesday night. You and Eddie went out to see Laura the next morning, but you wouldn't open a missing-person case."

"It hadn't been seventy-two hours yet. You know the drill."

"And then this afternoon, the call came that a body had been found on Rancho land."

"I knew it was her before we got there. It had to be."

"No wonder you were puking."

He was quiet for a moment, not looking at me, something working in his face.

"What?"

He shook his head.

"Tell me."

He took out his phone, poked at it, and turned the screen to me.

It was a text thread from Rose, ending with a video. "Look at the date on the last text," he said.

I took his phone and squinted at it. The text had been sent today, this morning, at 9:37 a.m. The text contained a video attachment.

"Holy shit," I said. "When did the coroner say she died?"

"He's not exactly sure yet, but preliminary determination is at least forty-eight hours before we found her."

"So somebody else has Rose's phone. What's the video of?"

"It's nothing," said Tyler quickly, trying to grab his phone back. But I was quicker. I turned away from him, shielding the phone.

"Don't, Jo," he pleaded, weakly.

I ignored him and pressed Play on the screen. It was a short video of Tyler on his back on a bed, thank God not the Apache Motel bedspread, spread-eagled, naked, eyes closed. The camera slid down his body to his erect cock, held in the hand of whoever was shooting this. Rose's hand. With her other hand, she turned the camera around on herself and put his cock in her mouth and started blowing him, looking up into the lens of the camera with a half-crazed expression of triumph.

I really, *really* wished I didn't have to look at it. I didn't want to see Rose and Tyler together for a slew of reasons. I didn't want to have to look at Tyler's beautiful naked body, not now, not when I was feeling so vulnerable and hungry for contact.

I handed his phone back to him as if it were red-hot.

"I thought she was blackmailing me. Scared me so much. Then they found her body. I didn't know what to think." He sucked in his breath and ran a hand over his face. "It's fucking weird. This whole thing is fucking weird."

"Rose's phone is missing," I told him. "I put a trace on it this morning, must've been around ten, right around the time you got the video. So it must have been turned off right after the text was sent, which would exclude the possibility of Rose having somehow put this text on an automatic timer before she died. So the question is, who has her phone?"

Tyler looked befuddled. "Why would anyone want to do that? Just to spook me? Maybe she gave her phone to a friend or something and told them to send it. That would be like Rose, that crazy bitch, to try to fuck with my marriage from beyond the grave."

Was he really this clueless? Or maybe he had something to hide and was deliberately trying to deflect me from the obvious conclusion: Rose's death had been staged to look like a suicide, and the person who did it had her phone.

Tyler rested his head in his palms and grabbed hanks of his own hair to anchor his skull in place. "If this video got out somehow, Linda would . . . I don't even know."

I knew Tyler's wife, Linda, had known her for more than sixteen years. She was a proper old-fashioned Catholic girl, and her marriage and family were everything to her. She was also very proud. For example, she didn't like me because I was Tyler's ex-girlfriend, even though I was no threat to her at all. My very existence irked her. So no wonder Tyler was bughouse. If she saw this video, she'd leave him in a split second if she didn't kill him first. And he'd implode without her.

"Jesus, Tyler."

"Yeah." He knocked back his whiskey and grimaced.

"Who else have you told about this?"

"No one. Just you. And it'd better fucking stay that way."

"So let me ask you this. What if I hadn't been there today, at the scene? Were you just going to let this whole thing go? Just shut up about it and assume the text was revenge porn or attempted blackmail by whoever killed Rose, so you could save your own ass?"

"Whoa," he said, leaning back. "Whoa, whoa, whoa. Who said anything about Rose being killed?"

So it was the first scenario. He really was clueless. Okay, maybe I shouldn't fault him too much, given what he was going through. But I had to settle the matter definitively. I gave him a hard stare. "Did you kill her, Tyler?"

His mouth fell open. "What?!" I watched him closely while he tried to figure out the best words to use to deny this in a way I would find crystal clear and completely credible. "No!" was all he came up with. "What the fuck, Jo?"

Not exactly convincing, but good enough. "Listen. If you're really not going to recuse yourself, then you need to open this case as a potential homicide. Do you understand? We need to work together on this."

"But what if the autopsy confirms that it was a suicide?"

"How did she get to the tree barefoot, Tyler? There were no marks on the soles of her feet. And no shoes anywhere that I could see, unless you found them in the bushes after I left."

"Maybe she flew there. Fucking crazy witch." I saw the whisper of a sickly grin on his face as he finished his beer.

"You're better than this, Ty."

"I'm really not."

"What about the triangle etched into her arm? I'm assuming it wasn't there the last time you saw her."

"She did it to herself?"

I shook my head, disappointed to see what a complacent, wisecracking, lazy provincial cop he'd become. I looked at my beer glass, tipping it so the beer slid up the side, swiveling its bottom on the table.

Tyler leaned forward. "So," he said in a low voice, with the conspiratorial tone of someone who desperately wants to change the subject, "that guy in the booth over there. Five seconds."

We used to play this game in bars back when we were at the police academy together, challenging each other to memorize strangers' faces at a glance in case we ever had to ID them.

There were three recessed booths along the back wall, cracked red pleather seats and fake-wood veneer tables, two of them empty, the middle one inhabited by a lone man. He was tall and pudgy, with dyed black hair that fell long over one eye, shaved on the sides, a pouty expression on his long horseface, slight buckteeth, and a big, velvety black mole on his cheekbone. He wore a lime-green mesh shirt. He was drinking a neon-green house margarita in an enormous stemmed glass.

Confident that I could pick him out of any lineup, I turned back to Tyler. "He looks familiar. Was he at school with us?"

"He was a year behind us at the U of A, actually," said Tyler. "Drama nerd. He runs CHIT now, took it over from the original founders."

"Do we know him?"

"No. I arrested him and his two girlfriends a couple of weeks ago on a drunk and disorderly. I doubt they remember me, or anything much about that night."

"That must be Noah," I said. "Kylie and Babette's boyfriend." I gazed at the bacon cheeseburger and mound of hot crispy fries that had been put in front of Tyler while I was scoping Noah. My salad, which had also arrived, looked unappealing in comparison, but I'd had a burger at In-N-Out yesterday, and it was too soon to eat another one. The prospect of turning forty this year made me feel scratchy and depressed, feelings I didn't want to face because they were a big writhing can of worms. "Why did you arrest them?"

"They were singing show tunes, naked, in the Circle K parking lot. Covered in body paint, but not covered enough."

I grinned, letting Tyler think his distraction tactic was working. Though, to be fair, it partially was. "All three of them?"

"Buck naked. At the tops of their lungs."

"What happened after you booked them?"

"A night in the drunk tank and a hearing scheduled for sometime next month."

"So you had to cuff them and load them into your car all naked and covered in paint?"

"I had to have the upholstery cleaned. It was smeared with glitter."

"Was it performance art? Was it drunken hijinks?"

"I'm not sure they needed a reason."

And that was that. The topic of Rose didn't come up for the rest of the evening, but only because we steered ourselves around it.

Tyler signaled the waitress for the check. "Do you need a lift somewhere? Back to the Rancho?"

"I drove," I said. "I'm staying at the Apache Motel."

"Really," he said. "Why?"

"It's totally free of memories."

He nodded as he paid the check. I let him. I figured he owed me. We walked out into the night air together and stood by our cars, which were parked side by side. We both hesitated, stalling, waiting for something. Even all these years later, we felt the old habitual tug toward each other.

"Jesus," he said, running a hand over his face. "Thanks for listening. I needed to tell someone."

"Go home and get some sleep," I said to him. "Then tomorrow, open the case. Yes?"

I waited for him to nod before getting in my car.

BACK AT THE APACHE MOTEL, I LAY AWAKE ON THE HARD, BLEACH-smelling motel sheets while headlights from Arizona Avenue slid over the ceiling and a drip from the bathroom sink beat time to the film I was projecting on the inside of my skull, like one of those old-fashioned shaky, silent Super 8 home movies. I imagined the violent motion and pain of those final instants of Rose's life. The short fall, the crack as her neck broke when the noose stopped her body in midair, and then, if she was lucky, unconsciousness, a quick death. If she was unlucky, she bucked in midair for a while, asphyxiating.

The potential fact of her suicide hit me with a slap of unbearable sadness, like an actual hand smacking my face. I viscerally felt the cold rage, the absolute, permanent fuck-you it took to do this act. If she had done it, she had meant to die.

But I didn't think she had.

Just as I was falling into a blank sleep, the motel landline on my nightstand rang. I clawed my way awake and picked up the receiver. "Hello?"

I heard silence, and in the background, a static-like noise. It sounded like flames crackling. It reminded me of something: the call at my office.

"Hello?" I said, awake now, my skin crawling. "Who is this?"

The line went dead.

I got up and peered out the front window through the stiff curtains at the parking lot, the empty road beyond it. I picked up the handset and dialed zero for the front desk and asked the sleepy-sounding night clerk if he could determine the origin of the call just now.

"We can't do that kind of thing here," he said thickly.

"Well, what did they sound like? Could you tell if it was a man or a woman?"

"I never talked to them."

"What do you mean?"

"It didn't come through the front desk," he said. "They must have called your room phone directly somehow."

I hung up and got back into bed and lay staring up at the ceiling. I hadn't told anyone I was here except for Tyler. He could have seen my room key at dinner, memorized the room number on it, and dialed my room directly. Unless someone else was following me. But whoever had called just now had to be the same person who had crank-called my office number yesterday afternoon, before I had even officially taken this case.

I stayed awake for hours. Nothing made any sense. Nothing added up. My chest was tight, my brain wouldn't go to sleep. And in the pit of my stomach, in my gut brain, I felt a cold, hard knot I hadn't felt in a very long time. Along with profound sadness, I felt fear.

NINE

THE SONORAN DESERT IS THE MOST BIODIVERSE DESERT ON EARTH. But it's also a brutal place in which most of the native plants and animals exist to hurt or flat-out kill you—Gila monsters, black widow spiders, rattlesnakes, coral snakes, bark scorpions, killer bees, and too many species of cactus and other toxic plants to name. I've been bitten by scorpions and threatened by pissed-off rattlers, have picked hundreds of cholla spines out of my flesh over the years. But like everyone who lives here, I've learned to coexist with them all.

It's the encroaching, invasive species that I find truly terrifying, the imported red fire ants, who swarm anyone unfortunate enough to disturb their mounds with lightning speed and sting repeatedly by grabbing skin in their vicious mandibles and injecting toxic venom. They are rapacious carnivores that eat bird eggs and rodents and sometimes even attack and kill newborn fawns and calves. These horrifying fuckers are closely followed in sheer evilness by the rampaging Argentine cactus moths, whose larvae consume entire prickly pears from the inside out. Even the harmless-looking buffel grass and fountain grass, not native to this region, cause widespread devastation. Wildfires aren't natural in southern Arizona, and no native plant here has adapted to withstand them. Their recent annual occurrence is caused by these upstart weeds that sit there like dry tinder waiting for a spark, sucking up water from native flora, killing them as they spread, then drying out and catching fire. How long would it be before we soft western white people, with our air-conditioned retirement de-velopments and strip malls, were forced out by the increasingly dire heat waves, fires, and droughts, like the Hohokam before us? Fifty years? A hundred? Not nearly as long as they had lasted, that was for sure. Humans were the most dangerous, rapacious invasive species of all.

Early the next morning, I got up and threw on my running clothes and ducked my head under some cold water to wake myself up. I went out into the parking lot and did a few bullshit stretches just for show in case anyone was watching, maybe my crank caller. No matter how unsettled I was feeling, I wanted them to know I was not going to be intimidated by their amateur scare tactics. I drove up Arizona Avenue to Bella Luna Road and down past the Rancho driveway to park in the spot where I'd parked yesterday, got out and did a couple more half-assed stretches to impress my invis-ible stalker, then ran out the rutted hunters' track into the desert.

My sneakers crunched in the packed sand. The air was cool and dry and smelled spicy and clean, that morning desert smell I love. I headed up the flank of the hill and followed the ATV track for a couple of miles, pounding up steep slopes and down through gullies and straight up inclines and straight down into washes again, breath-ing hard, feeling my blood pumping, feeling alive and less afraid. In high school I ran cross-country, and I used to do this same run in the mornings before school. My body remembered this track, my feet bouncing automatically off the sides of the raw, red, rocky ruts, taking steep dips at full speed, using the momentum to propel me up the next flank, caroming off the deeper ruts and flying over the crevices. There were no switchbacks, the road just went straight up, straight down. I was alone out here, no Jeeps or ATVs full of deer hunters in camo hanging off the roll bars, guns strapped to their backs. They came up here during the season from as far away as Wisconsin and

Texas. I used to know a couple of different groups, and occasionally I passed their camp in a deep wash way back in the mountains on my long runs.

After several good, hard, fast miles, I stood on a high ridge looking out over the valley, breathing deeply, doing squats to show anyone hiding in the buffel grass what was what, almost pissed off to think they might be lurking out there. I looked out to the mountains, where the track kept going, south, following the curvature of the land up to the top of Mount Lemmon. I could see where it was crisscrossed by a few other rough tracks that went farther back, east, into these foothills, where the hunters had their camps, where the outlaws once hid out. It was so beautiful up here, the quiet absolute and alive. The flank of the slope rising behind me was covered in barrel cactus. The low washes were shaggy and diffuse shades of green, mesquite and cottonwood trees. Off to my right was a ridge extending into the valley, thick with sagebrush. Unseen animals watched me from every crevice and branch, insects and birds and reptiles, rodents, coyotes, javelinas, probably a bobcat or two.

I turned around and ran back the way I'd come. My legs had that pleasant shaky feeling that meant I had worked them hard. I looked forward to drinking the bottle of water I always kept in my car. Down near the road again, I took a detour into the desert along the bottom arroyo, heading back to the cottonwood tree.

As I ran, I felt that distinct and definite sense that I was being watched by someone, not hypothetically but deliberately. They were just behind me and to my left. I stopped running and stood very still, eyes and ears on high alert, but all I heard was the wind rattling through the mesquite and dry brush. Nothing moved. But when I started running again, my footsteps crackling into the silence, the feeling persisted, that uncanny sense of another sentient creature close by, on my trail. I've never been wrong about this sense. It might have been a person, or a coyote, or a bobcat. Whoever it was, they weren't making themselves known. As long as they didn't attack me, I was okay with them, at least for now.

I came to the cottonwood tree. It spread its branches over the wide bend in the sandy wash, a sunlit mass against the deep blue morning sky. I stood under it for a while, looking up at the branch where Rose had hung, then wandered higher up the wash, slipping through the barbed wire when I came to fences, skirting mesquite and sagebrush, clambering over rocks. I saw prints of cows, horses, and humans. I didn't see any discarded shoes, or anything else that struck me as suspicious. I was thinking about Rose. I let memories flood me. And as I headed back to the tree, I felt those eyes on me again, unseen, hidden somewhere just ahead of me now. I waited.

A tiny figure stumped into view. Not a coyote.

"What the hell," I said to Ophelia.

She looked up at me with what I could have sworn was a questioning expression.

"Did you walk all the way here from the Triangle A?"

It suddenly occurred to me that she was a dog without a person, which is always a sad thing.

"Were you looking for Rose?" I asked her. "Following her scent?"

She stared at me with her bug eyes. Poor kid. I headed back the way I'd come, and she trotted along at my heels back to my car, where I guzzled most of my bottle of water and offered her the rest, poured into my cupped palm so she could lap at it. With her in the back seat, I drove to the Apache Motel and unlocked my concrete teepee, leaving the little dog on the concrete apron in front of my door. After I showered, I came out with my bag, and there she still was. I went to the front office and checked out. The desk clerk on duty, the one I'd talked to on the phone in the wee hours after the crank call to my room, turned out to be another squat mushroom-pale person who looked to be a close relative of the clerk who'd been at the desk when I checked in two nights ago. He even had a large pink wart on the same spot on his forehead. What were the odds?

"Didja figure out who called you?" he asked me.

"Not yet," I said.

Ophelia looked expectant when I came out again. I unlocked my car, and she leapt into the back seat again as I drove along Arizona Avenue and parked in front of the Arroyo Cafe, in the shade of a mesquite tree. Ophelia had settled herself into a curled heap of teddy bear fur. She was probably tuckered out from her long trek and needed a snooze. In case she was thirsty, I scrounged up another bottle of water and poured a good dollop into an empty fast-food beverage cup from a while back, the top part torn off enough to give her snout a chance. As soon as I set it down, she dove right in and started lapping with her weird little troll's tongue.

I left the dog there, windows all the way down, even though it wasn't hot yet. It was early, but the cafe was already hopping. A town full of senior citizens is an early-bird place. I waited a few minutes by the door before the hostess plucked a big, laminated menu from the holder and parked me at a little two-top by the plate-glass window, right by my car. Good. I could keep an eye out, make sure no one dognapped Ophelia, about whom I was beginning to feel uneasily protective.

The Arroyo Cafe was relatively new, less than a decade old, but it felt like a throwback to the seventies, with macramé plant hangers full of coleus and spider plants, walls painted sunflower orange with harvest gold and avocado trim, a mostly vegetarian menu, heavy on the seitan and tempeh, with a few grudging concessions to rabid carnivores like me, and the Lovin' Spoonful's "Daydream" wafting from the speakers. They clearly knew how to keep their clientele happy. I glanced around at the occupants of the cafe and saw bald and gray heads, wrinkles, reading glasses, purple handwoven tunics, relaxed-fit jeans, and the kind of wide, flat sandals that were easy on the bunions.

THE ARIZONA TRIANGLE 93

My phone rang. Laura Gold's number popped up.

"Hello, Laura, how are you?"

"Oh, Jo," she said in a hollow voice, sounding like Greta Garbo in *Camille*. "I'm never going to be all right again. I was awake all night."

"Have you heard from the cops or the coroner yet?"

"Yes," she said, "and it's just awful, some terrible woman without a shred of human feeling told me it takes ten days to two weeks to get the autopsy report." There was an agonized silence. "They're cutting her up, Jo, my little Rose."

"I'm so sorry," I said. That was standard, but they needed a better way of dealing with bereaved family members.

"Ben is convinced that Rose wouldn't do something like this. He insists that she would never take her own life. Do you think he's right?"

"I don't know yet. But I have my doubts, as well."

"He thinks I should ask you to keep investigating."

"Did you talk to the cops?"

"They're saying it was a suicide, pending the coroner's report. I just don't know who to trust anymore. Can you help me, Justine?"

"Sure I can," I said, suddenly furious at Tyler. "Of course. Our contract and retainer are already in place, so we're all set as far as that goes."

"Thank you," she breathed into my ear. "I need to know. If someone did this to Rose, they need to be caught. If she killed herself, I want to know why. You're the only one I trust to find out."

"I'll do my best."

As I hung up, the waitress appeared, a slim, dark-eyed young Latina with a serious expression, enormous eyes, and a firm, plush mouth. I was checking her out, I realized, until I saw her name tag: Lupita. Small town. This was quite possibly the same person who was emailing with Rose about Sunset Shadows.

"Good morning," she said with a warm smile. "What can I get you?"

"Spinach omelet with a side of sweet potato hash and the biggest cup of coffee you can muster. Did you know Rose Delaney, by any chance?"

She looked shocked. "I heard what happened. I knew her."

"I'm a private investigator," I told her, opening my wallet and showing her my license. "Rose's family has hired me to look into her death."

An elderly hippie chick three tables away from us raised a finger and called, "Miss!" Lupita smiled and raised a finger back at her. "I have to go," she told me. "Can we talk later?"

"Whenever's good for you."

"I get a short break at eleven thirty."

"I'll come back and pick you up."

I inhaled my breakfast, slugged back an extra cup of coffee, and paid my check.

OPHELIA HAD CLIMBED INTO THE FRONT PASSENGER SEAT WHILE I was in the cafe. She rode shotgun with her paws braced against the dash, staring out the windshield. While I drove, I called Tyler's cell phone, and when I got his voicemail, I said, "It's me. Call me back as soon as you can, Ty, it's urgent."

I parked in my usual spot in the Bella Luna's main courtyard, just below the old ranch house. It was starting to feel like a habit. I wondered if my mother had been bracing herself since I'd shown up, girding her loins for me to knock on her door. I planned to do it today. I'd put it off long enough. I couldn't spare her my unwanted presence forever.

Ophelia at my heels, I hotfooted it up the path to Laura and Leo's house, knocked on the door, and waited. Jason answered, looking as if he hadn't slept in a year. His eyes were puffy. His jowls sagged a little. He was only in his early thirties, but his sister's death had turned him middle-aged.

"Rose's dog is running loose," I told him. "I brought her here. I'm not sure what else to do with her."

"Rose had a dog?"

"Her name is Ophelia."

We looked down at her. She was sitting in my shadow, looking up at me.

"What is she?"

"Angela said affenpinscher. She might be hungry. She could probably use some water too. I found her out in the desert earlier."

Jason squinted at me, as if he suspected me of pulling a fast one on him, rooking him. It was the expression of someone who can't trust anyone because he isn't trustworthy himself. "My dad is deathly allergic," he said shortly. "It can't stay here."

"Okay," I said. "I'll figure something out, I guess." I made a sudden gesture, chopped the air with my forearm. This sometimes works to distract and disarm people who are hostile to me. "When was the last time you saw Rose?"

"We talked last week."

"On the phone?"

"Yeah. She's been up here the past month."

"When she was living down in Tucson, did you see her very often?"

"We haven't been close in a while. Is this an interrogation?"

I was peering into Jason's ferrety face, gauging his microexpressions, trying to suss out whatever was making him act like this toward me, whatever he was feeling underneath all that. "Jason, I'm so sorry about your sister's death."

"Okay," he said, and started to slam the door in my face.

I stopped the door closing with my boot. "Hey. I've been hired to help your family. I'm not your enemy. I work for you. If you can tell me anything to help me, that's good for your mom and for you. Not me."

He stared down at my boot as if it were caked in dogshit, then gave me a look so cold, it chilled me in the heat. "Okay," he said again.

I moved my foot. He closed the door with more force than necessary.

OPHELIA STILL IN TOW, I HEADED DOWN TO THE U-SHAPED COMplex just above the rundown old stables and yard. Bella Luna's art studios are housed in a horseshoe of airy and ample workrooms with small, high windows. Each studio has two doors, one to the inner courtyard and one to the railed porch that runs along the back of the building, looping around all three sides. The courtyard is paved with adobe bricks and has an outdoor kitchen, two large pottery kilns, and a generous, two-tiered patio with a fire pit near the kilns. White cast-iron furniture is scattered here and there under a shaded overhang. The courtyard is green with pots of succulents and bird-of-paradise plants.

Solo Petersen tossed me a cold bottle before he even said hello. "Well, look who drifted up on the tide."

I caught the beer and cracked it. It was nine thirty in the morning, the old party boy. He always stocks his studio fridge with twist-offs for easy access and budgetary pragmatism. "Hi, Solo," I said.

"Oh, Jo, you're a sight for some very sore eyes."

Solo's real name is Frank. His nickname is from the 1970s, like everything else around here. People didn't start calling him Solo because he was a flinty-eyed lone-wolf type, riding the range alone, often on the wrong side of the law. No, he got the moniker because he was as harmlessly pretty as Harrison Ford and as earnest and dorky as the entire Star Wars franchise. It fits him. He is a man who is singularly affectless in a wholly benign way, with a psyche as clean and simple as a bowl of oatmeal. I've never seen him lose his shit, never seen his emotional temperature rise even one degree. Even now that Rose, whom he'd been close to her whole life, had died suddenly, he appeared to have absorbed the shock with his usual stoicism. He was sad, I could tell from the way his eyelids and mouth sagged a little. But shit happened, people died. And you went on, until you died too. I had always liked this about him. He was soothing to be around.

I perched on his worktable and took the pack and matches out of my jeans pocket and fired up a cigarette, inhaled with relief. Apparently I was letting myself smoke again. I told myself this was okay, and that as soon as I figured out what had happened to Rose, I'd stop again.

The other thing I liked about hanging out in Solo's studio was that he was always perfectly happy to sit in easy silence. While I smoked, he sat at his foot-powered wheel and shaped a lump of clay with both hands, pedaling away, the wheel humming, adding water every so often to keep the bowl he was making nice and wet. The way the clay leapt upward with only the gentlest nudging looked like magic, as if it were a primordial creature coming to life in his godlike hands.

I was thinking about the tangled web of romantic shuffling and lifelong friendships here. Solo's ex-wife Patty was originally married to Leo Gold until Laura stole him away shortly after she arrived here. A few years later, Patty got together with Solo. They got divorced in the late nineties, and these days, Patty lived alone, and Solo was shacked up with an experimental filmmaker named Priyanka, ex-wife of Pablo, who was now living with a much younger woman named Glenda, who came here for a horse workshop nine years ago with her best friend, Sylvan, and never left. Sylvan was sort of with Jeremy for a while a long time ago, and in recent years he'd sort of been with Andy, Jeremy's ex. It was always hard to keep up. What made it easier is that no one ever left. This has always been the Rancho's entire organizational system, everything and everyone gets repurposed and reused. Nothing goes to waste or gets thrown out if anyone can help it. Cast-off things are stored in the old ranch house until they're useful or needed again. Cast-off people find one another and regroup. And no matter what fights or rifts or feuds erupt, everyone stays civil or at least connected or at least present. It's what has made this place work for almost half a century. Now, the youngest original members were almost seventy, and the oldest were pushing ninety. They'd come this far together; they'd go the distance.

But I wondered what would happen as they became incapacitated and started to die off. We now-grown-up kids of Della Luna came back sporadically to visit, but none of us lived here; we were all scattered far and wee. The twenty-some members of the Rancho owned it collectively, and there was no infrastructure for end-of-life care and no plan that I knew of for carrying the place forward after the original members died. It had become a geriatric commune.

Considering all this, I realized that Sunset Shadows made a kind of pragmatic sense, if you looked at it sideways.

The worktable I was sitting on was cluttered in an orderly fashion with piles of unfired clay bowls and pots of glaze and a rack of fired tiles. On the shelves on the wall by the main kiln were stacks of plastic-wrapped blocks of raw clay and an array of finished light fixtures, vases, and small and large bowls. Solo's work was all unpretentious, utilitarian stuff. One of my favorite possessions for years had been the large, plain, brown-glazed mug with a sturdy handle he'd given me when I left to move down to Tucson just before my freshman year of college. I drank my coffee out of it every morning.

He wasn't exactly my surrogate dad, because Solo isn't fatherly, but after my father died, he was the older adult male I knew I could trust to tell me the truth and have my back: my confidant. He was also, I knew, Rose's confidant. She and Leo were never close, and her own father was thousands of miles away. She'd counted on Solo's easy low-pressure, nonconfrontational counsel as much as I had. I suspected Solo knew things about Rose that she might not have felt comfortable confiding in anyone else around here. Whether or not he'd tell me was anyone's guess. Solo never betrayed a confidence.

"Laura hired me," I told him. "First to find Rose. And now to look into her death, uncover anything that might explain it."

"What have you learned so far?"

"She's apparently been having a fight with her roommate, the drummer in her band." This was a gambit. I was hoping Rose might have told the details of this rupture to Solo, and that he'd be uncharacteristically willing to spill them to me.

But Solo just nodded. "Yeah, that seems pretty normal in bands." He himself played bass in a Grateful Dead–like assemblage of old dudes who got baked and indulged in hours-long, meandering two-chord blues jams in the studio courtyard. I would have bet there had been zero drama between them all for the thirty-odd years they'd been playing together.

So I told him everything else I knew, including Rose's recent affair with Tyler. I didn't mention the video, because Tyler had sworn me to secrecy, but that was the only thing I left out.

"Rose was a troubled girl," said Solo. "I was always sorry you and she had that falling out. It was harder for her, not having you."

"She couldn't forgive me for whatever she thought I did. That was on her, though."

He was silent a moment.

"You don't agree," I said, bristling.

"I don't agree or disagree. I understand. Adolescence is a hard time. Friendships are intense at that age."

"What do you mean when you say she was always a troubled girl? Because of the divorce between her parents? Because she had mental issues?"

"Yes to both," he said. "Some kids are more resilient. Rose took everything harder than other people. She felt everything so deeply."

"Her father died three years ago," I said. "That must have been tough. Weren't they extremely close?"

He gave me a searching look. He seemed to be about to say something. His knees rising and falling with the pedals, he worked the lip of the bowl he was fashioning to make a thick, sturdy rim. After a while, he said, "It was complicated, from what I understand. Rose had a complicated family life."

"Her family always seemed like the happiest family I knew."

"Nothing is what it seems, which I am sure you know from your line of work."

"So please tell me," I said. "Is there anything you know that might help me figure out what happened to her?"

I saw a flicker in his eyes, a quick shift. "I will say this about the eldercare facility they want to build. I'm against it in principle. But I signed off on it because we need it. And frankly, I'm glad it means the Gonzalez brothers won't be herding their cows here anymore. Good riddance to them."

I was genuinely surprised by this. The Gonzalez family and their herd had always seemed like a neutral, accepted part of life here. "Why's that?"

"I always got the feeling they thought we were a bunch of dirty hippies. Especially Paco. That guy rubs me the wrong way. He has an attitude. Judgmental. Makes me want to pop him one in the jaw." I saw something in Solo's face that startled me, a squinty-eyed, tight-mouthed meanness I'd never seen before, his pretty features all bunched up. Then just as suddenly it was gone. "Oh, and there is one thing, not necessarily related, but you never know, you might want to check it out. Suzie Cummings mentioned to me that her horse was standing outside the corral on Wednesday when she went down to ride him. Just standing by the fence, waiting to be let in. She thought I might have let him out. Of course I didn't. You might want to ask her about that."

The back of my neck prickled. Rose could have ridden Suzie's horse to the tree. That would explain the lack of marks on her bare feet and how she managed to tie a noose and hang herself a foot above the ground without anyone's help, if it turned out she really had hanged herself. And the horse knew the way home.

"I will," I said. "Right now. Thank you for the beer, Solo. For everything."

I HEADED DOWN TO THE STABLES TO LOOK AROUND FOR LAURA'S borrowed hiking boots, which had stuck in the back of my mind. It would all be so neat, so conclusive, if Rose had just put on her mother's boots, walked from the Triangle A to the stables here, discarded them near Bilbo's stall, and taken Bilbo to the tree. Everything would make sense. I would have a clear picture of how it all fit together. And I could let Laura know the case was closed and move on down the road back to Tucson, the next case.

But the hiking boots weren't anywhere.

I stood by the fence, leaning on a post, watching Bilbo and the two other horses, Susanna and Buddy, munch hay in the shade and shoo flies with placid flicks of their tails. I fished out my phone and called Laura.

"Hello? Justine?"

"Laura, I'm wondering if Rose ever returned those hiking boots she borrowed the other day."

"No?" said Laura in a voice that told me she thought this was a weird question but was humoring me because I was the professional here.

"Could you take a look and see if they might have been put back without your knowledge?"

"Hold on," said Laura. There was a brief silence. "They're still missing," she said. "You know, it's all right, I never use them, they're ancient."

"Thank you," I said. "I'll keep you posted."

I looked a second time through the stables, in each stall, in the open yard, in the tack shed, and in the land around the stables. Then I stomped my way around the perimeter, peering under the bench by the tack shed, behind every ocotillo and prickly pear. No boots. This didn't mean my theory was wrong. It just meant the boots were still missing. But nonetheless I felt that gnawing little sense of frustration at a missing jigsaw piece, that one letter you couldn't get in the crossword.

The boots had to be somewhere.

I needed to pay my mother a visit, but first I needed to talk to Suzie. Because my mother's house was directly on the way to Suzie's, I took the long way, the path that twisted up from the stables through dry sandy patches of sagebrush and ocotillo and Indian paintbrush. I had to open and close two gates in barbed-wire fences and scuttle around piles of boulders, but I didn't mind. I needed some time to think.

TEN

EVERYTHING WAS SO QUIET, NOT A PERSON IN SIGHT. THE PLACE was deserted and eerie feeling. I was surprised by the lack of commotion on the Rancho grounds. I had expected the whole community to be milling aimlessly about in collective shock. But I could feel something in the air. The silence had a shattered quality.

Suzie Cummings lived in a little cottage near the old empty water tower, which was commonly thought of as her water tower by dint of longtime creative possession. She'd once turned the shaggy cylindrical wooden shell into a pinhole camera, had staged a historically correct miniature replica of a Hopi village inside, and had re-created the Mad Hatter's tea party scene from *Alice in Wonderland*, letting people in one at a time to be Alice. She was a former elementary school teacher, so her aim was educational as well as aesthetic; she always invited the local elementary school classes on field trips to see her displays.

Her front door was whimsically decorated with gourds and jingle bells and chili peppers strung together. When I knocked, it whipped open instantly, as if Suzie had been standing there waiting for me.

"Oh, Jo," she said, pulling me inside. "Sit down, please. Oh, I'm just frantic. Oh, our dear Rose. No, don't sit there, dear, sit here so I can look at you. It's been a while, hasn't it!"

She was right; it had been a while. Over the years, I'd always kept my distance from Suzie. She was an intensely focused, ungainly, scattershot British woman with flyaway straw-colored hair and protruding, watery-blue eyes and a thick mouth that she twisted to one side in quizzical anxiety. She talked in breathy whispers, soft and childlike, her voice fading at the end of each sentence so you had to lean in to hear her. I'd always regarded her with suspicion, as if there were something didactic and needy underlying her effusive generosity.

Suzie hovered at my side, staring at me with avid anxiety. She seemed on the verge of breaking down.

"How are you, Suzie? I imagine this has been a shock."

"Oh," she said. "Thank you. I'm devastated, we all are."

"I heard from Solo that you found your horse outside its paddock on Wednesday morning."

"Yes, that's right. It thought it was odd, since Bilbo hasn't jumped the fence in at least ten years. I don't think he's able to anymore. Why do you ask?"

"I don't know. Just a theory." I glanced around at her house, which despite the heat outside was pleasantly chilly, thanks to the ceiling fans and swamp cooler. Every curtain rod and shelf, behind the stove and along the back of the couch, was thronged with creatures, the fanciful imaginary animals and fairylike beings Suzie carved from mesquite wood, dressed in cloths she made from natural desert fibers, painted with dyes she made from plants and crushed minerals. She sold these little dolls to collectors and buyers. En masse, they were compelling, if strikingly creepy. Along with several live cats curled on cushions and sprawled on braided rugs, the place bristled with a sentient, watchful audience.

"Do you think . . ." Suzie drew in her breath and covered her mouth, looked at me. "It was Rose, wasn't it? She was trying to communicate with me, send me a message, a cry for help. It was her spirit, trying to talk to me through Bilbo, wasn't it? Trying to let me know she was in trouble." She gave a strangled shriek in the back of her throat.

I considered setting her straight on the actual, very physical theory I had for how Bilbo had got out of his paddock that morning. But what was the point?

"I always take Bilbo out for a ride in the mornings," she was saying in an anguished half whisper, "every single day. Rose knew that. Her spirit knew. But I didn't listen. I couldn't hear her!"

"There's no way you could have known," I said, my voice neutral, flat. Often this works to lull very upset people when I need to get information out of them. Distressed people seem to find this grounding and sometimes even comforting. "Was there any sign at all that someone might have ridden him? Did he have a saddle on, a blanket, a bridle, sweat marks, anything like that?"

"I don't remember. No, he just had his usual old halter on."

"Was there a lead rope attached to it?"

"I don't know. Yes, I think there was. Oh, dear. I feel responsible somehow." Her teeth were chattering.

"It's all right, Suzie. You did nothing wrong. Just sit down."

She perched on the edge of a chair across from me at the table, still lost in her spiritual reverie about her horse. "He seemed normal," she said. "Just standing there. Wait." Her eyes bulged at me. "What if the message wasn't meant for me. What if Rose's spirit was trying to communicate with somebody else. With *you*!"

"Oh really?"

"Yes, that's it!" She shuddered again, her shoulders actually trembling. "You know, dear, I'm a little psychic, I always have been, and I am getting a very strong sense that Rose is trying to tell you something."

"Okay," I said with a glance toward the door.

"It's just a feeling, but it has to do with her wanting you to know that she forgives you."

Genuinely startled, I blurted out, "How do you know this?"

"Well, you know, dear, she confided in me about her difficulties with you, how terribly painful she found it when you got together with the boy she liked. I tried to help her, but who knows, she was so distraught for so long."

So Rose had been trash-talking me at Bella Luna all these years, ratting me out to the grown-ups, shaping her story, turning herself into the wronged victim.

Before I said something I regretted, I left Suzie to the peaceful company of her handmade doll collection.

"Goodbye, dear," she said, blinking in the harsh sunlight as she watched me go. "Keep your eyes and ears open for signs! The dead speak through the *anima mundi*, the great spirit world of animals!"

As Suzie's door closed behind me, I had that familiar sense of being watched by someone or something. I wasn't surprised when, somewhere off to my right, I heard Ophelia sneeze and turned to see her lying in the shade of the front patio, staring at me. "Hey, Rose," I said jokingly. "Bless you." She didn't answer, but she followed me along the winding path to my mother's casita.

I TOOK A DEEP BREATH AND KNOCKED ON THE DOOR OF THE HOUSE I was born and raised in. My mother's front door, unlike Suzie's, was neither whimsical nor decorated. It was plain, no froufrou.

When Marianne caught sight of me, she scowled, her standard reaction whenever she sees me, as if my very existence pisses her off. She swept me into one of her awkwardly didactic hugs, an iron-lung clench I emerged from a little dizzy from her skull knocking against mine.

"Hello, Mom."

"Justine," she said. Her refusal to call me Jo feels like another of her endless rejections of me. "You're up here looking into Rose's death, of course."

"Laura insisted on hiring me."

"Well, you're the one she wants," she said, her tone a little brusque, a little accusatory, but why, I had no idea. I couldn't parse it. I can never parse my mother.

She hustled me through the small front room she used as a painting studio, back to the kitchen with its uneven tile floor, old appliances, pots of herbs growing on a shelf in front of the big window over the farmhouse sink.

Marianne was the only child of two Boston Brahmins, Charles and Margaret Bass, Chaz and Mig, both frigidly neglectful and imperiously demanding of their daughter. She was talented and ambitious, but according to her, she was never encouraged, only criticized and pushed. She was valedictorian of her class at Abbot Academy and graduated from Radcliffe summa cum laude with a degree in art history. When she came of age and inherited her trust fund, she left her horrible childhood and parents behind for a life of freedom and art. In New York, she painted and hung out in the Village, hobnobbing with bohemians. She hitchhiked around the country with a loose series of friends and boyfriends, backpacked through Europe and Asia with the same, and settled at the Rancho in the 1970s, where she met and married a Mexican expatriate painter named Diego Bailen, embraced life in the desert, and gave birth to me, although I'm pretty sure I was not part of her life plan.

I do know that I was deeply loved by my father. He died in a stupid, horrifying car accident when I was little. A drunk driver swerved into his lane and hit him head-on, killing them both instantly. I imagined my life might have turned out completely differently if he was still alive. After his death, my mother and I lived in this house alone together, both of us spinning in our separate grief. I was only eight, but my childhood was over. My tender, ebullient dad was the one who made us feel like a family. My mother forgot about me for hours at a time while she painted, left me to fend for myself, never seemed to notice or care that I spent most of my time over at Rose's. She didn't know how to be maternal or generous. Her own upbringing had caused her to cloak herself in defensive self-protectiveness. She was so busy trying to repair her own damage that she had no caretaking left to offer her daughter. She forgot to buy me new clothes, never checked on my homework, and had only the vaguest idea of who I was.

I realized early on that the best thing, the only thing, I could offer my mother was to understand and forgive her limitations. She taught me to survive on my own, fostered my innate predilection for autonomy and independence. So we struck a mutually standoffish détente that lasted until I graduated from high school and moved out. My mother has lived here alone ever since.

I seated myself at the round wooden table while she put the kettle on to boil and puttered noisily while the water heated, clearing dishes from the drying rack. Having me around always seemed to make her uncomfortable, and she was extra agitated today. She fumbled with the box of tea bags, then banged her hand against the stove and tried to pretend it didn't hurt.

"Oh, Mom!" I said. "Be careful."

She huffed. She had always resented any sign of caretaking on my part. "I'm fine." Her voice was snippy. I could feel her generating a powerful force field to keep me at bay. I should have been used to it by now, but the old wound was deep, had never healed.

As for me, my toe was tapping against the table leg, my fingertips drumming like mad against my knee, keeping agitated time with impatience to get out of there.

"You heard about Rose," I said.

"Yes." My mother and Laura have never been each other's favorite people, to put it mildly. I have my theories as to why, but no firm data to back it up: as far as I could make out, they were both queen bees as younger women, both very beautiful, and the Rancho must have felt big enough for only one of them. I also suspect that Rose's and my rift came as a secret relief to them both, confirming and augmenting their own. "It's just tragic. Do you think they'll rule it a suicide and close the case?"

"I'm not sure," I said. "And even if they do, Laura wants to know why Rose killed herself."

"That makes sense, that she would want that, of course she would." Was that a softening I heard in her tone, a slight whiff of empathy for a bereaved fellow mother? Surely I was imagining it. But maybe not. "Why don't you let Tyler Bridgewater handle the case, if there is a case? Isn't that his job?"

I clenched my jaw. My mother had never approved of Tyler, which was one of the many reasons he had appealed to me so powerfully back in high school. Ditto my line of work, which she always felt was beneath my potential. She wanted me to be a college professor and a writer. For her, detective work was on par with being a plumber or a mailman, which I also considered perfectly fine professions, but my mother was an elitist snob through and through.

"They haven't opened a homicide case yet, that I know of," I told her, not rising to any of her bait. "They're waiting on the coroner's report. Standard procedure."

"I always knew that Rose had her demons." And there was that tone again, that nearly empathetic softness in her voice, but not without an edge of judgment. "It was never easy for her in that family, being Leo's stepdaughter, half sister to the boys, having to go back East every summer to see her real father. It's tough for a kid."

I shook my head at this version of Rose. "She was hardly Cinderella. She loved New Jersey, she thought her dad was the bomb. Her brothers and stepfather adored her. I know a lot of things went to shit recently for her, but her family life was always solid." I was tempted to add that I had envied her for this, but that wasn't fair. It wasn't my mother's fault that we lost my father. I knew she missed him. I knew she kept the steer antlers he'd found in the desert hung above the couch, and the three small portraits he'd painted of young

Marianne holding infant me above the sideboard. His navy canvas jacket still hung on a peg by the front door. I knew she wore it sometimes and had never washed it, along with his old Stetson, sweat stained and tattered, which she used as a gardening hat. As far as I could tell, she'd been single, even celibate, since the accident almost thirty-two years ago. My dad was the love of her life. And if she couldn't have him, she didn't want anyone.

Including me. She'd closed herself off in her grief, rejecting me, her grieving eight-year-old daughter. I hadn't had any clue what to do about it, how to win her back. Eventually, I gave up trying, and pushed my pain and sadness way down deep where they couldn't hurt me anymore. As I grew up, I taught myself not to need my mother.

Or so I tried to convince myself.

Just as the kettle gave its rising shriek, I heard a knock at the front door.

"That must be them," said Marianne, as she poured boiling water into the teapot. "Will you get the door?"

"Who's them?" I asked. It was just like my mother to neglect to tell me she was expecting visitors.

I opened the door and was surprised to see Jason Gold standing in front of me, dressed smartly in a suit and tie. He looked even more surprised to see me, and I caught a fleeting look of alarm on his face, which he quickly masked with a forced smile.

"Hello again," he said. "I wasn't expecting you here. These are my business partners, Chad and Phil." He gestured behind him at two soft, balding guys in business suits, carrying rolls of paper and files tucked under their arms, their faces bland and incurious. "We have an appointment with your mother."

"Come in!" My mother's voice echoed from the living room. "I won't bite."

Jason stepped past me, and I eyed his associates as they followed on his heels. They were a type I had come to know well growing up in Arizona, indoor guys with financial savvy, identical, as if each of them was stamped out in some android plant and shipped to every town all over the Southwest and installed prominently in every bank and office, swathed in yards of beige or navy serge in the chill of air-conditioning, ready to invest your money or sell you insurance or build you a condo. I'd gone to high school with an uncountable number of adolescent versions of Chad and Phil, with their Baptist-pastor haircuts and snub noses and downy mottled-red cheeks, who goofed off in Spanish class and played second-string JV football and had perky, pretty girlfriends, and then went on to join investment firms and manage car dealerships. They were the kind of guys who said things like "I'll circle back and touch base when I have the bandwidth to do a deep dive, let's break down the silos and run it up the flagpole and move the needle," all that bullshit self-important empty jargon that made me want to hurl.

"Well, sit down, then," said my mother to the newcomers. "Help yourself to some tea."

As the men seated themselves around the living room, I watched with amused half admiration as Marianne set the tea tray on the coffee table with a plate of gingersnaps. An innocuous little whiff of steam rose from the teapot's spout. It was ninety-five degrees outside, but my mother, true to her British roots, believes that hot tea is the appropriate beverage for this climate, just as her forebears did when they were colonizing sunbaked India and exploring the sweltering Amazon and going on safari in Kenya. Hot tea all around.

"Thank you for agreeing to talk to us," said one of the development boys. Chad? Phil? I was having trouble telling them apart. "We appreciate you taking the time to meet with us today."

My mother ignored him and turned to Jason. "I'm surprised to see you here, Jason. You must be feeling such terrible shock after what happened with your sister."

My mother was always able to be warm and empathetic with

other people's kids. Just not her own. In spite of my determination not to mind, it still made me wince inwardly.

"Yes," said Jason, clearing his throat. "Of course, we all are. But I didn't want to pass up the opportunity to meet with you and discuss our proposal for the Sunset Shadows development, since you are the only member of the community who hasn't signed off on it yet."

Oh, so that's why they were here. My mother was the lone hold-out, of course she was. I felt almost proud of her and glad, for once, not to be the subject and recipient of her stubbornness.

"I'm sorry, but you're wasting your time," Marianne said, pouring herself a cup of tea since nobody else seemed interested. "I'm not signing anything."

The three men exchanged a quick, nervous glance.

"We understand that you've got questions," said the other one, with what he clearly thought was delicate tact. But I sensed that these guys wanted to clonk my mother over the head with a shovel and bury her with the bulldozers. "This is an all-or-nothing deal, so of course we need you on board."

My mother sat back and made a pleasant humming noise, which I knew meant there was nothing more to be said on the matter; her judgment was final. But you were welcome to try to change her mind all you liked. Good luck with that, boys.

"So what exactly is this Sunset Shadows thing?" I asked. Clearly relieved to have an audience, Jason and his associates went into full sales mode, unrolling plans, spreading them out on the table while my mother grudgingly moved the tea things to make room, pointing to various features on the professional-looking maps and drawings.

Sunset Shadows, as far as I could tell, consisted of a sprawling complex of hexagonal adobe-colored buildings, two parking lots, a swimming pool, a new road built straight in from the highway, bypassing the Rancho entirely. The development would sit on a hundred-acre plot of Bella Luna land purchased for the ludicrously low price of a hundred dollars by the development company, Innovative Integrations, Inc., which seemed to consist solely of the three men sitting before me. In return, all of the permanent longtime founding residents of the Rancho would be able to enjoy the luxuries and privileges and services offered to the paying-in-full guests with an "aging-in-place option" to stay in their own original houses, and full use of the medical staff, cleaning services, and gym and spa facilities. As Jason made clear, there would also be "infrastructure upkeep and improvements" for Bella Luna itself.

"That means repaving the driveway, renovating outbuildings and the main house, and updating the septic," one of them said, maybe it was Chad.

"These aren't negligible expenses," Phil chimed in. "Innovative Integrations would carry all of it, one hundred percent."

Also, apparently, there was a pressing deadline to get signatures on the contract before some nebulous time-sensitive opportunity expired, I wasn't entirely clear what, but I suspected it was largely manufactured to gin up a sense of urgency to get my mother to sign.

Well, what choice did the Rancho have, really? Everyone was getting old. No one had much money left anymore.

But my mother was adamant in her opposition. She explained that the main problem she had was with the parcel of land that they were after, a wild valley that lay south of the ranch buildings. Poppies covered the sunny flanks of the hillsides in springtime. A pack of coyotes had their den there. There was a forest of old yuccas. Tucked in the rolling low foothills, crisscrossed by the cows' grazing trails, you couldn't hear traffic or see any sign of human life. That valley was timeless, quiet, pristine. I had the sense this wasn't the first time she'd told them this.

"It's such a lot to give up," said my mother.

"You're not losing anything, Marianne," Jason said.

"The poppies will be gone," she snapped. "Of course I'm losing something."

"Maybe we can save them for you. Meanwhile, that land is just sitting there doing nothing. This is about ensuring your own long-term health and comfort. Sunset Shadows will provide round-the-clock care and upkeep for the ranch."

"But why does it have to have such a terrible name?" I could feel my mother's patience wearing thin. "Might as well call it Death's Door. I'm only sixty-eight years old, for God's sake."

"Everyone else has signed," Jason said with soothing unctuousness. "All twenty-six of them. Some are even younger than you are."

My mother sipped her tea and looked into the middle distance and said nothing, just shut down. It was another one of her maddening traits, or social survival skills, depending on how you saw it. I suppressed a grin; I was totally on her side here.

"Well," said Chad or Phil, clearing his throat while the other one gathered up the maps and drawings. They could clearly tell they were barking up an empty tree. "Why don't you take some time to think it over, talk to some of the other folks who've signed already, and we'll circle back in a few days."

"Would you mind leaving the drawings here?" I asked. "It would help for us to be able to look them over."

"Sure," said Jason. "They're just copies."

"I don't believe a word out of their mouths," my mother said as soon as the door had shut behind them. "As far as I see it, the instant we sign that land away, they'll go and do whatever they want with it, mine it for uranium or build a megamall. There's nothing in any contract that holds them to anything. But I seem to be the only one around here who thinks that. Everyone else is signing the damn thing and pressuring me to do it too. It makes me so mad."

She picked up the plate of cookies and thrust it in my direction. She herself was not going to eat even one, that was a given. These cookies were for me, her galumphing daughter. My mother is a cricket with anorexic tendencies, whereas I'm built like my father, tall and strong, with a layer of padding like a dolphin and gargantuan appetites of all varieties. My mother has always been hyperaware of and competitively pleased by our physical differences. Right now she sat curled in her chair, one long, spindly leg wrapped around the other, her white pageboy falling just so around her gaunt face. My eyes narrowed at her as I took a gingersnap and crushed it between my molars, then took another one and pulverized that too. My mother's self-denial always makes me rebelliously ravenous.

"I know it's much too early for this conversation," I said, between bites, "but what is your plan for your very old age? Of course I'll do whatever you need. But somehow I doubt you'd want to live with me."

"God no," she snapped without the slightest pause. Ouch. "I want to stay right here in this house until I die. I don't want anyone fussing over me."

"Okay, but realistically, wouldn't it be convenient to have a medical staff and all those facilities nearby, available if you needed them?"

"I'd rather walk out into that wild land, lie down, and let the coyotes and the birds eat me."

When I laughed at this, she looked startled, since she hadn't meant to be funny.

"I'm serious," she said. "I can't stand this whole for-profit industry that preys on the elderly. I hate everything about it."

"Well, I agree with you. And I happen to know Rose did too. She was fighting to stop it. She and Lupita Gonzalez, from the cattle family."

"Oh, you can't stop something like this. It's inevitable."

"Does that mean you're going to sign?"

"I can't be the lone holdout forever. I was hoping Solo would see the light at least, but he was the first one to go for it. Stupid man." My mother glared at me as if this were my fault. "By the way, the open-studio full-moon party is still on, but we've decided to make it a memorial for Rose instead. You'll come, of course."

This was the first I'd heard of it. "I'm not sure I'm invited."

"Of course you are."

"Rose and I weren't exactly close."

My mother gave a high, disapproving whinny in the back of her throat. "You're investigating her death, aren't you? Seems awfully close to me."

A question suddenly floated into my brain as if it had been on a delayed timer. The cottonwood tree that Rose had been hanging from, what if it was on the hundred-acre parcel that Jason and his cronies wanted to develop for Sunset Shadows? I sifted through the maps and drawings on the coffee table, found a satellite image of the land, and there it was, the dirt road, the boulder-strewn wash, the large cottonwood tree, right smack in the middle of the land.

"Do you think you could at least try to get the word out about the memorial?" My mother had poured herself another cup of tea and was retreating now to her worktable in the corner of the room. "Laura and Leo are inviting everyone who knew Rose."

My brain was jumping in my skull. "I really have to go now, Mom, I'm sorry, I have an appointment. But I'll see you tomorrow."

I rolled up the map, tucked it under my arm, and left Marianne at her worktable with pencils and sketch pad, drawing the aloe plant in front of her, turning its spikes into fat limbs sprouting from a headless block of torso. This was her artistic jam, turning plants into meat, the ascetic's vicarious pleasure. She always worked whenever she was tense or upset. It was her primary source of comfort, much the way actual fleshly pleasures were mine. In my mother's case, though, it resulted in impressive, accomplished, weirdly beautiful works of art that people admired, bought, and hung in their houses. In my case, it just resulted in more flesh.

ELEVEN

THE DAY HAD CHANGED WHILE I'D BEEN AT MY MOTHER'S HOUSE. Fat squashy raindrops spattered my windshield. Cool wind billowed through my rolled-down windows as I drove, smelling of wet rock and resiny plants. The velvety-soft gray sky looked freshly lit, brightening as the clouds raced and thinned overhead, then darkening just as fast with more splats of rain. Ophelia rode shotgun the way she had before, paws on the dashboard, slitting her eyes as rain splatted her face. I could have sworn she was smiling. I was finding myself fighting a growing affection for this winsome little beast. I had no room in my life for her. What this said about my life, I didn't want to articulate.

As I pulled into the Triangle A parking lot, my phone rang. "Jo Bailen."

"This is Michaela D'Ambrosio speaking." The speaker's voice was husky, New York accented. "Mickey. I'm Rose Delaney's roommate. Her mom just called me; she gave me your number and said I could call you." Aha. So this was the roommate Rose had been fighting with.

"Hi, Mickey," I said. "I was going to call you, actually."

They took a deep, sucking breath. "Holy shit. I'm just . . . Is it true? Did Rose really kill herself?"

"It looks that way," I said. "I'm trying to find out why."

I heard some ragged, wet noises. "Are you finding out anything?"

"I'm trying to put a picture together of her life leading up to this past week. I understand you and Rose were friends?"

"Best friends and roommates, and we were in a band together. For a lot of years. Through a lot of shit." Mickey sniffed hard. "I apologize for my emotionality, I'm just kind of . . . This is so awful, I do not know what I'm gonna do without her. No idea." Their voice crackled in my ear. "She *killed* herself? It's a literal shock. Out of the freaking blue."

"Listen, Mickey, I'm heading back down to Tucson later on, if you're free. I could come by."

"Absolutely, I'll be here."

"And I've got Rose's dog with me. I would like to drop her off with you, if you can take her."

"Rose's what?"

"Her dog. Ophelia."

"Rose doesn't have a dog."

"She did, apparently. Maybe it's a recent adoption."

There was a silence. "I can't believe she got a dog. Our landlord doesn't allow pets. Was she not going to move back in with me? Why the hell would she get a dog?"

"Okay then," I said. "I'll make other arrangements. And I'd really appreciate the chance to talk to you."

"Oh please, come over. Anytime." Mickey gave me the address, and we hung up.

SINCE SHE SEEMED WILLING TO FOLLOW ME EVERYWHERE, I LED Ophelia up the porch steps of the Triangle A main house and knocked. Angela answered right away in a blue bathrobe, her hair up in a clip, hugging a mug of something to her clavicle. "Good morning, Jo," she said, opening the door wider to let me in. "I heard what happened, they found her body. Jesus."

"I know," I said. "I came to tell you, in case you hadn't heard."

"Her mom called over here last night. Kylie talked to her. Come in, everyone's here. Kylie just made coffee. There's plenty of breakfast, Noah made pancakes."

"I can't, I need to get going," I said with some regret. I would have loved to hang out here for a while, eat pancakes, and talk to these beautiful women about Rose's death. "I'm just here to drop off Ophelia. She keeps dogging me, but I can't take her. And she's probably hungry."

"Come on, Ophelia," said Angela, making a kissing sound. "Come have breakfast."

"Rose's roommate, Mickey, didn't seem to know she had a dog."

"She didn't," said Angela. "Ophelia showed up out of nowhere one day a couple of weeks ago, started hanging around here. Rose decided to keep her, but I guess . . ."

We both looked down at the little creature, lying right inside the doorway at Angela's feet. She had rolled onto her side and was energetically licking her nether regions.

"She seems to think this is home," I said hopefully.

Angela sighed. "For now, she can stay here," she said. "I guess we could keep her overnight. But I already have a dog and I don't want another one. I'll take her to the Humane Society tomorrow and let them rehome her."

"Okay," I said. "That sounds like a plan. I'm off now, but I'm sure I'll be back at some point." With a wave, I headed down the steps into the strong, wet wind.

As I drove, I called Ronnie. She picked up after one ring. "Hey, Bailen."

"Hi. I'm still up in Delphi, and this case seems to be lasting awhile. But I'm heading back down to Tucson later, if you need me to come by the office for any reason."

"Why the fuck would I need you in the office? Just solve the goddamned case."

It was bracing to hear her voice, the real reason I'd called. I was feeling a bit queasy up here, stalking Rose through my hometown. "I'll come by to check in," I said.

"Just hand it to me!" she said so sharply my phone jumped in my hand. "No, not that one, you fuckwit, the right one!"

I heard an apologetic male voice in the background, then the line went dead.

Slightly cheered, I hung up and stowed my phone and pulled my car in front of the Arroyo Cafe. Lupita was waiting in the doorway, shielded from the rain. She landed in my passenger seat, saying something in very fast Spanish about how her boss was getting on her nerves and she wanted to quit but the tips were too good.

"I don't speak Spanish," I told her.

"What?"

"Well, not beyond high school."

"Your last name is Bailen?" She pronounced it the Spanish way. "*Dígame.*"

"My Mexican dad was killed in a car crash before he could really teach me."

"Shit. I'm sorry. Where was he from?"

"Monterrey," I said, not rolling the *r*'s. "But my mother is a WASP from Boston. White as the driven snow."

"You're still a *chicana*," she said.

"I don't feel like one. My father told me all about his racist family telling themselves they were white Europeans. They obsessively traced their lineage back to Spain and talked about their 'pure' blood that was uncorrupted by a drop of Indigenous genes, so proud of being *güeros* instead of *mestizos*. Screw them. I've never met them. I've barely even been to Mexico, aside from a few trips to Nogales to get drunk. We took a high school class trip to Mazatlán once."

"They can pretend they're not real Mexicans, but everyone there has *some* Indigenous blood." Lupita laughed. She had a good laugh, smutty and wicked. "And your accent sucks. You say *mestizaje*." In her mouth, the word sounded beautiful. "That's what I am."

"Speaking of which," I said, "did Rose ever tell you she was part Navajo?"

"Yeah. She told me her real father, her biological father, belonged to the Navajo Nation. She talked a lot about feeling out of place in her family, since they're Jewish and Anglo, and feeling like she didn't belong in the world of white people."

"I hate to break this to you, cowgirl," I said on a fresh rising wave of gobsmacked outrage at the sheer bald-faced bullshit of this, "but Rose's father was a New Jersey Irish-American white boy. She had not one drop of Native blood. None."

"What?"

"Rose was white. Pure white."

Lupita looked genuinely shocked. "No way. She talked about trauma and identity, she told me to think about my own heritage."

"No doubt," I said. "But I'm telling you, she made it up. Complete fiction. To put it kindly."

"I can't believe it. Why would she make that up? Why would she lie about it?"

"It got her a teaching job, for one. Probably made her seem interesting. I'm sure there was a deeper reason, too, a psychological explanation; there generally is. Something in her must have wanted to be part of that collective memory. I guess one of my assignments here is to discover why."

"Tell me when you find out. I want to know. Making that up? Jesus."

I turned off Arizona Avenue and headed us up Coyote Loop Road, a dirt road that runs uphill through a sleepy bunch of houses, eventually crests over a ridge, skirts the town, and loops back down again.

Lupita peered through the windshield. "Where are we going?"

"For a drive. When do you have to be back?"

"Fifteen minutes."

"Got it." Plenty of time; I slowed down to an easy twenty-five. "How well did you know Rose? Did you see her recently, while she was back up here?"

Lupita turned to me, curling her spine into the seat back, resting her feet up on the dashboard. Her dark silky hair fell across her cheek. I caught a whiff of lemony shampoo under lingering scents of bacon and coffee. "You don't remember me, do you?"

"Should I?"

"I was three years behind you in school. All the way through. I remember you, anyway."

"Wait, I said, casting back, A small, dark girl emerged from the fogbank of my memory, watching me in the halls of our high school, trying to talk to me at a football game, sitting next to me at a Triangle A party. She was so young, barely a kid, a skinny, scrappy freshman when I was a senior, almost a grown-up. "I do remember you. Why didn't you say something right away, at breakfast?"

"Oh, I'm just messing with you." Her eyes gave off light at me. "I had a mad crush on you that year. You were the older woman of my dreams. Too bad you're straight. You were with Tyler, anyway." She paused. "You are, right?"

"What, straight?" I looked sidelong at her, grinning at her directness. "I would say I'm . . . omnivorous." I let the moment pass because I was working. But she definitely had my attention. We started talking about other kids we'd gone to high school with, people I hadn't thought about in years and didn't much care about.

I was just wondering how to bring the conversation back on track when Lupita said straight out, "Okay, so how can I help you here? What do you need to know?"

"You're a Gonzalez, right? You're related to the cattle family?"

"My dad and uncle inherited the business from my grandfather. My cousin Tono's the one who saw Rose and called 911, he was moving the herd yesterday."

"You and Rose were emailing about a land deal. Was it Sunset Shadows?"

"It's a bad thing, for my family and for hers. Stupid, wrong. But both our families are for it. We can't make them listen."

"Why is it bad for your family?"

"We've always had a deal with the Bella Luna to let our cattle graze on their land. The developers are offering my father and uncle money to buy them out of their contract. It's not enough."

"I gather that Rose was fighting with her brother Jason about this."

"Same way I'm fighting with my dad and uncle. She and I were working together to stop them all from giving it away and letting them ruin it."

"Everyone is signing," I said. "Even my mother. I just talked to her."

"See, it's a tragedy. My family's cows have been grazing on that land since the 1940s. There are water rights that come along with it, too, good water, not that radioactive shit from the valley, so the cows can drink it. We manage a hundred acres for the Rancho, we keep it wild and healthy, and our cows get fat on the grass, which reduces the risk of wildfires. And we pay them for the use of the land on top of that. What better deal is there for them?"

"What did these guys offer your family? Because it looks like they're taking it."

"It's only a one-time payment, to agree to cancel their ten-year contract. Not that much money."

"Where will the cows go?"

"There's a tract of land across the highway—do you know the Maclean Ranch? But it's not as good. Less open land, more restrictions, and no water. It's not the same."

My car crested the ridge and went around the little loop at the top and started back down the switchback. A dog behind a chain-link fence in a scruffy brown yard lunged and snarled as we went by. Next door, another dog sat in the shade, chained to a pole. Most Arizona domestic dogs aren't coddled or walked, and they don't sleep inside. They live alone in hot yards, many of them on too-short chains. Their purpose is to bark at and attack intruders. I've always been horrified by the cruelty of this. But there's nothing anyone can do about it.

"Why did your dad and uncle take the bait?"

"Because those *pendejos* made them feel like they couldn't say no, like they owed it to the Rancho people to let them have this amazing retirement community."

"By 'those *pendejos*' you mean Jason too?"

She grimaced at his name. "He's the worst one of all."

BY THE TIME WE GOT BACK TO THE ARROYO CAFE, IT HAD STOPPED raining, and the sky was clearing. The sun was evaporating the rain into a shimmering mist. A breeze blew in through my open window, and I could hear the popping sound of water soaking into dry land. The instant I came to a stop, Lupita slid out and closed the door. She turned back and ducked her head in the passenger window to say, "Hey, hit me up if you ever want to get a drink."

I drove away smiling, in spite of everything. Maybe I was just happy to be heading down to Tucson, back to the big city, leaving all this death and history behind, if only for a day.

TWELVE

WITH THE RADIO TUNED TO THE CLASSICAL STATION, I CRUISED down to Plato Valley with mountains rising on my left, open desert all around, listening to two violins and a viola and cello swirling the air around my ears, four voices chit-chattering, discussing, disagreeing, and coming back together in unexpected harmony. I've always loved string quartets for the clarity of their conversational threads, so much like verbal discussions, a similar rhythm and density. These four were chewing on something that elicited a lot of joyful crunching from the cello and viola and fluid folksy birdsong from the violins. I settled into it, and the miles slipped by, wild desert stretching away outside my small speeding pod, aural civilized beauty inside. Humans are terrible: we pollute and befoul and kill, inflict pain and violence, destroy oceans and forests. But then, on the other hand, there are string quartets.

Just after I hit the town of Acantilado and the highway widened to four lanes past Plato Valley's retirement communities and developments, the quartet ended, and the mellifluous deejay informed me that this had been the American Quartet by Dvorak, performed by the New York Philharmonic Quartet. I turned off the radio, my mind now clear and full of ideas, my mood uplifted, ready again to face the immediate and pressing question of suicide and ecological despoilment and emotional entanglements.

Closer to Tucson, as I passed one mattress store and fast-food place after another, the highway widened to six lanes, fresh blacktop thick with traffic, heat squiggles rising in the midday sun. I turned left onto Ina Road and funneled myself into Tucson's grid of wide avenues, jogging in a zigzag pattern west and south and thus down to the university district.

Rose had lived with Michaela D'Ambrosio on a dusty, quiet, windblown residential side street in a stucco bungalow set back from the sidewalk in a scruffy half-wild yard of cactus, sand, rocks, and several trees—avocado, lemon, and palo verde. I parked in front of the house and got out of the car and heard all the outdoor, fenced-in dogs barking all over the neighborhood, heralding my arrival. I was familiar with this part of town. All those years ago, Tyler and I had shared a house a few blocks from here, our own very similar little bungalow. We picked oranges from our backyard tree in the morning, avocados and limes from our front-yard trees to make into guacamole and squeeze into our tequila in the evening.

I knocked on the door, saw a face briefly appear in the front picture window, checking me out, and then the door opened. "Hey." Mickey was a short, wide person. They wore a sleeveless denim shirt and Bermuda shorts that revealed very white, stocky limbs, red hair buzzed short on the sides and spiked on top. I recognized them as the drummer in the video of Rose's band.

"I'm Jo Bailen," I said, flashing my PI license. "We talked on the phone earlier."

"I'm Mickey. My pronouns are they/them. Come in."

The shining floors smelled of pine and looked freshly mopped. The little living room with its wooden beams and white stucco walls and brick fireplace was neat and bright and stylish: a midcentury modern aquamarine couch, black leather club chairs, orange laminated Formica coffee table with Danish modern tapered legs, shelves of books that covered the entire far wall. A Navajo blanket, which every gringo in Arizona seemed to own, hung on the opposite wall. A flat-screen TV hung over the fireplace mantel. There was a stripped-down drum kit in the corner, two guitars in cloth cases by the wall.

"Someone has good taste," I said.

Mickey visibly vibrated with sorrow, hands fluttering in the air by their shoulders as if the invisible puppet master was drunk. "Rose," they said. Their face was flat and square and puckish, with deep dimples in both cheeks and sparkling blue eyes. "It was all her. I have the taste of a truck driver. No offense to truck drivers, I've been one. But Rose was the genius around here."

So Mickey had been in love with Rose.

"How did you know Rose?" I asked.

"We both worked at Club Head after college. I was bartending, she was cocktailing. Instant friends. Back then I still identified as a cis-female lesbian, and she was deep into women's studies and feminist poetry. Rose and I talked a lot about female identity. We started a band together. Our first one."

"So you and Rose were close for a long time."

Their face started to crumple, and then they remembered their manners. "Can I get you a beer? Or, like, water? That's about all I've got. Rose dealt with groceries. I'm your basic frat boy."

My heart went out to this person. I could see it all: almost twenty years of pining for a woman who could never love them back but who was their roommate, bandmate, and best friend. "A beer would be great."

I used the brief moment of solitude to snoop around the bookshelf and found heaps of poetry, as well as reference books, southern Arizona bird-watching and hiking guides, and classic novels. If Rose had had a secret penchant for trashy bestsellers or Harlequin romances, she had stashed them elsewhere.

Mickey came back with two bottles of dark Mexican beer and handed me one. I took a swig of bitter, yeasty brew and wiped my mouth on the back of my hand. As I perched on the couch, Mickey flopped into a club chair and slung a bare leg over to rest ankle on knee.

"I have to be honest," they said. "I'm having a lot of trouble coming to grips with this. Can you spell it out for me, exactly what happened? Rose's mom was pretty emotional, and I didn't feel right grilling her for details. She didn't tell me till this morning. When did it happen?"

"We're waiting on the coroner's report for the exact time," I said. "But as far as we can guess, it was early Wednesday morning." I described it briefly, just the facts: branch, tree, rope, barefoot, white dress.

"That does sound like her," said Mickey with a wry half smile. "But fuck me, I feel like I should have known! Why didn't she call me? Yeah, she was having problems. But she was not, like, suicidal."

"What kind of problems?"

"Well," they said, "to be honest, she and I had been fighting."

"Why?"

"Well, there was this boy. Her student."

"Chayton Griffiths."

"Oh, so Babette and Kylie filled you in. Chay was her *student*. A *teenager*."

"She slept with him?"

"She's an idiot. I mean, it was flat-out wrong, all that shit she did. Pretending to be Native? Getting work and fellowships and a publishing deal because of that?" Mickey shook their head, mouth tight. "That was effed-up, and I told her so, and she lost it on me. Said if I loved her, I wouldn't judge. I said part of love is telling someone when they're acting wrongly. She stopped speaking to me and went up to Delphi."

"I understand she was heartbroken over the kid, on top of her book being canceled."

"She really loved him." Some of Mickey's feelings about this flashed across their face. "But she said it was worth it in the end because of the poems she was going to get out of it. That was her motto: Turn pain into work. But yeah, she was psyched about her new book. She said it was going to put her on the map. Then it got canceled, and so did she."

"Was she upset about losing her teaching job?"

"Sure, I guess she was, but teaching wasn't her life. Writing was. She said she'd start waitressing again if it came to that; she really didn't give a shit about academia. Although she loved her students, the place. She liked teaching, but she said it took her away from writing. And it didn't really pay that well. She could make twice as much cocktailing, working fewer hours. And our band had been getting some great gigs lately, paying ones."

"Sounds like she was planning to get on with her life," I said.

"Yeah." They paused. "And I have to say again that I highly doubt that any of this would make her kill herself. She was facing it all."

"Do you mind if I take a look at her room?"

"Oh sure, of course. This way."

Mickey led me into a short hallway and gestured to the doorway on the right. Relieving me of my empty beer bottle, they vanished into the kitchen to let me prowl around.

ROSE'S ROOM WAS SMALL AND BEAUTIFUL, MADE DIM BY A PAINTED three-panel shoji screen in front of the only window. The midnight-blue walls were hung with a cluster of small, framed, black-and-white photographs of desert landscapes, stark and stylized: cliffs, saguaros, a broad wash running with water. I recognized Catalina State Park. Her queen-size bed had a handmade, polished-mesquite headboard and was covered in an orange-gold woven bedspread embedded with tiny mirrors. On top of a tall mahogany bureau was a matching orange cloth on which sat a large, matching mirror, in front of which were arranged small enamel and ceramic bowls filled with jewelry.

To the side of the dresser top stood a carved and decorated

wooden doll, about nine or ten inches tall, with a handwritten label on the bottom that said "Navajo-Made Crow Mother Kachina Doll." She was finely made and looked rare or at least old and expensive and of high quality, a collector's item maybe. Two feathered wings bristled on either side of her head, and she held a potted yucca plant in her hands. Above a green, feathered ruff around her neck, her small precise face was black and fierce and geometric. She wore a red-and-black-striped headdress, a black dress, moccasins, and a cape. The significance of the Crow Mother, according to the website I found by quickly looking it up on my phone's search engine, was that she "participated in the initiation of children by whipping them with her yucca blades." And then they whipped her back. I found this fascinatingly kinky. The Crow Mother, matriarch of all the kachinas, powerful and mysterious and quintessentially Native, struck me as exactly the sort of figure that Rose would identify with, whose iconic presence she would covet, and whose handmade imaginary likeness she would have on her dresser top.

I put the Crow Mother back in her place and resumed my prowling around the room. I looked in her bureau drawers and closet: neatly folded and hung clothes and shoes on racks, nothing of interest. I looked under her bed and felt around in the crevices of her mattress and under the pillows. Hidden behind the tripaneled shoji screen, unexpectedly, I found a small writing table and chair tucked next to the plain, large sliding window, which looked out on a double driveway and the house next door, a nothing view partly blocked by a large spiky blooming ocotillo that grew directly in front of the window. Its neon-bright orange flowers pressed against the pane. On the writing table was a stack of books. There were six in all, all of them poetry collections: *A Radiant Curve* by Luci Tapahonso, *Evidence of Red* by LeAnne Howe, *Conflict Resolution for Holy Beings* by Joy Harjo, *The Radiant Lives of Animals* by Linda Hogan, *When My Brother Was an Aztec* by Natalie Diaz, and a Norton anthology of Native Nations poetry called *When the Light of the World Was Subdued, Our Songs Came Through*. I flipped through all these books, one by one, to see if anything fell out, if there were any marginal notes, if Rose had left any personal messages or clues of any kind in any of them, but there was nothing. No suicide note, no confession, nothing of interest that I could ascertain except that Rose clearly had an interest in Native poetry, which I had already known.

On the nightstand by the bed was a collection of framed photos. In a triptych of hinged frames, there was a shot of Rose and her brothers as kids, sitting at their family dinner table, the three of them laughing hard together. The middle photo must have been taken just before senior prom, Rose in a form-fitting long white gown and green gloves, her little brothers flanking her, Ben pinning on her corsage, Jason lifting her arm up dramatically as if they were ballroom dancing together.

The boys looked completely in Rose's thrall, their older half sister, clearly the little betas to her absolute alpha. That sweet, innocent photo had been taken at the beginning of the night that ended with Rose and Tyler and my druggy threesome. The third photo showed Ben at three or four years old, wearing a tutu and tiara, Jason in a cowboy hat and kid-size chaps and spurs with a bandanna around his neck, and eleven-year-old Rose dressed in a full red skirt, a scarf in her hair, bangle earrings, Mexican peasant blouse. Halloween, maybe?

Another framed photo was of Rose and her mother. Rose must have been in her twenties when it was taken, Laura in her late forties. I never thought the two of them looked remotely alike. Laura was ethereal and golden, Rose sturdy and dark haired like her father. But in this photo, a close-up of their faces side by side, both looking straight at the camera with identical moody, dreamy expressions, I could see they had the same cheekbones and softly rounded chins and deep-set eyes. This photo was, I knew, a rare moment of tenderness between them. Their default mode with each other, even when Rose was little, was a prickly, snippy mutual disappointment and reproach. Laura rarely give Rose the validation and attention she craved, and Rose was never the adoring, respectful daughter Laura wanted. Both of them wanted the spotlight, the praise. Their egos clashed, and their needs and predilections dovetailed too precisely. They were too much alike.

I WENT BACK OUT TO THE LIVING ROOM AND SAT ACROSS FROM Mickey. "So what kinds of things did Rose tell you about her family? How did she get along with them, anything in their history, that sort of thing?"

Mickey's face rippled slightly as their eyes darted away and then back to my face. I knew that look. It meant a person was wondering, briefly, whether to reveal something, and then deciding not to. "She loved her family. There was some shit with her dad when she was young. She didn't really talk about it, but I knew it was a big deal for her to go and see him when he was dying. She forgave him in the end, and she was glad she did."

I flashed on the fact that Rose hadn't written about her father at all in her journals. "Do you know what kind of shit it was?"

"I always had this sense of, like, weirdness around him. She wouldn't say what it was."

So maybe he'd molested her? If so, this was yet another huge thing in my former best friend's life that she'd never breathed a word of to me. Well, anything was possible. Just the mere thought that this could be true made me feel sick. "Anything else with her family?"

Mickey's face rippled again with internal debate, the desire to spill something batting against the instinct to keep their trap shut.

"Leo, her stepfather, she liked him, right?"

"Sure." No doubt there. So not that.

I kept probing. "Her mother? Her brothers?"

"It was complicated with her mom, but nothing bad. And she loved her brothers." Again: Eyes darted to the wall, back to me. Deep breath, eyes steady on my face. Here it came, and boom. "So actually, and I'm sorry if this is weird, but she had a thing about you."

"So you know who I am." This was starting to be a theme.

"I recognized your name, for sure," they said. Now that they'd opened the floodgates, the water was rushing out. "She talked about you. And that guy, Tyler, that guy you went to high school with. She had an obsession with him. And you too. Like, a fixation on you guys."

"Really."

"Oh yeah, Rose talked about you a lot."

"I've been hearing that," I said, flexing my hands at the untenable weirdness of Rose's obsession with me, wishing I could erase it. Swamped with a weary, helpless sadness that was beginning to feel all too familiar, I added, "And now she's dead, so there's nothing I can do to fix it."

At the word "dead," I saw Mickey cave in around the emptiness of Rose's absence. It was time to get a move on, but it made me melancholy, the thought of leaving Mickey to grieve alone in this quiet house that was chock-full of Rose. They went by plural pronouns, but they still had a poignant-seeming singular identity that no language could alter. Then I remembered. "There's a memorial for her on Tuesday evening, up at Rancho Bella Luna. It starts at five. You're welcome to come."

"Oh, that would be cool," they said, perking up very slightly. "I'll definitely be there."

"Just one more thing. The student Rose was involved with, do you have a phone number for him?"

"Chay Griffiths," they said with a tinge of vicarious or maybe loyal bitterness. "I don't have his number, but you can find him on campus, I bet. It's small."

THIRTEEN

"YES, I REPORTED HER TO THE DEAN FOR INAPPROPRIATE BEHAVIOR," Chayton Griffiths told me. "But there is a lot more to the story than that."

I waited, letting him spit it out in his own time at his own pace, and looked around at this idyllic little campus perched on the eastern flank of the Tucson Mountains above Saguaro National Park, with a view over the city all the way to Mount Lemmon. It was Sunday afternoon, the student body at large and unscheduled. I had parked in the visitors' lot and wandered around the campus, soaking up the ambience of this exclusive artsy summer camp of an institution of higher learning. Saguaro Early College, nicknamed "the Simon's Rock of the West," was a small school that was reputed to be stocked with rich arty kids. The grounds were landscaped naturally, with a bare minimum of water-wasting lawns. Mission-style adobe buildings were set into plazas paved with adobe tiles and made green and lush with cacti and shrubs and native flowers. Birds thronged palo verde trees, chirping away in the afternoon sunlight, flitting overhead. Hummingbirds buzzed at the cactus flowers. Tiled fountains splashed here and there, peaceful, oasis-like. I could imagine never wanting to graduate from this place. It looked like a country club or resort hotel.

My mother wanted me to finish high school here, transfer as a junior and graduate with an AA after two years, then go to an Ivy or one of the Seven Sisters. She could afford it, since she still had some of her trust fund. She never said this directly to me, she just left brochures in my room for Saguaro, Simon's Rock, Interlochen, Fountain Valley, Thacher, Putney. I'd pawed through them and looked at all the attractive, arty, smart kids in the photographs, ostentatiously busy with test tubes and violins and lacrosse sticks, the trappings of preppie ambition, and then I stayed right where I was at Plato Valley High School, singing "Eye of the Tiger" along with the marching band at pep rallies, drinking beer at the Triangle A on Saturday nights, and getting straight As without really trying. I liked it where I was, and frankly, I couldn't leave Tyler. He felt like my security blanket, the person who kept me warm. So maybe I missed out on the stellar education my mother wanted for me, but in the plus column, I stayed local, low-key, and pragmatic, all good things in my profession.

By going to the Student Union and asking around, I had eventually found Chay sitting alone in the grass by the quad fountain, playing a guitar and singing, looking every bit the tender young male poet with a lock of hair falling just so over his forehead, his rosy lips pursed in song, his tenor voice floating on a spring breeze. He wore a billowing blue button-down shirt that matched his eyes, blue jeans rolled up at the ankle, and his feet were bare. He had long legs and a sweet neck, bent over his instrument. He looked fully conscious of his beauty, and not at all innocent or carefree. He also looked uncannily like Tyler Bridgewater had at that same age.

He stopped playing and looked up when I approached him, his face impassive. I showed him my license and introduced myself and told him I was investigating Rose Delaney's suicide.

This made him sit up straight and pay attention. It was the first he'd heard of it, and he was gobsmacked by the news, I could tell. It clearly gave him a strong urge to talk to me, as if he were absolving himself, defending against an accusation I hadn't made. It all came out in a rush. I barely had to ask. He explained it all as articulately as I'd ever heard anyone say anything, and it made me marvel anew at the way so many of the members of his generation know how to offer up their inner lives in social-media-ready, sound-bite-digestible form. The dignified habit of guarding your deepest secrets seems to be a lost art.

As an offshoot of his work in her creative writing class, Rose had offered to help young Chay with his poetry in individual sessions, which morphed into late nights with glasses of wine at her house. He was eighteen and she was his teacher. She pursued him with aggression and insistence. He felt stalked by her, as if she objectified him. He did finally give in and sleep with her, against his instincts, a total of three times. "It was . . . it made me a bit . . . she kind of freaked me out. She was intense. Like, really emotional. And when I ended things, she acted like . . ."

I waited some more. I had all the time he wanted to take.

My snap first impression of Chay, which hadn't changed since I'd started talking to him, was of summers sailing off Cape Cod, family house in leafy, moneyed Connecticut, elite prep school, trust fund, father a gentleman lawyer, mother arty somehow, amateur poet or watercolorist. He was clearly precocious and bright, but his grades hadn't been good enough for the Ivies, and he was the second- or third-born, so he had the freedom not to have to go to Harvard and study law or medicine. Instead, he got to come to southern Arizona and write sad ballads in the grass all day instead of grinding away in Cambridge or New Haven. This kid had clearly been raised to feel entitled to expect the best from life, although I picked up some ongoing confusion around what he really wanted. A black sheep in the making, possibly a ne'er-do-well dreamer, he'd grow up to be the glamorous uncle who was always jetting in from Peru and Indonesia and Kenya to wow his older, go-getter siblings' offspring with thrilling stories and exciting advice and winsome company, but he'd forget birthdays and flake out on long-term plans.

"But," he went on after a moment of silence meant to be "thoughtful," during which he stared at the tussock of grass he was uprooting, blade by nervous blade, giving me time to fabricate this entire past, present, and future for him, "it didn't feel right for her to blame me and treat me like a villain, when she was the one who seduced and pursued *me*. I was the one who had been taken advantage of."

I made an encouraging therapist-like hum that I hoped implied Bad Rose. "You were a teenager. Her student."

"Exactly," he said. "And I mean, to be honest, I like girls my own age. I was sort of seeing someone. Sleeping with Professor Delaney, Rose, that whole thing, I did it for her, definitely not myself. She seemed to want it so much, and I didn't want to offend her."

"Sounds like a recipe for trouble," I said. To my ears, my voice sounded as disingenuously soothing and nonjudgmental as a good cop's, while the bad cop waited in the wings of my brain with a cudgel. I could feel myself egging him on, eliciting this story. It made me feel like just another predatory older woman. So be it. This kid wanted to talk, I was just handing him lines.

"The first time," he was saying, "it was late and I was tired and she was so . . . needy. And I thought I must owe her that, for helping me so much. And it was easier to do that than to keep saying no, and I felt sorry for her, like it was mean and selfish to deny her. It happened a couple more times."

He fell silent. He chewed his lower lip, plucked more grass, added each little green spear to the careful pile he was creating. His cheeks were downy, and his fingernails were beautifully kept, manicured and filed. His tanned forearms were covered in soft golden hair. The knee that poked through the hole in his jeans was bony and boyish. He was so young, just a kid still. Rose! I thought. Your teenage student! But the bad cop in me was squinting skeptically at him.

"So it didn't end well," I said.

"No," he said. "I'm a guy, you know? I'm not used to this treatment. It made me understand a bit more how women feel sometimes with men."

I listened very hard to all of this, parsing out his inflections, his word choices. There was something practiced-sounding about it, alongside the real emotion in his voice. This story of a charged, emotionally messy bramble came out fairly coherently articulated. He was naturally well spoken, like most kids of his cultural sophistication and background. And of course he had said all this before, likely more than once. He didn't sound defensive or aggrieved, he sounded sad, regretful, resigned. But I was still wary. I didn't buy his victimhood here. He struck me as too canny for that.

"And I could have just left it there. Right? No harm, no foul. But here's the thing, here's why I had to tell the dean." His eyes narrowed, looking directly at me, as if he'd snapped suddenly into the psyche of a shrewd, assertive, grown-ass man. "After I broke it off, she said she couldn't have contact with me anymore because it was too painful for her to see me. I wasn't in her class this semester, but I was her student last semester. And she didn't write a letter of recommendation for me for the summer internship I'm applying to. I was turned down for the fellowship for next year that she had told me she would make sure I got. I had told my parents I'd get it."

This last bit seemed to be the real insult and blow: he'd lost face with the senior Griffiths and possibly also with a condescending older sibling or two. So Chay had slept with Rose because she offered the fellowship, the contacts, the praise and support as enticements and had led him to expect great rewards for his sexual favors. Then, when he cut her off, reneging on his side of the deal, Rose had reneged on hers by refusing to make good on her promises or to mentor or help him any further.

Of course, no matter what, she never should have proposed such a deal in the first place. It was sleazy and wrong. She screwed him, and then she screwed him over. Losing her job must have been a blow, no matter how she spun it to her friends, but being exposed for bribing a beautiful young male poet to sleep with her and then getting dumped by him couldn't have been great either.

I wondered whether Chay was the only student Rose had been involved with. It was possible that others could be on the verge of coming forward. Maybe Rose hanged herself to escape the private pain and public shame of it all. And then, when she took refuge in Delphi and finally got Tyler into bed, he had ended their affair. The extra added pain of that must have brought it all home to her. This was as good an explanation as any I had stumbled on, for the moment, anyway.

"I see," I said. "So going to the dean for you was about justice."

"Right," he said, looking relieved that I understood. "I wasn't planning to until she did all that."

"When did you report Rose to the dean?"

"I wrote a letter to Dean Duby's office about a week ago and laid it all out."

"How did the dean respond?"

"I guess she fired her."

"Did you also write anonymously to the dean and Rose's editor to expose her for not being Navajo?"

"What?"

I repeated the question.

He looked horror-struck. "She's not?"

"Nope. And someone outed her."

He gasped, a ragged indrawn breath. "That wasn't me. I didn't know. I mean, that was our entire connection. My mother is Hopi, and Rose convinced me to . . . She was the whole reason . . . the Hopi and Navajo tribes are cousins, she told me. So we were deeply connected, with a powerful shared history."

My entire image of Chay shifted all at once. "Wait. You're Native?"

"Half. My mother doesn't talk about it, she's left it behind, she doesn't even see her family anymore. But Rose made me see that it's something I need to honor and learn about. She sent me up to the reservation to visit my aunties and cousins and learn about my culture. She gave me a kachina doll. She told me to 'write my bloodline.'" He stared at me. His face looked bleak. "She's not Navajo?"

"No," I said with as much compassion as I could muster.

"I wish I had never gotten involved with her," he said, leaning back on his elbows to form a curved hammock of his body, his bare feet crossed at the ankles, his locks lifted by bursts of breeze, his chillaxed posture totally at odds with what he was saying, the hollow tightness in his voice. "So she killed herself. Whoa."

"I know," I said. "It's a lot to take in."

After a moment, he sat up straight and looked into my eyes. "It feels like a cop-out to me. Like she won by cheating."

"If it's any comfort, Chay," I said, not unsympathetic to the self-aggrandizement of an eighteen-year-old boy, "I think Rose absolutely did not win."

"Okay." I caught a glint of self-awareness in his thick-lashed eyes. So much about this boy reminded me of teenage Tyler Bridgewater, the lissome beauty, that same cocky but vulnerable naïveté, even his inflections when he said certain words. The likeness was strong and unmistakable.

"By the way, there's a sort of memorial gathering on Tuesday up in Delphi, at the little artists' colony where Rose grew up. You should come if you want, and bring any others of her students who might want to pay their respects. It starts at five."

"Sure," he said. "Yeah, that might actually be kind of nice."

After we had exchanged contact information, I left Chayton Griffiths to his guitar and hoofed it back to the parking lot and slung myself back into my car, which was now hot enough to roast a chicken. I cranked all the windows down and blasted the AC until it blew frigid, then zipped the windows shut and drove myself down the mountain and went back to my apartment to give myself a much-needed night off.

ON THE WAY, I STOPPED FOR SUPPLIES, NAMELY BOOZE AND GROCER-ies. Carrying two brimming paper bags, I let myself into my dim, deserted-feeling apartment, fired up my music system with some vintage funk to cheer me up. I went into my galley kitchen and got out my corkscrew, opened a bottle of Rioja, and poured myself a glass.

When he was alive, my father loved music, he loved to cook, and he loved Spanish wine. And by passing those loves on to me, he gave me a way to feel close to him and remember him for the rest of my life, even though he was gone. Glass of wine at my elbow, shaking my booty to Bootsy Collins, I chopped an onion, threw it into a frying pan with some olive oil, added some chopped mushrooms, and let it all sauté. I threw three cut-up Yukon Gold potatoes onto a sheet pan, tossed them in oil and salt, and put them to roast in the oven. Then I laid a couple of juicy chicken thighs into the skillet, browned them well on both sides, poured in a mixture of cream, Dijon mustard, and tarragon, and left it all to simmer while the potatoes finished and I made a salad.

I took my loaded plate and wineglass to sit at my little table, looking out at the stucco wall of the opposite wing of my apartment building. I spied on my neighbors as the sky darkened and their lights came on, watching a family isolate themselves at five different blue-lit screens, an old couple playing Scrabble, three low-life-looking dudes on a couch playing video games and drinking beer, some kids rolling around a floor with a dog, squealing so loudly I could hear them across the courtyard.

As I was finishing my second plateful, my phone rang, caller ID blocked. I answered it. It was my crank caller again: the other end of the line sounded like a yuletide fireplace in full swing, logs burning merrily.

"Hello," I said in a bored voice, just for show. There was no answer, of course. "Hello?" I said again. After the line went dead, I rolled my eyes theatrically and tossed my phone back on the table. But the skin on my arms was crawling, just a little.

Who the hell was this? Blocked callers were tricky to trace, but maybe I could get Freddy Lopez to hack it, especially if whoever this was decided to call again.

After I did the dishes and took a long, cool shower, I sprawled on my couch in my shortie pajamas and watched a nineties rom-com on my laptop while I finished the bottle of wine. I brushed my teeth, drank a big glass of water, and went to bed early, where I slept the sleep of the righteous and innocent even though of course I was neither, if only because no fully alive adult was.

I woke up very early the next morning and made a pot of strong coffee. Loins girded, brain refreshed, I wrote down all my notes from the previous two days, organizing and recording everything I knew about Rose Delaney. I looked closely at all the pictures I had taken at the scene: the knot, the position of the rope on the branch, the distance between her feet and the ground, the ground around the tree. With a knot in my stomach, I stared at the close-ups of Rose's body: the triangle scratched on her forearm, the angle of her neck, her expression, her dress.

It was possible that very early on Wednesday morning, Rose had walked the two miles from the Triangle A to Rancho Bella Luna. Maybe she wore her mother's borrowed hiking boots and then ditched them by the stables when she borrowed Suzie's horse and rode him, barefoot and barebacked, to the cottonwood tree, in a white dress, with a rope, and hanged herself. I considered this. She had some convincing reasons to want to die. And everything about the death scene, every single detail, pointed to the dramatic suicide of a poetess, with no sign whatsoever of coercion, foul play, or prior violence or harm.

But I was stuck on the small triangle scratched on her arm. She could have done it herself, but that didn't seem right. All I needed was one more thing that didn't fit, one more indication that someone had forced her up into that tree against her will. Despite everything, I owed her at least that much.

I reread the return emails I'd received from Rose's academic dean, Lena Duby, and Felix Mantooth, her editor, both expressing concern at the news of Rose's disappearance. At my request, they had attached the anonymous emails concerning her fake identity. These were identical, to the point, and evidently untraceable: "To whom it may concern: Rose Delaney is not at all Navajo, she's white and has no Native blood whatsoever. She's faking this identity for her own benefit and profit. It is my hope that you'll take appropriate action once you have ascertained the facts for yourself. Sincerely, Anonymous."

The lowercase "white" suggested that this was written by a white person. I stared into space and chewed on the tone and wording and syntax, which I found huffy and vaguely corporate and more than a little bit threatening: "whatsoever" and "appropriate action" and "ascertained" made me squinch up my face and point my mental finger at Jason, who naturally knew his sister wasn't Navajo. No one in Rose's inner circle knew, or at least admitted that they knew. Jason had been fighting bitterly with Rose. Maybe he was so angry with her for trying to screw with his own professional success that he felt the need to wreck hers. The wording of the email sounded to me like a financial guy trying to sound smart for bookish people; this explanation made more sense than anything else I could come up with.

I read through all my notes, adding and augmenting and drawing connections, but I didn't have a lot to go on. There was too much I didn't know, so many open questions. I still didn't know who had Rose's phone, or who had sent Tyler the video, or who was making these annoying crank calls to me.

And I didn't know whether any of this connected to the anonymous emails to Rose's academic dean and book editor. Well, no matter what came of it, talking to them both seemed like a good next step. It was Monday, so I might be able to find them both at their workplaces. On the Saguaro College website's faculty page, I saw that Lena Duby had office hours from noon to two. I jotted down her campus address. Then I found the website of Catalina Press and called the main number.

"Catalina Press," said a lilting, velvety female voice.

"My name is Jo Bailen. I'm a private investigator. I'd like to meet with Felix Mantooth to discuss Rose Delaney at his earliest convenience."

"Rose Delaney? Is she suing us?"

"Suing you?"

"I figured, if she's hired an investigator, she must be trying to get back at us for canceling her book."

So Rose's former publishers didn't know she was dead. I'd tell them in person. Much better that way, for a number of reasons, the main one being that I wanted to see their reaction to the news for myself. "She's not suing you, and she didn't hire me. I'm working for her mother. I'm looking into who might have sent you the anonymous email about her ethnic background."

"We have no clue. Let me save you the trip."

I didn't respond. I let the silence grow, fill to the brim with air, and pop.

The woman on the other end made an impatient huffing noise. "But you're welcome to come to the office today. He'll be here."

"How is two o'clock?"

"That works."

AS I WAS CHANGING INTO MY GYM CLOTHES, MY PHONE RANG: Laura Gold.

"Jo?" Her voice was wan and quavering.

"Good morning, Laura. How are you?"

"Well, it's just awful. I'm calling about Ben. I just heard from his sponsor. He relapsed badly last night. They said he OD'd. They brought him back but just barely, the medics. He almost died. He's in the hospital, in a medically induced coma, all the way up in Phoenix, no visitors allowed yet. Not even me. I'm just frantic."

My heart gave a lurch in my chest. Poor Laura. Poor Ben. "Oh, that's awful. Do you know what happened?"

She was hyperventilating a little. "His sponsor says he doesn't think he meant to kill himself, it was a bad batch, laced with fentanyl, they're everywhere right now apparently, it's so dangerous."

"Is he going to be okay? No permanent damage?"

"It's too early to know. My sweet Benny." She broke down into wordless sobs. "He was doing so well," she managed to say. "It was just too much for him, losing his sister." She took a ragged breath. "I don't know how I'm going to get through this."

I felt so sad for her. Her husband was going, her daughter was gone, and now she might lose her son as well. Laura was never coming back from this, I could hear it in her voice.

"I'm so sorry," I said helplessly. "Is there anything I can do?"

"No. I just needed to tell you, that's all. You and Rose used to be so close once, such an inseparable pair, somehow talking to you helps me to feel closer to her."

As soon as we hung up, I headed straight to the gym. I needed to give my brain and heart and soul a rest and make my muscles do all the work for a little while.

FOURTEEN

MY EX-COP TECH BUDDY FREDDY LOPEZ WAS WAITING FOR ME OUT-side the men's locker room as usual, looking ripped and buff in his black drop-arm tank and moisture-wicking shorts. His thick black hair looked freshly clipped, and his lean, symmetrical face was blisteringly close shaven. If I didn't know him, I would have pegged him as an exotic-looking gay model, not a very straight, very nerdy computer tech ninja.

"There's still no sign of life from that phone," he said as soon as he saw me. He talked fast, without inflection, his voice high and nasal. We're the same height, five nine. We meet at exactly eye level, although he outweighs me by a good thirty pounds of pure muscle. "It's been dead or turned off this whole time. You sure it's not in a dumpster somewhere?"

"Someone out there has it. They sent a text after she died."

"It wasn't on a timer?"

"Can you find out?"

"I can try," he said. "So I'm guessing I should stay on it?"

"Definitely," I said. "It's all I've got right now."

"You sound like you're running a case. Don't they have a detective working this? DA's office?"

"Nope. Cops think it was suicide. This is off-book."

"Copy that."

We headed to the weight room and got right down to it. After we did our side-by-side stretches, I lay on my back on the short, padded bench like a helpless beetle, pressing a rack of weights upward with all the muscle strength in my arms. Freddy loomed over me, making sure I didn't crush my own neck.

"So what's new with you?" I grunted, hoisting. Freddy and I see each other twice a week for these sessions, but I always ask.

"Britni and I broke up."

"That sucks."

"It's okay. She got on my nerves."

"Why?"

"She's obsessed with her weight. Like, if she thinks she maybe gained three ounces, none of which I can ever even see, she stays at home. She cries about it all day. It's all she can talk about. I swear she's got two percent body fat. But she hides in her room crying and won't leave."

"Doesn't she have to go to work?"

"She lives with her parents," he said. "They support her."

My arms were quivering. I held the weights aloft and waited for my muscles to quiet down. "Is she fourteen?"

"She's twenty-nine!"

"Poor girl," I said. "She needs medication. Therapy."

"That's above my pay grade," said Freddy. "I'm just bored."

"Got it," I said, bringing the weights down with relief, then stubbornly lifting them again. What an odd means of getting strong this was. In the olden days, people just did physical labor all day, chopping and scrubbing and hauling and carrying. Now we paid money to expend energy on repetitive motions that served no purpose beyond the obvious.

"You're pressing seven pounds more today than you did last time," said Freddy. Was that a note of pride? He fancied himself my weight-training mentor and guru; of course he took credit for my progress.

My answer was a primal noise in the back of my throat as I pressed upward.

When it was Freddy's turn to lift, I tried not to notice or mind that he automatically racked up so much more weight onto the machine than I had lifted. His superior strength was genetic, sex based, and that was just the way things were.

"Can I ask you something?"

"Go for it," he said easily. His grapefruit-size biceps flattened and slid around his upper arms as the weights shot upward. He was just warming up. He hadn't even added the full weight yet.

"I've been getting these calls from a blocked number, about three or four now. No one's there when I pick up, it just sounds staticky, like someone's holding a phone next to a crackling fire."

"That's not at all creepy."

"Is there any way I can find out who's doing it?"

"Maybe. Depends on how elaborate the block is. Of course, whoever it is would need to call you again, I would need to be locked in and ready on my end, and then you would need to keep them on the line for maybe like a minute or so. So, yeah. It's complicated."

"Forget it then."

We were silent for a while as Freddy bench-pressed more than my own weight, and I'm not small. When he'd finished his reps, we moved on to barbells and dumbbells, then squats and lunges. Freddy has some kind of OCD, so he always keeps our workouts on pace and precise, like a human metronome. "Careful of your rotator cuffs," he likes to say. I roll my eyes, but secretly appreciate the reminder.

As we were toweling ourselves and the machines off, guzzling water from the bubbler in the corner, I said, "How's your *abuela* doing?"

"She told me it's time to get married," he said. "Yesterday."

Freddy's grandmother, Carmen Lopez, is a political science and law professor, tenured at the university for decades, as well as a pro bono lawyer and fighter for social justice and immigrant rights. She's also the hawkeyed defender of her four grown children, nine adult grandchildren, and four great-grandchildren, all of whose lives she manages with iron precision. Freddy is terrified of her.

"She's going to choose a wife for me. No more *chicas tontas*." He wiped his mouth on the back of his hand.

"But you love silly girls," I said.

"I do," he said.

"But you're going to do what she says."

"I have to."

"I know."

"My life is over."

"Maybe not over. But definitely changing."

We went off to our separate locker rooms to shower and change. Afterward, we met at the gym's juice bar, a surreal, futuristic chrome-and-Lucite establishment tucked into a corner of the lobby. Brightly lit, gleaming with a bank of high-tech juicers and blenders, its walls and fixtures all in clean fruit colors, its counter display case bristled with every healthful ingredient known to humankind. Freddy, a big believer in the postworkout protein shake, ordered the Plant Power Smoothie, a thick green sludge made of pea-protein powder, spirulina, kale, and hemp seeds; I got the Tango Shake, a kid-dessert concoction of oat milk, peanut butter, mango, banana, and cinnamon. We sat on side-by-side stools at the Disney-like bar, sucking down our calories, our muscles all pumped and tired, our hair wet, relaxed and at ease after the intense physical ordeal we'd just been through together. There's always a cozily postcoital feeling about this ritual.

"By the way," said Freddy. "Do you want me to get you the location data for that phone I'm tracing before it was turned off?"

I looked at him, slack-jawed. "Wait, you can do that?"

"Yeah, dude."

"Why the hell didn't you tell me before?"

"Uh, 'cause you didn't ask?"

"Yes!" I said. "Let me know as soon as you can."

I parted ways with Freddy in the parking lot and drove over to the office to check in with Ronnie and see if Erin was back from Phoenix yet.

"Hello, Jo," said Madison with weird perkiness as I came in. She actually looked awake today.

"What's up, Madison?"

Her face burst into sudden dazzling bloom: a smile. "I got into film school at the University of Southern California!"

"Congratulations," I said. "I had no idea you'd even applied."

"Oh my God, it's been my dream forever. I sent them a short film called *The Zen of Tricky*. I can't believe I got in and I get to go!"

Tricky was her pet rat. She had been obsessively filming him as long as she'd worked here, almost two years.

She was still smiling, rapturous and alight, as I walked away. I went into my office, marveling at the way people could surprise me, especially when I radically underestimated them.

"Bailen," said Erin Yazzie from my doorway as I sifted through today's mail, a bunch of junk and circulars. The worst thing about all meaningful correspondence going online is that it has totally eradicated the pleasure of getting letters.

"Yazzie," I said. "Welcome back. How was Phoenix?"

"Major suckage," she said. "It's a pit of hell. Why do people live there? Also, I shot a guy. I'm still rattled."

"Whoa! What happened?"

"Had to. He was shooting at me."

"Did you kill him?"

"He's in the hospital with a big hole in his shoulder. I tried to minimize the damage. But I had to stop him. Anyway, when he gets out, he's going to rot in Supermax till he croaks."

Erin is still a kid, only twenty-seven. She's worked at the agency since she got her PI license two years ago. Unlike Rose Delaney, she is an actual, full-blooded Navajo, from Tuba City, born and raised on the rez. She's skinny and wiry, a whippet, with a plain, wide face. She wears glasses because of an allergy to contact lenses, and she keeps her straight black hair shoulder length, with cute librarian bangs. She looks shy and meek, but she has a black belt in mixed martial arts and her firearm skills are formidable. This girl kicks major ass and fears nothing. And she's sharp as a razor blade.

She looked cool and professional as always in a white fitted button-down shirt and tailored khaki slacks, dark brown loafers with no socks, and pearl earrings. She hides behind long sleeves, ashamed of the vitiligo that runs down her brown arms in white splotches. She was teased cruelly for it as a kid. Worse, she was sexually abused for years by her family's white church pastor, starting when she was four. At eight, she was misdiagnosed by the psychologist hired to administer IQ tests to reservation kids, pegged as mentally handicapped. This was apparently a regular and ongoing scam supported by the reservation, classifying kids as special needs to bump up the school's government funding. So, small-for-her-age, super-bright-but-traumatized, myopic, quiet little Erin was shoved into remedial classes, which caused her to be mocked even more. What didn't kill her made her the toughest person I've ever met.

"What've you got cooking right now?" she asked me, parking her bony rear on the edge of my desk. "Still taking porny pictures of MILFs?"

"Nope," I said. "I spent the weekend up in Delphi. My childhood best friend was found hanging dead from a tree by her neck."

She gave a low whistle. "This was the pretend Navajo?"

"Yup."

She gave me a look that brimmed with the half joke she wasn't making: Look what happens when you mess with the Diné gods. "You okay with this case? Very close to home."

"It couldn't get much closer."

"Something about the way you phrased it makes me think you don't believe it was suicide."

"I'm not sure. I've been getting weird crank calls at different numbers, someone keeping tabs on my whereabouts. Rose's phone went missing after she died. Also, there was this weird . . . triangle scratched on her forearm." I realized I was massaging my right earlobe, something I do sometimes when I'm stymied and upset. "And I know her, or I used to anyway. I don't think she'd do this. She was dramatic, yes, but not a suicide."

Erin pushed her glasses up her nose, squinting sideways at me, sucking in her cheeks to make hollows under her cheekbones: her thinking face. "You never know for sure who will or won't."

All at once, I remembered that Erin's much-older sister had killed herself, years ago.

"You're right," I said, chastened.

"I didn't say that to make you feel guilty because of my sister, dumbass. I said it because it's true. Something to keep in mind."

"You're still right." I gave my colleague a level look. "She had reasons. Her life was a mess. When Rose got caught pretending to be Navajo, she lost her job and her book deal."

Erin gave me a level look right back. "As well she should have."

"Hey," came Ronnie's foghorn blat. "Get in here, let's have a pow-wow."

"A what?" Erin said, her voice bland.

"A damn *reunión de trabajo*," said Ronnie in her terrible Spanish.

"Offensive," said Erin as we traipsed to Ronnie's office.

"I'm calling HR," I said.

"A kibitz, you fuckwads," said Ronnie. She was slouched in her chair with her feet up on her desk, daintily crossed at the ankle, looking into a compact mirror while she slathered cherry-red lipstick on her cherubic mouth. She wore a dusky-rose miniskirt and matching little jacket with a cream silk camisole and high-heeled black lace-up espadrilles. Career Barbie was on point today. "Park your asses."

Erin and I sat in the two chrome-and-leather chairs opposite Ronnie's desk, which is vast and shiny and elegant and made of some endangered rainforest wood. The agency's offices were hastily patched together with glue and pasteboard and popcorn ceiling tiles, but Ronnie's furniture is top-of-the-line. Somehow, knowing Ronnie, this makes perfect sense.

"Happy Monday," she said. "Yazzie, what's up."

"Wilson is in the hospital on his way to prison," she said.

"Good work. Archer Insurance wants you to investigate an arson claim down in Benson, and some rich dude wants you to do a background check on his fiancée. I'll email you the deets. Bailen?"

I snapped to attention.

"Good work on the Cortez case, that dickball George is reaming his soon-to-be-ex-wife as we speak, and I don't mean in the biblical sense. Of course we're on her side, but business is business." She sucked hard on her vape pen a few times and exhaled mint-scented steam. "Solve the missing-daughter case yet?"

"She turned out to be dead."

"Great, submit your report."

"Her mother and brother asked me to keep investigating. They want to know why. Also . . ." I chewed the inside of my cheek. "Something feels fishy to me. Several things."

"Fishy as in maybe murder? Murder adjacent? Murder-*ish*?"

Erin gave a soft snort.

"I don't know yet," I said. "Possibly murder. But maybe not."

"As long as they pay you, you're of course very happy to continue."

"That's what I told them."

"I'll be up in Sedona. Keep me posted."

"Vacation?" asked Erin with a knowing glance at me.

Ronnie never takes vacations, because she doesn't believe in them, because they're an expensive waste of perfectly good billable hours. "Of course not. My oldest and richest client has a bad feeling about her new paramour. She's paying me a fuckton of dough to spend a few days up there sussing him out, picking up his vibrations, sensing his chakras, also doing a complete and thorough dive into his life to make sure it all adds up." She slung her feet down to the floor, stood up, snapped her laptop shut, and slid it into her bag. "I'm packing my bikini for prime tanning hours."

"I'm off to Benson," said Erin, standing up and walking out.

"And I'm going back up to Saguaro Early College to meet with the academic dean during her office hours," I said, but no one heard me. My colleagues were both already on the move.

FIFTEEN

LENA DUBY'S OFFICE DOOR WAS OPEN, BUT I KNOCKED ANYWAY, JUST to show my manners. The title "dean" had led me to expect a serene suite of glossy, oak-floored, high-ceilinged rooms with Victorian furniture and bay windows and maybe an ornamental fireplace. But her office in the 1960s-era Neville Hall, a Soviet-bloc-type textured-stucco construction with concrete walkways and scuffed linoleum floors, was fluorescent lit, chaotic, and crowded with unpacked cardboard boxes and a strong odor of air-conditioned dust. Lena Duby turned out to be as unprepossessing as her digs, a hobbity creature with a rounded jaw and small far-apart eyes, her gray hair tousled and chin length. She motioned me in, blinking and bumbling like a female Mr. Magoo.

"Rose was such a good teacher," she told me after offering me a wooden classroom chair and handing me a glass of ice water poured with clumsy haste from a sweating pitcher on her book-piled desk. "Her students loved her, and I felt very much that she connected with them, inspired them." Her voice was wheezy, hesitant, with odd pauses between words, as if English weren't her native language even though she'd lost any trace of an accent. "I was so disappointed to get that email, to hear she wasn't Navajo after all."

"I can imagine the tough position it put you in."

"It was anonymous," she said. "Do you have any idea at all who the sender might have been?"

"Anyone who knew the real truth about her. Old friend, family member, lover, someone she drunkenly confided in at a party. No idea at the moment."

The dean made a soft clucking noise. "Whoever they were, they wanted her to be punished for it. May I ask, why are you investigating this email? Did Rose hire you to find the person?"

"No," I said. "Oh, I am sorry. I assumed you knew."

Her face was genuinely blank. "Knew what?"

"Rose was found dead this weekend. It appears that she hanged herself."

The dean's face went stony. "Oh my word," she said. "Hanged herself."

"I'm so sorry to tell you like this," I said. "I shouldn't have assumed that you'd been notified." This was disingenuous, of course, because I had been hoping to catch her off guard with this news.

"Rose is *dead*? That's—I'm absolutely shocked. I had no idea. She *hanged* herself. Oh my." She licked her lips, took a quick, hard breath, fumbled her glass of water to her dry lips, and took a loud gulp. When she could talk again, she went on in a rush, eyes blinking rapidly like a nervous tic. "Rose seemed to accept the fact that I had to let her go, no hard feelings, no anger whatsoever, she wasn't nearly as upset as I had feared she would be, not defensive at all."

"How so?"

"She apologized for the deception," said the dean. "Sincerely. And we had a very productive conversation about it. She was articulate about her reasons for it. In fact, in the end I encouraged her to write an essay about it, and she said she would think about it." She put a hand over her eyes and gently rubbed her temples with thumb and forefinger. "Oh poor Rose."

"Can you tell me about this conversation you two had?"

Now she steepled her two hands together, resting her chin on their tips, looking up at the ceiling, remembering. "Well, I made it clear that of course this lie she told went against everything we at Saguaro believe in and stand for, and she was terminated, no question. We strive to promote inclusiveness here, so six years ago, we offered Rose the job over several other highly qualified candidates. Our preference for her was of course strongly based on her ethnicity, her identity as an Indigenous American. We felt she would bring a valuable perspective and wealth of experience to our students."

"She was a diversity hire."

"That's right. Although she was also qualified, of course. But her BIPOC status was what ultimately caused us to choose her over the others." Dean Duby took another sip of water. She stared at me for a moment. "She *hanged* herself?"

"From a tree."

She said something guttural and curt in a language I didn't recognize; it could have been Serbian or Urdu, a profanity or a prayer. "Maybe I was too harsh. Maybe she was more upset than she let on."

"Too harsh how?"

"I told her that her need to pretend to be something she wasn't, in any way, is a sign of professional, personal, and artistic weakness. She took this job away from a real minority. She co-opted the experience and history of a vulnerable culture not her own. She lied in the classroom, in her work, to her students, as a community member." The dean made an angry laughing snort in the back of her throat. "Do you know, there is another, I mean a real, Navajo Nation member on our faculty, and when the truth came out about Rose, he and I had lunch to discuss his feelings about it all. And he told me that Rose often berated him for speaking insufficient Diné. For not being involved enough in sustaining the old ways of their people. He said she seemed really angry at him for walking away from his culture to the degree that he had."

With a bleak smile, I pictured Rose self-righteously haranguing her Native colleague. "I can imagine his reaction to the news that she was faking it."

"Yes, Rose was a champion of cultural knowledge," said the dean. "She encouraged all her students to write from their own authentic traditions, to learn everything they could about their bloodlines, to ask their living elders to tell their stories. She had them all keep a 'roots journal,' as she called them. White kids from Iowa were writing about their Swedish and German immigrant ancestors. Descendants of colonizers, in other words, old family East Coast white kids and kids of British descent, were reckoning with the sins of their own forebears."

"I bet they had a blast doing that."

"Oh, they loved it. They were crazy about the whole project. Many of them have let me know, recently, that they feel that she betrayed their trust. They're deeply confused and hurt."

"I've known Rose since she was four," I said. "She was the daughter of two white people."

"I know," said Dean Duby. "When I asked her for any sort of proof that she had Native ancestry, even her mother's verbal corroboration, any old family record, she said, 'It's over. I confess. I'm white.' As if she were being interrogated by the Stasi."

"Did she give you any reason for the lie? Other than that it was a handy professional attribute?"

"She talked about her father. She told me he was very proudly Black Irish, and that's where she got her coloring. Rose referred to the Irish as the 'n-words of Europe,' as persecuted and traumatized and oppressed and maltreated as any people on earth. But she pointed out that because people of Irish descent are white, there is no language for their descendants to use to articulate their inherited trauma, no recourse, no reparation. Irish Americans are white people in a white-dominated country where Jews and black and brown and Indigenous minorities are free to identify with their oppression."

"So Irish Americans are doubly oppressed. Because they're white." I shook my head at the twisted logic of it. "Okay."

"She said that as a woman of Irish descent, she carried a double whammy of, as she called it, 'enforced silence.' She believed that all Caucasian women share a bond of oppression, but they're forced to bury it now to be allies with their BIPOC sisters. But she said the pain is only going underground, it's not healing."

"So calling herself Navajo felt real and justified to her, because she belonged to a different traumatized culture and was a woman."

"Yes!" Dean Duby looked at me with approval, as if I were one of her bright students. "That is exactly it."

"What a crock," I said. I couldn't help it. It just came out.

"I think she had a point," said the dean. "It doesn't excuse what she did. But it does explain it, to a certain extent. She said she believed in contextualizing all personal experience in creative writing, especially trauma and identity. To her, these were inseparable. The irony was that she taught her students that the trauma of their own ancestry and sexual identity is their own to explore freely."

I shook my head briskly at Rose's gobbledygook rationale. "But that wasn't the only reason she was fired, was it? You got another letter about her, signed by one of her students."

"That matter is confidential," said the dean. "I have to protect the student involved."

"His name is Chayton Griffiths. I already spoke to him. He told me what happened. He said he didn't send the Navajo letter, just the sexual-impropriety one."

"Oh. Well, it did strike me as . . . odd," said the dean. "Two letters coming around the same time. I did wonder if they were both from Chayton, seeking revenge, perhaps."

"He says not. And he doesn't seem exactly vengeful. More like he's aware that he learned a valuable lesson."

"And you believe him?"

"I don't know," I said. "Should I?"

"I don't know either."

"Did you know he's part Hopi?"

"Of course," she said. "His scholarship is predicated on that fact."

"Thank you, Dean," I said, after a brief silence. My work here was done.

"Please call me Lena. I am happy to help in any way I can."

I gave her my phone number and invited her to the memorial at the Rancho the next evening, then walked back through the campus to the parking lot. As I went, I thought I glimpsed Chay in a group of kids, lounging on the steps of the student union, but he was too far away to identify for sure.

WITH MY CAR WINDOWS OPEN TO LET IN A RUSH OF HOT AIR, I drove down the winding, steep mountainous roads toward the city center. It was time to tell Felix Mantooth that Rose was dead and talk to him about her canceled book.

Catalina Press was housed in a small industrial building on East Stevens Avenue, down by the train tracks, just across the narrow street from a tidy little park. It had a facade of ornate brick with plain stucco sides and was surrounded by a large dirt yard behind a chain-link fence on one side and a corrugated-iron fence on the other. The land it sat on was an entire triangular little city block. I parked on the empty street right in front, got out, and stood looking at the building's brick front for a while, not sure where the entrance was. A roll-up doorway over a small loading bay and two large windows on either side had been bricked up, leaving their shapes in the facade. The brickwork was ornate and geometric, with arches over the windows and an inlaid vertical pattern of pale brick below a dentiled cornice.

I strolled around the fence, peering in at the bare yard. On the east side of the building, toward the back, I saw a large glass-block window, about six by eight feet. I went through a small opening in the fence, and as I approached the glass block, I realized that there was a steel door next to it, camouflaged, painted the same off-white color as the stucco. This place was as well defended as an armory or treasury.

I pressed the intercom button next to the door and heard the buzzer squawk inside.

A moment later, the fisheye in the door darkened: someone was checking me out, no doubt making sure I wasn't an armed robber come to steal all the books.

"Hello?" came a distorted voice over the intercom.

"I'm Jo Bailen," I said loudly, flashing my PI license at the fisheye. "Felix Mantooth is expecting me."

I heard the sound of three dead bolt locks being sprung. The door opened.

"Sorry for the third degree," said a woman. She was short and stocky, I guessed her age around fifty or so, with square shoulders, over one of which was slung a thick black gray-streaked braid that rested on her jutting monoboob shelf. She wore a denim jumpsuit, a chunk of turquoise on a leather thong around her neck, and feathered earrings. Her cheekbones were gleaming planes in her wide face. Her eyes were black and direct. "I'm Connie Shelltrack," she said. "Felix's executive assistant. Please come in."

"You've got some tight security here," I said in a bright voice to let her know I wasn't complaining, just approving.

"This place used to be a storage warehouse."

"For what?"

"All kinds of things."

I followed her past a big desk, I assumed hers, cluttered with piles of books and manuscripts almost obscuring a large, shallow bowl full of Hershey's Kisses. I resisted the urge to sneak a handful as she rapped twice on a closed metal door. "Felix," she called. "Jo Bailen is here."

I heard a muffled "Come in."

Connie opened the door and stood aside so I could enter.

I walked into a small windowless room that I quickly realized wasn't small at all; it was just stacked floor to ceiling, in some places two or three deep, with boxes of manuscripts, manila envelopes of manuscripts, bound manuscripts, and loose manuscripts held together with rubber bands, pile upon pile upon pile. In the midst of this dense forest of unpublished work sat a desk, and behind that desk sat a man.

He stood up as I came in. He was of medium height, with a narrow build, and he looked around Connie's age, ten or so years older than me. Thin dark hair grew winglike over his ears, parted over his right temple in what looked like a cowlick, and lay haphazardly on his freckled forehead. He wore baggy, threadbare chinos into which was tucked a faded chambray shirt, a leather belt embroidered with beads cradling a tidy paunch, and a small copper hoop in one ear. On his feet were dirty white canvas sneakers.

"I'm Felix Mantooth," he said. "Come on in, excuse the mess. Have a seat."

"Can I get you a coffee or water?" Connie asked as I looked around for a place to sit.

"I'd love some coffee, black is fine." I spotted a small folding chair dwarfed by piles of written matter, a toadstool among the towering trees, and perched carefully on it, hoping nothing came crashing down on me.

While Connie went off to get the coffee, Felix seated himself behind his desk, a battered metal thing that looked like a relic from the days when this place was used for industrial storage. I could see a harried inventory clerk sitting behind wire baskets marked PAYABLES and RECEIVABLES brimming with invoices and bills of lading in triplicate.

"Thanks for taking the time to talk to me, Mr. Mantooth."

"Felix, please! Mr. Mantooth is my dad."

I grinned politely at his Gen-X stab at humor. "I have a few questions about Rose Delaney," I said.

Coming back into the office with a ceramic mug of coffee, Connie cleared her throat loudly, I gathered not because of a frog stuck in there, but to convey an opinion of Rose that was not complimentary. I had wondered when I met her if she was Navajo, and now I guessed she must be. She went back out to her desk, muttering, closing the door behind her.

I took a sip of coffee. It was bitter and lukewarm and tasted as if it had been sitting in a turned-off coffee machine since early morning, which it probably had.

"Go ahead," said Felix. "Ask away."

"I don't know if you've heard, but Rose was found dead on Saturday. Preliminary determination seems to be that it was suicide."

"Yes, I was so sorry to hear that," said Felix.

"Oh," I said, surprised. "From my conversation with Connie on the phone earlier, it sounded as if you didn't know."

"The grapevine, meaning the literary community here in Tucson, is closely knit. Rose, despite recent events, was well liked. Everyone is, of course, shocked." He let out a small gasp, as if something were just now occurring to him for the first time. "You don't think . . . her canceled book? You know about that? Could it have been—"

"It's unclear why she did it," I said. "I'm trying to figure that out, in addition to a number of other things."

"Whom are you working for? Rose's family?"

"That's right."

"What do you want to know? I'm delighted to be of any help I can." He said this earnestly, and I believed him. He was clearly all eagerness to take part in a real private-eye investigation, oddly piqued and even excited by the idea of a poetess hanging herself. My snap assessment of Felix Mantooth was that he was the type to be far more enamored of the idea of things than of the actual things themselves, who sat by a campfire and recited poetry aloud and drank expensive whiskey but didn't really like being outside, who cooked elaborate recipes with esoteric ingredients but didn't much care what the end result tasted like, who prided himself on giving exquisite oral sex without being particularly lusty himself. I would have bet he was a fan of the most grisly Scandinavian crime fiction, all that cold, bloody darkness on the page at a safe remove from his own life.

If I told him that Rose had ridden a horse bareback at dawn, barefoot in a white dress, to hang herself from a cottonwood tree in an arroyo, he'd pass out from the aesthetics of it all.

"Do you do your own printing on the premises? This building looks big enough to accommodate a press."

"In fact we do!" His freckles glowed in his milk-white face. "We're a rarity in this. Our editing house is a small outfit, just Connie and me and three interns, university students who do a lot of the initial weeding out of manuscript submissions and some freelance editing. The actual press is in the back of the building, a pair of brothers runs it. They also print a couple of literary magazines and run a vanity press for authors willing to pay to publish."

"How long have you occupied this building?"

"Only fifteen months. Before this, I ran the press out of my house." He looked sheepishly around at all the manuscripts. "You can imagine how much my wife loved that. We got a grant, enough to sign a lease. We share the building with the printing press, we have a contract with them to print our books, and they pay the lion's share of the rent. Couldn't be a better situation. At least so far." He didn't knock on wood, but the urge hovered in the air by his knuckles.

"I'm here," I said, "because I'm wondering about Rose's book being canceled. I'm hoping you can fill me in on how she took it, anything you noticed about her at the time when you told her."

"Well, she was deeply upset, as you can imagine. But our hands were tied. The press has a serious commitment to amplify underrepresented voices. Rose's pretense went directly against everything we believe in and are trying to do. Connie is Navajo, and this felt especially insulting to her. She edits a lot of our poetry and is a poet herself. In the process of working together on this book, she and Rose had become closely allied in their interest in Native culture and traditions. To find out that Rose was faking it, well, that was hard. A real blow."

"I read the book," I said. "To me, it seems to be more about climate catastrophe and biodiversity collapse than Native identity."

"She writes in a collective tribal voice, as a Navajo, unequivocally." He sounded defensive and aggrieved. "You just can't do that if you're not Native."

"Isn't that what 'poetic license' means? That you can be or say or do whatever you want in writing, as long as you do it well?" Of course I knew full well what the deal was, but I was being disingenuous on purpose. I wanted to see his reaction.

"Once upon a time, and for a very long time, white writers could get away with appropriating BIPOC cultural experience and identity. But that is no longer the case, and thank God for it. Now it's seen as what it is, yet another form of colonization, or to put it more personally, identity theft. And Rose knew that as well as anyone. But I think she convinced herself that her identification with the Navajo people was so deeply felt, it had become authentic. And that wasn't her choice to make."

"I see," I said.

He huffed. "You can't just decide to belong to a minority culture. It's not like being trans or queer, which is innate. Rose wasn't, let's say, born in the wrong ethnicity, that's not a thing. She was flat-out faking it."

"Successfully too," I said. "For a long time."

He looked sheepish. "I believed her."

"So did the dean up at Saguaro Early College. So did her closest friends."

"Well, I also want to say, to be perfectly frank, in my opinion, it didn't serve her poetry. In other words, this new book was not her best. We were proud to publish it because we believed in Rose as an artist, but in truth I found this new work a trifle . . . heavy-handed. That is to say, it's not as nuanced or technically accomplished as some of her earlier stuff."

Although I wasn't qualified to compare this new book to her other poetry, which I hadn't read, I couldn't disagree with the "heavy-handed" part.

Felix was writhing a little in his chair, his hands crossed and pressed against his breastplate. "Oh man, I really loved her first book. It was so brilliant, so authentic and raw. Really fucking original. She burst out of the gate with this incendiary, magical collection. We didn't publish that one, I wish we had. It rocked."

"What's the title?"

"*Love Triangle*. Terrible title—it sounds like a bodice-ripping beach read, and it's about adolescence, thwarted teenage obsessive passion, but it's absolutely powerful stuff. Knocked my socks right off my feet."

"*Love Triangle*," I repeated. An icky feeling chilled the back of my neck.

"There's one particularly extraordinary poem called 'Prom Night' about three-way sex. That's tricky and hard, to fuse poetics with sensual experience without being pornographic or maudlin or clichéd. She pulled it off. To put it mildly. That poem remains her best, I think."

"Oh," I said as mildly as I could, despite the fact that I was hyperventilating. How had I never known about the existence of this book? Did Tyler know about it? I would have bet not. I was gripped by a burning curiosity to read this thing and an equally strong itch to get the hell out of this paper-jammed room, so dense with words, claustrophobic, and hemmed in. "Would it be possible for me to see the printing press?" My quizzical tone was meant to imply that this was essential to my case, but really, I was just feeling antsy, and I wanted to talk to Connie.

Felix almost leapt up from behind his desk. "I'll gladly give you a tour of the premises," he said grandly.

"I was hoping Connie might have a minute," I said. "Since she was Rose's actual editor, as well as her friend, I'd like to get a chance to talk to her."

"Of course." He subsided back into his chair, his hair quivering on his brow from all the ups and downs. "She'd love to give you an earful, I am sure."

SIXTEEN

CONNIE TOOK MY EMPTY COFFEE CUP AND SET IT DOWN NEXT TO the bowl of Hershey's Kisses. When she saw me eyeing them, she said, "Help yourself. I keep them there for the interns, to reward them when they're good." She laughed. "Which is all the time. They're nice kids."

"Are they around somewhere?"

"They only work three days a week, and this is one of their off days."

As she led me through yet another reinforced steel door toward the back of the building, I unwrapped a candy and shoved it into my mouth. I was instantly lulled by the familiar chalky melt on my tongue, that weird Hershey's sour tang underlying the supersweet, milky chocolate. It erased the taste of the coffee.

"We're old-school here at Catalina Press," Connie said over her shoulder, as she led me down a short hall past several closed wooden doors with transom windows overhead. She stopped walking and turned to address me directly, eye to eye. "We only accept physical manuscript submissions on actual paper, never online documents. Our equipment is all twentieth century. But we also print our books and magazines on unbleached recycled paper, which is very twenty-first century. The guys who run the press are committed to making beautiful objects, not mass-produced corporate products. We want to be an alternative to those shiny disposable commercial books from conglomerate houses. We have a very small design team of artists who do our covers."

"How can you afford all this? Isn't it expensive?"

"Of course it is. And we can only do it because we're partially subsidized by several rich patrons, which come to think of it is very nineteenth century." She reached out and caressed a plain old round doorknob as if it were a relic from that time, from the age of romantic poetry and beautiful, finely wrought objects. "They also happen to be among our authors. Our patrons, I mean. And we do get a fair number of federal and civic grants as well. Also, believe it or not, our books sell. Some collectors have all of them."

We were both leaning against opposite walls of the hallway, which was illuminated by daylight filtering down from a large skylight, so it wasn't as airless feeling and closed in as it could have been.

"Why do you think Rose pretended to be Navajo?" I asked.

Connie snapped into a new kind of attention, sharp and hot. "I am so angry at her. It makes me feel like a patsy. I hate that feeling. I didn't even think to question it. She seemed genuine to me. I just feel like, who would pretend to be Native? Why would she bring that kind of trouble on herself?"

"You must feel blindsided."

She gave me a look. "It seems so creepy. The conversations we had, me talking straight with her like she was my cousin. Things one Native woman only says to another one, like code talking, that shared understanding and context. Now I think she was drinking in my own truth and reflecting it back to me. Sucking it out of me, appropriating it, making it her own. A vampire. I noticed she started talking like me, my accent. I heard her using it. Mirroring me. But I thought she was authentic, so I let it go."

"She studied you."

"Yeah." Connie's eyes gave off glints. "I feel used."

"Do you have any idea why she chose that particular identity? I mean, any underlying reason?"

"You mean beyond the fact that she benefited from it? Used it to advance herself? To me, looking back now, it just seems like a way to get the attention and success she was craving. Maybe she thought people were less likely to question a Native identity than if she had claimed to be black, say, or Latina. Who knows? She was obviously smart, because it worked."

I nodded. Her anger burned like dry wood, snap crackle pop. "Was there anything else you picked up? Any kind of personal identification that went deeper than ambition or attention mongering?"

"Oh," said Connie. She rolled her eyes. "Well, yeah, I mean I guess she talked about collective trauma a lot. She said she would never have children, to spare them quote-unquote 'inherited personal and collective global trauma.' As for me, I have three kids, and like I told Rose, they're all grown up now and doing fine, they have jobs and don't waste resources. But she liked to talk about this study that shows the way suffering and pain are passed down genetically, imprinted in blood and DNA, so your descendants inherit it. Rose talked about the Irish, the Jews, black people descended from slavery, other oppressed groups, how they're all genetic victims of their ancestors' persecution and abuse. I think she saw the history of humans as 'man hands on misery to man.' Or woman, to be fair."

"Her new book was very much about that," I said.

She snorted. "That stupid book. Come on, I'll show you the press. They're printing today."

I followed her through the steel door at the end of the hallway into a cavernous, high-ceilinged room that was clanging and churning rhythmically with various large, active machines. A couple of young guys stood on the floor, watching the books get made. They both had thick brown wavy hair springing back from wide brows. One of them, the beefier and shorter of the two, had a handlebar mustache and wore a white T-shirt with mustard-colored Carhartt work pants, suspenders, and work boots. The other, tall and lean, had a goatee and wore a poufy-sleeved white blouse, a Utilikilt, and scuffed motorcycle boots. Both of them wore black aprons and work gloves. I guessed they were brothers, and I was proved right when Connie introduced them to me as Jack and Caleb MacGregor. While they squired me around the shop, pointing out all the gewgaws and doodads, the old letterpress with its accoutrements, the cabinets of paper stock and inks, the typesetting machine, the binder, the trimmer, the offset lithography press, I nodded and asked questions and made appreciative noises of admiration, but I kept my radar attuned to Connie. Underneath her pride in this establishment and evident fondness for these two hipster blokes, I could feel a thin hard wire of rage. I'd plucked that wire when I got her talking about Rose, and it was still vibrating; I could almost hear it through the din of printing machinery.

As we walked back through the connecting hallway, I asked, "What's in these rooms off this hallway?"

She started opening doors. "Storage in here, our backlist. This is the general office, the interns work in this room when they're here, and this room here is officially mine, but I only use it to write in. I like working at my desk by the front door so I can keep an eye on things."

I poked my nose into all three rooms, which were windowless, each about fourteen by sixteen feet. The backlist storage room was crammed with metal shelves filled with stacks of printed books. The interns' room had three small metal desks in the middle, a coffee station against one wall, and the rest of the space was possibly even more cluttered with manuscripts than Felix's. Connie's room was comfortable and cozy, with a large Navajo rug on the floor, which looked totally natural in this room, unlike the ubiquitous Navajo rugs that hung on all the gringos' walls. A generous wooden desk was piled high with manuscripts, an armchair with a standing lamp next to it, and boldly vivid watercolor paintings on the walls, of desert landscapes.

Back out by Connie's desk, I took another Hershey's Kiss to stall for more time. I was waiting for her to say something; I wasn't sure what. I was listening to that vibrating taut string, trying to tune my antennae to its frequency.

On a swift, clear hunch, as Connie and I were making preliminary goodbye noises, I asked, "Who sent that anonymous email, the one about Rose?"

Her eyes met mine, as hard and glinting as obsidian. "I don't know," she said. "But Rose sure did, She knew who it was right away."

Bingo. "How did you know that?"

"Because she said so. When I told her about the email, showed it to her, she said, 'That motherfucker. This is war.'"

I waited. When Connie didn't say anything more, I asked, "What else?"

"That's it."

"'That motherfucker,'" I repeated, thinking. "'This is war.' That was really all she said? You didn't ask her who she meant?"

"She said it under her breath. Not to me. I didn't care who sent it, I only cared that she had lied to me."

"So we don't even know if it was a man or a woman."

"Motherfucker. That sounds like a man. Do women call one another motherfuckers?"

"Yup," I said. "Rose used it for everyone she was mad at. She once called me a motherfucker. Many years ago."

"You knew her?"

"Long, long story," I said. "And I've taken up enough of your time."

I said goodbye, thanked Connie, and headed out through the rubbled yard to the street.

Back in my car, I drove straight to Rose and Mickey's bungalow, parked on the street in front. When I knocked, Mickey came to the door in pajamas, looking bleary-eyed.

"Sorry if I woke you, and sorry I didn't call first," I said. "I'm here to pick up a copy of Rose's first book."

"I wasn't sleeping," they said, opening the door wider to let me in. "Just mourning. It involves a depressing amount of whiskey. I can't tell if I'm drunk or insane from lack of sleep."

"God, I'm so sorry," I said.

Mickey slumped on the couch as if they'd been sitting there since I'd left the last time. They gestured feebly toward the bedrooms. "Go on back if you'd like, she probably had a copy or two in her room. Feel free to take whatever you want."

In Rose's room, I scanned her bookshelves. She had a fair number of each of her two published collections. I snagged a copy of *Love Triangle* as well as her other published book, *Wingtips*. They were the same handy size, both slim, both published by the University of Arizona Press.

Exactly as I had done with Connie just now, I dawdled, hesitating, feeling as if Rose's room itself had something to tell me, if only I could align my inner ear with its pitch. I often do this when I'm stuck in a case, just stand around, taking in the ambient emotional noise, hoping something clear emerges. Sometimes it jars something loose. Not always. I was thinking about Rose's use of the words "motherfucker" and "war," both of which she had aimed at me, back when we were fourteen and I "broke the girl code" by going to the movies with Tyler. I recalled the sound of her voice, harsh with emotion: "God, Jo, you're such a motherfucker." I replayed it a few times in my head, amplified by memory, slowed it down, listening to every inflection and syllable. And then, right before she stomped away, she had added, "This means war." Grandiose and melodramatic, yes, but she meant it, this was as serious as a heart attack, as the saying goes. She was hurt, furious, and maybe worst of all, her ego was crushed. Rose's ego was the engine that made her go. Anyone who injured that vulnerable and crucial part of her was the enemy.

Motherfucker. This means war.

Whoever had written the emails had very likely done some heavy damage to her ego. Someone she had been close to. Someone who had wanted to punish her, as Lena had said, and who knew exactly how.

I hadn't been Rose's lover, except for that one drug-fueled night with her and Tyler after prom, and maybe this person hadn't either. But just like Rose's intense love-turned-to-hate with me, there was something intimate at work here, something deep, something lover-*ish*, lover adjacent.

I ducked behind the shoji screen in front of her bedroom window and sat at the little table. I set the two poetry books down, squaring them off, edge to edge. This was where Rose had done her writing, I could feel it. Her private little refuge, her workroom. The chair was a comfortable and expensive office chair, padded, ergonomic, bouncy, with armrests. I wheeled myself back and forth, my fingertips lightly pushing me off the rim of the table. I looked out the window, saw the plain two-car driveway partially obscured by the ocotillo. The house next door was just across the driveway. A large window looked into this one. I saw a refrigerator in the gloom of a kitchen. Someone probably stood at that window to load the dishwasher, scrub vegetables. I wondered who it was, and whether this neighbor was as aware of Rose sitting here writing as Rose must have been of him or her over there, going about their business.

I opened *Love Triangle* at random and saw the line "You, ancient enemy, evil shadow, fatal woman." I was no poetry expert, but I was pretty sure this meant me, as did the references, which I found as I read the whole book, starting from the beginning, to Lady Macbeth, Circe, and, most flatteringly, Mata Hari, the beautiful spy who seduced and killed. I was also a hyena, a Venus flytrap, and a rutting bitch in heat. I had heft and power. But poor Tyler was, variously, Adonis, Apollo, and a hapless, spineless Hamlet. He was a willow tree, a "fatly glistening" daylily, and all manner of delectable food: ripe fruit from figs to mangoes, tender lamb, a loaf of soft bread, and warm, bursting cheese. He was a leggy fawn, a silky suckling babe, a wholly objectified, dehumanized creature made entirely of words, owned entirely by Rose.

What struck me, even more than the writing itself, was the fact that Rose had invested two totally ordinary Arizona teenagers with all this timeless mythological and elemental fascination. It made me wonder about all the based-on-real-life (mostly female) muses immortalized by (mostly male) geniuses throughout history, these Maud Gonnes and Annabel Lees and Belles Dames sans Merci, normal girls elevated to demigoddesses, their real-life counterparts likely just as goofy and flawed as Tyler and I had been. This seemed to me like Rose's way of owning us. This was how she kept us close, she stole our breath with her succubus zeal, co-opted our souls. She pinned our simulacra to the paper, used language to hold us fast in her sticky web.

I came to the poem Felix had told me about, a long, dense, five-part prose poem about what happened with the three of us the night after our senior prom under the cottonwood tree. In my memory, we were three kids on drugs, pawing one another's bodies with lustful curiosity. Rose was the first girl I ever had sex with. I wasn't attracted to her in particular, and we had that complicated history, but that moment with the three of us was the first time I knew for sure that I liked girls' bodies as much as boys'. So it was important for me in that way. It woke me up to a certain truth about myself, my own fluid sexuality, and planted the seed that grew in me, flourished. Realizing this fundamental truth about myself, that I was primarily hungry for variety and autonomy in a way that far outstripped my parallel need for intimacy and stability, had determined my life's course as an independent, omnivorous singleton. I broke up with Tyler shortly afterward, which couldn't have been a coincidence.

Clearly, it had been significant for Rose in a wholly other way. In her language, through her eyes, I felt my own body with her hands, looked at myself with her eyes. She wrote about a psychic fusion of three minds, three hearts beating in the same rhythm. She had to vanquish me. She had to possess him. Neither one of us was real to her. We were the objects of her voracious hunger. The sheer visceral physicality of the language had real force, blunt and Anglo-Saxon, frank, headlong. It was a short book, and I had time, so when I finished, I went back to the beginning and read it again.

About halfway through, as if it were real, a wash of electricity rode the currents of the air in this room. I felt Rose everywhere, hovering in the air all around me. They had been so all-consuming, her feelings about me, their power had stayed behind like a residue. Jesus fucking Christ, I thought, impressed. I had never felt a fraction this strongly about anything, ever, in my entire life.

I sat very still, slapped by the waves of obsessiveness emanating up from the page. Tyler had recently slept with Rose. Not once, but several times. I thought about that video of his prone naked body with his erect cock grasped in her hand. She had recorded her victory as proof, a trophy. She had finally gotten something she'd wanted since she was a kid.

How could Tyler have been such an idiot, to give her that power over him? How could he have been so weak?

The last part of "Prom Night" described the aftermath of our three-way make-out session, when Rose was caressing us both, gazing into our eyes. She described the sensation of sliding into the sight line between Tyler's and my eyes, into the tight, strong hammock strung between us, so her own psyche swung there, its weight held fast in Tyler's and my love for each other. She wanted to stay there forever. The moment stretched, lasted, ballooned in the light of the rising sun. We were a trinity, a fusion of satisfied desire.

The poem ended, and Rose's ghost evaporated, poof, leaving me sitting in her chair, staring out the window, massaging the hell out of my earlobe to calm myself the fuck down.

I opened Rose's second book, looking with no small amount of trepidation for any more poems about Tyler and me. But this book felt like a catchall for the incidental poems she'd written as palate cleansers during her marathon obsession with us. The opening poem, "Boardwalk," was a paean to the Jersey Shore, funnel cakes, Bonne Bell Lip Smacker lip gloss, all those gritty, hazy summers in Trenton with her father. The book moved between southern Arizona and New Jersey, delineating the disparate emotional geographies of Rose's youth, mother in the West, father in the East, the cultural displacement of belonging in both places and neither place, the yearly disruption of the bounced-around only child of divorced parents. In a poem called "Dressings," she described shopping for clothes with her father at a megamall, trying outfits on in the dressing rooms and modeling them for him, then playing dress-up games with her little brothers in Arizona, putting clothes on the two younger boys and acting out stories with them, the power of those games. Another poem, "Force of Nature," was about Jersey itself, a sort of paean, as far as I could tell, to casinos, wise guys, and glam women doing coke in ladies' rooms.

I could see what Felix Mantooth had meant: Rose's first book was her masterpiece. She had shot her poetic wad on Tyler and me, and once we were safely caught between the covers of that book, a lot of the power drained out of her subsequent work. This second book felt clichéd and pedestrian, dramatic when it should have been understated, coy when it should have punched directly. I couldn't figure it out. Maybe I just didn't get poetry.

Tucking both books under my arm, I went back out to the living room and sat in the chair opposite Mickey. Their hair was flattened on one side, smooshed against their skull. Their pajamas were cotton, light green with parrots on them, and were a little wrinkled and grimy. The air in this house smelled dankly of sadness and booze.

"I am not okay," said Mickey. "I know I'm not. But I feel stuck here."

"Want to take a walk with me? Slowly, just around the block? It's a nice day out."

"The thing I don't get," they said, "is why she did it while she and I weren't speaking to each other. How could she just leave me there? We were so close. I know she thought I was judgmental. And she was right. But I couldn't believe she would lay herself open to being exposed like that. You know? Like, maybe don't fuck your teenage student. Maybe don't pretend you're something you're not. She was just so totally amazing exactly the way she was. Then she kills herself. No note, right? Just boom, she's gone forever. No resolution. We could have worked it out. I only acted that way out of love, I wasn't mad at her, I was just so worried about her. And now I'll never see her again. How am I supposed to live with this? What do I do with this? How do I go on?"

I was aware that these were the thoughts that had been running like a ceaseless current through Mickey's mind since Rose died, and all they were doing right now was externalizing them. If I drove away right now, this circular pattern would loop around and around while they drank more whiskey and sweated alcohol into their pajamas and lay with their head on the throw pillow, smooshing their hair even more.

"A walk might be good for you," I said. Mickey's sorrow was hard to watch. It was so helpless and poignant. "Fresh air. A change of scenery. Move your limbs."

"I can't. I can't leave this house. I'm waiting for her to come home. I feel like that Japanese dog whose owner died and who went to the commuter train station every day to wait for him. I am that dog."

"Well, I think there was more to Rose's death than meets the eye, and I'm working as hard as I can to find out what it is. Do you know anything about who might have written those anonymous emails to her editor at Catalina Press and the dean at the college? Apparently Rose knew who it was."

This seemed to perk Mickey up a little, the opportunity to talk about Rose in a way that was useful rather than heartsick. "No, but I'm pretty sure it was her brother Jason. That guy is a sneaky weasel. He came over here last month for dinner, and he and Rose got into a huge fight about some real-estate deal he was making, selling off some of their parents' ranchland."

"Why do you think Jason sent the emails?"

"Because he literally told Rose that night that she'd better watch her back. If she fucked up this deal for him, he'd get revenge. He meant it. I believed him. After he left, I told her to be careful, and she laughed it off, saying he's my little brother, he's harmless. I told her maybe she didn't take him seriously enough. I think that might have been the start of it. She got mad at me for interfering, said she felt like I was taking his side. I swear, all I was doing was warning her."

I was running my fingers over the spines of Rose's books, tapping them lightly with my fingertips, thinking about the things Solo hinted at but didn't say during our conversation, all the things he knew about Rose's family life. "But as it turned out, she didn't fuck up the Sunset Shadows deal for him."

"Well, she sure wanted to. Part of why she took that residency up there was to be closer to the whole thing, keep an eye out and make sure her parents didn't sign it, make sure no one at the Rancho did. She wanted to protect them all from Jason. She thought he was a snake. You know, the whole 'he's my brother and I love him, but I don't trust him,' that kind of thing."

I didn't know, because I had no siblings, but I could imagine. "So you don't think it could have been the boy she was sleeping with, her student?"

Mickey was sitting up a little straighter for the first time since I arrived. Some color was coming back into their face. Their voice even sounded a little less defeated. "I mean, not that Chay *wouldn't* have done that? But I feel like that kid had no idea she wasn't what she said she was. Whereas Jason was her brother, so he knew perfectly well what her background was and wasn't. He knew, and he had a good reason to tell on her. And he seems like the kind of kid who ratted his sister out every chance he got. When they were little, he told on her all the time. It would be in character for him to do that."

"Did you ever get the sense that he might harm Rose physically? Did he seem dangerous in that way?"

"I don't know about physically. But he definitely wanted this deal to go through, and he wasn't going to let her stop him. I wouldn't be surprised if he was celebrating right now. He's a cold-blooded socio-path."

"What about their younger brother, Ben?"

"Poor Ben. He loved Rose so much. She was more than just a big sister. She was also like a second sponsor. Did you know he was in NA?"

"I did."

"I heard from Babette that he relapsed over the weekend and OD'd and almost died. He sounds like he's in worse shape than I am."

"You know, I knew those two boys when they were young," I said. "Really well. Ben always struck me as a vulnerable little boy. Sweet. But he got upset a lot. Wouldn't eat his dinner, had tantrums over spinach or liver. Jason was quiet. He always wanted the violence in our pretend games to go further. He pushed the outlaw stuff, the pretend hangings. Sometimes it made Ben cry hysterically, and no one could comfort him. Even when they were little, Ben was hyper-sensitive and Jason was fundamentally cold. It's funny how people are who they are, even as kids."

Mickey almost smiled. "Rose told me Ben was always a little jeal-ous of his brother, how nothing ever seemed to bother him or make him sweat, everything just rolled off his back, while Ben would be devastated. It's weird how totally different siblings can be."

I got up. "Thank you," I said. "I have to go now, but I'll see you at the memorial tomorrow night?"

"I'll try. Hey, can I ask you something?"

I paused at the front door with my hand on the doorknob and turned and looked Mickey in the eye. "Of course."

"If you end up finding out that Rose didn't actually commit suicide, can you please tell me right away? Of course it would break my heart in a whole other way if she was killed. But it would also mean that she didn't do this to me on purpose."

"I promise," I said. "I'll tell you as soon as I know anything."

"Thanks. I'm going to take a shower now," they said, heaving themselves up off the couch. "And then I'm gonna eat a damn vegetable."

As I unlocked my car and tossed Rose's poetry books onto the passenger seat next to me, my phone rang. It was Freddy Lopez.

"I've got the last location grab on that phone before it was turned off," he said. "Are you ready?"

"Give me a sec." I fished around in my glove box for a pen, found one, and opened *Love Triangle* to a blank page. "Ready."

"Okay. The date is Wednesday of last week, the time is 5:26 a.m., and the location is . . . Delphi, Arizona."

"Can you get any more exact than that?"

"GPS puts it about two and a half miles southeast of the town. Looks like there isn't much out there. It's sort of close to something called Rancho Bella Luna?"

That was roughly the location of the tree where Rose was found hanging. So she did have her phone with her when she died. Or at least the person who was with her did. And it also put a pin on her time of death. "Anything else?"

"Yeah. There's a short window at 9:37 a.m. on Saturday when it looks like the phone was turned on again for about a minute or so."

The text with the video to Tyler. "Did you get a location for that?"

"Yes, hang on . . ."

I waited, tapping the butt of the pen against my front teeth.

"It's in Plato Valley, address 10458 West Clementine Road," said Freddy. "Looks like an office complex of some kind."

I scribbled down the address. "Thanks, Freddy. I owe you big-time. And call me right away if that phone goes live again."

"No doubt."

A quick search of the address led me to the website of Innovative Integrations, which I dimly recalled was the smarmy, euphemistic name of Jason's development company.

Okay then.

I called up Jason's phone number and hit the green icon to call him. Of course my call went to voicemail, and of course Jason's impatient-sounding outgoing message informed the caller that he was "out of pocket" at the moment but would return my call "ay-sap." I left an equally impatient-sounding message of my own, asking him to call me back as soon as possible, enunciating the latter four words with undue emphasis. Fuck him and his ASAP.

Finally, I had a lead.

As I slipped my car into the dense river of traffic and hauled my ass north, Bluetooth and Spotify flooded my ears with the song stylings of Taylor and Billie and Ariana and Beyoncé. Their voices kept me company, bossed me around. Perfection was a disease of a nation, and I needed a bad girl to blow my mind, and to stay beautiful, and not to abuse my power. I could get behind all of that. I sang along and the miles slipped by, my little self-contained pod speeding through the bright open land.

SEVENTEEN

I DROVE THROUGH THE UGLY, SUBURBAN, CORPORATE, OVERDEVEL-
oped sprawl of Plato Valley, the faux-stucco corporate complexes and
newish "senior living" development hospitals that lined both sides of
the six-lane road bizarrely named Clementine. When I reached 10458,
I switched Cardi B off mid–cheap ass weave, so the British-accented
voice of my GPS butler, Nigel, could politely guide me along the twisty
blacktop lanes of a labyrinthine corporate complex. With impeccable dulcet politeness, he threaded me through a series of identical
one-story adobe buildings set in rolling hills, landscaped with native
plants and trees, with a commendable lack of water-sucking lawns.
When Nigel told me to park, I parked. When he told me to complete
my journey on foot, I turned off my car, got out, and hoofed it through
the fiery breath of Hades to the glass doors whose virtual footmen
opened them automatically at my approach, to admit me to an Icelan-
dic paradise. A curved, plant-covered green wall was inlaid with two
brushed stainless steel panels, sheets of water streaming down their
surfaces to splash into an ornamental rock catchment. Directly behind the entryway was a spacious, peaceful waiting lounge, filled with
sleek chairs and curved couches arranged in conversation groups, positioned to face the floor-to-ceiling plate glass windows for a stunning
view of the corporate park itself.

I approached the reception desk, a polished slab of red sandstone,
behind which sat two young blond women, both wearing neat little
linen suits in jewel tones, one of whom was busy at a computer, the

other eyeing me with polite wariness. She looked young and impatient and unimpressed, her face blandly pretty, distinguished only by a lip ring, which probably drove her parents crazy, which was probably the point. I imagined myself as she must see me: a tall stranger with no business here, my hair tufted and windblown, scruffy and out of place in my vintage cowgirl boots, dusty bootcut Levis, and black T-shirt. I was not the kind of person who generally walked through that door. I had no appointment. Maybe I also had a certain cheeky, subversive glint in my eye, as if I didn't take any of this corporate aspirational-living claptrap seriously enough, or at all.

I checked my attitude and introduced myself like a proper grown-up, flashing my PI license.

"I have a meeting with Chad and Phil at Integrated Innovations," I told her.

She must have believed me because she hopped on her office phone and moved her lips silently and replaced the receiver and asked me to have a seat, someone would be out to get me.

I obediently parked myself in a geometric wingback chair uphol-stered in moss-green pleather and drummed my nails on my knee and kept an eye on the doorway next to the reception desk to see who would appear. The chair faced the parking lot and seemed to be bolted to the floor, so I had to twist around and crane my neck, but I wasn't going to let anyone sneak up on me. I was betting it would be Phil, who struck me as the beta to Chad's alpha, but maybe Chad wanted to bustle out all-importantly and intimidate me. Or maybe they'd send their assistant to get rid of me.

As it turned out, I was dead wrong. The person who walked through the doorway was none other than Tyler Bridgewater in his police uni-form. He saw me at the same time I saw him. He didn't seem glad to see me at all. He looked miserable.

"What are you doing here?" we asked each other simultaneously.

"You first," I said.

"I had a business meeting."

"What business is that?"

"None of yours," he said. He licked his dry lips. "Seriously, Jo, what are you doing here?"

I paused for a moment, debating with myself how much I should reveal. Right now, the facts as they stood were that someone had sent Tyler a text with an incriminating video of him having sex with a woman who was now dead, from that dead woman's missing phone, which had been located here at this address in Plato Valley, where Tyler himself just happened to be when I showed up to investigate. Could Tyler have sent himself the video from Rose's phone? But that would mean he had Rose's phone, which would also mean . . . My brain was in too many knots. I decided to play my hand and loosen the whole damn snarl.

"I traced the GPS location of Rose's phone retroactively, pinned it when that text was sent, the one with the video of you two together."

"How did you do that?"

"I have methods. Anyway, her phone was here."

Tyler looked around in bewilderment, as if the phone were floating around the lobby in midair. "Where?"

"Somewhere in this building. Or at least within a hundred-foot radius of it. At 9:37 a.m. on Friday, whoever it was turned Rose's phone on, sent you that text, and then turned it off again a minute later."

"Wow," said Tyler. "Are you sure?"

"Positive."

I studied his face. He seemed genuinely freaked out. "Holy fucking shit."

"Yeah," I said. "Now it's your turn. What are you doing here? Who were you meeting with just now?"

He was silent, so I took a stab. "Does it have to do with Jason Gold? Innovative Integrations?"

He glanced over his shoulder, shifted his gaze to the bluestone pavers under his feet.

"Are you investigating them?"

"Not exactly." His voice was weak.

"So why are you here?"

He turned and walked out of the building.

"Hey, come on," I said, trotting after him to the parking lot. "Whatever it is, you can trust me."

"Maybe. But not here."

I followed him to his cruiser, which was parked around the corner, out of sight, which explained why I hadn't seen it when I drove in. He opened the door. "I have to head back to the station quickly. Meet me at the first Circle K parking lot in Delphi in half an hour, and I'll tell you everything."

I watched Tyler drive away, mulling it all over. What could be so disturbing that he wasn't willing to talk about it in the parking lot of an office building with no one around? Was there some kind of surveillance system here? What the hell was going on?

I needed to go back in there and persist until I talked to either Chad or Phil. As I headed back toward the sliding glass doors, I spotted Jason Gold out of the corner of my eye, scuttling along a walkway on the side of the building, fishing a key fob out of his front chinos pocket and aiming it at a white Lexus. For a brief moment, I considered accosting him, then I decided to take a subtler tack. He hadn't seen me yet. I could use that to my advantage.

Ducking down, I slipped between the rows of cars until I reached my Honda and slid into the driver's seat, slouching below the window as his car drove by. I turned on the ignition, pulled out slowly, and followed behind him at a safe distance. I'm always happy when I'm tailing someone. I love having a clear objective whose essential protocols are not to lose the quarry and not to be seen, two things that often come into conflict with each other. It takes skill to ride the razor-thin line between visibility and invisibility, anticipating my mark's moves, constructing a theory of where they're going and why, slipping through traffic like a ninja. Every time I do it, I feel like I'm in a Bond movie.

This time, when the white Lexus turned left onto the highway toward Delphi, it was disappointingly easy to keep on his tail and guess where he was headed. So I decided to up the pressure a little.

"Nigel," I said to my Bluetooth. "Call Jason Gold."

"Calling Jason Gold," Nigel informed me in his soothing British accent.

The phone rang a few times. I could see Jason, two cars ahead in the other lane, as his voice came over the speakers.

"Hello? Who is this?"

"Why was Rose's phone at your office after she went missing?" No point in beating around the bush. I had the element of surprise, so I might as well use it.

"Who is this?"

"Why was Rose's phone at your office after she went missing?"

"Jo? Is that you?"

"Did you text Tyler from Rose's phone?"

"I have no idea what you're talking about."

The highway banked right and began to climb into the foothills, narrowing to two lanes. We were separated now only by a red van. With a broken yellow line and nobody on the immediate horizon, I zipped into the opposite lane and floored it past the van.

Unlike 007's superfast, cool cars, my old Honda doesn't have much pickup, even on level ground. It took me an embarrassingly long time to get past the van and overtake Jason's Lexus. As I inched my way up alongside his car, the looming form of a hulking eighteen-wheeler appeared over the horizon, coming toward us from the opposite direction. I had to make this quick. "Who sent that letter about her not being Navajo? Was it you?"

I looked over at Jason as I drew level to watch his face as he answered. Glancing over at me, his eyebrows shot up over the rims of his aviators. "What are you doing, Jo?" His voice came over my speakers as I watched his lips move. "Are you trying to kill us?"

I was almost half a car length ahead of him, but the eighteen-wheeler was bearing down fast, almost close enough now for me to make out the driver's face. Jason didn't slow down or move over to let me pass. He was enjoying this, I could swear it.

Taking evasive action, I tapped my brakes to let him get ahead by a nose and darted in behind his Lexus at the last second, just as the behemoth barreled by us, horn blaring. Jesus, that was close. Way too close.

"You're insane!" Jason yelled through my speakers. "Do you know that? You should be arrested for reckless driving."

"You could have at least slowed down to let me pass."

"All right, that's it. This is harassment."

"Wait," I said, before he could hang up. "One more thing. Can you think of anyone who hated Rose?"

"She hated you, that much I know." I could feel the daggers in his eyes behind his aviators boring into me in his rearview mirror.

"Look," I said, making one last feeble attempt to get anything I could out of him. "I know there was tension between you two. I know you and Rose were having heated arguments about the Sunset Shadows land deal. And I know that someone has her phone. They've been sending videos and texts from it since she died. One of them came from your office building. Was it you?"

"You need to check your shit, Jo." He spat my name like a curse. "My sister killed herself, all right? My brother's in the hospital right now in a coma. My mother is a wreck, and my father is turning into a vegetable. And now you're accusing me of murder and trying to run me off the road? I'm not the psycho here."

"Jason . . ."

"Seriously, go fuck yourself."

There was a double beep, followed by Nigel's voice informing me politely that my call had ended. The white Lexus accelerated away, leaving me in its dust.

By the time I got to the Delphi turnoff, Jason had no doubt already arrived at Rancho Bella Luna. I swerved onto Arizona Avenue and swooped into the Circle K parking lot, turned off my engine, leaned my chair back, and closed my eyes. I was trembling a little, visualizing that huge truck barreling toward me, horn blaring. My dad's fatal accident had happened on that same stretch of road. I couldn't believe I had been so reckless. Jason was right, my behavior just now was deranged. I was so hell-bent on proving his guilt, I'd endangered myself and everyone around me. All for nothing. And now he was convinced I was a lunatic.

I felt a little lightheaded and shaky. I realized that all I'd had to eat or drink today was bad coffee and Hershey's Kisses at Catalina Press, and before that, the postworkout shake with Freddy Lopez. It was almost five thirty, the shadows were lengthening, and my stomach was growling.

In high school, during our stoner days, Tyler and I used to mainline convenience-store microwavable frozen snacks. Buoyed by a wave of remembered weed-infused satiation, I went into the Circle K, peed in their grungy little bathroom, washed my hands and face, and prowled around the store, putting together a sad-looking car supper. I got a couple of bean and cheese burritos with a few packets of hot sauce, a bottle each of iced tea and lemonade to mix together in the paper cups I purloined from the stacks near the soft drink guns, a handful of Slim Jims, and a large pack of peanut M&M's.

While I nuked the burritos in the little microwave next to the coffee and paid for everything, I was mentally girding myself for the inevitable call from Laura. I could already hear her distraught voice on the other line asking what on earth would possess me to accuse her precious son of murdering his sister while I tried to run him off the road, and then telling me that my investigative services were no longer required, and that it would be better for everyone if I stayed away from her family for a while.

But the call didn't come. Maybe Jason hadn't told her. I had no idea why he wouldn't or what it meant that he hadn't, but I was too wrung out at this point to speculate.

Tyler pulled up in his cruiser just as I was walking out. I got in the front passenger seat and started unpacking the bounty I'd assembled. He turned his police radio's volume down low so it just crackled a little and we couldn't hear the dispatchers' voices.

"Thanks," he said, eyeing it all. "I've barely eaten today."

"Same." I handed him a piping hot burrito and squirted a packet of Valentina on mine and bit into it. Refried beans and melted cheddar and flour tortilla and hot pepper sauce hit my tongue with that old, familiar sensation of pure pleasure: fat and carbs and spicy, savory softness.

"Unnngh," I grunted. "So good."

Tyler looked down at his food, not moving.

"Lost your taste for teenage stoner food?"

"My stomach hurts."

I looked closely at him. He looked panicky and haunted, the way he'd looked the other day at the scene of Rose's death. "What's going on?"

"I can't talk about it."

"To me? Come on, Tyler. I'm probably the one and only person on earth without a dog in any of your fights who you can absolutely trust."

He turned to look me in the eye. His were bleary. "Can I?"

"I'm on your side. I'm the vault of secrecy. And I just want whatever is best for you."

"Why?"

"Because I care about you, you dumb shit. I always will."

He took a deep, shaky breath. "So that video I showed you of me and Rose. That's just the tip of the iceberg. I'm in up to my balls in all this."

A lump of burrito stuck in my throat. I swallowed hard. "Meaning?"

"Linda doesn't know any of this. I can't tell her, she'd absolutely kill me. I invested our savings in Sunset Shadows. Jason told me about it, he said it was no-fail and guaranteed to give me a return of minimum two hundred percent. Meaning my money doubled, or more."

"Two hundred percent? For investing in yet another retirement community development in the land of retirement community developments? What is this deal, exactly?"

"So they get the land from Bella Luna for basically nothing, like a hundred dollars, and with that, they get the water rights that are attached. That's what they're really after, the water rights."

"But they're planning to actually build the whole community, right?"

He sighed. "I thought so at first. But now I'm pretty sure they're just playing with investors' money. I suspect it's part of some Ponzi scheme they're running, but I can't prove anything. They're advertising it as 'natural spring-fed land.' People are buying in. Not Rancho people, other investors."

"But that's a total lie. There's no spring."

"There used to be one, and it still shows up on survey maps, which they bring to every meeting with their other investors."

"Wow." I took a gulp of my Arnold Palmer. "If it gets out that all the water is gone and those rights are worthless, they're going to be in some trouble."

"They don't care. They got it for free. And it's all about appearances. What they can make it look like to investors."

"Jesus. What are they getting people to invest in, if they're not really doing anything with the land?"

"They claim they're going to subdivide it. So they have start-up costs, running utilities out to the subdivision, grading and landscaping, and there's all the construction costs for the houses."

"So let me see if I've got this right. The Rancho just gave them a hundred acres for a dollar an acre in exchange for providing twenty-four seven aging-in-place medical services to their elderly, and it sounds like they're collecting investors' money to quote-unquote 'develop' it. So they'll make noises about construction delays to the Rancho people, and stave off their investors, and just fucking *sit* on the land and all that nonexistent water. And then they turn around and use the investors' money for the next scam. Yup, sounds like a Ponzi scheme to me. They've got themselves the twenty-first-century equivalent of a gold mine."

"It's my kids' college fund," Tyler said mournfully. "And they're lying to all of them, your mother, all those old people."

"How did you figure it out?"

"I put two and two together, woke up in the middle of the night with a light bulb over my head. Something wasn't sitting right with me. There are all those other planned developments in Plato Valley that have stalled or gone nowhere because of lack of water, lack of buyers. Or maybe they're scams too. How is this one different? So I went to confront them today, to ask if I can pull out of the deal. I even threatened to tell all the investors and the people at the Rancho what they're doing."

"What did they say? You're law enforcement."

"They laughed in my face. They told me if I tried to take them down, I'd lose everything, all the savings I put in."

"Fuckers," I said. "Motherfucking fuckers."

Tyler looked at his burrito as if it might bite him back. "Anyway, I can't do jack shit now. The contracts are ironclad. Everybody has signed already, handed over the land. These guys are untouchable."

"Not everybody," I said. "My mother still hasn't signed."

"Wait. Are you serious?"

"Yeah. I was just there with her yesterday when Jason and his cronies came by the house and tried to get her to sign. She refused."

"Holy shit. Maybe I'm wrong then. Maybe there is some hope, after all."

"You need to eat that," I said, nodding at his burrito. "Before I do."

Tyler took a bite, another bite, and then, his hunger ignited, he shoved his food into his mouth as fast as he could. We ate and drank in silence, chewing our Slim Jims in tandem, passing the M&M's packet back and forth. When we'd eaten everything, I wadded up all the trash, got out, threw it away, and came back to the cruiser. "Want to go for a little drive?" I asked.

He started the engine and pulled out onto the road. He drove us in the direction of Delphi State Park, a mile or so out of town.

"Did you ever read Rose's first book of poetry?"

"No. Should I?"

"It's all about us. What happened on prom night. She loved you and hated me with equal force. She was obsessed with us. Even into adulthood. It gave me the willies. I mean, to me, what happened was kind of sweet, it's funny. But to her, it was cataclysmic."

He shot me a look. "No shit," he said.

"I cannot believe you slept with her, Tyler. How could you let her in like that? How could you—"

I stopped. Tyler's face was contorted, his mouth working.

"Hey," I said. "Come on, Ty, it's okay, it's over, she's gone."

"I'm such a fuckup," he said, almost choking. I was worried he'd run the car off the road. "If I lose all our money. If Linda ever sees that video. What was I thinking?"

"Midlife crisis maybe?" I said. "Not to minimize it, I'm serious. We're turning forty. We're all freaked out. You made some questionable choices, but at least you didn't do what Rose did, and at least you're still alive."

"I'm going off the rails."

"You're going to be okay."

"How do you know?"

"Because we're going to find whoever sent you that video and make sure Linda never sees it. And we're going to make sure that land deal never goes through, and shut Jason and those scumbags down, and get you your money back. We'll get the FBI involved if we have to."

Tyler turned into the state park, drove slowly to the parking lot, and parked. We looked out through the windshield at the rolling green desert hills in the bright, late sunlight. To our right was the hewn-timber kiosk with its big-framed trail map, hikers' information pamphlets, trash can, and lockbox for park fee envelopes. No one was here but us. The parking lot was deserted. The trail leading off into the hills glinted, quartz and fool's gold in the rocks catching the late light. A covey of quail poked around a nearby clump of brush, their red caps flashing.

"Okay," he said, nodding to himself. "Okay. You're right. Fuck those douchebags. Let's take them down. And if I get through this without losing everything, I'm never going to do anything stupid again."

I chuckled. He laughed then, too, a painful sound, but it comforted me a little. We sat there in silence for a while, watching the quail dart through the shrubs and peck at the ground.

"You think Jason did it, don't you? Murdered his sister and took her phone."

"I don't know," I said. I decided not to tell him about our little run-in on the highway. "But it's the only logical conclusion I can draw, at least right now. The only problem is I have no way of proving it."

"So sending that video to me was a threat? Telling me to back off?"

"Maybe. And it's not just you. Someone's been calling me too.

Blocked caller ID. No voice, just weird static like crackling fire on the other line."

"Should I bring Jason in for questioning?"

"Not yet. I need to do some more digging first. Jason is a wily customer, and we need to have our shit together before we move, or we'll lose him."

Tyler went quiet for a moment. Then he shook his head, to clear it, or in disbelief, or both. "Okay. I'm going to let you drive this thing, Jo. I trust you because I don't trust myself anymore."

After he dropped me off at my car, I climbed in and sat there for a moment, wondering what to do next. I had planned to go and tell Laura Gold everything I'd learned, but Jason was probably still there, and I had no idea what he'd said to her about me. Besides, all I had right now were dark suspicions. Better to hold off saying anything to anyone until I knew for sure what Jason was up to.

My phone rang. It was Erin Yazzie. "Hey, Yazzie."

"Hey, Bailen. So the guy I shot."

She sounded worried. She needed reassurance. I knew the feeling.

"That scumbag," I said. "He shot at you first."

"He did, right?"

"You had to defend yourself."

"He was trying to kill me."

"You had to shoot him. And you just wounded him, remember? He's alive and well except for the hole you put in his shoulder. Lucky bastard."

"It's a weird feeling to shoot someone. I don't like it."

"It has to be done sometimes in our line of work. One of the bad parts of the job. How's Benson?"

"It's nice down here. It's peaceful. How's the fake-Navajo case?"

"Confusing."

"Good luck," she said with a smile in her voice. Good, I'd cheered her up.

"You too," I said.

After we hung up, I called my mother's number. She picked up on the third ring. "Justine." Her tone was curt. I was interrupting her. "Is everything all right?"

"Everything's fine, Mom. I'm still up here working this case. How are you?"

"How am I? I'm fine, why wouldn't I be?"

"Good. You still haven't signed that contract for Sunset Shadows yet, have you?"

There was a silence on the line.

"Mom?"

"I had to," she said. "Jason came over just now, and he was so upset about everything that's happened to his poor family, I couldn't say no. Did you know Ben's in a coma? It's just terrible."

I held the phone to my chest and opened my mouth to scream, but nothing came out. That motherfucker, I thought. This means war.

EIGHTEEN

MY SECOND THOUGHT AFTER HANGING UP WITH MY MOTHER WAS that I had overplayed my hand and lost. Tyler was screwed, my leverage was gone. Worse, I had tried to intimidate a viable suspect in a dangerous and reckless manner, thus giving Jason all the reason he needed to get me thrown off the case. And he knew it.

At the moment, the only ironclad piece of incontrovertible evidence I had to go on was the location of Rose's phone when that text was sent to Tyler on Saturday morning. Whoever had Rose's phone was at the scene of her death, I knew that too. And the only other person I knew who was connected to Rose and the office building in Plato Valley where Innovative Integrations was headquartered was Tyler.

But he would have had to have staged Rose's murder to make it look like a suicide, and then sent himself a video of the two of them together from her phone. It seemed outlandish. Unless of course it was designed to shift the blame onto someone else, like Jason.

Jesus, I needed a drink. I didn't want to drink alone, that much I knew. And I had no desire to go anywhere near the Rancho right now. I needed a break from all things Rose tonight, so that ruled out the Triangle A cohort. There was nothing for me in this town, but the drive back down to Tucson seemed long and lonely, and there was no one waiting for me at home.

Lupita Gonzalez answered on the second ring. "Hey, *mamita*. I was just thinking about you."

"Want to get a drink?"

"Come over," she said. "It's my nephew's birthday, we're having a party. We have a ton of food and beer. You know where I live, right?"

"Just up the highway. I'm not dressed for it, though."

"It's a cookout, you can wear pajamas if you want. Pull around back, we're near the corrals."

Bar H Ranch was just a mile or so north of Delphi, off the highway, down a long red-clay road punctuated with cattle guards. I drove past a bunch of contented-looking cows in a pasture, munching on mesquite and buffel grass. I waved to them as I got out to open and close the main gate, then drove through and pulled into the ranch yard. The large, extended family lived in the ranch house and several structures and outbuildings around it, including a prefab cedar timber cabin, a double-wide trailer on cinderblocks, an enormous RV, and an old adobe casita. The ranch house itself was a sprawling one-story stucco structure with a deep front porch and a peaked roof with two chimneys. The Gonzalez family had been here since the early twentieth century, raising about sixty head of Black Angus cattle at a time, sustainably, conserving water and managing their land and the land they leased from neighbors. I knew this because I'd visited the ranch with my high school Arizona History class, back when they taught things like the history of cattle ranching.

I pulled around past the windmill and corrals to a tangle of mesquite trees and a clearing, where I saw smoke drifting from a couple of grills and a small crowd of people sitting around tables. When I parked and stepped out of my car, a few barking, scruffy, midsize dogs raced over to inspect me, sniffing my knees and crotch, panting up at me. I smelled meat and smoke and heard tinny ratcheting mariachi trumpets through loudspeakers, a hubbub of laughter and voices.

As I made my way toward the crowd, Lupita separated herself from everyone and came to greet me. "Hey," she said, giving me a warm hug. She wore gold hoop earrings and a short orange T-shirt dress, her hair pinned up on her head in a sexy, messy bun, her legs long and smooth in orange-and-white cowgirl boots, really cool ones, low-heeled and tall, with inlaid firebird wings.

"Nice boots," I said.

She flashed me a grin. "Come get a beer," she said, leading me over to a couple of galvanized tubs in the shade, full of ice and beer and soda. A nearby table was full of amazing-looking food. I glimpsed the remains of a pan of enchiladas with green sauce, a platter of grilled chicken pieces, another of carne asada, a bowl of yellow rice studded with chopped bell peppers and scallions, a pan of refried beans with crumbled cotija cheese on top, a stack of corn tortillas, and a platter of sliced avocado, jalapeno, tomato, cabbage, and jicama.

"Help yourself," she said.

"Damn!" I told her. "I ate already. If I'd only known."

"Come and meet everyone then. You might get hungry again later."

I fished an icy, dripping bottle of beer out of the tub and opened it as Lupita brought me over to a group of men sitting apart from everyone else. They were talking in rapid-fire Spanish, and from what I could glean, it was something about a guy they'd seen recently driving through the back of their land in an ATV, probably taking a short-cut to his hunting camp back in the mountains. They didn't like it. It was trespassing. "Papi, Tio Chuy, Juancito, Tono, this is my friend Jo Bailen. Jo, this is my dad, my uncle, my brother, and my cousin."

We all nodded solemnly at one another. All four of these guys looked familiar to me. The Gonzalez men had long, bony faces with thick eyebrows. Lupita's father was the one that Solo had told me thought all Rancho people were dirty hippies. Looking at him, I could see how this might be the case. Paco Gonzalez was fiercely impeccable and proper, in a wide-brimmed white straw cowboy hat, pressed white button-up shirt, bolo tie with a silver clasp and a large inlaid chunk of turquoise. He had an impressive handlebar mustache. He fixed me with a look. "*¿Creciste por aquí?*"

"Yeah, she's from Delphi," said Lupita in English. "She grew up at the Rancho Bella Luna."

"*¿Eres una de las hijas des esos artistos?*"

"Her mother is a painter," said Lupita. "*Su padre es muerto.*"

"*¿Ella no puede hablar, Guadalupe?*"

"Come on, speak English."

Paco waved us away, unsmiling, but I thought I caught a gleam in his eye. I met Lupita's mother and two aunts, another brother, more cousins, her sisters, nieces, nephews, including the birthday boy, Pedro, a stout little man-toddler all of three years old, in a miniature cowboy hat and a black felt vest with appliqué bulls on it, and another uncle, Carlos, who sat bent and silent in his wheelchair. "He was born like this," said Lupita. "He's my mother's baby brother. We all take care of him."

She and I sat down with a group of women, who had separated themselves from the men. They all smiled at me, nodded, and went right back to their conversation, which was about a woman they knew who was opening a craft store in Delphi. Some of them thought it would be fine. Others were sure the store would be gone by next year. I had no idea why this would be controversial at all, or a topic of discussion, but they were all getting into it. Lupita's Tia Ana, who looked as skinny and bitchy as my mother, went into a diatribe about how Delphi didn't need another craft store, one was enough. "Oh," I said to Lupita. "Does your aunt own the craft store by the church?"

She gave me an odd look. "I thought you didn't speak Spanish."

"I didn't say I didn't understand it."

"You should have told me you did." She leaned back in her chair looking up into the mesquite tree we were sitting under, lifting her chin in a sudden cool breeze, and touched her beer bottle to mine. "I'm glad you came over."

"It's so nice here," I said. I was aware of a pang of something in my chest, a tightness that felt like nostalgia or wistfulness. Lupita was lucky to have this clan, this place, this food. Most of the time, I was pleased with the fact that I belonged to nobody and traveled through the world alone. But right now, compared to this, my life struck me as depressingly empty. "Does anyone ever leave this place? I can see why you wouldn't."

"The only ones who still live here now are my parents and Chuy and Teresa, plus me and my cousin and my brother, Juan; we help out and pay rent, and my brother will take over as manager when my father retires. Everyone else moved off the ranch. My uncle Eduardo is a lawyer, my aunt has her store, two of my cousins are in business school. Yeah, like that."

An hour later, the party started to break up, people taking their dishes and waving goodbye and driving off, others collecting paper plates and empty bottles, tamping down the embers in the grills. Lupita nudged me and said with a sidelong look, "Want to go for a walk?"

We grabbed a couple more beers and set off in the indigo light of early evening, the moon just coming up, back into the hills behind the ranch, ambling at a clip through the brush. She was almost as tall as me, and we walked at a similar pace, fast but easily. "It's always good, seeing my mother with her girlfriends and sisters," she told me. "She gets along so much better with women than men. She and my father have been married since they were kids, but I never understood what they have in common. They make it work, though. But she has a close friendship with a woman who goes to our church. They even take trips together sometimes. She stays over there a few nights a week. I wonder about her."

This seemed like a personal thing for Lupita to be telling me. We hardly knew each other. It felt like a lead-in to a bigger conversation, so I said, "What do you wonder, exactly?"

"I think she's queer, like me. But I can never ask her. Or tell her about myself. My family is superconservative. Not politically really, just socially. I have to be careful. They want me to get married, to a man. Of course, I don't have to."

I thought of Freddy Lopez and his autocratic grandmother. "Of course you don't have to, but . . . ?"

"But I will. Just like my mother did. I'll find myself a nice hard-working *chicano* Christian boy."

"You should marry my friend Freddy Lopez," I blurted out. "His grandmother told him he has to get married, and all he wants to do is date hot little babes, one after another. You guys could be each other's beards."

"Give me his number," said Lupita bleakly. "He sounds perfect."

We climbed up to a ridge overlooking the lights of Delphi just to the south, scattered through the high valley, and sat side by side on a boulder, watching the almost-full moon climb the sky. The land was splashed with cold, liquid silver. "What did you think of Rose?" I asked her. "Knowing she was pretending to be Navajo?"

"Honestly? I have to admit, it really makes me laugh. Come on, it's funny. Pretending to be Native, what a crazy-white-girl thing to do. I know Rose was complicated, she wasn't easy, but I really liked her. She had a lot of spirit. She was funny. She believed in things."

"That's all true," I said. "About Rose."

"So you two were tight, and then you weren't. I remember something about it back then, people talked at school about how she hated you and Tyler, how she was jealous. What was that all about?"

"I was her best friend all through our childhood," I said. I had been trying to avoid thinking about Rose for a night, but somehow I found myself wanting to talk to Lupita about her. Maybe I just wanted to talk to Lupita about anything. She made me feel more comfortable and open than anyone had made me feel in a very long time. "Starting from the age of four, we grew up together. But when Tyler and I got together, she freaked out. I thought it was because she was in love with him. That's what she told me at the time. But I read her diary from that year recently, and now I feel like I don't know anything. She never wrote one word about me. We were inseparable our whole childhoods. I was invisible to her. But man, I loved her so much."

"You mean romantically? Sexually?"

"Maybe? Maybe I felt things for her that she didn't know how to deal with. Maybe she . . . picked up on my own energy, maybe she knew I was sexually fluid way before I did. I think my attachment to her might have confused her. She was straight, as far as I know. But . . . we were so close. And I know I project a masculine energy sometimes. Anyway, it was really messy and complicated, our breakup. I mean, we were kids, right? We didn't have a language or any context for that level of intense feeling, we just sort of took each other for granted. And I don't think she ever figured it out. Sometimes best friendships can be too close."

"Why did your friendship end?"

"I told her I was going to the movies with Tyler."

"She ended your friendship because of *him*?" Her voice crackled with gratifying skepticism.

I leaned into it for a split second, feeling warmly vindicated, but my innate sense of fairness and blunt honesty made me say, "See, for Rose, it was an unforgivable betrayal. She had a crush on him first. The problem was that she never mentioned it to me. I told her I was going out with him, and she freaked out, so I swore I'd cancel, but the damage was done, there was no fixing it, the cat was out of the bag that he and I liked each other. That was it for her. She didn't speak to me for the rest of high school. Then it got weird." I told Lupita what had happened on prom night: the tabs of Ecstasy, the three-way sex under the cottonwood tree.

Lupita gave me a sidelong look. "So Rose was your first kiss? I mean, girl kiss."

I laughed. "Is that really what you took away from the story?"

"No." She smiled. "I took away that you like your work. You like analyzing people, figuring them out."

"Yeah, I do. It suits me. It takes intuitive thinking and a kind of obsessiveness, different from Rose's, the need to know things and do whatever it takes to find the truth. I like working alone. But I confess, I was feeling kind of lonesome when I called you."

"You did sound a little blue."

"I'm glad you invited me over."

She turned to look at me. She didn't say anything, but in her face I saw a question, a flickering uncertainty. I was pretty sure I knew what she was asking.

"And I meant this to be a date," I said clearly.

"Good," she said. "If you hadn't called me first, I would have called you."

As she leaned against me, without even thinking I slid my arm around her shoulders. She encircled my wrist with one hand and kissed me on the mouth. She tasted like smoke and beer, and her body was warm and strong and humming with vibrant life. I kissed her back, my loins catching fire, a little dizzy with wanting her. She hiked up her dress's short skirt and straddled me with one leg hitched over my hip, angling her crotch against mine, and we started dry humping like kids, my hands on her thighs, pulling her hard against me. My whole body felt hot and electric. The rock we were sitting on was very uncomfortable and not at all ideal. "Hey, come spend the night with me," she said breathlessly, with her mouth on mine.

"Won't your family know?"

"A sleepover with a friend, I have them sometimes."

We speed walked back down the hillside to the ranch in the moonlight, touching each other the whole way, her arm encircling my waist, my arm around her shoulders, my dangling hand grazing her taut little breast with its erect nipple. We had to stop to make out a couple of times when our desire got too charged. She led me up the steps of her cabin and into its one room and over to a wide, low bed covered in a woven wool blanket. Our clothes came off, our boots, and she stripped the blanket back so we could lie in the cool sheets. Her bed smelled like lemons. Her skin was warm and smelled smoky from the barbecue grills and musky from her own smell. I buried my face in her silkiness and drank her. She wrapped her entire self around me. Naked in the moonlight, her hair was loose, her rib cage narrow and elegant. Her hips were curved, lush. All the things I'd been holding inside, pent-up and tight, for the past few days came flooding to the surface. I concentrated all of it into my mouth, hoping I was doing it right, feeling out of practice, gratified when I felt her tense and quiver and go silent for a long moment before she relaxed, breathing hard. She pulled me up her body until we were pressed together, scissoring our legs, undulating against each other slowly, kissing open-mouthed, probing, soft, letting our breaths still. I wanted to bite her earlobe, her neck, her shoulder, and wrestle her around, get combative and sweaty, but I was a little shy, still feeling my way into this, hoping she was enjoying it. I didn't want to put her off with my frank rapaciousness in case she didn't like that sort of thing, so I behaved myself. She turned me over onto my back and moved her mouth down my body with fluid assurance, her hands stroking me. It was madly sexy, fucking someone so sexually confident but deeply closeted, her whole disapproving family apparently within earshot. It was a highly underrated aphrodisiac. She lapped at me, slid her mouth and tongue in and out of me in easy rhythm with my undulating hips, until I arched my back and came hard, trying not to make too much noise.

We fell asleep without a word, intertwined and naked. I sank slowly down, down into the deepest sleep I'd had in longer than I could remember. At one point in the night, it must have been hours later, I felt Lupita get up, very slowly, trying not to jostle me, and my conscious brain hovered at the surface while I waited for her to come back to bed. A little while later she wrapped her arms and legs around me, and I slipped back down, deep into the bottom of my brain's ocean where all the eyeless creatures lived.

MUCH LATER, I WOKE UP IN VELVETY DARKNESS. THE MOON HAD set. I heard Lupita breathing softly and evenly next to me and felt a rush of euphoric happiness. The pilot light in my loins was lit, ready to ignite into high flame any second. I wanted to wake her up and molest her, but I lay very still. It occurred to me that something must have woken me up. Then I heard it, a faraway put-putting engine, like a faint high-pitched buzz saw, and I remembered that Lupita's father and uncle had been talking about some frequent trespasser on his ATV. No doubt he was riding up into the mountains right now for some dawn wildlife poaching.

Daylight was just beginning to seep around the edges of darkness, and I looked at my phone to see what time it was: 4:37. Then I saw that I had several texts. The first was from Freddy Lopez: Phone went live at 3:20 a.m. near Delphi. Couldn't get exact address. Went dead in less than a minute. Did he ever sleep? The second was from Rose Delaney's phone number. There was no text, only an attachment. It was a video.

I got out of bed, put on my T-shirt and underwear, and slipped outside, closing the door behind me as quietly as I could. On the little front porch of Lupita's cabin, I perched on the railing and leaned against a post. My heart pounding, mouth dry, I hit Play on the video. I saw a close-up of Rose's anguished face, shot from just below her. The person holding the camera stepped back a little to frame Rose on Suzie's horse with the cottonwood branches directly overhead. Rose wore a noose around her neck, and the other end of the rope was knotted and tied to the large branch above her. She looked straight into the camera and said in a shaky voice, "This is your fault, Jo. You did this. I blame you for all of it." Then she looked directly at the person who was holding the camera. "I love you. I am so sorry," she said. Her voice was despairing, harsh. "I am so, so sorry for what I did."

From off camera came a sharp sound. As the horse bolted, startled by the hard slap on its flank, Rose's expression turned from pleading abjectness to pure shock: she had clearly not expected this, had not thought the person would actually kill her; she'd thought it was just theater. The camera stayed on her, and I stared into my phone, watching her jerk as the rope pulled taut and hanged her from the tree by her neck. She twitched and writhed and died and went still, her body swaying a little. Then a hand came into the frame, wearing a plain white cotton glove, and scratched a triangle in her forearm with a knife blade. Rose's skin started to ooze blood, and then the video ended.

I watched it again, and again, and again, as if it were a vivid nightmare I had woken up from and had to replay in my mind to make it seem less real. Each time, I was horror-struck anew by Rose's accusation of me, her apology to her murderer, the bloody triangle. And no matter how much I deeply, childishly wished I could change the ending if I just watched it enough, it always went the same way.

BACK IN THE CABIN, I PULLED ON MY JEANS AND BOOTS AS QUIETLY as I could. Lupita stirred, yawned. "Come back to bed."

"I have to go."

"Stay, I'll make coffee."

"I have to work. I'll call you soon."

As I drove south and across the highway, less than a mile to the Triangle A, I thought about sending the video to Tyler. If nothing else, it would force him to finally open a homicide investigation. But I couldn't be sure he wasn't the one who'd filmed it—as crazy as that still sounded to me. I decided to wait awhile and show it to him in person when the time was right. If it really was Tyler, I wanted to be able to observe him closely while he watched it. If there was a cold-blooded killer hidden away somewhere in there, I would know it.

NINETEEN

I PARKED IN THE TRIANGLE A'S LOT NEXT TO AN UNFAMILIAR LITTLE white Kia. Before I got out of my car, there was one person I had to tell right away.

Mickey D'Ambrosio answered on the first ring. "Jo?"

"Hey. Sorry to call so early. I have some tough news for you, Mickey. It's the news you asked me to give you."

"About Rose?"

"She was killed," I said. "She didn't commit suicide. I have proof. I can't get into it any more than that, but I wanted you to know right away."

"Thank you." I heard a soft sound that was either a sob or a drunken hiccup, maybe both. "This breaks my heart, but it's just good to know she didn't do this to me."

I got out of my car and trundled over to the ranch house. Angela came to the front door in her bathrobe, her hair a loose tumble of red curls, but I barely noticed her gorgeousness this morning. I was in a welter of emotion, simultaneous new lust for Lupita and cold horror at the video I'd watched so many times I had memorized it frame by frame.

"Hey, Jo," said Angela. "Come on in, have some breakfast."

I followed her back through the house to the kitchen, where I saw Kylie and Babette at the table with the guy from the Delphi Inn the other night, Noah, the third member of their throuple. He looked like a little boy this morning. His longish, wispy dyed-black hair was tousled rather than artfully plastered to his head for maximum emo drama, and he was wearing black pajama bottoms and a gray T-shirt with "BLM" in black letters on the front. Kylie wore a pale-blue baby-doll nightie, Babette a black bathrobe. Everyone looked sleepy. I started to mentally parse out the potential interpersonal dynamics inherent in being in a three-way and bugged out at the complexity of it all. No thank you. A duo was intense enough.

I poured myself some coffee from the pot on the stove and took a seat at the table.

"How's the investigation going?" Kylie asked.

"I have a few questions for you guys, I hope that's okay."

"Of course, we'd be happy to help," said Kylie while Babette murmured something. Noah just watched me.

"There are reports of an ATV trespassing up at the Bar H Ranch, crossing their land to get to the mountains. Have you heard or seen anyone suspicious over here, anyone who doesn't belong?"

"An ATV?" said Angela. "Um, yeah, all the time. I hate to say this, but that's hardly unusual. Everyone has them. We have one here."

"I have one too," said Noah. His voice was languid. He was still watching me.

"So," I said. "In other words, you have heard one nearby recently."

"Sure," said Kylie. "Just a few nights ago, I heard someone driving somewhere out there in the desert."

"Which night? What time was it?"

"Actually I think it was more than once, a couple of nights maybe, just in this past week. I don't remember when exactly. Like, around three a.m.?"

"If you would think hard about it, Kylie, and see if you can pinpoint which nights this happened, it might be important."

"Is this somehow related to Rose?"

"I don't know," I said. "It could be."

"ATVs are terrible," said Babette. "They tear up the desert. I wish we could outlaw them."

"I don't disagree," I said. My brain was running on its own track. I was thinking about the fact that the Bar H Ranch ran along the valley and up through the foothills and abutted Rancho Bella Luna's land, where they grazed their cattle, the place where Rose was found, the proposed site for the fictitious Sunset Shadows project. There was a whole network of trails back there, and an ATV could cross the back of the Bar H from the north and reach the Rancho that way.

"Have we met before?" Noah asked, peering at me. "You look familiar."

"I saw you at the Delphi Inn the other night when I was having dinner. I heard you run CHIT now?"

"That's right," said Noah. "We've been busy over there."

My cop friend told me he arrested you guys the other night on public nudity and drunk and disorderly charges, I was very tempted to say, but did not say, to him. Instead, I asked him about the theater's current incarnation, the projects they were working on.

"We're making joyful avant-garde site-specific videos of life in Delphi for our YouTube channel," he told me.

"Videos," I remarked out loud.

"That's right." He sounded proud and defensive. "We consider ourselves the town's unofficial Chamber of Art. You know, instead of Commerce. We're creating a brand. Trying to drive destination tourism to bring people to our theater."

Admittedly, it sounded pretty harmless. It also answered my question about what the three of them had been doing the night Tyler arrested them. I pictured him corralling these three and putting their naked, spangled bodies into the back seat of his cruiser and smiled. "Sounds like fun," I said mildly.

Noah leaned his head back slightly and flared his nostrils, looking down his long nose at me. "The cop who arrested us didn't think so. The one you were having dinner with the other night. He's a bully."

"Tyler?"

"Oh, he put his hands wherever the hell he wanted to."

"Did he hurt you?"

"Only psychologically."

Internally, where no one could see, I rolled my eyes. Externally, I changed the subject. "What did you think of Rose pretending to be Navajo?"

"Rose was toxic." Noah's emotional temperature seemed to be set on cool. His face, as he spoke, was without expression. His eyes looked straight into mine with chilly clarity, no subterfuge, no affect. "Total egomaniac. She treated Kylie and Babette and Mickey like she was a cult leader with her followers. The band existed to give her a platform. She held them back musically, and I think she brainwashed them."

"She did not brainwash us," said Babette with a soft snort.

"She kind of did?" Kylie scrunched up her nose. "I mean, we always did things her way. If we questioned her choices, she would get so upset. Like lose it on us."

"She was a tyrannical monster," said Noah. "And a pathetic fake. I really hated her poetry. I hated the way she sang; she had no talent at all, no sense of phrasing, her voice sucked. Babette and Kylie are brilliant musicians. She treated them like session hacks, like she was the rock star and they were just hired to help her realize her vision."

"This is kind of true," said Kylie. "I loved Rose, but I was a little bit scared of her."

"Major power trip," said Noah.

"Bullshit," said Babette. "She was crazy, but who cares. I was just having fun."

"She had no interest in getting a record contract; she refused to even talk to any manager or producer who approached them," said Noah. "She said she wouldn't lose control or sell out. As if accepting money was bad."

Babette grinned at him, nudged him with her elbow. "Noah, she was pure."

"I would live or die for my art, but I would never refuse financial support, and I'm not afraid to collaborate or take direction." Noah was talking quietly, but I heard steel running through his voice. "Rose was a control freak who couldn't listen to criticism; she literally couldn't take it. Of course she didn't want a record contract. She didn't want a producer coming in and telling her how to sing."

"Are you going to take her place in the band now?" I asked.

He gave his girlfriends a sidelong look. "If they'll have me."

Kylie slipped her hand into his, and he squeezed it.

Babette looked stern. "You have to behave yourself."

"I'll do anything you ask," said Noah.

I stood up. "Thanks for the coffee," I said. On my way out, I turned to find all four of them staring after me, silent. "Kylie, if you remember the time and day . . ."

"I'll let you know," she said. "I promise."

As I walked past the Art Barn to Rose's casita, I heard little toenails clicking on the flagstones behind me. So Ophelia had been spared the trip to the shelter, at least for now. I was strangely glad to see the little troll again.

"Hello, little trooper," I said. "You look thirsty."

She followed me into the casita and sniffed at the water bowl on the floor. I emptied it in the bathroom sink and filled it up again with fresh water. She lapped at it, then jumped up and lay on Rose's bed, watching me. Sitting at the worktable, I powered up Rose's computer. Slowly and methodically, I went through every single thing on the laptop, every photograph, every file. I didn't know what I was looking for, but I felt a strong sense of urgency, a hunch that something I had missed before might tell me something I didn't already know.

As I searched, a little mouse scratched at the floor of my mind, maybe something someone had said, something I'd heard but hadn't paid sufficient attention to. On the other hand, maybe it was just a mouse.

As the morning wore on, I steeped myself in Rose's life, her presence, her language and images and history. Scrolling through her bookmarks, I found and opened her Duolingo account. She had been studying Navajo. I clicked on a lesson and heard a Native man or woman speaking this ancient, complex language for the benefit of anyone who cared to learn it. The voice sounded elderly, hoarse. I listened to some Diné phrases, trying to say them, pretending I was Rose learning this language in order to take on the identity of one of its speakers.

In her documents folder was a file called NEW WORK. I clicked on it and started scrolling through what I guessed she'd been writing while she was up here doing this residency. These new poems were completely different, her former pretentious plaints to her purported Navajo foremothers giving way to something blunter and fiercer, written to someone she called alternately "red-lipped Narcissus," "cruel beauty," and "heartless young god." The poem felt like a heartbroken aria of unresolved desire and profound pain. "I walk in beauty," the most recent poem ended, "to forget you, to forget you, to forget you." Chay, I assumed.

I opened a zip file marked FAMILY PICS and started clicking through photographs taken of old analog snapshots. There were a few of Rose's dad, Jimmy Delaney, standing on a beach boardwalk, suntanned, his black hair slicked back from his forehead, decked out in 1990s summer duds, aviator shades and white chinos and a pink polo shirt, boat shoes with no socks. Beside him stood preteen Rose in a glittery gold tube top, denim miniskirt, and wedge sandals. She wore blue eye shadow and pink lipstick and looked sullen, face turned away from the camera. In the next photo, one of her dad's arms was slung around his daughter's slight shoulders, the other around the waist of a pretty brunette woman with huge boobs and a salacious-looking grin. There were a couple more daddy-daughter shots, presumably taken by Jimmy's girlfriend, or whatever she was. I focused on Rose's obvious misery, her gawky preadolescent body displayed so frankly in these clothes. At home in Delphi, on weekends and after school, she generally wore overall shorts, sneakers, and rugby shirts. Tomboy clothes, like me. I knew she dressed differently in New Jersey because she brought all these duds back with her and trotted them out for various occasions, a school dance, a party. I looked at her father, a creature of that place and time, fast, easy, nineties tristate money and all sorts of underhanded ways to get it. It occurred to me that Rose's brother Jason should have been the son of a Jersey mobster instead of a doctor like Leo Gold. Jason must have been jealous of Rose's summers in the East, going to shindigs with her rich, sleazy dad. It was just a hunch, but I bet I was right.

AFTER A COUPLE OF HOURS, I CLOSED THE COMPUTER AND STRETCHED. Feeling stiff and sluggish from sitting so long, I went out to my car and fetched my workout clothes from my gym bag and went back to Rose's casita and put them on. Ophelia watched me from Rose's bed, her head cocked.

Leaving her to snooze in the shade on the patio, I set off at a good clip. Once I warmed up, my body felt zingy and supercharged, thanks to my night with Lupita and the shock of that video. The day was cool, overcast. But no rain fell, despite faraway lightning flashes and thunder in ominous charcoal clouds. I pounded down the Triangle A's dirt driveway to the highway, ran across it and headed down on the shoulder toward Delphi, then took the old stagecoach road that disappeared into the desert.

After a mile or so, I turned onto the hunting track that went up into the foothills, followed that for a while, leaping over rocks and ruts, springing off the hairpin turns, slingshotting myself up steep inclines. At a crossroads, I swerved onto another track that headed north toward the Bar H ranchland. I pounded along, slipping through barbed-wire fences, climbing over cow gates, staying on course, my sneakers slapping the hard clay earth.

When I hit the road that ran up into the hills, I stopped, hands on my hips, breathing hard, sweat trickling between my boobs and down the small of my back. A few fat drops of rain hit the top of my head like the first few kernels of corn exploding in the pan, and then the sky let loose with a frenzy of popping. The air sizzled alive with the smell of plants and rocks thirstily sucking up the warm water.

Out of nowhere, prickling the surface of my arms, came that eerie sense of being watched, the preternatural awareness that something sentient was stalking me, animal or human, and I was in their sights.

My hair plastered itself to my skull as water streamed into my eyes. I looked up and down the valley, scanning the expanse of it, the cluster of Bar H Ranch buildings and the mesquite grove below, and to the south, the Delphi water tower at the highest point in town, and the town itself sprawled downhill from and all around it. I turned and peered through the rain up the hill's steep flank above me, the raw red dirt track climbing the foothills into the mountains, straight up at a fifty-degree angle, cresting the ridge and disappearing into the heavy, dark, monsoon clouds as rainwater flowed down the track in runnels.

Just as I was getting ready to run again, I heard the loud crack of a rifle report echoing around the valley. I froze, my ear trying to gauge exactly where the shot had come from. Then I heard a second crack, this one preceded a split second before by a whizz and thump close by my ear. I whipped my head around and saw a neat little hole where a bullet had lodged itself in a barrel cactus just up the slope from me, not three feet away. There was no doubt: that was meant for me.

This was technically not the first time I'd been shot at; I was trained for this in cop school. But it was the first time it had ever happened with real bullets. Instinct took over, and I turned and bolted back the way I'd come as fast as I could go, rocketing down the wet clay, slipping and panting hard, zigzagging and ducking to minimize their target surface. As I ran, I braced myself for the next crack of the rifle, anticipating the hot flash of pain as the bullet ripped through my skin. But it never came.

By the time I got back down to the safety of civilization, the rain had stopped and the sun had come out and was evaporating all the water into a low, drifting mist. I fetched my go bag from my car, then headed back to Rose's casita, soaking wet, splashed with red mud, heart pounding in my skull. I stripped and sat hunched over naked and shivering on the bed, staring at the floor in shock. Someone had taken a potshot at me. I had no idea whether they were trying to kill me or simply scare me, but it hardly mattered. Getting shot at was terrifying.

Sensing my agitation, Ophelia jumped up and started licking my face, my arm, my neck, anything she could get her little troll tongue on, trying to soothe me, or at least distract me. It worked. I smiled at her and petted her head, and she lolled her little tongue out, panting, and smiled back.

"Good dog," I said. "It's okay. I'm okay."

I took a long, hot shower, lathering up with Rose's organic herbal shampoo and conditioner, then dried myself on her towel and changed into a clean bra and T-shirt and underwear from my go bag, sliding back into my jeans and boots. Ophelia watched me the entire time with an anticipatory cock of her round little bug head, and when I closed up the casita again and headed to my car, she trotted along with me and tried to hop up into the driver's seat before I could get in. I let her in the back passenger door. She rode in the back seat, relaxing back on her haunches, eyes slit shut.

"Don't get any ideas," I told her. "I don't do relationships."

Before the shots, as I ran, I had been chewing over an unresolved question, the fact that, along with negating my entire existence, Rose's journals hadn't mentioned her summers in Trenton with her father. It was time to get some answers.

I parked in my courtyard spot by the Rancho main house and headed down to the studios and found Solo arranging an assortment of his bowls on a big table in his cleaned, tidied workroom, getting ready for the memorial. I barged right in.

"Hello there," he said mildly.

"How much do you know about Rose's father?"

"Jimmy Delaney?" He looked surprised, but he rolled with it, the way he always rolled with everything.

"Wasn't he some kind of mobster?" My voice sounded loud, but I didn't care.

"He ran a waste management company in Trenton, New Jersey. You do the math."

"What else do you know about him?"

He hesitated. "Rose confided some things. She asked me not to tell anyone."

"This is no time to keep secrets, Solo. I need to know whatever it is."

He set a large, round bowl on the table and slid a white cloth handkerchief out of his hip pocket and rubbed it so the blue glaze shone. "I know a few things," he said. "I know Jimmy was abusive to Laura when they were married. Rose saw it happen. He drank, he had a temper, and Laura would get on his nerves with her drama. So he whaled on her. That's how Rose told it to me. She said she was glad when they left New Jersey and moved out here when she was little."

I nodded. This made sense. "Because of the custody agreement, she had to visit him in the summers till she turned eighteen. So she spent July and August in Trenton with him. I missed her. She didn't come back until right before school started."

"What do you know about those visits?"

"It sounded fun out there," I said. "She told me about hanging out on the boardwalk when he took her to the Atlantic City casinos. He took her shopping for outfits to wear to glamorous-sounding parties up in Philly. As far as I could tell, her dad spoiled her. She always seemed depressed and kind of distant when she got back. I figured it was because she was disappointed to be back in boring southern Arizona, and because she missed her father. But I'm getting the feeling now that there was stuff she wasn't telling me. And I think you know what it was."

Solo opened his little fridge and handed me a beer and opened his own and took a swig and wiped his mouth on the hankie. "Yes," he said. "You're right."

I swallowed. "Tell me."

Out it came, just like that. "Rose's father sexually abused her. She didn't tell me until a couple of years ago, right after Jimmy died, when it was too late to do anything about it."

Oh God, poor Rose. I felt a sharp pang of sorrow for my old best friend. And I felt so stupid. I should have known somehow, should have guessed. "Why am I just learning this now?"

"I was sworn to secrecy. As long as she was alive, I couldn't tell anyone else, I promised I wouldn't, it was her truth to share when she was ready. I'm only telling you now because she's dead, and you're investigating. If it can help you figure out why she died, my breach of confidence will be justified." He looked at me, his face wrenched. "And God, Justine, it's been agony keeping this to myself. Watching her life go off the rails. She wouldn't ever see a therapist. I begged her to. She said she found solace in her work. I have felt so helpless. It's hard to know something like that. It's painful."

"Solo, she never said a word to me. The whole time we were friends."

"She was ashamed, she said. She felt it was somehow her own fault."

"So no one ever knew, all those years? She dealt with it alone? She kept it all inside? How did she survive?" I was hyperventilating with shock and rage. "Her father *raped* her?"

"It happened the last summer she was there, she said. But it all started early. The grooming. The sexualized dynamic."

"What do you mean?"

"She said even when she was little, she always felt like his date for the summer. A mini girlfriend. Like he paraded her around, showed her off. Made sure she looked a certain way. Sexy."

"How? In what sense?"

"He took her shopping and dressed her. She described it as Jersey mob girl."

"Right," I said. Now that I knew the truth, everything made sense; in a horrible, nightmarish way, it all was clear now. "She brought all those clothes home with her. I remember I was jealous. A seven-year-old with glittery tube tops and miniskirts and platform shoes."

"When she was a little girl, he started taking her to dinners and parties as his date, and he always gave her some of his beer; he poured some of every beer he drank into a small glass for her. But the worst part . . ." He shook his head and pinched the bridge of his nose between two fingers.

"What's the worst part?" I asked with visceral horror.

"She had to sleep in his bed with him. He required her to."

Oh Rose. I wanted to pound my head on the floor. "She had to sleep with him?"

"She told me it was like the way you'd sleep with a dog, he wanted a warm body next to him. He didn't like sleeping alone."

"Jesus," I said.

"Also, about the Navajo thing, Rose identifying as Native," said Solo. "It reminded me that she said that her dad was Black Irish, and she looked like him, and he taught her to be proud of that."

"Black Irish," I said. "But did he have any Native heritage? Navajo in particular?"

"Jimmy Delaney?" Solo looked baffled.

"I didn't think so," I said. "Oh Solo, why didn't Rose ever tell her mother about this? Does she know?"

"She couldn't tell Laura," he said. "When it was all going on, Rose didn't want to upset her mother or force her to face Jimmy in court again. The first time, the divorce and custody battle, he apparently trotted out all Laura's 'histrionic behavior,' as he called it, and the judge was a sexist prick who agreed that she was crazy. Laura almost lost custody entirely, but luckily all Jimmy wanted were summers. So that's why Rose didn't tell her anything. When she told me all this a few years ago and swore me to secrecy, she said she felt like there was no point in upsetting Laura now. Rose was dealing with it, she said. She had it under control."

I looked at Solo and he looked back at me.

"Thank you for telling me," I said. My mouth was dry.

He looked stricken. "I hope it helps your case. Now that it's too late to help Rose."

We sat in silence for a while. I finished my beer, and Solo took the bottle and put it in the recycling bin. Everyone knew that recycling was a scam and a crock in Delphi, but they all did it anyway, maybe hoping it might turn out to be real, like the Easter Bunny.

When Rose came back from Trenton before freshman year, only months before our rupture, she had seemed weirdly angry at me. I'd forgotten about this until now. She lashed out at me for nothing, nitpicked my eating noises, jumped if my arm brushed hers, meanly criticized my clothes. I felt as if she'd outgrown me, like she thought I was a provincial doofus. That went on for that whole first semester of ninth grade. I thought maybe now that we'd started high school, she was pushing me away because I wasn't cool enough for her. Rose, in her slinky minidresses from back East, her white go-go boots and platform shoes.

So I might have flung my date with Tyler at her in mean, small triumph to show her that at least he liked me, even if she didn't any-more.

That's what I did. I remembered it all now. I used Tyler to show Rose that I wasn't a loser.

She was an underage girl who was being sexually groomed by her father. She couldn't tell me, she could only pick at me and push me away. Instead of confronting her and demanding to know what was going on with her, like a real friend would, I flung my date with Tyler in her face. To her, that really was a sickening betrayal. Never mind that she had never told me she liked him. She could see my triumph, and she took it to mean I thought I'd beaten her. And that was why she never stopped hating me.

What was wrong with me? Why couldn't my best friend in the world trust me enough to tell me her secrets? What kind of person was I that she had been in so much pain right under my nose and I couldn't see it?

"Poor Rose," I said. "Oh, my God."

"I know," said Solo with a slight sigh, which for him was a palpable gust of grief.

TWENTY

SINCE THE 1970S, WHEN THIS PLACE WAS FOUNDED, BELLA LUNA has hosted a "Luna Llena" party once a month on the full moon—open studios, beer and wine, a live band or a jam session of the resident musicians, everyone gathered in the courtyard of the artists' studio complex. It's the most important, and often the only, big social event here. People get their work-in-progress ready to show, bring food to share, invite friends and neighbors, get a little gussied up. It's an excuse for all the communal loners and solitary souls to commingle and have some fun together. The Luna Llena parties also serve as memorials when someone close to the community dies. They'll probably keep up this tradition until every last one of them is gone and there's no one left to throw the parties anymore.

At five o'clock, with my gaze set on X-ray, my ears attuned to subaural frequencies, I walked with my mother from her house over to the studio courtyard, carrying our offerings. My mother had the bottle of Rioja I'd brought tucked into her arm, while I lugged the heavy pot of her signature Arizona beef-and-bean chili, secret ingredient dark chocolate. It smelled so good I wanted to tip the entire pot into my mouth before we even got there. My mother would, of course, not be eating one morsel, just crudités and sparkling water for her.

The courtyard was buzzing and humming, people setting up tables in the shade on the terrace, Solo behind the bar stocking the fridge with beer, Pablo taking bottles of wine out of boxes and setting them on the bar top, a few others by the long food table arranging compostable paper plates, napkins, and cutlery. I hadn't seen a lot of these people in months, so I got swept into hellos and hugs and how-are-yous, passed from one avidly welcoming old character to the next until my face hurt from smiling and I was sweating in the hot sun. Dina the filmmaker, Pablo the sculptor, Glenda the whatever-she-did, Celia and Tom Dixon the organic gardeners from across the road, and then I got a glimpse of Laura and Leo bringing a large urn of branches and flowers.

It felt like a party, although the mood was somber and subdued out of respect for Rose and her family and a collective sense of shocked disbelief at what had happened. Still, also in honor of Rose, all the old folks had put on their cheeriest finery—print sundresses and Hawaiian shirts, guayaberas and caftans. They looked like a flock of large, sad, but colorful jungle birds. The table of food was crammed full with a potluck hodgepodge of homemade offerings from salads to casseroles to cakes. All the studio doors around the courtyard were open to let people mill around inside, gawking at the work, most of which had discreet price tags on the wall next to them in case anyone was buying. All in all, it looked like what it was: a full-moon party after a death.

Marianne got instantly waylaid by Carmen Ellis, a rich arts patron who loved to motor up to Bella Luna's parties from her Tucson mansion to rub noses with the local bohemians. She was always trying to get my mother to paint her portrait, even though Marianne emphatically did not paint portraits. Disturbingly to me, my mother always turns into a little girl in crowds and at parties, the neglected child she used to be decades ago, as if she's correcting the damage, soaking up any attention and courting as much of it as she can get. As far as I can tell, it's never enough. "Gee, I'm so flattered you keep asking me," I heard her say in a child's voice to Mrs. Ellis, breathy and coy. Cringing, I headed to the bar alone.

"Hey there," said Solo, handing me a cold bottle. "There's a bunch of kids making trouble by the stables, I believe."

Interested to see what constituted "a bunch of kids making trouble" around here, I sauntered down to the horse paddock with my beer, too warm in my jeans and boots, glad I was wearing my best T-shirt, which was blue-green and fit me nicely, or so I'd been told by an admirer a while back. I saw the gaggle of people hanging out by the tack shed before they saw me, and I recognized quite a few of them: Jason and a couple of older Bella Luna kids, now in their late thirties. I saw Noah standing with Angela, Kylie, Babette, and Mickey, who was wearing spiffy linen shorts and a button-down white shirt, and who gave me a wan little wave when they saw me. Lupita, looking foxy in a tomato-red shirtdress and flat leather sandals, stood off to the side with her cousin Tono, both of them inspecting the horses and talking softly.

No one was making trouble that I could see. Solo just had an odd way of putting things sometimes.

As I approached the group, everyone turned to look at me, hands shading eyes. I headed for Lupita. Her black hair was loosely piled on her head with a clip, her face was unadorned by makeup, and she wore no jewelry. We smiled at each other. There was something guarded in her face. She was with a family member. Of course. I got it right away and tried to telegraph a neutral friendliness.

Tono Gonzalez looked younger than his cousin by a few years, a tall, serious guy in a white button-down shirt and bolo tie, khaki pants, and cowboy boots. "Hi, Tono," I said.

"Hello," said Tono. "I am so sorry. My condolences."

"He was the one who found Rose," Lupita told me. "We came to pay our respects."

"That must have been terrible," I said.

He looked upset at the memory. "Honestly, at first I thought it was a bunch of plastic trash bags, caught in the branches. Until I got closer. I'm sure I will remember that image of her for the rest of my life."

"Me too," I said.

"We're only here for a minute, we're on our way to church," Lupita told me.

"Church," I echoed, disappointed. "On Tuesday?"

She looked proudly at her cousin. "Tono is the junior pastor, he's leading Bible group tonight. We'll say a special prayer for Rose. It's good to see you."

I wanted badly to ask if she wanted to meet up later, but I didn't dare in front of her cousin.

As I watched them leave, someone behind me called, "Jo." I turned, and there was Tyler, movie-star handsome in a white embroidered cowboy shirt and blue khakis. I was surprised to see him here. He had brought his wife. I nodded at Linda. It was generally awkward those rare times when she and I met. This time was no different: she smiled tightly and said, "Hello, Jo" with the slightest edge in her voice. She was serious and self-contained, with very pretty, straight, shiny black hair and huge brown eyes. She had been Linda Martinez when we were in cop school, back when she worked at the reception desk at the academy. All the male students had crushes on her. All the female students thought she was a bitch. She ignored almost all of us, especially me, except for Tyler. Now, she kept him on a short leash, but it wasn't short enough.

I found her very dignified and touching, actually. She was dressed in a tailored navy-blue dress with a white collar, low-heeled pumps, a small cross on a delicate gold chain around her neck, and a gold stud in each earlobe, as if she were going to Mass. She was honoring a dead woman she hadn't even known, not realizing that Rose had been her husband's mistress. And I guessed by the absence of kids that she was even paying for a babysitter to do this.

Her attitude toward me was hostile and wary; I sensed how much she wanted to wipe me out entirely from his past, and possibly also from the planet. I could imagine the thermonuclear explosion if she ever found out about her husband and Rose. Perversely, I liked Linda for her propriety and her stubborn adherence to old-fashioned norms. At least she stood for something. I wished we could have been at least cordial. But Tyler was not the kind of man who inspired alliances among the women who loved him. He was too sheerly beautiful for that. He made women want to possess him. Not me, not anymore. But Linda didn't know that.

I wandered over to stand in the shade of a mesquite tree with the Triangle A crew and Mickey. We drank our beers and agreed that this was a very strange day, a strange thing to have to commemorate. Noah wore a shiny silver jumpsuit and pointy-toed rocker boots. He was bouncing gently on his heels as if he were warming up for a race, intoning soft "mi-mi-mi, la-la-las" under his breath.

In a clump, we "kids" drifted up to join our elders in the courtyard to say hello and get more drinks. It was nice in a way to be folded into the group like this. Whenever I was at Bella Luna in the past, I unconsciously braced myself against that never-ending, dark, unasked-for antipathy from Rose. Our mutual fixation on each other had colored everything for me here. If she were alive and here, I'd feel her smoldering spitefully at me. With Rose gone, the entire tenor of this place had changed for me, neutral and free of conflict. I felt a little lonely, to be honest.

I moved slowly along the terrace, dissolving into the background, watching. Leo sat at a table with a small group of his old cronies, Pablo and George and Tom, all of them talking intently, still with important things to say after almost half a century together. Leo looked like his old normal self, but I could see his friends leaning in to hear him when he spoke, as if he didn't have the energy anymore to be fully audible, or the capacity to make sense. They looked worriedly puzzled at whatever he was saying. I saw Patty put an arm around Laura's shoulders and lead her to a bench.

I stared at Laura, seeing her anew in light of what Solo had just told me, confirming my direst fears about what happened in Trenton. Did Laura not suspect anything when her young daughter came back from visiting her physically abusive ex-husband with a suitcase full of little hooker outfits? She hadn't protected Rose at all. In fact, Rose had protected her. I was outraged on Rose's behalf all over again.

I cornered Jason by the drinks table, feeling protected by the benign presence of Solo, who was bartending, and forced him to acknowledge me.

"I'm so sorry about your sister," I said. I felt like forcing the issue, even though I knew it wouldn't get me anywhere. "I really am."

Jason actually rolled his eyes, just a flick, but I caught it. I flashed on the video of Rose telling me she would die thinking it was my fault. Had Jason shot it? Was it his hand that had made Bilbo bolt, and scratched the triangle in her arm? Was he the driver of the ATV, early in the morning? I stared at his face, searching for any flicker of guilt or nervousness. But I felt myself blocked by his pure iciness.

The truth, which had been clawing at the back of my mind all day and which I was trying very hard not to face, was that no one benefited more from Rose's death than Tyler. Not even Jason. Rose's protests of the Sunset Shadows land deal had hardly been effective. Everyone in her family had signed already. Tyler, on the other hand, was having an affair with Rose and stood to lose his marriage, and possibly custody of his kids, if Linda found out. Maybe he decided to bring me in on it because he knew that I trusted him, and he could easily manipulate that trust to make me help him pin her murder on someone else, like Jason.

I tried to imagine Tyler killing someone. It was hard for me to envision. I'd never seen that violence in him, that desperation. Sure, he'd caved when wads of drug money were thrown at him, but he didn't strike me as someone with the soul of a murderer. The person who shot that video was methodical, cold, and purposeful. Tyler was emotional and weak. It didn't add up.

But as crazy as it seemed, there was no avoiding it: Tyler was the only person who had sufficient motive to kill Rose. His life was vastly improved by her death. He was also the only person who knew I was staying at the Apache Motel that first night, when my anonymous stalker called the phone in my room. And he plausibly could have been at every location where Rose's phone had turned up. In other words, he had means, motive, and opportunity.

Could he have been the one who shot at me today, trying to scare me off? I had to be more careful around him, keep him close, but not tip him off that I suspected him. If he had done it, and had sent me the video of Rose's death, the fact that I hadn't brought it to his attention yet might spook him. I would have to do something about that, and soon.

"JUSTINE," CALLED LAURA AS SHE CAUGHT SIGHT OF ME FROM THE shaded bench where she was sitting.

I went over to sit next to her. I looked closely at her face under the broad-brimmed straw hat she wore, finely woven, with a black band. Her eyes were huge and shadowed. Her cheekbones were as sharp as blades. I felt grudging compassion for her. She had failed her daughter badly, but she was old now, and so vulnerable. "How are you holding up, Laura?"

"I've been wanting to ask you, have you heard anything new about Rose? We haven't had a chance to talk. Is there anything at all you can tell me? I feel that if I can understand this, even a little, I can survive it."

I said with great care, "I am working on it night and day."

Laura didn't answer. Her eyes didn't waver from mine. She waited, as if I had more to say.

"How is Ben?" I asked her.

"They're still keeping him in a medically induced coma. There is no telling what degree of permanent damage there will be."

"Have you seen him?"

"We're going to visit him tomorrow. His primary doctor told me it might be good for him to hear my voice. Jason and I are driving up to Phoenix in the morning."

Just then, Rose's old bandmates moved onto a makeshift stage on the upper terrace, where a small cluster of mikes and amps had been set up. Kylie picked up a guitar and strummed some chords, Babette strapped on a bass and plucked a couple of low notes to test the volume, and Mickey seated themselves behind the drum kit. Noah stepped out of the crowd and stood in front, grasped the mike, and said in a sultry whisper, "Rose, we love you, we miss you, rest in peace." What a hypocrite, I thought. As we all held our drinks up in a toast, he nodded to the others, and the music started. Noah sang in a sultry falsetto; this wasn't the Sisters of Percy's usual dance music, it was a bramble of sound, repetitive and lush, with a hard, trancey drumbeat. Noah looked totally stoked to be up there, performing with his girlfriends.

While the band went through their set, I moved through the crowd. Someone had made a huge vat of boozy punch, potent and delicious, with passion fruit and guava juices and tequila and who knew what else. I got myself a glass. The music ended, and we all started toasting the air as various people delivered short speeches about Rose. As the band started in on their second set, I made chitchat with Connie and Felix and their three young interns from Catalina Press. I greeted Lena Duby and a couple of Rose's other former academic colleagues when they arrived. All the while, I kept a bead on Tyler, aware of where he was, whom he was talking to. I looked for an opportunity to get him alone, but every time I looked over, Linda was at his side.

It was almost dark when a few students from Saguaro Early College showed up: Chay and four others of varying genders and races, all of them looking very young and sensitive and a little shy. I caught Chay's eye and waved at him. He waved back a little awkwardly, but didn't approach me. After spilling his guts to me so freely, he seemed to feel a need to keep his distance. They stood in a clump together on the terrace with glasses of punch. Once they'd drunk enough to vanquish their timidity, they started going in and out of the studios, chattering among themselves, curious about the artwork. I eyed them, wondering if Rose had seduced any of the other kids she taught, wondering how they all really felt about her.

I lost track of them entirely for a while, and when I walked into Pablo's studio, there they all were, looking at his newest enormous sculpture, the only thing in the room. It was a gigantic steel agave plant, stylized and abstract, with sharp spears shooting out from a solid trunk and tapering to needle points, coated with an acid-green iridescent glaze that glistened like oil spilled in a puddle. There was a cordon around it so people wouldn't get stabbed by it or have their eyes poked out.

"This is so beautiful," said Chay to me when he saw me. He appeared a little startled at the sight of me, wary but friendly enough.

"And dangerous," I said. "Like most things in the desert."

He smiled at this, just slightly. "Thanks for inviting us."

"I'm glad you came."

I left Rose's students to admire the treacherous steel agave and started wending my way through all the studios, giving myself a little tour of everyone's artwork. As always, I was impressed by the industry of these old artists, still going strong in their old age. I noticed how varied their work was, still, even after almost fifty years of working and living so closely together, how distinctive their respective styles were. I didn't even need to check the placards, I instantly knew whose paintings and photos and sculptures and ceramics were whose. I spent some time looking at my mother's weirdly gorgeous flesh-plant watercolors and ink drawings, her aloe plants with their hairy strongman arms, agaves with sharp talon-like fingernails, thinking about what a mystery Marianne had always been to me, the one cipher I could never figure out, the great unsolved case of my life. I might have been a little tipsy myself.

BACK IN THE COURTYARD, THERE WAS STILL SOME DAYLIGHT LEFT, but the shadows lay long on the ground, and the atmosphere felt a little warmer now, with music and booze and the release of all being together. Now that the music and speeches and toasts were over, the air had quieted down, everyone gathered to sit in little groups at the tables under the covered part of the terrace. Pablo lit the fire pit by the kilns into a nice blaze that gave off mesquite-smelling smoke. Solo and Patty fired up the grill and threw burger patties and hot dogs on it. A few of the old-timers took over the makeshift stage with acoustic instruments and sang earnest old folk songs.

As twilight started to shade into indigo, I found myself sobering up a little, standing on the terrace by the studios, slightly apart from everyone. I kept an eye on Tyler, unable to shake the feeling that he was covering his ass by being here. He rested his hand on the small of his wife's back as they talked to Solo and Glenda, two people he neither knew nor cared about. While I spied on him, I eavesdropped on a conversation to my left—a few of the resident artists telling one another what geniuses they all were and how important their work was to the history of art, the usual ego-boosting hot air everyone had always liked to blow at one another around here. "You've elevated folk art to real greatness," Patty was saying to Suzie. "It's remarkable how you've blended mythology and representation." I didn't look, but I would have bet Suzie was glowing, even preening. They all did this at every single full-moon open-studio party through the ages.

As if he'd felt me staring at him, as if my gaze had unintentionally pulled him to me, Tyler ditched his wife, left her trapped listening to Solo telling one of his old stories. He approached me from the right and stood next to me, looking out at the crowd with me from the relative invisibility of this spot.

"Hey," I said without looking at him.

"Hey there."

"Surprised to see you here," I said. "With Linda."

"Rose was an old childhood friend."

Our shoulders weren't touching. We didn't look at each other. I was talking quietly to the air in front of my nose. No use pussyfooting around. We only had a second before Linda would sense us talking and put a quick end to it.

"I got a text from Rose's phone early this morning. It was a video of her death. Someone filmed it. She was murdered, Tyler."

"What? Why didn't you tell me?"

"I'm telling you now."

"Can I see it?"

"Not now and not here. I'll be at the Apache Motel later, same room as last time."

"I'll meet you there."

Linda waved sharply at Tyler, motioning him to join her as she headed for the drinks table. I watched him go, then parked myself in a chair and leaned back against the wall. My heart was pounding slowly. He had fallen right into my little trap, the galoot, he'd let on that he knew my room number at the Apache Motel. So he must be my crank caller. I went back over every encounter I'd had with him, starting with him retching next to Rose's body. If he'd killed her, he ought to win an Oscar. I had underestimated him in so many ways.

The strings of lights along the eaves of the buildings had been turned on. The full moon was rising over the roof of the summer kitchen. I felt my eyes slide half shut like a cat's. My mind stayed totally alert, but my body relaxed into the drifting mesquite smoke and the soft plunking of guitars and the faraway chattering of many voices and the aftereffects of a day filled with boozy emotion ranging from withheld to bursting. It was pleasant, like being underwater, every-thing around me muffled.

My phone buzzed in the right butt pocket of my jeans. I fished it out. It was a text from Freddy Lopez: Phone went live at 6:48 for forty seconds, Delphi again.

Instantly tense, I scanned the courtyard, focusing one by one on everyone, seeing who was sitting where and with whom. Not one person had a phone out that I could see. Laura was sitting with Suzie and Patty. Jason stood by the fire pit with Kylie and Noah and Babette, and Mickey was talking to Leo and his pals on the terrace. Chay and the other college kids thronged the food table, hoovering up the remnants of the potluck. Chad and Phil had evidently ingratiated themselves with Solo at the bar; the three of them appeared to be deep in conversation. And Linda was talking to my mother, of all people.

Where was Tyler? I leapt up and strolled around, looking for him. A small pack of ranch dogs went running by, Ophelia in their midst. They all looked happy and delighted with this fresh summer night.

My phone buzzed with another text. This one was from Tyler. Found something. Meet me in the middle studio with the huge steel sculpture.

I crossed the courtyard and went into Pablo's studio, aware that I could be walking into a trap, preparing to defend myself. It was dark in here; the only light was from the fire pit and strings of lights outside. I could see Tyler's outline in the dimness, standing in the middle of the room.

"Got your text," I said as I hit the light. "Why are you in the dark?"

The room flooded with brightness, and I blinked. Tyler stood in the middle of the room, staring at something right in front of him. He looked shocked.

"Tyler?"

He didn't move. It took a couple of seconds before I realized he wasn't moving because he was impaled on the huge steel agave sculpture, three of whose razor-sharp, thin, pointed spikes had been thrust through his chest. His arms hung limp, and his eyes were fixed on nothing.

His phone was on the floor. Near it, blood congealed at his feet in a dark shiny pool. He was dead.

"Tyler." It came out as a croak. My heartbeat crushed my breath in my throat, but there was no time to react or lose my shit. As I dialed 911, I looked around in the few seconds it took the dispatcher to answer. I forced myself to examine Tyler's position on the spike, the viscosity of his blood on the floor, the waxy paleness of his skin, the direction his eyes had frozen in. The way things looked, he had been dead for a few minutes. So the person who had killed him had sent me that text. They had wanted me to find him, to walk in and see this.

I thought fast, piecing it all together. The studio had a back door that led to the parking lot. Whoever had done this could have come through the back or simply walked in the door I'd come through. So they had Rose's phone and had sent Tyler a text when the phone went briefly live, telling him to come in here. Of course he obeyed right away, wanting to find out who'd sent the video. When they had Tyler in here alone, they must have positioned him in front of the sculpture in just the right spot, with his back to it, caught him off guard enough to shove him very hard into the spikes with enough force to pierce his heart. He had died instantly, the expression of total surprise frozen on his face because he hadn't been expecting this from the person who had killed him.

He had known this person. Whoever the fuck they were.

I bent down, my eye caught by something, and saw a small triangle scratched into his inner forearm, seeping blood.

"What is the nature of your emergency?" came the dispatcher's voice after two rings.

I hardly knew where to start.

TWENTY-ONE

IN THE WHIRLWIND THAT FOLLOWED, I BECAME A PERSON OF IN-
terest in the FBI's investigation of Tyler's murder, as both a suspect
and a witness. The investigator, Doug Kepler, was pale and expres-
sionless, short and slight with a bland face, buzz-cut white hair,
mild blue eyes, and a flat voice I had to work hard not to be fooled
or soothed by. Our lengthy conversation took place downtown the
day after Tyler died. I spent almost five hours sitting in a hard chair
in Kepler's office at the FBI field office on Commerce Park Loop. As
I told him everything I knew, I understood how self-incriminating it
all might strike an astute and intelligent listener. My old frenemy had
apparently killed herself, but maybe I had killed her when I learned
that my old lover had been sleeping with her. After I was hired to investigate Rose's death, I killed Tyler in an ongoing fit of jealousy, and
then I was the first on the scene, the one who discovered the body. If
this were *Peyton Place* or *Days of Our Lives*, I would absolutely have
been the double murderer.

But this was not a soap opera, and I was not a vindictive ex-
girlfriend. I was an innocent bystander, one of the grieving wounded
left behind, and an investigator myself. I hoped Agent Kepler might
make the connections and see the big picture I was missing. Prefac-
ing it with the context in which it was sent, and my own innocence,
I showed him the video I'd received from Rose's missing phone: her
accusation of me, the murderer's gloved hand slapping the horse to
make her fall to her death, etching the triangle in her flesh, identical

to Tyler's. I told him everything I'd learned in the course of my brief inquiry into Rose's death, including Tyler's and Rose's and my entire history, the subjects of Rose's poetry collections, and Solo's description of Rose's Trenton summers with her father. I told him about the mysterious local ATV rider, the Gonzalez family's relinquishment of their grazing lease on the disputed piece of Rancho land, the missing hiking boots, Suzie's horse, the fallout of Rose's affair with Chay and her long-standing ongoing Navajo pretense, her various friendships, Tyler's dubious relationship to money, his marriage, his affair with Rose. I revealed what I knew about Sunset Shadows, the theory that Jason Gold was a scam artist and the fact that Tyler had sunk all his savings into what he had been sure was a Ponzi scheme, that Jason and Rose had been fighting about it, that Tyler had confronted Jason in the Innovative Integrations office the day before he was killed. I told him that Jason had been in Delphi the morning Rose died; he had also been at Rose's memorial the night Tyler died. I told him that someone had shot at me while I was on a run back in the mountains that same day and offered to take him out into the desert and locate the bullet, which I imagined was still lodged in that barrel cactus, so ballistics experts could examine it. I looked forward to revisiting the scene in the stalwart company of FBI agents, but to my disappointment, Kepler didn't take the bait.

As I talked, cold air blew from an overhead vent, and a piece of paper on Agent Kepler's desk flapped gently. I heard myself sound alternately angry, sad, and bewildered. I drank so much water, requested so many bathroom breaks to pee, I felt as if my body were demanding a constant stream of hydration to fuel the emotional flow of words emerging from my mouth.

"Thank you, Ms. Bailen," said Agent Kepler when I finally ran out of things to reveal. "I'll call you if we have any further questions."

IT WAS ALMOST THREE O'CLOCK ON WEDNESDAY WHEN I WAS RE-leased, free and presumed innocent, back to the wild, back to the enormous question mark burning a hole in my head. A triangle has three sides. I stood by my car in the sunny afternoon heat, blinking around the parking garage, wondering what was going to happen next. It had been an odd sort of relief to be questioned by Agent Kepler, to let someone else drive, to spill what I knew. But now I felt a little sheepish about how much I didn't know and mildly hungover from my hours-long verbal information dump.

And I also felt queasy and nervous. As I drove myself to my office, I could not shake the certainty that I was next. I was such a clear and obvious target, Jason might as well walk up to me on the street in broad daylight with a gun and shoot me point-blank in the head. Feeling a little chickenshit, if prudent and cautious, I stayed in my office until seven thirty and worked a potential fraud case from the comfort of my computer, with the remote help of Freddy Lopez. I drove straight home and stayed there all night, ordered a pizza, drank half a bottle of wine, watched a movie on my laptop, turned in, and slept badly. On Thursday morning, I went to the gym and lifted weights and did burpees with Freddy as usual and enjoyed our postworkout smoothies together and filled him in on everything. "Be careful" was all he said. "I'm always here if you need me." I went back to the air-conditioned safety of my office and spent the day catching up on paperwork. Erin was down in Benson on her arson case, Ronnie was still in Sedona, and Madison was all aglow with her acceptance into film school, so the office felt like a peaceful haven. Exhausted by stress and grief, bone-tired in both brain and body, I drove home, made myself a turkey sandwich for dinner, watched a few old episodes of *Murder, She Wrote*, and brushed my teeth. I got into bed, put my head on the pillow, settled my body under the sheet and cotton blanket, felt myself sink down, down, down, and I was out.

Just after two o'clock in the morning, I was pulled out of an intensely deep sleep by my phone's obnoxious and insistent ringtone. I blindly reached out a hand and slapped my nightstand to locate it, squinted through one half-open eye, saw CALLER ID BLOCKED, and sent whoever it was straight to voicemail. I did not need another creepy flame-crackling crank call right now. Fuck whoever that was. Fuck Jason Gold and his little scare tactics and his Lexus and his aviator shades and his whole evil little Ponzi empire.

As I tried to sink back down again, an emotional electric shock wave crested over my body and zinged me awake. Tyler was dead. My old high-school sweetheart and lifelong friend was gone. Someone had killed him. I'd never see him again. Our entire shared history was wiped out, and all the love I'd felt for him had nowhere to go, ever again. An old familiar feeling was there, too, that this was all my fault. How could I ever have suspected him of murdering Rose? I should have protected him instead. Burning with rage and guilt and sorrow, I lay awake the rest of the night. With heavy head and foggy brain, I forced myself out of bed as soon as early daylight seeped through my blackout blinds, pulled on my shorts and sneakers, and ran through the cool, quiet dawn streets of my neighborhood, keeping an eye out for a white Lexus containing a lurking murderous douchebag. I felt slow and headachy at first, but by the end, I'd regained some brain-power and energy.

Back at home after a shower, as I was breakfasting on a piece of sourdough toast paved with a thick layer of peanut butter and a pint glass of sweet creamy iced coffee, my phone rang. It was Laura Gold.

"Laura," I said, "how are you?"

I heard the wet sounds of crying. I waited, suddenly worried Ben's condition had deteriorated, or worse.

"Oh Justine," she said.

"Is Ben okay?"

"Oh! Ben, yes, he's doing a lot better." She took a deep, ragged breath. "I just went up yesterday to see him; he's out of the hospital and staying at his sponsor's house, Lou Scarlatti and his wife, they're both such wonderful people. I think he's going to be mostly all right. He's fragile, but he's determined to get clean again."

"Oh," I said. "Laura, I am so glad to hear this. Thank you so much for calling to tell me." But why was she crying? "Is there something else?"

"Oh God, yes, that's why I called."

"What happened?"

She choked it out. Jason had apparently just been arrested on suspicion of murder and taken into FBI custody. He was considered dangerous and a flight risk. Bail was set at one hundred thousand dollars.

Sweet relief flooded every cell in my body, along with a childish sense of vindication.

"Leo and I don't have that kind of money." It sounded like her teeth were chattering. The poor woman was frantic. "Our child, stuck in that awful place. I'm so afraid for him."

Poor Laura, losing all three of her kids at once, one dead, one in a coma, one in jail. But thank God Jason was locked up and wasn't going to be allowed to go free to await trial. Thank God he couldn't finish his psychopathic murder geometry. Hallelujah. I wanted to kiss Agent Kepler on his thin, dry lips.

But underneath my relief was that little mouse scratching again. I still hadn't answered the question of *why* Jason had done any of this. Sure, Rose was a thorn in his side, but murdering his own sister? His motive for killing Tyler seemed even more unlikely. And me? The third side of a defunct sort-of love triangle from a quarter of a century ago? Why the fuck would Jason care? What did he even have to do with any of it?

"He's innocent," Laura was saying into my ear, her voice trembling but insistent. "Jason is innocent, they've got the wrong person."

"I know it must seem that way," I started to say.

"Please find the real killer," she said. "I'm begging you."

In fact, I had been planning to wait a certain amount of time to submit my invoice to Laura out of respect for her bereavement and the ordeal of Ben's current medical situation. The case was therefore still technically open.

"Who do you think it is?" I asked her. "Because frankly, Laura, I don't have a clue. If it wasn't Jason, who? Do you have any ideas?"

"No," she said. "But it's not Jason. It can't be Jason. He's not a killer. I know my own son! Some of his business tactics might be a little sneaky sometimes, I'll grant you that. But a murderer? His own sister? Killing Tyler like that? Jason would never, ever do that. I swear to you, Jo."

My brain was chewing on all the questions I had about this family. I couldn't ask Laura directly right now, or maybe ever. What mother ever knows the full deep, dark truth of what's going on with her adult kids? But I knew who might be able to help me. I scrounged around for pen and paper. "Would it be possible for me to talk to Ben? Can he have visitors?"

"Oh yes, good idea," she said. "I just spoke to Tricia before I called you, Lou's wife. She's a lovely, kind person. I'll call them back right now and let them know you're coming."

As Laura gave me Lou and Tricia's phone number and street address, my heart sank a little. I felt a little bad about needing to talk to Ben, which would traumatize him all over again.

"You're sure Ben can handle this?"

"He said it might actually be good for him to talk about Rose now."

"Okay then," I said.

I DRESSED IN FITTED NAVY TROUSERS AND A SHORT-SLEEVED WHITE cotton blouse and charcoal-brown midcalf boots, my freshly shampooed hair nicely combed, cowlicks and rogue waves tamped down with gel. I was trying to appear professional, nonthreatening, and benign. I had never shot up fentanyl-laced heroin and overdosed, nor had I been in a medically induced coma, nor had I lost one sibling to apparent suicide just before my other sibling was arrested for her murder, but I could imagine that having all this happen in one week did not make for a robustly sunny outlook. I intended to tiptoe around Ben Gold on little cat feet, let him tell me whatever he wanted to say, make sure he was stable and okay afterward, then get the hell out of that blighted part of the world.

After I filled my tank with gas at the Circle K, I went in and bought cold bottles of unsweetened iced tea and fancy lemonade, snagged a large paper cup from the soda station, and hit the road, my car and me fueled and hydrated. My old Honda felt a bit wonky on its pins, something wrong with the steering, a slight pull to the left. All that recent rumbling and jouncing over the dirt roads and cattle guards of Delphi must have jolted it out of alignment. I compensated for the drift with a firm hand on the wheel and tried not to imagine a big bomb strapped to the bottom of the chassis, about to blow me to smithereens as I drove through the cotton fields around Chandler and Casa Grande.

I always had mixed feelings about seeing these acres of white fluffballs in the desert, although of course this time of year they were just getting started, so now they were only seedlings. The Hohokam grew cotton here thousands of years ago, so it's nothing new. And it makes a nice alliterative contribution to the famous-around-here "five Cs" of Arizona—the other ones being citrus, cattle, copper, and climate—but it seems wrong that this non-native, high-water-use crop should be so prevalent in this parched state, two hundred thousand acres these days, enough cotton to make an annual pair of jeans for every single American. As the Colorado River dwindles to a trickle, there's less and less water left for this or any crop. Or a sprawling megalopolis, for that matter. So it's only a matter of time, I guess, before the cotton and the people have to find somewhere else to live. That was fast. The Hohokam's sojourn here lasted almost a millennium and a half.

My thoughts on the drive up to Phoenix are generally of this caliber: dire, apocalyptic. The Valley of the Sun makes me cranky. It's a gigantic, polluted, beige grid, crisscrossing wide melting-asphalt thoroughfares chockablock with a slow-moving glut of traffic trying to get through Phoenix, Glendale, Mesa, Tempe, Scottsdale, miles upon miles of chain restaurants, malls, title-loan offices, and cookie-cutter housing developments. It has no pedestrians or downtown or character. It's soul-crushingly hot, dusty, and often humid, the sky overhead ripped with sonic screams of airplanes landing and taking off and the constant ratcheting of police surveillance helicopters. You can legally text while driving, which may explain the traffic clusterfuck permanently bringing everything to a bumper-to-bumper crawl on I-10. Golf courses are everywhere; homeless shelters are nonexistent. The cops are famously racist and corrupt, the VA hospital is known for not giving a shit if veterans die or go insane waiting for treatment, crime is rampant, panhandlers accost your car at every intersection, and way too many people are fake blond and surgically enhanced. On the plus side, the tacos are good and there's an IKEA.

The Scarlattis lived near I-17 in the Alhambra neighborhood, off North Twenty-Third Avenue between Bethany Home Road and Camelback. I threaded through a labyrinth of sunblasted, dusty streets of mid-twentieth-century cinderblock ranch houses with carports, either scruffy brown lawns or sandscaping, as I called it, dotted with mesquite, ocotillo, and palm trees. This was supposedly a predominantly Hispanic neighborhood known for its high crime rate, but at the moment, the streets were deserted, sleepy, and calm, except for a woman in sneakers walking a fluffy white dog along the sidewalk, so maybe all that crime happened after dark, what did I know?

I parked by the curb in front of the Scarlattis' place on West San Juan. Their beige stucco house was a little more shipshape than its neighbors but was otherwise identical to them in layout and size, with the same slightly pitched red shingle roof. Their small front lawn was bright green, and when I leaned down to feel it, I touched the dry sharpness of plastic. The picture window by the front door and the two smallish front windows were all smooshed full of closed beige curtains. The carport and driveway held three midsize sedans of about the same vintage as my own, two white and one blue. Between the concrete apron of the driveway and the fake lawn was a paved strip of fake brick. Nothing alive grew anywhere on the property. It was all sterile and spotless and sealed up tight.

I walked up the short, curved walk to the front door and mashed the doorbell button. I heard two-tone chimes inside and waited under a corrugated metal canopy held up by a trellis as the woman and her dog walked by. She saw me standing there and nodded at me while her dog peed at the edge of the fake lawn.

The door opened. "Are you Jo?" asked a tiny woman with a cloud of dark hair and gigantic purple-framed glasses that almost hid her face. She peered up at me. Her face, the little I could see of it, was a pale oval with small, appealing features. She wore a belted purple tunic over black leggings and sparkly sandals. She offered me a cool, soft hand to shake; my own hot, callused mitt swallowed it. "I'm Tricia Scarlatti. Come on in."

I stepped into a climate so chilly I almost gasped. The baby-blue wall-to-wall carpet had vacuum-cleaner skid marks, and the air was full of competing artificial scents, air freshener mixed with furniture polish spray mixed with scented candles.

A young woman was in the entryway directly in front of me, blocking me. It took me a split second to recognize Ben's girlfriend, Savannah. She looked awkwardly upset. "I was just leaving," she said, but to whom I wasn't sure. "Sorry, sorry."

Before I could say hello, Savannah slipped by me and flung herself headlong down the little walk, turned right, and fled on foot along the sidewalk, slim and leggy in a baby tee and high-waisted shorts, flat-footed in leather sandals, out of sight.

"That's Savannah," said Tricia. "Ben's girlfriend. She just came by to bring him some things."

"We met already," I said. "She seemed upset about something."

"She'll get over it. A small misunderstanding with my husband earlier."

As Tricia led me through the house, I had a quick impression of a Danish teak hutch and dining set in a small dining room. In the adjoining living room, two facing snow-white couches sat on the continuation of the baby-blue carpeting, along with a Lucite coffee table holding oversize art books and a side table arrayed with coasters and candles. A wall held a mounted flat TV screen and suspended white shelves festooned with crystal geodes and an assortment of Native pottery and baskets. I had only been in this sterile, cloying interior for a matter of seconds, but I already urgently wanted to escape.

"Out here," said Tricia, pulling open a heavy sliding door.

I stepped back out into the normal weather. It was a relief to breathe hot, polluted, dusty air again. I could see why Ben was sitting outside.

The patio, shaded by an overhead canopy, was crowded with an eight-piece outdoor furniture set made of slatted acacia wood and cream cushions, two facing love seats, and two sets of facing double chairs, with two aligned coffee tables in the middle. In one corner stood an elaborate gleaming gas grill, possibly never used. Beyond the spotless stone pavers of the patio, bright green artificial grass covered the backyard, which was bordered by a spanking-clean cedar fence. It all looked like a stage set, not one molecule out of place, every blade of fake grass aligned, patio furniture in a perfect square. Clearly, no kids or pets lived here. Maybe the Scarlattis were cyborgs who never ate, sweated, or shat.

Tricia indicated the love seat facing Ben, and I obediently sat in it. "I'll fetch you guys some iced tea," she said, and traipsed back into the house.

Ben sat hunched over with his elbows resting on his knees, his hands clasped and limp, his neck bent. A cigarette burned between his fingers. He looked up at me through his eyelashes.

"How are you, Ben?"

He took a drag and exhaled. "Tired." His voice was flat. The skin on his face sagged. This was going to be even harder than I'd expected.

I cleared my throat, acutely aware of the imposition of my presence here. "Thanks for agreeing to talk to me. I won't stay long."

He pulled himself up so he was sitting normally. I could see the effort. His face was blank, eyes unblinking, still fixed on me. I couldn't read his expression, but he looked exactly like what he was, someone who had been through absolute hell and was still going through it.

"Are you up for this conversation? If not, I can go. I don't want to make things worse for you."

"How could things be worse?"

"Good point." I tried to give him a reassuring smile, but it felt fake. "I just saw Savannah on my way in. She seemed upset."

"Oh, she's mad because Lou is being protective. She just brought me some clothes." Every word he said sounded painful to spit out, as if each one were a jagged pebble. "It was nice of her. She stayed to talk, but Lou wanted her to go right away, to let me rest. It wasn't necessary, I love her company. I don't know what I would do without her."

"Does Jason have a girlfriend?"

He rolled with the abrupt shift in topic as if it were a perfectly rational segue. "Jason is asexual, I'm pretty sure. Maybe also gay. Although who knows? But the answer is no, he's single."

Tricia came bustling out carrying two glasses full of clear amber liquid and clinking ice cubes. She set Ben's on the table next to the ashtray and handed me mine. I took it, wishing fervently that it would turn out to be a very strong rum and Coke, but it was iced tea made from powder, much too sweet. I set my glass down on the table in front of me. Ben hadn't touched his.

"So now Jason's in jail," Ben said after Tricia had vanished back into the house, quick and light as a cartoon pixie.

"The FBI arrested him for killing your sister and Tyler Bridgewater."

Ben crushed his cigarette butt under his sneaker and lifted it into his hand and held it there for an instant before he deposited it into the ashtray. "What evidence do they have?"

"I don't know."

"What did you tell them? You were investigating."

"Everything I know, which isn't much. But really, nothing in particular that implicated Jason."

"You must doubt he did it too. Otherwise what are you doing here? If you thought the FBI had the right person, you'd stay home."

"I sincerely hope they have the right person." I was watching him closely. He looked as if he were disintegrating, dissolving from the inside out.

"Want a cigarette?" He held the pack and lighter out to me.

I took one, lit up, and handed the paraphernalia back. He lit a fresh one, and we puffed away for a moment. I took a gulp of fake iced tea. The combination of harsh smoke and cold sucrose in this scorching, dirty air was weirdly bracing.

"My brother didn't do it," said Ben. "Jason wouldn't kill anyone. He's too much of a pussy."

"What do you mean, Jason's a pussy? Is that connected to his being asexual? Do you mean it literally, or is it more of a suggestion that he's passive, or physically remote?"

Ben's mouth twisted. "All of the above."

"Is it okay if I ask you some more questions about your family?"

"Like what?"

"About growing up, Rose and her dad, your own home life. She wrote a lot of poetry and essays about trauma." I couldn't bring myself to tell him about Rose's father. Maybe later, when he was less fragile.

Ben grunted. "I assume it must have been connected to whatever happened in high school with you all."

I sighed. This shit again. "You mean with me and Tyler getting together."

"My sister was a hot mess."

"Jason told me he and Rose were close."

"Depends on how you define close."

"And you? Where did your own trauma come from? I always thought you were the ideal nuclear American family. I romanticized you guys."

"No family is perfect. Every family is fucked-up."

"Can you describe how your family was fucked-up?"

"Jesus," he said. He let out a breath that sounded like a gasp in reverse. "I don't see how this is going to help you understand why my sister died."

I squinted at him. "It might."

"I think you're asking because you're curious, because it's personal for you."

"I ask questions, Ben. That's how I do my job. I ask and ask and ask like a pesky little fly buzzing around until the answers start adding up. Sometimes I ask the same question again and again until I understand the answer. If you know of a better way to go about this, please, I'm all ears."

"Okay," he said. "Ask."

I took another sip of tea. The icy sweetness made my teeth tingle. The cigarette smoke felt pleasantly caustic in my throat. "What was Leo like as a dad?"

"Jewish doctor father, terrifying interrogations at dinnertime about what we'd learned at school that day, big kisses and hugs and tucking in at bedtime. Confusing as fuck. But we knew he loved us. That was never in question."

"What's it like to have him have dementia?"

"Heartbreaking, just what you would expect, you never know what you're going to miss until it's gone. My dad had a sharp brain, and he was intimidating. Now he's like a little kid, confused, emotional."

"Do you think Rose ever felt left out in your family, since she wasn't Leo's daughter?"

"There was definitely favoritism in Jason's direction, and maybe mine at times, although I was younger and therefore less important. My dad and Rose got along fine, but they weren't close."

"Did Rose resent you and Jason for that?"

"Resent us?"

"Was she competitive with you guys?"

"Possibly." His eyes shuttered. "That's enough. I can't talk anymore. I'm sorry." He slowly slumped to one side to rest on one elbow, holding his cigarette in his free hand. His whole body looked caved in on itself. His face was averted from me. He went completely still and silent except for the smoke billowing from his mouth.

After an uncomfortable moment, during which I tried to think of something to say to soothe him or give him some kind of assurance, I stood up. "I'm sorry," I said. "Thank you, Ben, I hope you feel better soon. I'm rooting for you."

He didn't answer, just gave me a half-assed wave goodbye, a sideways flap of one hand. It felt heartsick to me rather than dismissive, full of conflicting resignation and turmoil.

I COULD HAVE ESCAPED BY THE SIDE GATE, BUT INSTEAD I CARRIED both glasses back into the house, acting as if I were being polite, but

I was really just looking for an excuse to talk to Tricia and Lou, if he was around. I found Tricia in the kitchen, nervously wiping the immaculate white granite bar top with a brand-new sponge and a spray bottle of chemicals. She wore a blue apron tied around her child-size waist and pink rubber gloves. Her cloud of hair and huge glasses made it impossible for me to see her expression.

"Thanks for the tea," I said as I scooched by her and set the glasses by the sink. Safely installed in her sight line, I turned to face her.

She stopped futzing with her cleaning apparatus and peered up at me. "That was fast."

"Ben doesn't seem in any state to talk to me about any of this. I feel bad for coming."

"He said he was willing to help."

"He's been here since yesterday?"

"We went and got him at the hospital as soon as he was released. Lou thinks he needs to be in rehab. We're working on that."

"Lou is his sponsor in NA?"

"Yes. We're both former addicts. Lou's drug was heroin, I did crystal meth. We met in rehab." She spoke without drama, just stating facts. "We've both been clean and sober for twelve years as of last week. We have the same recovery anniversary, in fact."

The front door opened, and a man came into the kitchen carrying two paper grocery bags. He set them on the counter and turned to look at me. "You're Jo? I'm Lou."

He was bald and trim, broad shouldered, with gleaming olive skin and azure eyes, radiating low-key charisma and raw sex appeal. As soon as he walked into the kitchen, his wife visibly relaxed; all her agitation went to ground and her face lit up. She started unpacking the groceries and putting them away, but her eyes were on her husband. As for me, I had developed an instant crush on him.

"Hi, Lou," I said. "I just talked to Ben, and I'm worried I upset him, did more harm than good."

"He's stronger than he looks," said Lou. His eyes flashed at me from thick black eyelashes. His mouth was firm and well shaped. I even liked his voice. It was warm and gravelly, with a knowing glint, the voice of a man who'd survived a lot of shit and could laugh at himself. "He's ready to get clean again, he swears this was a one-time thing, and I believe it. Especially after what happened. He almost died."

"Were you there when he was brought in?"

"His mother called me afterward. Said no visitors. He contacted me yesterday and asked me to come get him. I told him only if he agreed to stay here with us. He wouldn't go home with his mother, and he can't be alone right now."

"Laura said she came up to see him yesterday."

"They spent almost an hour sitting out on the patio in near-total silence. She left crying. Poor woman. He wouldn't even let her go to his place to get his things, told her Savannah would do it."

"Where does he normally live?"

"Ben? His apartment is not too far from here; he could walk there if he wanted to."

"What about Savannah? She was just leaving when I got here. She seemed upset."

Tricia and Lou exchanged a quick, pointed look.

"You don't like her," I said.

"It's not that we don't *like* her," said Tricia carefully.

"I don't like her," said Lou.

Tricia cleared her throat. "She's young."

"She makes everything about herself," said Lou. "Everything. That's not helpful to Ben right now. He has to focus on his own recovery."

Tricia gave me a frank look, one woman to another. "When she came over earlier, Lou asked her to give Ben some space. She stayed a whole hour after that. She doesn't like to be pushed around."

"She wasn't happy," said Lou. He lifted his hands, palms up. "Tough shit. Ben's as fragile right now as he's ever been. You know his brother was just arrested for the murder of their sister."

"As well as the murder of a local cop," I said.

Tricia looked stricken. "It's a lot for him right now, on top of his relapse."

I shot her a look. "Ben says Jason didn't do it."

"He means he hopes his brother didn't do it," said Lou.

Tricia continued to gaze steadily back at me. I could finally see her eyes behind her glasses, shrewd and bright, more intelligent than I'd given her credit for. "What do you think, Jo?"

"I have no idea. It seems that Jason's trying to con a lot of old people out of their land and a lot of rich people out of their money. At least the FBI is looking into it."

"He's in custody?" Tricia clucked. "Their poor mother, my heart went out to her yesterday. All three of her kids . . ."

"And her husband," I said. "Ben's dad was recently diagnosed with dementia. They're expecting me later this afternoon." I checked my wrist, a symbolic gesture only, because I wasn't wearing a watch. The digital clock on the microwave said 1:38. I wanted to be in Delphi by four to talk to Linda Bridgewater before I saw Laura Gold, and I was planning to stop for some takeout tacos on my way, so I needed to get a move on.

"Can you do me a favor and tell Laura that Ben is going to be okay?" Tricia asked. "I know it doesn't seem like it right now, but he really will. Lou will help him."

"What did the doctors say exactly about his long-term prognosis?" I was trying to be tactful, but I needed to know. "He doesn't seem like himself to me, but maybe it's the aftereffects of the drugs? Not just the overdose, but also the medications he was on in the hospital. Laura said they induced a coma."

"He'll pull through," said Lou. "When I came to pick him up

yesterday morning, he was waiting outside. He checked himself out. He didn't want to be there another minute."

"Which hospital?"

"They took him to Maricopa. I guess it was the closest one when he OD'd."

"Do you know who his dealer is? Or where he got the stuff?"

Lou looked at Tricia. She shook her head very slightly. "Frankly," he said, "I don't recommend messing with them."

Okay. So I'd have to track them down on my own, whoever they were.

"Right," I said. "I'm just curious about the fentanyl. I'm wondering if it was deliberate." This question had been hovering in the back of my mind, the possibility that someone had tried to kill Ben, or that he had tried to commit suicide.

"It's going around," said Lou. "Some of the dealers are even stocked with Narcan just in case."

"It's terrible," said Tricia. "Dealers cut their drugs with it, and then they bring back the addicts who OD on it so they can buy more."

"I'm glad I got clean before that shit went into circulation," said Lou. "I'd be dead a hundred times over by now."

A few minutes later, I thanked the Scarlattis and left them in their neat, sober, immaculate house with the broken version of Ben Gold, but only temporarily broken, if Lou was right, and I hoped he was. I was feeling jumpy and sad. I thought a bunch of tacos might cheer me up a little.

TWENTY-TWO

ON THE DRIVE BACK DOWN TO DELPHI THROUGH THE MILES OF BUR-geoning cotton fields, I mulled over the facts. The visceral brain in my gut was hard at work, collaborating with the cerebral brain in my skull. At the moment, all I had was a gnarly glut of feelings, information, sensory input, impressions, inflections, and inferences. The neurons in my intestines were suffused with raw data, and they were chewing on all of it, churning it around. I could not rush this process. It was like digesting food, only what came out was a synthesized nugget of truth instead of shit. Much cleaner, much more useful.

The two murders felt meticulously planned, more psychological than violent, more symbolic than cold-blooded, and their success had relied on the fact that the murderer was well known by both victims.

All three times Rose's phone had gone live, it had been just long enough to send a video and then a text to Tyler, and a video to me, and Freddy had pinpointed its location as Jason's office building or somewhere in Delphi.

Whoever had done it might have been trying to implicate Jason, but that didn't mean it was Jason. Just about everyone in this town seemed to own or have access to an ATV.

And even those white cotton gloves in the video of Rose's death made it impossible to tell whether the hand inside them was male or female or otherwise. Anyone could have been wearing them: Jason, Chad, or Phil, Linda Bridgewater, any inhabitant of Rancho Bella Luna, any of the Triangle A crew, including Noah and Mickey, any member of the Gonzalez family, including Lupita. It had not escaped my attention that she had gotten out of bed in the night at the same time the video was sent to my phone.

The truth was that I had been so focused on Tyler and Jason, I'd neglected to really consider anyone else. Chay Griffiths could have killed Rose, and he had also been at the Rancho the night of Tyler's murder. For all I knew, it could have been Connie Shelltrack or Lena Duby. Maybe it was Leo Gold, pretending to have dementia to cover his tracks. Maybe it was the desk clerk at the Apache Motel.

Rose had pissed off a lot of people. Tyler had been at the scene when Rose's body was found. I had been pulled into the case. Her killer had no doubt planned for that, as well, likely setting me up as a prime suspect from the very beginning.

Those forearm triangle scratches, whatever they were, those cattle brands—a triangle meant three. And I couldn't shake the dark suspicion that I was meant to be the next dead body.

The only thing I knew for sure right now was that I had to watch my back. But I was also starting to understand that the only way I was going to figure this out might be to let myself get ensnared, take whatever bait was offered. I had to wait for the signal that I was up. Rose was gone, Tyler was gone, and now it was my turn, and the only advantage I had was that I could feel it coming. But I had no idea where it would come from, or from whom. I didn't trust anyone, because I couldn't.

In the midst of all this cogitating, I was swamped by a physical bodily reaction so strong I almost had to pull my car off the road, an internal earthquake that mimicked intensely painful nausea but was psychological in origin. I thought it was caused by fear at first, but when I thought about being sucked into the killer's web, whatever trap he or she had laid for me, I didn't feel afraid, I felt awake and weirdly excited. Out of nowhere, I pictured Tyler's face, remembered with acute specificity his expressions, the sound of his voice, our final conversations. My oldest friends were both gone. I'd never see Tyler again. And even more painfully for me, I'd never see Rose again. I hadn't fully realized until I lost her how much love I still felt for her, how much a part of me she had always been.

It was too sad to bear. I had no way of articulating any of it; my brain shut down in the face of it. My body was expressing my grief. My body always knows things my mind can't. And it tells me what it knows, if I just listen, if I just turn my brain off and power down my analytical engine and go inward. My heart was crying so hard it ached. There was no other way to put this feeling into words. My chest cavity felt rhythmically pummeled.

I pulled over onto the shoulder and hit my hazard lights and pounded my fists on the steering wheel and cried hard for a few minutes.

Then I pulled slowly back onto the highway, the jackhammer of grief still ratcheting away in my rib cage. I had a job to do. I had to keep myself moving forward, steadily on track.

My phone rang: my boss.

"Hi, Ronnie," I said, trying to sound normal. "What's up?"

"When you're finished with the case up there, I have a job for you and Yazzie."

This was much-needed good news. I loved working with Erin. "What is it?"

"Some shenanigans going on at the Ocotillo dog park. Someone's stealing dogs? I don't know, sounds like a shitstorm anyway, and apparently the cops are quote-unquote 'worse than useless.'"

"Why does it take two detectives to solve this?"

"Because the woman who called sounds like she can afford it. Rich as fuck, in other words. And she asked for my two best PIs."

"I'd be flattered if we weren't your only two PIs."

"She said she'd pay top dollar, as long as it takes. So wrap up that case and get back down here. Let's milk this."

At 4:00 p.m. on the dot, I pulled off the highway onto Arizona Avenue, back in Delphi again. I turned up Coyote Loop Road, drove along the ridgeline through mature trees and tumbled boulders, shaggy old telephone poles strung with thick looping black wire, houses set well back from the road and separated by long empty stretches of forested land. I'd called Linda Bridgewater yesterday, and after some initial stiff resistance to talking to me at all, I'd convinced her to help me find whoever had killed her husband. So now I was headed for the house where she and Tyler had lived, raising four kids, making a family together. I had never been there, so I watched the house numbers until I came to number 615, which had a helpful hand-painted wooden sign on the chain-link fence, right by the mailbox, that said THE BRIDGEWATER FAMILY. It looked as if one of their kids had made it, maybe for a Mother's Day present for Linda, maybe not.

Set back from the road in a dirt lot shaded by a grove of large old trees, cottonwood, palo verde, hackberry, mesquite, the house was the usual sprawling one-story midcentury stucco ranch. It looked well cared for, spruced up with new gray siding on the entrance, fresh tomato-red paint on the trim. A white SUV was parked in the gravel driveway, which was bordered with sparkling white rocks, mica catching the sunlight. I parked behind it and got out of my car and looked down at the valley stretching out for miles in front of the house, up at the mountain peaks rising behind it. Nice view up here.

The land around the house was cluttered with an assortment of kids' bikes. Through the open garage door, I saw an ATV. The sight of it almost made me laugh out loud. Of course.

I tapped the brass knocker on the spanking-white front door and heard kids shrieking, a dog barking. The door was opened by a tall, skinny boy. I guessed he was around twelve. He looked so much like Tyler at that age, handsome and serious and sweet, I felt weak, sandbagged by loss.

"Hi," I said. "I'm Jo Bailen. I'm here to talk to your mom. Is she around?"

"Pleased to meet you," he said. He opened the door wider to let me in, the man of the house now. "I'm Dylan Bridgewater."

I followed him into the kitchen. The house felt bright and open, homey and friendly, full of comfy couches tufted with dog hair and Lego pieces, a big rug cluttered with beanbag chairs, books piled next to a set of interlocking wooden train tracks, two low tables strewn with crayons and construction paper, glue and scissors. The kitchen was a big, open room in the back of the house, with a linoleum floor, Formica counters, stainless-steel appliances, and a big table and chairs in one corner. Next to the table, a set of sliding glass doors opened out to a back patio and fenced yard. I caught a glimpse of a trampoline, a swing set, two sparkly hula hoops, a gas grill.

Three kids of various sizes and ages sat at the table with glasses of milk and a big plate of cookies. Dylan rejoined his little brother and sisters, sliding back onto his chair, taking a big gulp of milk as if the trip to the front door had made him thirsty. Linda Bridgewater stood behind the kitchen bar, shaping dough into balls and putting each one on a greased cookie sheet. There was enough dough in that bowl to feed every kid in Delphi. A steel cooling rack at her elbow was filled with the latest batch of freshly baked chocolate chip cookies.

"Hello," she said to me, flicking a glance in my direction without meeting my eyes. "Give me one sec to get these in the oven and I'll be right with you."

"Of course," I said politely. For almost seventeen years, Linda and I had shared the odd but common bond of two women who have no real history together and no relationship with each other whatsoever, except for both loving the same man. She had always been weird with me because I was his high school sweetheart, and because we had once shared a house together in Tucson. Of course, by then we were only friends, but I'm sure Linda didn't see it that way. In her mind, I was the one who broke his heart and got away. I had never had any problem with her, but that was only because I had him first and let him go. That was just how this worked.

As I hung out by the two-door fridge, I found myself mesmerized by the table full of Tyler's kids. They were so cute, a combination of him and Linda. The smaller boy's name was Troy, I learned. The girls were Sophia and Alexa. I was terrible at guessing kids' ages, but if Dylan was twelve, then Sophia might have been ten, Alexa eight, and Troy maybe five or six, all of them far too young to lose their father. I knew all too well how that felt. But at least they all had one another.

Linda slid the rack into the oven and brushed her hands on the front of her short denim skirt and came out from the kitchen area. Her dark hair was held back by a pink headband. She wore a white sleeveless blouse and pink Keds with no socks. She looked like a TV mom in a classic old sitcom, Laura Petrie or Carol Brady, so fresh and young, except for her eyes, which were clouded, vacant, stunned with grief.

"Guys," she said to her kids, "I'm going to talk to Jo for a little while. Dylan, when the timer goes off, take the cookies out, use the mitts, and turn off the oven. If you need anything, go ask Grandma, she's in her room."

Linda led me into a room off the kitchen, a small, dim study with a desk, two chairs, and three filing cabinets side by side against the wall. Piles of paper were stacked on every surface, as well as on the floor by the wall. "This is my office," she said. "I work from home, I'm a CPA now. Please excuse the mess, I'm still digging out from tax season."

I sat in the chair by the door. She seated herself behind the desk. We were only about three feet apart. This was the first time we had ever been alone together.

"Linda, I'm so sorry," I said. "I can't wrap my head around it."

She made a soft sound in the back of her throat. "Can you find the person who did this?"

"I'm trying."

"It wasn't Jason Gold. No way."

"What makes you say that?"

"He and Tyler were buds."

"I know they had some business dealings . . ." I said cautiously.

"You don't have to protect me. Did he think I wouldn't notice that all our savings were gone? Tyler was so gullible. He was terrible with money."

"I remember," I said before I could stop myself.

"Of course, you know. He was a gambler and he loved schemes and he believed he'd get rich quick someday. I know he was doing it for us, and I forgive him, but I'm still mad as hell at him. I also know that he was having an affair recently, so you don't have to protect me from that either. I just don't know who it was with." She shot me a look. "Was it you?"

"God, no," I said, I hoped with enough force that she'd believe me the first time and we wouldn't have to go through a rigmarole. "No way. Tyler and I had a high school thing, that's all. Whatever happened between us belongs to the distant past."

"I have to admit I'm relieved to hear it. Who was it? Do you know?"

"It was Rose Delaney."

I could see her pupils contract. "No."

"I'm sorry."

"How do you know?"

"He told me."

Another flinch. "When?"

"The night after her body was found. He told me only because he was being blackmailed and he needed advice."

"Blackmailed how?"

"A video. I'll spare you the details. It was sent from Rose's phone, which went missing after she disappeared."

"He could have told me."

"He was afraid you'd leave him. His worst nightmare was losing you."

"I would never have left him." She ran a hand over her eyes, but she wasn't crying. "Never. Not for any reason. Not for losing all our money, and not for sleeping with that crazy bitch."

"You knew Rose?"

"Just the way everyone knows everyone in Delphi."

Linda was sitting very still, very straight, her hands folded on the desk, her eyes flickering with evident discomfort at my steady gaze. I felt a wall of coolness between us, her ancient rivalry with me, her inability to countenance this big part of her husband's past. I had no way to show her how nonthreatening I was except to be as cool as she was, to meet her reserve with my own sense of propriety and boundaries. But all I wanted to do was to grieve with her at losing a man we had both loved.

Instead I said evenly, "I'm going to find the person who did this."

"Do you have any idea who it is?"

"I'm circling them. I can feel myself getting closer. But I probably won't know who it is until they jump out at me."

She looked puzzled. "Don't detectives usually hunt for clues?"

"In this case, there aren't many to be found."

"Okay," she said, still looking puzzled, which I interpreted as doubt at my professional capabilities. "So how can I help you?"

"By telling me if anything has occurred to you, anything you've thought of, any detail, no matter how insignificant it may seem."

"I have absolutely no clue," she said after a moment. "Who would have done this? No. I don't know."

I found myself asking her about living in Delphi after growing up in Tucson. "Do you miss the city? I know this is a very small town." Ben was right, often my questions are just personal, pure curiosity, totally unrelated to the case at hand. Sometimes it pays off. Most often, it just satisfies my own need to know things about people.

"I love it here," said Linda. "We're going to stay put."

She walked me to the front door to see me out. "Call me anytime," I said. "You have my number."

I got into my car, thinking about the fact that Tyler's pension and life insurance policy would go to his widow. He had squandered their savings and cheated on her, and now she was set for life. Linda had good reason to wish Rose dead. She could have been pretending just now not to know who Tyler was sleeping with. These facts passed through my head without any particular suspicion attached to them. But I was aware of all of it, all the same.

I drove down the other side of Coyote Loop back to Arizona Avenue, thinking that if I were inclined to a cynical view of things, which I was, Linda's little cookies and milk scenario might have been calculated to give the impression of normalcy, a good mother taking care of her heartbroken children in the wake of their dad's murder. I couldn't help wondering how they acted together now, as a family, when there was no visitor observing them. This made me think about the limitations of how much anyone can ever really know about anyone else. I wondered if Linda had it in her to kill anyone.

I TURNED ONTO RANCHO BELLA LUNA ROAD, PREPARING MYSELF TO talk to another bereaved woman. Laura was expecting me at five, and I was a little early, but I didn't think she would mind. On the phone earlier, she had sounded intensely eager for my company.

As I pulled into the Rancho's front courtyard and parked, I saw her waiting for me, perched on the main house's patio wall. She wore a pale-green silk pantsuit and floppy-brimmed black straw hat, oversize sunglasses against the glare of the late afternoon sun. On her feet were low-heeled tan mules. She was elegant even amid the worst tragedy of her life, and maybe even more so, when she most needed to prop herself up with her movie-star persona. From a distance, as I walked toward her from across the courtyard, I saw her strike a pose, one hand curled at her breastbone, the other resting on one slender knee, her head angled upward so her face caught the light.

As I climbed the steps, she leapt up to cling briefly to me as she pecked my cheek. "I thought we could talk right here," she said as my hand went up to wipe off any lipstick she'd left behind on my cheek. "No one is around, and Leo is in one of his moods right now. Patty is with him. She's very good at calming him down. She's been so good through all of this, I don't know how I'd do it without her."

I sat in a wrought iron wingback chair and put my feet up on the low wall so I was facing Laura and neither of us was looking directly into the slanting rays of the sun. The sunlight threw her face into stark relief, illuminated the topography of skin sagging at her jawline, crepe-like skin collapsing in the hollow of her neck. Her mouth was a tragic slash. When she lowered her sunglasses to look directly at me, her eyes were as hooded as a lizard's. She looked wrecked but admirable, a woman who had lived life fully and was determined to rise above this crushing sorrow. I couldn't take my eyes off her.

"I just went up to see Ben," I told her.

"How did you think he seemed?"

"A bit shaky, but his sponsor thinks he'll be okay."

"He was terrible yesterday when I went up. Just awful, could hardly speak. I was devastated. But I spoke to him a few minutes ago on the phone. He told me Lou, that excellent man, has found him a place at a rehab center. Ben is checking himself in this evening. He's assured me that he's going to be all right."

"I'm so glad," I said.

"And I have good news from Jason as well."

This gave me an uneasy feeling. "What is it?"

"His lawyer spoke to the judge and convinced her that he isn't a danger or a flight risk, and she reduced the amount of bail. I managed to raise half of it, and Chad and Phil put up the other half. Those angels! Such good people are looking out for my sons. Jason's being processed and released; he's going to call as soon as he's free. He'll be on his way up to Delphi tonight. His lawyer is confident he can prove Jason's innocence on all counts. Another piece of good news. All at once, just this afternoon. Oh, it's been agony."

"I can well imagine." The hair on my arms was standing up. So Jason would be out of jail and in Delphi tonight. Okay then.

"The only thing I need to know definitively now," Laura was saying, "is about Rose. What have you learned in your investigation? Anything?"

It was long past time to show Laura the video of her daughter's death. I had planned to show it to her after the memorial the other night. But then Tyler had been killed, and the FBI had questioned me, and Jason had been arrested. Now I felt as if I had waited too long, and at the same time, I frankly wished I could wait forever. Telling Mickey had been one thing; the news had helped and comforted them, upsetting as it was. It would do nothing good for Laura. It would only intensify her grief and freak her out. And possibly make her suspect me.

"There's something I need to show you," I said. "You know Rose's phone has gone missing since she disappeared. Someone out there has it. I received a video from that phone. A video that shows Rose's death."

"She filmed her own suicide?"

"Her killer filmed her murder."

"Her killer."

"She didn't commit suicide, Laura."

"Oh thank God. I want to see it." Her voice was firm.

"It's hard to watch."

"I don't care, I need to see it."

I cued it up and handed her my phone. She pressed Play. I watched as she took it in. I heard Rose's voice coming from my phone, listened for what felt like the thousandth time to her accusing me. I could have mouthed the words along with her.

Laura made a choking sound, clutched her breastbone, poked at the phone, and watched it again. A third time, a fourth. She handed my phone back to me. "Why does she blame you, Jo? To whom was she apologizing?"

"I don't know yet. That's what I'm trying to find out."

"You didn't do this, of course."

"Of course not!"

"No, of course you didn't, I'm sorry for even suggesting it. But then who did? Who killed my girl?"

Her voice deepened and quavered on the word "girl," so unerring, so true. A director would have kissed her hand and called "Scene." I marveled at this woman's strength, which seemed to derive from her ability to play herself impeccably at all times. Just as I had wondered earlier about how Linda and her kids acted when they were alone, I wondered now about what Laura did when there was no one around to watch her and she was stripped to her true essentials. Did she cease to exist in some fundamental way without an audience? Or did she allow herself to exist fully in the absence of anyone watching her? Self-consciousness was an interesting thing. To observe emotions being performed for my eyes was always telling. I knew that Laura was heartbroken, devastated, and would never be whole again after Rose's death. But I couldn't help feeling that she had already perfected the role of grieving mother.

Leaving her with assurances that I would keep working on her behalf until the truth was revealed, I headed up Arizona Avenue. I checked into the Apache Motel again, like old times, wordlessly exchanging credit card and key fob with the odd creature behind the front desk. After I had settled into my grungy little teepee, I took myself out for dinner at the Delphi Inn, where I sat alone at the table where I'd sat with Tyler and ordered a cheeseburger and fries and jalapeno poppers and a beer with whiskey chaser, in honor of him, a little grief ritual. While I ate every bite and drank every drop, I talked to

Tyler, speaking out loud to the empty air across the table from me. I told him everything I wanted to say to him. I felt a couple of times that he was really listening. But he couldn't tell me who had killed him, no matter how much he may have wanted to.

I looked over at the booth where Noah had been sitting the other night and remembered how Tyler had goaded me to check him out, our old ID-the-perp game. The three cracked-leather booths were empty tonight, and so were most of the tables around me, but in my current state of mind, the whole place felt alive, shivering with ghosts.

TWENTY-THREE

FULL OF MEAT AND FAT AND BOOZE, I PAID MY CHECK AND DROVE
the quick minute or two to the Apache Motel. Back in my teepee, I
locked the door and latched the chain, closed the curtains tightly, and
turned on one soft lamp by the bed. I took my .40-caliber Sig Sauer
semiautomatic handgun out of its case and loaded it and put it on the
nightstand, the safety on, but easily reached. I'd brought my smaller
Glock 27 as well, and I considered it for ease of concealment, but I
preferred the Sig Sauer, and I didn't care if anyone figured out that
I was armed. Lying on top of the blanket, feet crossed at the ankles,
fully dressed, I fell into a light doze.

By two o'clock, I was wide awake again, staring into the darkness,
feeling extra alert, watching intermittent headlights slide their glowing bars across the ceiling.

I texted Freddy, You up? You checking the phone?

On it, he texted back.

My heart pounded slowly. My breathing was shallow. I was waiting, I realized, for my turn. I could feel them out there, whoever they
were, getting ready to pull me in. They must have known I was able to
track Rose's phone, since they seemed to know everything else about
me. I got out of bed and sat in the chair at the little table by the window, my gun at the ready. I was tapping my toe, ginned up, my muscles flexing.

I didn't have to wait long. Freddy called me at 2:35 a.m. to let me know that Rose's phone had gone live and was staying on, for the first time, instead of winking out after less than a minute the way it had all the other times. He was zeroing in on its exact location, somewhere just outside of Delphi.

It was my homing beacon. My summons.

While Freddy triangulated his locator in ever-shrinking possible locations, I put on the headset, phone tucked into the butt pocket of my jeans, so Freddy spoke directly into my ear, and I spoke into the mouthpiece. I strapped my pancake holster on the right side of my waist and slid my gun snugly into it. Then I pulled on my night camouflage: black sneakers with no reflective tape, a long-sleeve black turtleneck, and a balaclava over the headset.

"Got it," he said as I readjusted the phone in my pocket, making sure it wouldn't fall out. "It's in the hills behind Rancho Bella Luna. I'll talk you in. Just stay on the phone."

I felt my butt buzz and fished my phone out and read a text from Rose Delaney's phone: I know you're tracking this phone, so you know where to find me. Come alone. If you bring anyone with you, you'll never know the truth.

I read it aloud to Freddy.

"Fuck," he said. "Okay."

"Jason's out on bail. If this is Jason."

"Only one way to find out. But you still have to have backup. I need a way to get you out of there."

"Do it," I said. My voice sounded calm, but adrenaline was pumping through my veins. "But they have to be invisible. I mean it. They have to hang far back, out of visible range and earshot. And I don't want them to move one toe until I tell you to deploy them. Otherwise this asshole is going to disappear, and I'll have to watch my back for the rest of my life."

"Roger that," said Freddy. "You make the call."

———————

I STEPPED OUT INTO THE NIGHT AIR. IT WAS COOL AND FRAGRANT with the exhalations of sleeping plants, bright with a still almost-full moon. I chirped my car unlocked and got in and drove to the Rancho and parked by the stables. Solo had always kept his dirt bike in the shed, his precious and beloved 1978 vintage Yamaha two-stroke Enduro Symphony. I shoved the door open, and there it was. With my mental fingers crossed that it had enough gas in it to get me where I was going, I kicked the engine to life and got on and put-putted along the wash behind the stables to the fire road. Solo had always kept the bike in mint condition, and the moonlit night was bright enough for me to steer clear of rocks, so it maneuvered well over the sand. I made pretty good progress, avoiding the worst ruts and boulders, slithering around fences and climbing up into the hills. The moon shone at my back and cast my shadow ahead of me, a large, looming figure I would have been intimidated by if I'd seen only the shadow. I kept the headlamp off and navigated in the moonlight. I heard the pack of coyotes off in the valley, yipping away, announcing their intention to hunt anything edible.

"You're getting closer," said Freddy after a while. "Your backup is just down the valley from you, getting into position."

"Who'd you send?"

"Two police, one squad car. I told them the deal. You won't see or hear them, but they're standing by. They have the coordinates of the phone too."

"I'll go the rest of the way on foot," I said softly, "slower but not as obvious."

"Keep going," he said.

I ditched the bike and started hiking, staying low down, in the shadows of mesquite and palo verde trees, as much as possible. Breaking into the open, moving as fast and silently as I could, I clambered to the top of a steep hill and stared into the wilderness that stretched back to the mountains. I was close to the spot where I'd been shot at a few days ago, maybe a ridgeline away. The edge of the Gonzalez ranchland was just in back of me.

"It's halfway up the next hill," said Freddy. "Straight ahead." I bushwhacked down into the gulch, picking my way through deep crevices and loose rock and thick underbrush, sidewinding as I started up the next flank, making as little noise as possible, trying not to dislodge rocks, checking behind me and around me often to make sure no one was sneaking up on me. The slope was very steep, and I was going at a good clip, but my heart thudded with regular rhythm in my throat, and I wasn't out of breath. I felt like a cat, nimble and easy in my limbs. This, right now, was why I was so fanatical about exercise. I could feel all the muscles in my back and arms and abs flexing, ready for action. My gun sat snugly at my waist.

"Bear to your right just a hair," said Freddy in my ear. I corrected my course, climbing steadily. After a few minutes, I realized where I was headed. It was the old outlaws' hideout Rose and I had found as kids, the remnants of Crazy Davy Thatcher's shack, weathered boards held together with handmade nails, the roof long gone, plants growing from the dirt floor. We used to spend hours there, playing Crazy Davy and his sidekick, Silver Pete. Rose always got to be Crazy Davy, the hotheaded hero, shouting her own version of nineteenth-century-criminal epithets and doing little jigs to show how crazy he was. I played the stalwart Pete, who was entirely fictitious and without a real-life counterpart, as a tobacco-chewing, swaggering roustabout who liked to say things like "I'll be gol-dad-nabbed!" and "Why, that's a stellar notion, Davy!" We shot pretend guns at pretend rabbits and skinned and cooked them over pretend campfires, singing "Red River Valley" with fake drunkenness as we swilled pretend jimsonweed tea.

Ben and Jason had played those games with us. I remembered how Ben had sobbed hysterically when Rose pretend-died. In those games,

I was the sheriff, and Ben and Jason were my deputies. What struck me now, remembering, was Jason's odd, cold expression, watching Rose's theatrical death throes. A weird little smile, maybe of pleasure.

I overshot the hideout in an arc to its right and circled back, creeping up on it from above. When I was almost on top of it, I sheltered behind a boulder for a minute, peering down at the moonlit shack, watching for movement, a glint, a flash of light, anything. It looked deserted. I crept down the slope, keeping to the shadows, moving silently. "I'm going in," I whispered into my mouthpiece.

"Be careful," said Freddy.

"Yeah," I breathed.

"If anything happens, tell me; I'll send the cops in after you. They're in position."

I circled the shack slowly, hardly breathing, scanning the dirt and rocks for a likely ambush. On the way here I'd had plenty of time to speculate about what I was walking into. Someone had turned on Rose's phone and led me here, exactly the way they'd been sucking me in all along with these texts and videos and crank calls, and I could only surmise that they did this because they were playing on my need to know the truth, and eventually they intended to kill me. On the other hand, this was likely the only way I would ever find out who they were. So here I was, willingly walking into a trap, allowing whoever it was to have their shot at me.

I saw the light from a phone screen, probably Rose's. It sat out in the open, on a flat rock several yards from the entrance to the shack. I heard and sensed no movement from the shack, no sign of human life anywhere.

This felt wrong. I turned slowly, scanning the land all around me. I didn't trust the stillness, the silence, the absence. The back of my neck prickling with apprehensiveness, I picked up the phone, waiting to be jumped. But no one emerged from the darkness. I seemed to be alone here.

"Something isn't right," I whispered to Freddy. "There's no one here."

"Get out of there," he said. "Go now."

Grabbing Rose's phone off the rock, I melted into the shadows, moved off down the slope, sidewinding like a fast-scuttling crab toward the gulch at the bottom, staying low and invisible.

I heard the ATV as it crested the top of the hill I was about to climb, that unmistakable low roar punctuated with the whine of revving and the farting of exhaust. I saw it, too, because whoever was driving it had the headlights on. It came bouncing down the slope, straight toward me, its lights picking me out of the background and illuminating me. There was nothing to do but wait, no possibility of outrunning it, nowhere to hide.

"It's showtime," I whispered to Freddy. "They're coming for me."

"Your backup is ready," he said. "I'm here."

I tucked Rose's phone in my other hip pocket and drew my gun from its holster on my hip, flipped the safety, and planted my feet in the dirt, ready for action. The ATV stopped a few yards away from me. The engine cut out and the rider dismounted and took off a helmet to reveal a cascade of long dark hair. It was a woman, slim and I guessed young. She tossed the helmet onto the seat and walked toward me, into the light of the high beams. Lupita? Linda? Babette?

And then in a flash I recognized her.

"Savannah," I said with a mental slap on my own forehead. I had not seen this coming. Not at all, not in a single one of my calculations. "What the hell?"

"Who the fuck is Savannah?" Freddy asked in my ear.

"Ben's girlfriend," I muttered.

"Okay, that's random," said Freddy.

I raised my gun and pointed it at her with both hands. "Stay right there," I said.

She stopped and raised her hands. "You don't have to do that.

I'm unarmed. You should watch what's on that phone. You have it, right?"

Holding the gun in my right hand, I fished Rose's phone out of my hip pocket with my left hand and balanced it in my palm.

"Watch the video," she said with a hint of impatience, probably because I was supposed to have done this the minute I found the phone, and I'd messed up her plan. She seemed relaxed, if a little out of breath with excitement. This was probably fun for her. "It's cued up. Just press Play."

"What's happening?" Freddy sounded like a little kid pestering his sister while he's missing the exciting part of a movie.

"I'm watching the video now," I said to Freddy while pretending to say it to Savannah. Keeping my gun trained on her, I jiggled the phone to bring it to life, and pressed the Play arrow with my thumb.

Rose's face filled the screen. Behind and above her was a cotton-wood branch with a rope tied to it. Her face was contorted with emotion. "I am so sorry," she said. "I don't want to say it out loud." The video joggled and she looked briefly terrified. "I don't want to have to say it." Another joggle. "Please don't make me say it." It was her death scene, an earlier part of it that I hadn't seen yet. She was weeping. Someone offscreen was goading her because her eyes widened and fixed on something. "Okay, okay, I'll say it. Okay." She took a breath. This was hard for her. "I forced you guys to dress up like Tyler and Justine." She took another breath, clearly following instructions from the unseen interrogator. "I made you pretend to be them." Joggle. "I made you pretend to be them and have sex with each other, and I watched." She wiped tears from her cheeks as if she were slapping herself. "And then I punished you for it." Another pause, her eyes fixed with fear. "I'm sorry. It was so sick, and I'm so sorry." She held out both hands. "I was fucked up back then." Another joggle. "I know it wasn't okay. I was fucked up, all right? I was—I'm so, so sorry I made you do that. I haven't been able to live with myself ever since."

I thought I might vomit. I whispered, "Jesus."

"What is it?" said Freddy in my ear.

In the video, Rose was holding out both hands. "Please forgive me. Please accept my apology. It's all I can do now. I can't change what happened. I love you so much, I'm so sorry." She looked straight into the camera and added in a shaky voice, "This is your fault, Jo. You did this. I blame you for all of it—"

I stopped it. "I've seen the rest," I said. "I know how it ends."

Savannah huffed, the little bitch. "She blamed you up until the very end."

"But who was she apologizing to? Who was filming? Was it you?" Except my brain had already landed on the truth while my mouth was moving. I'd suspected the wrong brother.

But it couldn't be Ben. That was impossible.

"I'll tell you why," said Savannah, answering a question I hadn't asked. "That's why we're here. When they were kids, Rose made Jason have sex with Ben. Jason was dressed like Tyler. Ben wore one of your old dresses from when you were little. Do you understand me? They were ten and eight years old. It happened more than once, a total of four times. Four. When they wouldn't do it, she beat them up. She was fourteen. Way bigger than them."

"That's . . . so terrible, I can hardly believe it. Rose did that to them?"

"And it's your fault."

"How is it my fault?"

"And Tyler's," said Savannah, as if I hadn't spoken, as if she were reciting lines.

Wait, of course. Savannah was playing a part. She must have written a script. She *was* reciting lines.

"Okay," said Freddy's voice in my ear. "I'm sending in the cops now."

"Not yet." I was about to tell Freddy what I'd realized when Savannah glanced over my shoulder at something behind me. I whirled around, but I was too late. Something sharp jabbed me in the neck, and I felt myself go limp. I dropped Rose's phone and my gun as I toppled and fell, conscious but unable to speak, with a dead thud to the ground. There I lay like a trussed-up fly in a spider's web, caught and ready for killing, looking up at the face of Ben Gold hovering above me, blotting out the moon. Whatever drug Ben had stuck me with had paralyzed me, but I was fully aware. So, some sort of fast-acting neuromuscular blocking agent.

"Jo! What just happened?" I heard Freddy's voice say in my ear but was unable to answer him.

"Let's see who you've been talking to all this time." Savannah leaned over, stripped the balaclava off my head, found the headset, and took it off me. She lifted my phone from my back pocket and checked the screen to see the caller ID.

She strapped on the headset. "Freddy, it's under control," she said into the mouthpiece. Her voice was my voice, same timbre and inflections. Her mimicry of me was perfect. So Ben hadn't been kidding about her acting skills. "I've got Jason here, he's cuffed and ready to talk. I'll let you know when this is finished and you can send the cops to pick him up. It'll be a minute, so tell them to hold tight."

Freddy must have said something because she gave a low chuckle that sounded just like mine. "Yeah, Jason's not too happy right now," she said in my voice. She hung up and picked up Rose's phone and my gun and tossed them into the canvas bag in the back of the ATV.

The two of them began to undress me, pulling off my gun holster, shoes, socks, jeans, T-shirt, and turtleneck, until I was down to my underwear. The ground was hard and cold. I'd fallen on one hip and a shoulder. I could not move a single one of my muscles. Whatever drug this was had no painkiller in it. They obviously wanted me to feel every bit of whatever they were about to do to me.

As Ben stood over me, silently watching, Savannah rummaged around in the canvas bag and pulled out a rope. Together, they lashed me tightly by the waist to the rear bumper of the ATV. Then she got back into the seat, started up the engine again, and dragged my inert body up the hill to the shack, rough hard ground eroding my bare skin, embedding rocks and cactus needles in my flesh, making me bleed. Ben came walking behind, watching everything.

When my head banged hard against a big rock, I briefly lost consciousness. I came out of the blackness a very short time later to find myself vertical, with a powerful headache, a deep chill on my skin. I was still immobilized, but now my hands were tied in front of me, and my torso was attached from under my arms to something hard and solid against my spine. *Quick*, my numbed brain prodded itself, *wake up and figure this out*. I was lashed to some sort of pole or tree trunk. My feet were tied together, too, and rested on a pile of mesquite wood, twigs, and crumpled paper. Savannah was off to my side. Ben sat nearby in a folding chair, smoking a cigarette. Behind him sat the dark bulk of the outlaws' shack.

I got it: I was tied to a stake, and I was about to be burned to death like a witch. I tried moving my hands and feet. They responded to my brain's signals. So the paralysis was wearing off. That was fast.

"She's awake," came Savannah's voice from somewhere to my left, close by.

"Hey, Jo," said Ben, his voice uninflected.

"Hi, Ben," I said with a thick tongue. I opened my mouth wide and worked my jaw, feeling my brain coming back online. Pain throbbed through my whole body like a live animal inhabiting me. I was thirsty. They'd dragged me over here, stripped me, and tied me up like a shot deer waiting to be gutted. "You're supposed to be in rehab."

"That's where I am, as far as my mother knows," said Ben. His cigarette end glowed red as he sucked in smoke.

"And you were just in a coma. In the hospital."

Savannah cleared her throat. "Hello, Mrs. Delaney," she said in a throaty, professional voice, sounding suddenly like a harried, professional middle-aged woman. "This is Dr. Montrose, Ben's attending physician at Maricopa County Hospital. I'm calling to update you on his current status. We're keeping him in a medically induced coma until it's safe to wake him up. We're not permitting visitors yet, but we'll notify you as soon as that changes. I'm going to give you my personal cell number, as I'm sure you'll have questions and concerns. Please call me anytime."

"Oh." It came out sounding something like a groan. I had been such an idiot. No wonder he'd come out of that coma so fast. Ben and I were staring at each other with enough intensity to make the air sizzle. You might have thought we were in love. "It was you all along."

Ben flicked his lighter a few times. If he meant to scare me, it worked, but it looked more reflexive and nervous than menacing. "I'm giving everyone something they want before they die, a little parting gift. With Rose, I accepted her apology. She begged me to, and I did." He said this without any apparent awareness that this was not actually an act of generosity if you were killing someone. "And I promised Tyler never to send that video to Linda. I let them both die with peace of mind by telling them what they needed to hear."

"How thoughtful," I said. "What's my parting gift?"

"Knowledge. You get to know why this is happening to you. That's what you want, isn't it?"

I already knew, or thought I did. "I get it, Ben. You blame Tyler and me for what Rose did to you."

"Gosh. Spoken like a true detective. It's always somebody else's fault, huh?" He sounded sad, tired. He flicked the lighter again.

I turned to Savannah. "Why are you doing this?"

"She loves me," said Ben with the ghost of a smile.

I coughed and felt a searing pain on my side. So one of my ribs was broken. "Listen," I said to Savannah. I needed to scare her. Local cops didn't sound threatening enough. "There's an entire SWAT team less than half a mile away. They know exactly where we are. If I'm not back soon, they're going to come looking for me. And trust me, they will find you. You're an accessory to the murder of three people. That's at least twenty years in jail. If you turn yourself in right now and cooperate, and tell them Ben coerced you into doing it, you can walk away from this. Think about it. You're still young, you have your whole life ahead of you."

Ben looked at Savannah. "You see? I told you she would try to mess with your head. That's what she does, she messes with people's heads. She did it to Rose, and now she's trying to do it to you. She goes after the ones she thinks are weak because she's evil. But you're not weak, are you?"

"Don't listen to him, Savannah. Don't be stupid."

"Sorry," she said, sliding her dark hair off her head, a wig, to reveal blond hair. "There is no Savannah." She tossed the wig onto the woodpile at my feet, I guessed so it would burn along with me. The FBI would sift through the ashes and find its remnants. Not that that was much of a consolation, since I'd be long dead by then. "I'm Molly McDevitt. I'm a receptionist at Innovative Integrations. I saw you come in the other day."

"Right," I said, recognizing her now. The lip ring. "So *you're* the one who sent those videos. It was you. You had Rose's phone this whole time."

"Yeah," she said. "That was totally me."

"She's a great actress," said Ben. "Her imitations are genius."

"I'm also good at being invisible," said Molly/Savannah. "I bet you didn't even know I was at the memorial party for Rose. Jason brought some of his staff, but you didn't give me a second look, did you? I'm just a receptionist, who cares. You probably feel pretty stupid right now."

She was right. "Did you kill Tyler, Savannah?"

"I made sure the coast was clear. Ben did the rest. Snuck in the back, snuck right out again."

I looked at Ben. He looked back at me. Ben Gold, Rose's cuddly, cheeky little brother with his wild frizzy hair and absurdist sense of humor, the little boy who loved Magic cards and Harry Potter. He looked so bleak and lost right now. Poor, damaged kid. I was fighting a deep sense of compassion for him, even though he was about to murder me.

"You were living out here when you were supposed to be in the hospital?"

"I went in the back door of the studio," said Ben. "No one saw me. Molly guarded the front door as soon as Tyler went in. He was so confused when he saw me. He died so fast. He was impaled through his black rotten heart."

I shook my head. Jesus. "What about Rose? How did you get her into the tree barefoot with no marks on her feet?"

"I'm her little brother. She trusted me, and she felt so guilty about what she did to me she's never been able to say no to me. I woke her up at four in the morning and told her to put on her white dress and to come with me. She was confused, but she did what I said. I drove her to our stables and made her get on the horse and led her out there. I already had the noose waiting in the tree. She thought it was just that old game at first, a way for me to make her confess and apologize."

So he'd made her think the horse and noose were just theater, just like we playacted when we were kids, that the apology was the whole point. The outlaw always had to confess before he got hanged. That was always Rose's favorite part, her dramatic recitation of bloody crimes. She always came up with some gruesome ones.

"Then you hanged her for real."

"She didn't see it coming."

"So who shot at me the other day? Was that you, Ben?"

"I shot at you." Savannah/Molly's snotty little voice was getting on my nerves. She held my gun almost jauntily, relishing it. "I'm a good shot, my dad taught me. We borrowed Jason's old hunting rifle from his parents' closet. It was Ben's idea. He wanted to plant a bullet near you in case the FBI needed more evidence against Jason. Scared you, didn't it?"

I refused to spend the last minutes of my life talking to this girl. I kept my eyes on Ben. "Rose's father made her sleep in his bed with him, all those summers when she went to visit him, and he raped her the summer before senior year. Did you know that?"

From Ben's dumbfounded expression, his silence, I could see that he hadn't had any idea.

"He started when she was little, dressed her up like a little sexpot and took her to parties. Like his date." I drove it home again so he'd really hear it. "She slept in his bed with him. He forced her to. The last summer she was there, he raped her. That's why she never went back again. She never told anyone until after her father died. She told Solo, and Solo just told me. I didn't know until now."

Ben was shaking his head. He clearly didn't want to forgive Rose, or understand her, or hear anything that would take away his aggrieved sense of her as evil. "It doesn't matter." Everything about him was blank, negative, flat, as if he weren't fully present, as if a whole part of him were being powerfully suppressed. "It doesn't change anything."

"It doesn't make up for what you did to him," said Molly/Savannah. Why was she still here? It was past her bedtime. "You have no idea, do you? How much Ben has suffered because of you?"

"Oh, go to hell." I snapped at her. "You think all of this is justified? Murdering people because your psychotic boyfriend thinks they're evil? Listen, one day you're going to wake up out of the warped little dream you're living in right now and realize what you've done, what you've *actually* done, the true horrors that you have *actually* committed. And they will haunt you for the rest of your life. You'll never be able to live with yourself after that." I could tell by her expression that I'd pierced her shell.

Ben sighed. "She won't have to," he said, and stood up. Cupping both her hands in his, he slid my gun out of her hand and took a step back.

"What are you doing?" she said, alarmed, surprised. "Babe?"

I'd taken the safety off earlier when I was aiming at Savannah, so all Ben had to do was hold the muzzle to her temple and pull the trigger. The silencer muffled the blast to a dull thud as a burst of blood and brains and skull fragments splattered to the ground, gleaming in the cold silver light. Ben and I watched the rest of her slide down to lie in a heap at his feet.

"Look what you made me do." A sob caught in his throat as her body writhed in a series of spasms and went still. "I didn't want to. But what choice did I have? What choice did I have with any of you?"

TWENTY-FOUR

I MOVED MY MOUTH, TRYING TO FORM WORDS, BUT NOTHING came out.

"This is your gun, Jo," he told me, holding it up so I could see. "Do you understand? You killed poor innocent Molly McDevitt, then Jason got away after he killed you. That's what this is all going to look like." He took a bandanna out of his pocket and swabbed the gun thoroughly.

"That's very clever of you," I said. My teeth were chattering. My body shuddered with cold and terror and pain. Burning to death was going to hurt. I was going to have to smell my own charred flesh as I died.

"But Ben," I said. I knew the rules: I got to ask questions until I knew everything, then Ben would light the fire and watch me die. As long as I could talk, I might stay alive. "Why is Molly McDevitt's body here in the first place, in your staged scenario?"

"The receptionist said too much to the FBI when they questioned her about the company's illegal dealings. So Jason used her as bait to get you here, in retribution. That's the narrative they'll construct."

"Freddy heard me call her Savannah," I said. "Loud and clear. That leads directly to you. You didn't plan on that."

"One girl looks like another girl at night, in the dark."

I wasn't so sure. I wasn't so sure about that, or any of his logic. He'd gotten away with all of this so far, as well as framing his brother, but maybe this was where it fell apart. Maybe I could talk my way out of this. And if I couldn't, I felt a shred of hope that the FBI might piece enough things together to tip them off.

"Why are you framing your brother for something he was forced to do to you?"

"He had a choice," said Ben.

"Rose beat you guys up when you refused."

"He'd rather rape his little brother than take a beating." Ben's voice held pain, scorn, and rage. "Pussy. He should have stood up to her, protected me. Instead, he held me down."

"So this is your revenge on both of them. Rose and Jason."

"Shock, isn't it? Sweet innocent little Ben with all his sad addiction problems. Yeah, I turned my rage on myself for years. I wanted to die. Finally I realized I didn't have to. I deserve to live. But I had to bring them both down to do it."

"But why kill Tyler?"

"He was part of it. And you too, Jo. You're the last piece." There was something final and resigned in his tone. He stared at me hard.

Time to change the subject, keep this conversation going. "Savannah's been a busy girl," I said. "Talking to the FBI, bringing you clothes up in Phoenix, working for Jason, acting like your girlfriend."

"She really was my girlfriend. And she played her part so well. I wish I hadn't had to kill her. I wish none of this was happening." Unlike Savannah or Molly or whoever she was, Ben didn't sound pumped up with excitement by this endgame. He sounded exhausted, let down. This was probably not as satisfying or thrilling as he'd originally imagined it would be. It was possibly anticlimactic now that he was in the final stage of his plan. Once I was dead, the whole thing would be over, and nothing would have changed for him. He was always going to be a fucked-up victim of childhood sexual abuse. This wouldn't heal him, not even close.

"So you've been camping back here in the hills while you were killing everyone, and Molly's been bringing you supplies on the ATV at night."

He sighed. "I like it here. It's peaceful. Except for the trip up to Lou and Tricia's, that was hard. But I like being out here in the mountains, sleeping outside."

"Are Lou and Tricia actors too?"

He looked genuinely startled. "No. They're good and decent people who believe I'm recovering from an overdose caused by grief at my sister's death."

"Do you really go to twelve-step meetings?"

"I have eighteen months of sobriety, thanks to them."

"Did you really overdose?"

"Not this time. But I have, before. I was suicidal for a while. Then I realized I had to slay my dragons so I could live. That's when I got clean."

"Are you really enrolled in the social work master's program?"

"Getting straight As."

"Where are your mother's hiking boots?"

He looked thrown off guard again. "What?"

"I assumed Rose put them on when you abducted her from her casita."

He shook his head. "She was barefoot. What hiking boots? No idea." He looked consternated by this detail, stopped short.

"Did you send Tyler a text from Rose's phone at the memorial to meet you in Pablo's studio?"

"Molly had Rose's phone. I came in the studio back door and waited. Her text to Tyler said to come alone and he'd get important information about Rose's death. He showed up curious to know who I was and ready to negotiate about that video. He never saw it coming."

"Then you texted me from Tyler's phone."

"I wanted you to find him. Like I wanted you and Tyler to find

Rose. The timing was important. You all three needed to be connected in death, or the triangle wouldn't be complete."

"What is this obsession with triangles?"

"They're ancient symbols of eternity, of the deity and holy union. Rose and Tyler got inverted triangles, pointing downward. Did you notice? They're feminine and symbolize water and earth and purification. You'll get a fire triangle, masculine and pointing upward, symbolizing fire and air, hate and anger and passion, also spiritual ascendance. You should feel honored that I chose it for you."

I had to suppress the urge to tell Ben how much I was not feeling honored in that particular moment, and how his esoteric symbolism sounded like something from a web page about Wiccans. I moved on instead to the next item on my list of survival questions. "The crank call to my motel room. How did you know I was there? How'd you bypass the front desk?"

"I trailed you from the Rancho that night and broke into the room next to yours. I just popped the lock. A room-to-room call."

"Clever," I said, with desperate clarity. "And I guess the crackling sounds were meant to symbolize the flames that I'm about to be burned to death by. That's nice foreshadowing."

A dark cloud moved over his face. "Don't mock me, Jo."

"I'm not," I lied. "I'm admiring your design, your attention to detail. Truly. So that's why you had your mother hire me so soon after Rose went missing. You wanted to suck me in, get me involved, make me start investigating. You wanted Tyler and me at the scene, you wanted us to see her hanging there. The triangle had to be complete."

"Yes," he said. "That's right. My mother is easy to influence; I know how to play on her fears. I told her I had a bad feeling. I'm the one who was close to my sister. I'm the one she talked to. You never once thought it was me, did you?"

"No," I said. "God damn it. I didn't." With mounting terror, I could sense Ben starting to get restless, probably remembering that there were cops out there somewhere. He was itching to finish what he'd started, bring his plan to fruition. "Rose clearly trusted you. She looked completely shocked when she realized you were actually killing her, right before she died."

"I wasn't totally sure what I'd do when I had her there. I thought her apology might be enough. I thought I might let her go. But it wasn't. It didn't make things better. I couldn't stop."

"So you slapped the horse to make her fall."

"She had to die. And then I had to kill Tyler and you. It wasn't fair if it was just Rose. It had to be all three of you."

"Of course," I said.

"I hate you so much, Jo, you have no idea how hard it's been to talk to you like a normal person these past few days. You're a monster. You destroyed my sister's life and my brother's and my life. You're a witch. You have to die like a witch. I need you to die."

My voice rasped with dry panic. "How did you get Tyler to stand in front of the statue?"

He shook his head and flicked the lighter, flicked it again. Molly's body lay in a still heap. Her brains gleamed darkly on the ground.

"Wait," I said. "Is your whole social work thing for real? Wanting to counsel troubled kids, run a center for them?"

"Why wouldn't it be? Damaged kids need grown-ups like me who know what they're going through. Enough talking now."

"No," I barked. "What are you going to do now that you've accomplished your life's goal?"

He came toward me.

I was babbling, panicking, but also, everything was occurring to me too fast to slow down. "You needed to kill us all so you could move on. And you're going to get away with it, and your brother is going to go to prison for the rest of his life. He raped you. Why don't you kill him too? Right, because you need him to take the fall for you. And you want him to get raped in Supermax."

"Pretty little redhead like him." I thought Ben might be about to weep.

"But you know he was forced to do it to you, forced by Rose." He was listening; I had his attention again, oh thank God. He stood close to me, his eyes just to the side of my feet, not meeting my eyes. I could smell the high, sharp smell of flop sweat mixed with musky unwashed skin. "So you're sparing his life, because he was as fucked-up and damaged as you were."

Ben took a switchblade out of his pocket.

"I get it now," I said. My voice sounded high and shaky. I tried to modulate it into a flat, calm monotone. "My crime was being the person you were forced to impersonate while your siblings abused you. I stripped you of your identity from an early age, and now you're stripping me of mine and reclaiming your own."

"It's the only way I'll ever be free."

"The three of you were all caught in a cycle of pain and abuse."

"A *triangle* of pain and abuse," he said. "With me at the bottom."

I let out a yelp as he bent down and carved a small triangle in my right forearm. I could feel a trickle of hot blood oozing down my wrist, pooling in my palm. He slid the knife back into his pocket.

"Rose did this to you." I was hyperventilating now. "You're the triangle, you and your brother and sister. Tyler and I are just shadow puppets. We're not even real. Killing us is meaningless. Tyler and I don't matter."

His face, inches from mine, was contorted. "I had to wear your old dress and she called me Justine. I was just a little kid. She called my brother Tyler. She made me suck his dick. She made him stick his dick in me." He looked nauseated. "Do you understand? We tried not to, but she beat us, punched us, held us down. I was eight! So don't tell me who does and doesn't matter here."

"But you didn't know why." I started talking fast, talking for my life. "You didn't know about Rose's father. You thought she did that to you guys because of me and Tyler. You thought we were the ones who traumatized her. You thought all this time that it was our fault. But we were just teenagers. All Tyler and I did was date. That's it. How could that have caused Rose to behave the way she did, to do all those things she did, for so many years? That would be insane, Ben!"

When I took a breath, he started to interrupt me, but I steamrolled right over him.

"And I don't think your sister was insane, I think she was damaged and hurt and traumatized, and everything she did was in reaction to what her father did to her. She never told me about it, and I was her best friend. She didn't say a word. Instead, she shut me out. She abused her brothers. She identified as a member of a displaced, oppressed tribe. She did it to express her own sense of persecuted subjugation, by borrowing theirs. She seduced a student who looks like Tyler."

Ben was pacing around, shaking his head. "You don't know anything. Nothing."

"Ben, your sister was abused, just like you. She passed it down the food chain. It wasn't me and Tyler. It was Jimmy Delaney. It was her father. He's dead now, it's too late to kill him, but killing me is pointless. I'm not the one who did this to Rose. It's not my fault this happened to you. I'm so sorry it did. It was wrong. It was terrible. I didn't know any of it until now, none of it. I didn't understand either."

He gave a brief, strangled shout that sounded like a yelp of real pain. "Shut up. No more talking." He came back to the edge of the fire mound and gagged me with the bandanna he'd wiped the gun with, tying it behind my neck tightly enough to force my mouth open. My dry tongue stuck to the cloth. I suddenly regretted having spent this whole time talking instead of screaming bloody murder. I would die either way, but not being able to make a sound made me feel so much more helpless.

Ben rasped his lighter for real this time and lit one of the crumpled balls of paper. "I'm burning you with my sister's book, the one she wrote about you." He stepped back to watch the flames grow.

The fire caught, spread to the next ball of paper, licked at a piece of kindling. Ben returned to his chair to watch. Something caught my eye behind him, a small animal moving in the dark doorway, probably a rabbit. I wished it were a mountain lion or a cop.

"Once you're gone, I'll be free," he said.

Of course he wouldn't. I was surprised by the sadness I felt for this irreparably damaged man.

I heard a loud popping sound at my feet, a rain-dampened mesquite log catching. The heat from the flames was getting intense, and the heavy smoke stung my eyes and made me cough, which hurt like hell. But it was just getting started. The moon was setting. All around me was darkness, the emptiness of the land. I could feel its implacable coldness. Nothing out here cared. It was almost comforting. My death didn't matter at all.

But Tyler's did, and Rose's. They mattered, so much, to me. And Ben's lifelong agony mattered. As the bottoms of my feet prickled with pins and needles of heat, I finally did howl, through the muffling bandanna in my mouth, hoping with futile desperation that the cops out there might somehow magically get worried and come running, even though I knew that Freddy thought I had it all under control. So little time had passed since I'd been tied to this stake waiting to be incinerated, maybe fifteen, twenty minutes at the most, but it felt like eons. Molly was dead. Ben was watching me from his chair. His eyes gleamed in the firelight. Molly's wig caught fire with a burst of noxious flame, making my eyes water. I turned my nose to the side to find a breath of cleaner air to suck into my lungs.

As I squirmed up the stake, trying vainly to lift myself out of the fire, Ben leapt from his chair and picked up my gun and fired into the darkness beyond the circle of firelight. Almost immediately, he was blown backward by a loud shotgun blast that boomed and cracked in my ear. He fell to the ground and lay still. I swiveled my head as Lupita stomped into the circle of firelight in a plaid wool jacket over what looked like a cotton nightgown, and a pair of beat-up work boots. Her cousin Tono, carrying a double-barreled shotgun, came right behind her in pajamas and a canvas hunting jacket. While he stepped on the fire, kicking the wood hard so it scattered in the sand, smothering the flames with his jacket, Lupita untied me, squinting in the smoke, and tore the bandanna off my mouth. As soon as I was free, I leapt out of the flames and tumbled into her arms, heaving with my mouth open for breath. I couldn't feel any of my injuries. The pain would hit me later, along with the damage from the fire, but for now, I was alive, zinging with relief.

"It's okay," she was saying. "I've got you. You're okay."

I was hacking and coughing, my eyes streaming. Lupita saturated the bandanna with a splash from a water bottle and handed it to me along with the water bottle. I wiped my face and gulped cold water while she scrounged a blanket out of the canvas bag by the chair next to Ben's body and wrapped me in its warm, scratchy wool.

The small animal behind Ben's chair gave a sharp bark and ran toward me. I lifted Ophelia into my arms, and she nestled against my chest under the blanket. Her raspy tongue licked my chin. I croaked, "How did you find me here?"

"That ATV, trespassing on our land," said Lupita. "We heard it again tonight after this little dog came out of nowhere and kept barking at me and wouldn't stop."

"Ophelia," I said.

"She's yours?"

I looked at Ophelia. She licked my chin again. Apparently she was.

"We lost the ATV," said Lupita. "We followed this dog here, and then we smelled the fire."

"Yo. What was that guy doing to you?" Tono looked freaked out. "He tried to shoot me. You saw that, right?"

I was swaying, gripping Ophelia too tightly, but she didn't seem to mind.

"We need to get you to the emergency room." Lupita wrapped her arms around me hard, holding me up.

"I'm okay," I said, sagging against her. "I just need some salve and gauze bandages and painkillers. My clothes are out there somewhere, my phone. That's my gun Ben was shooting with."

"It's okay," she crooned in my ear like a mother, cradling me. It felt like heaven. "We'll find it all. Tono, call the cops."

"They're right nearby," I said. "I'm sure they'll be here in two minutes. They would have heard the guns." My teeth were chattering. I felt manic. I had to call Freddy. "We can take this other ATV, too, and I've got a bike stashed over the hill."

"*¿Que chingados?*" Tono was pacing around, shaking his hands out, staring at the girl's body. "What happened here?"

Tyler's partner, Eddie Gomez, came panting up the hill, closely followed by the young rookie who'd been at the scene of Rose's murder. No wonder I'd almost died. Jesus. They'd probably been waiting this whole time in their warm car with coffee, playing video games on their phones.

I looked down at Ophelia, nestling her lumpy little self against my clavicle. If she hadn't barked at them, if Lupita and Tono hadn't followed the ATV, if he hadn't brought his gun with him . . .

Hours later, sedated and medicated, my rib taped, salve on my burned feet, cactus spines picked out of my flesh, my lacerations bandaged, I lay in a hospital bed, where I'd agreed to stay for the night for observation. Lupita had followed the ambulance, stopping at the Apache Motel to fetch my bag for me. After I was admitted, she'd taken Ophelia home with her.

Despite the sedative, I was awake, listening to the night nurses chattering at the desk, various machines beeping and hissing.

"She's right in here," came a nurse's voice in my doorway.

And there was my mother, looming over my bed, her face pale and distraught. "Oh Justine," she said, and I could have sworn she was crying. "They called me and I came right away. What happened? Are you okay?"

I felt her cool, hard hand on my forehead, as if she were checking for a fever, the way she used to do when I was little.

"I'm all right, Mom, I promise."

She burst out, "Oh thank God you're okay. I can't lose you too."

"It was Ben," I said. "He's dead now. Poor Laura."

"Can I get you some water?"

I gestured to my IV drip. "They're pumping me full of fluids and God knows what else," I tried to say. My tongue felt thick with exhaustion. My eyes were fluttering closed.

She sat in the visitor's chair and pulled it right up to the rails of my bed. "Ssssh," she said, her hand still stroking my forehead, smoothing my hair back, over and over. "I'm just going to sit here till you fall asleep. You need to rest now."

But I wasn't quite ready to go to sleep yet. I wanted to soak up every minute of my mother's soothing presence at my side. I breathed deeply, eyes closed, alive and well and safe and warm, thinking about Rose Delaney, the girl I'd loved, the person she'd become.

If I'd known at the time what was happening to her in Trenton all those years ago, maybe I could have helped her somehow. Maybe just telling me would have been enough, having an unconditional ally, knowing she was safe with me. I would have encouraged her to get help, to tell her mother the truth no matter what. And if Rose had trusted me enough to confide in me, maybe she and Tyler and Molly would still be alive right now, maybe Jason and Ben could have grown up whole and sane. But instead, for reasons I'd never know, she stayed silent and pushed me away, and then I abandoned her. Her father's abuse of her made her warp and destroy her little brothers' lives. There had been no way to make any of this right, even though that was what

Ben had thought he was doing, in his twisted way. He was trying to make it right in the only way he could—violently, destructively.

I'd escaped his plan for me only because Lupita and Ophelia, together, had saved my life. Now I owed them both everything: a woman I was sort of newly involved with; a dog I didn't ask for. Normally, I would run away from all this complication, tell Lupita it couldn't work between us and take Ophelia straight to the Humane Society so she could find a real home. But I felt a new kind of curiosity, an urge to let myself get entangled, to stay and try to connect. Maybe I would fail, and that was the most likely outcome, but I would give it a shot, I swore to myself, just before I fell, finally, into a narcotic sleep. It was for my own good, of course.

But really, I would do it for Rose.

ABOUT THE AUTHOR

SYDNEY GRAVES IS A PSEUDONYM FOR KATE CHRISTENSEN, AN ARI-zona native and the author of eight novels, most recently *Welcome Home, Stranger*. Her fourth novel, *The Great Man*, won the 2008 PEN/ Faulkner Award for Fiction. She has also published two food-centric memoirs, *Blue Plate Special* and *How to Cook a Moose*, which won the 2016 Maine Literary Award for Memoir. Her essays, reviews, and short pieces have appeared in a wide variety of publications and anthologies. She lives with her husband and their two dogs in Taos, New Mexico.